TRUST ME

Also by John Updike

THE CARPENTERED HEN, *poems*
THE POORHOUSE FAIR, *a novel*
THE SAME DOOR, *short stories*
RABBIT, RUN, *a novel*
PIGEON FEATHERS *and other stories*
THE CENTAUR, *a novel*
TELEPHONE POLES *and other poems*
OLINGER STORIES, *a selection*
ASSORTED PROSE
OF THE FARM, *a novel*
THE MUSIC SCHOOL, *stories*
COUPLES, *a novel*
MIDPOINT *and other poems*
BECH: A BOOK
RABBIT REDUX, *a novel*
MUSEUMS AND WOMEN *and other stories*
BUCHANAN DYING, *a play*
A MONTH OF SUNDAYS, *a novel*
PICKED-UP PIECES
MARRY ME, *a romance*
TOSSING AND TURNING, *poems*
THE COUP, *a novel*
TOO FAR TO GO: *The Maples Stories*
PROBLEMS *and other stories*
RABBIT IS RICH, *a novel*
BECH IS BACK, *short stories*
HUGGING THE SHORE, *essays and criticism*
THE WITCHES OF EASTWICK, *a novel*
FACING NATURE, *poems*
ROGER'S VERSION, *a novel*

John Updike

TRUST ME

SHORT STORIES

Alfred A. Knopf   New York

THIS IS A BORZOI BOOK
PUBLISHED BY ALFRED A. KNOPF, INC.

Copyright © 1962, 1979, 1980, 1981, 1982, 1983, 1984, 1985, 1986, 1987 by
John Updike

All rights reserved under International and Pan-American Copyright Conventions. Published in the United States by Alfred A. Knopf, Inc., New York, and simultaneously in Canada by Random House of Canada Limited, Toronto. Distributed by Random House, Inc., New York.

The following stories were originally published in *The New Yorker:* "Trust Me," "Still of Some Use," "The City," "The Lovely Troubled Daughters of Our Old Crowd," "Unstuck," "A Constellation of Events," "Deaths of Distant Friends," "Learn a Trade," "One More Interview," "The Other," "Slippage," "Leaf Season," and "The Other Woman." "More Stately Mansions" and "Poker Night" first appeared in *Esquire;* "Pygmalion" and "Made in Heaven" in *The Atlantic;* "Killing" and "Beautiful Husbands" in *Playboy;* "Getting into the Set" in *Vanity Fair;* "The Wallet" in *Yankee;* and "The Ideal Village" in *The Ontario Review.*

Manufactured in the United States of America

to JOHN, JASON, *and* TED

trusting and trustworthy

Contents

TRUST ME

Trust Me

WHEN HAROLD was three or four, his father and mother took him to a swimming pool. This was strange, for his family rarely went places, except to the movie house two blocks from their house. Harold had no memory of ever seeing his parents in bathing suits again, after this unhappy day. What he did remember was this:

His father, nearly naked, was in the pool, treading water. Harold was standing shivering on the wet tile edge, suspended above the abysmal odor of chlorine, hypnotized by the bright, lapping agitation of this great volume of unnaturally blue-green water. His mother, in a black bathing suit that made her flesh appear very white, was off in a corner of his mind. His father was asking him to jump. "C'mon, Hassy, jump," he was saying, in his mild, encouraging voice. "It'll be all right. Jump right into my hands." The words echoed in the flat acoustics of the water and tile and sunlight, heightening Harold's sense of exposure, his awareness of his own white skin. His father seemed eerily stable and calm in the water, and the child idly wondered, as he jumped, what the man was standing on.

Then the blue-green water was all around him, dense and churning, and when he tried to take a breath a fist was shoved into his throat. He saw his own bubbles rising in front of his face, a multitude of them, rising as he sank; he sank it seemed for a very long time, until something located him in the darkening element and seized him by the arm.

He was in air again, on his father's shoulder, still fighting for breath. They were out of the pool. His mother swiftly came up to the two of them and, with a deftness remarkable in one so angry, slapped his father on the face, loudly, next to Harold's ear. The slap seemed to resonate all over the pool area, and to be heard by all the other bathers; but perhaps this was the acoustics of memory. His sense of public embarrassment amid sparkling nakedness—of every strange face turned toward him as he passed from his father's wet arms into his mother's dry ones—survived his recovery of breath. His mother's anger seemed directed at him as much as at his father. His feet now were on grass. Standing wrapped in a towel near his mother's knees while the last burning fragments of water were coughed from his lungs, Harold felt eternally disgraced.

He never knew what had happened; by the time he asked, so many years had passed that his father had forgotten. "Wasn't that a crying shame," the old man said, with his mild mixture of mournfulness and comedy. "Sink or swim, and you sank." Perhaps Harold had leaped a moment before it was expected, or had proved unexpectedly heavy, and had thus slipped through his father's grasp. Unaccountably, all through his growing up he continued to trust his father; it was his mother he distrusted, her swift sure-handed anger.

He didn't learn to swim until college, and even then he passed the test by frog-kicking the length of the pool on his back, with the instructor brandishing a thick stick to grasp if he panicked and began to sink. The chemical scent of a pool always frightened him: blue-green dragon breath.

His children, raised in an amphibious world of summer camps and country clubs, easily became swimmers. They tried to teach him how to dive. "You must keep your head *down,* Dad. That's why you keep getting belly-whoppers."

"I'm scared of not coming up," he confessed. What he especially did not like, under water, was the sight of bubbles rising around his face.

His first wife dreaded flying. Yet they flew a great deal. "Either that," he told her, "or resign from the twentieth century." They flew to California, and while they were there two planes collided over the Grand Canyon. They flew out of Boston the day after starlings had blocked the engines of an Electra and caused it to crash into the harbor with such force that people were cut in two by their safety belts. They flew over Africa, crossing the equator at night, the land beneath them an inky chasm lit by a few sparks of tribal fire. They landed on dusty runways, with the cabin doors banging. He promised her, her fear was so acute, that she would never have to fly with him again. At last, their final African flight took them up from the Ethiopian Plateau, across the pale width of the Libyan Desert, to the edge of the Mediterranean, and on to Rome.

The Pan Am plane out of Rome was the most comforting possible—a jumbo jet wide as a house, stocked with American magazines and snacks, its walls dribbling music, with only a few passengers. The great plane lifted off, and he relaxed into a *Newsweek,* into the prospect of a meal, a nap, and a homecoming. Harold's wife asked, after ten minutes, "Why aren't we climbing?"

He looked out of the window, and it was true—the watery world below them was not diminishing; he could distinctly see small boats and the white tips of breaking waves. The stewardesses were moving up and down the aisle with unusual speed, with unusual expressions on their glamorous faces. Harold looked at the palms of his hands; they had become damp and mottled, as during nausea. However hard he stared, the sea beneath the wings did not fall away. Sun sparkled on its surface; a tiny sailboat tacked.

The pilot's voice crackled into being above them. "Folks, there's a little warning light come on for one of our starboard engines, and in conformance with our policy of absolute security we're going to circle around and return to the Rome airport."

During the bank and return, which seemed to take an extremely long time, the stewardesses buckled themselves into rear seats, the man across the aisle kept reading *L'Osservatore,* and Harold's wife, a faithful student of safety instructions, removed her high-heeled shoes and took the pins out of her hair. So again he marvelled at the deft dynamism of women in crises.

He held her damp hand in his and steadily gazed out of the window, pressing the sea down with his vision, stiff-arming it with his will to live. If he blinked, they would fall. One little boat at a time, the plane edged back to Rome. The blue sea visually interlocked with the calm silver edge of the wing: Olympian surfaces serenely oblivious of the immense tension between them. He had often felt, through one of these scratched oval windows, something falsely reassuring in the elaborate order of the rivets pinning the aluminum sheets together. *Trust me,* the metallic code spelled out; in his heart Harold, like his wife, had refused, and this refusal in him formed a hollow space terror could always flood.

The 747 landed smoothly back in Rome and, after an hour's delay, while mechanics persuaded the warning light to go off, resumed the flight to America. At home, their scare became a story, a joke. He kept his promise, though, that she would never have to fly with him again; within a year, they separated.

During the time of separation Harold seemed to be slinging his children from one rooftop to another, silently begging them to trust him. It was as when, years before, he had adjusted his daughter's braces in her mouth with a needle-nose pliers. She had come to him in pain, a wire gouging the inside of her cheek. But then, with his clumsy fingers in her mouth, her eyes widened with fear of worse pain. He gaily accused her, "You don't trust me." The gaiety of his voice revealed a crucial space, a gap between their situations: it would be his blunder, but her pain. Another's pain is not our own. Religion, he supposed, seeks to close this gap, but each generation's torturers keep it open. Without it, compassion would crush us; the space of indifference is where we breathe. Harold had heard this necessary indifference in the pilot's voice drawling "Folks," and in his father's voice urging "Jump." He heard it in his own reassurances as he bestowed them. "Sweetie, I know you're feeling pressure now, but if you'll just hold *still* . . . there's this little sharp end—oops. Well, you wriggled."

He took his girl friend to the top of a mountain. Harold hadn't had a girl friend for many years and had to relearn the delicate blend of protectiveness and challengingness that is courtship. She was, Priscilla, old enough to have her own children, and old enough to feel fragile on skis. She had spent the day on the baby slope, practicing turns and gradually gaining confidence, while Harold ranged far and wide on the mountain, in the company of her children. As the afternoon drew to an end, he swooped down upon her in a smart spray of snow. She begged him, "Ride the baby chair, so I can show you my snowplow."

"If you can snowplow here, you can come down from the top of the mountain," Harold told her.

"Really?" Her cheeks were pink, from her day on the baby slope. She wore a white knit hat. Her eyes were baby blue.

"Absolutely. We'll come down on the novice trail."

She trusted him. But on the chair lift, as the slope beneath them increased and the windswept iciness of the higher trails became apparent, a tremulous doubt entered into her face, and he realized, with that perversely joyful inner widening the torturer feels, that he had done the wrong thing. The lift rumbled onward, ever higher. "Can I really ski this?" Priscilla asked, with a child's beautiful willingness to be reassured. In the realms of empathy, he was again standing on the edge of that swimming pool. The evil-smelling water was a long way down.

He told her, "You won't be skiing this part. Look at the view. It's gorgeous."

She turned, rigid in the chair as it swayed across a chasm. With obedient eyes she gazed at the infinite blue-green perspectives of wooded mountain and frozen lake. The parking lot below seemed a little platter tessellated with cars. The lift cable irresistibly slithered; the air dropped in temperature. The pines around them had grown stunted and twisted. Mist licked off the ice; they were in the clouds. Priscilla was trembling all over, and at the top could scarcely stand on her skis.

"I can't do it," she announced.

"Do what I do," Harold said. He quickly slid to a few yards below her. "Put your weight first on one ski, then the other. Don't look at the steepness, just think of your weight shifting."

She leaned her weight backward, away from the slope, and fell down. Tears welled in her eyes; he feared they would freeze and make her blind. He gathered all his love into his voice and rolled it toward her, to melt her recalcitrance, her terror. "Just do your snowplow. Don't think about where you are."

"There isn't any snow," she said. "Just ice."

"It's not icy at the edges."

"There are *trees* at the edges."

"Come on, honey. The light's getting flat."

"We'll freeze to death."

"Don't be silly, the ski patrol dusts the trails last thing. Put your weight on the downhill ski and let yourself turn. You *must*. Goddamn it, it's *sim*ple."

"Simple for *you*," Priscilla said. She followed his directions and began gingerly to slide. She hit a small mogul and fell again. She began to scream. She tried to throw her ski poles, but the straps held them to her wrists. She kicked her feet like an infant in a tantrum, and one ski binding released. "I *hate* you," she cried. "I can't do it, I *can't* do it! I was so *proud* on the baby slope, all I wanted was for you to *watch* me—watch me for one lousy minute, that was all I asked you to do. You *knew* I wasn't ready for this. *Why* did you bring me up here, *why?*"

"I thought you were," he said weakly. "Ready. I wanted to show you the view." His father had wanted to give him the joy of the water, no doubt.

Dusk was coming to the mountain. Teen-aged experts bombed past in an avalanche of heedless color, with occasional curious side-glances. Harold and Priscilla agreed to take off their skis and walk down. It took an hour, and cost him a blister on each heel. The woods around them, perceived at so unusually slow a speed, wore a magical frozen strangeness, the ironical calm of airplane rivets. Her children were waiting at the edge of the emptying parking lot with tears in their eyes. "I tried to give her a treat," he explained to them, "but your mother doesn't trust me."

During this same perilous period, Harold attended his son's seventeenth birthday party, in the house he had left. As he was rushing to catch the evening train that would take him back to his apartment in the city, he noticed a fresh pan of brownies cooling on the stove. This was odd, because birthday cake had already been served. He asked his son, "What are these?"

The boy smiled cherubically. "Hash brownies. Have one, Dad. You can eat it on the train."

"It won't do anything funny to me?"

"Naa. It's just something the other kids cooked up for me as a joke. It's more the idea of it; they won't do anything."

Harold as a child had had a sweet tooth, a taste for starch; he took one of the bigger of the brownies and gobbled it in the car as his son drove him to the railroad station. In the train, he leaned his head against the black glass and entertained the rueful thoughts of a separated man. Slowly he came to realize that his mouth was very dry and his thoughts were not only repeating themselves but had taken on an intense, brightly colored form in his head. They were squeezed one on top of another, like strata of shale, and were vividly polychrome, like campaign ribbons. When he swung down from the train onto the platform of the city station, one side of him had grown much larger than the other, so he had to lean sharply or fall down. His body did not so much support as accompany him, in several laggard sections. Walking in what felt like a procession to the subway entrance, through a throng of hooded strangers and across a street of swollen cars, he reasoned what had happened: he had eaten a hash brownie.

One half of his brain kept shouting prudent advice to the other: *Look both ways. Take out a dollar. No, wait, here's a token. Put it in the slot. Wait for the No. 16, don't take Symphony. Don't panic.* Every process seemed to take a very long time, while his ribbonlike thoughts multiplied and shuttled with the speed of a computer. These thoughts kept adding up to nonsense, the other half of his brain noticed, while it called instructions and congratulations throughout his homeward progress. The people in the subway car stared at him as if they could hear this loud interior conversation going on. But he felt safe behind his face, as if behind a steel mask. Wheels beneath him screeched. A code of colored lights flew past the windows.

He was in air again, walking the three blocks from the subway to his apartment. Something in his throat burned. He felt nauseated, and kept selecting hedges and trash cans to vomit in, if it came to that, which it did not, quite. It seemed the confirmation of a gigantically abstruse theorem that his key fit in the lock of his door and that beyond the door lay a room full of dazzlingly familiar furniture. He picked up the telephone, which had the sheen and two-dimensional largeness of an image on a billboard, and called Priscilla.

"Hi, love."

Her voice rose in pitch. "What's happened to you, Harold?"

"Do I sound different?"

"Very." Her voice was sharp as porcupine quills, black with white tips. "What did they do to you?" *They*—his children, his ex-wife.

"They fed me a hash brownie. Jimmy said I wouldn't feel anything, but on the train in, my thoughts got very little and intense, and on the way from the station I had to keep coaching myself on how to get from there to here." The protective, trustworthy half of his brain congratulated him on how cogent he sounded.

But something was displeasing to Priscilla. She cried, "Oh, that's disgusting! I don't think it's funny, I don't think *any* of you are funny."

"Any of who?"

"You know who."

"I don't." Though he did. He looked at his palms; they were mottled. "Sweetie, I feel like throwing up. Help me."

"I can't," Priscilla said, and hung up. The click sounded like a slap, the same echoing slap that had once exploded next to his ear. Except that his father had become his son, and his mother was his girl friend. This much remained true: it had not been his fault, and in surviving he was somehow blamed.

The palms of his hands, less mottled, looked pale and wrinkled, like uncomfortable pillows. In his shirt pocket Harold found tucked the dollar bill rejected at the subway turnstile, extremely long ago. While waiting for Priscilla to relent and call back, he turned to its back side, examined the mystical eye above the truncated pyramid, and read, over and over, the slogan printed above the ONE.

Killing

ANNE'S FATHER'S HAND felt warm and even strong, though he lay unconscious, dying. In this expensive pastel room of the nursing home, he was
starving, he was dying of thirst, as surely as if he had been abandoned in a
desert. His breath stank. The smell from the parched hole that had been
his mouth was like nothing else bodily she had ever smelled—foul but in
no way fertile, an acid ultimate of carnality. Yet the presence was still his;
in his unconscious struggle for breath, his gray face flitted, soundlessly
muttering, into expressions she knew—the helpless raised eyebrows that
preceded an attempt at the dinner table to be droll, or a sudden stiffening
of the upper lip that warned of one of his rare, pained, carefully phrased
reprimands. A lawyer, lost to his family in the machinations of cities and
corporations, he had been a distant father, reluctant to chastise, the din-
nertime joke his most comfortable approach to affection. He had spent his
free time out of the house, puttering at tasks he had no son to share. In
New Hampshire, over several summers, he had built a quarter-mile of
stone wall with his own hands; in Boston, there had been the brick terrace
to level and weed; in the suburb of his retirement, compost heaps to tend
and broken fences to repair and redesign. In the year past, his hand had
lost its workman's roughness. There was no task his failing brain could
direct his hand to seize. Unthinkingly, Anne had asked him, this past
summer, to help one of the children to build a birdhouse; manfully, chuck-
ling with energy, he had assembled the tools, the wood, the nails. His pipe
clenched in his teeth as jauntily as ever, he had gone through the familiar
motions while his grandson gazed in gathering disbelief at the hammered-

together jumble of wood. The old man stood back at last, gazed with the child, saw clearly for a moment, and abandoned such jobs forever. Dry and uncallused, his hand rested warm in his daughter's.

Sometimes it returned her squeeze, or the agitation that passed across his face caused his shallow pulse to race. "Just relax," she would chant to him then, bending close, into his caustic breath. "Re-lax. It's all right. I'm right here, Daddy. I won't go away."

Anne was reminded, in these hours of holding and waiting, of a child-hood episode scarcely remembered for thirty years. It had been so strange, so out of both their characters. She had been a cheerful child—what they called in those years "well adjusted." At the age of thirteen or so, the first of three daughters to be entering womanhood, she was visited by insomnia, an inexplicable wakefulness that made sleep a magic kingdom impossible to reach and that turned the silhouetted furniture of her room into presences that might, if left unwatched, come horribly to life. Her mother dismissed the terror with the same lightness with which she had explained menstruation, as an untidiness connected with "the aging process"; it was her father, surprisingly, who took the development seriously. As Anne remembered it, he would come home pale from one of his innumerable meetings—the cold of the Common on his face, the weight of the State House on his shoulders—and, if he found her awake, would sit by her bed for hours, holding her hand and talking enough to be "company." Perhaps what had seemed hours to her had been a few minutes, perhaps her recol-lection had expanded a few incidents into a lengthy episode. In her mem-ory, his voice had been not merely paternal but amused, leisurely, enjoying itself, as if this visiting were less a duty than an occasion to be relished, in the manner of the country world where he had been a boy, where sitting and talking were a principal recreation. He had not begrudged her his time, and she wanted not to begrudge him her company now. She would put him to sleep.

Yet she hated the nursing home, hated and fled it—its cloaked odors, its incessant television, its expensive false order and hypocrisy of false cheer, its stifling vulgarity. These common dying and their coarse nurses were the very people her father had raised her to avoid, to rise above. "Well, aren't you the handsome boy!" the supervisor had exclaimed to him upon admit-tance, and tapped him on the arm like a brash girl friend.

His body, tempered by the chores he had always assigned himself, had stubbornly outlasted his judicious brain; then suddenly it began to surren-der. A succession of little strokes had brought him, who a week earlier could shuffle down the hall between Anne and a male nurse, to the point where he could not swallow. A decision arose. "The decision is yours," the doctor said. His face was heavy, kindly, self-protective, formal. The decision was whether or not to move her father to a hospital, where he could be fed intravenously and his life could be prolonged. She had decided not. The fear that the ambulance ride would compromise her father's dignity had been uppermost in her mind. But from the way the doctor seized her hand and pronounced with a solemn, artificial clarity, "You have made a wise decision," Anne realized that her decision had been to kill her father. He could not swallow. He could not drink. Abandoned, he must die.

Her voice took flight over the telephone, seeking escape from this responsibility. Why had the doctors given it to her? Couldn't they do it themselves? What would her mother have done? Anne called her sisters, one in Chicago, one in Texas. Of course, they agreed, she had made the right decision. The only decision. Their common inheritance, their mother's common sense, spoke through them so firmly that she almost forgave her sisters the safe distance from which they spoke. Yet their assurances evaporated within an hour. She called her minister; he came and had tea and told her that her decision was right, even holy. He seemed hard-boiled and unctuous both. After he left, she sat and held in her palms, votively, a teacup that had been her mother's. Her mother had died two years ago, leaving her children her china, her common sense, and a stately old man disintegrating from the head down. The cup, with its rim of gold and its band of cinnamon-red arabesques, had become sacred in this extremity; Anne closed her eyes and waited for her mother to speak through the fragile cool shape in her hands. Sensing nothing but a widening abyss, she opened her eyes and telephoned her husband, who was estranged from her and living in Boston. He had lodged himself in the grid of Back Bay, a few blocks from where she had grown up.

"Of course, dear," Martin said, his voice grave and paternal, as it had become. "You've made the only possible decision."

"Oh, you can say that, you can all say that," Anne cried into the hard receiver, heavier than the cup had been. "But I'm the one who had to do it. I'm killing him, and I'm the one who has to go watch it happen. It's incredible. His mouth *wants water*. He's drying *up!*"

"Why visit him?" Martin asked. "Isn't he unconscious?"

"He might wake up and be frightened," she said, and the image released a sobbing so great she had to hang up.

Martin called back a judicious while later. Anne was touched, thinking that he had telepathically given her time to cry herself out, go to the bathroom, and heat some coffee. But it seemed he had spent the time discussing her with his mistress. "Harriet says," he said, authoritatively, "the other decision would be downright neurotic, to cart him to the hospital and torture him with a lot of tubes. Not to mention the money."

"Tell Harriet I certainly don't want to do anything that would seem neurotic to her. She can relax about the money, though; she is not one of his heirs."

Martin sounded hurt. "She was very sympathetic with you. She started to cry herself."

"Tell her thanks a lot for her sympathy. Why doesn't she show it by letting you come back?"

"I don't want to come back," Martin said, in his new, grave, paternal voice.

"Oh, *shit* to you." Hanging up, Anne wondered at her sensation of joy, of release; then realized that in her anger with this man and his presumptuous mistress, she had for the first time in days thought of something other than the nursing home, and her father's dying, and her guilt.

She could not make herself stay. She would hold his hand for minutes that seemed hours, having announced her presence in his deaf ear, having settled herself to wait by his side. His face as it dried was sinking in upon itself, with that startled expression mummies have; the distance between his raised eyebrows and lowered eyelashes seemed enormous. His hand would twitch, or her hand, wandering, would come upon his pulse, and the sign of life would horrify her, like the sight of roaches scuttling in the sink when, in the middle of the night, the kitchen light is suddenly turned on. "Daddy, I must leave for a minute," she would say, and flee.

Her step seemed miraculously elastic to herself as she strode down the hall. The heads of the dying bobbed about her amid white sheets. There was a little gauzy-haired, red-faced lady who, locked into a geriatric chair, kept crying "Help" and clapping her hands. She paused as Anne passed, then resumed. "Help." Clap clap. *"Help."* The barred door. Air. Life. Barberry and pachysandra had been planted in square beds around the entrance. The parking lot was newly paved. This mundane earth and asphalt amazed Anne. The sun burned like a silver sore place low in the gray November sky. She slid into her car; its engine came alive.

The neighborhood of the nursing home was unfamiliar. She bought dinner for herself and the children in the innocent carnival of an A&P where she had never before shopped. She let herself be fed a sandwich and a Coke in a diner full of strange men. She inhaled the fragrances of a gasoline station where a friendly fat man in green coveralls filled her tank so matter-of-factly it seemed impossible that the life of another man, whose seed had become her life, was draining away, by her decision, beneath this chalky cold sky in this city of utter strangers.

Dying, her father had become sexual. Her mother no longer intervening, his manhood was revealed. For a time, after she died, Anne and Martin had thought to have him live with them. But, the first night of his trial visit, he had woken them, clearing his throat in the hall outside their bedroom. When Anne had opened the door, he told her, his face pale with fury, the top and bottom of his pajamas mismatched, that no one had ever hurt him as she had this night. At first she didn't understand. Then she blushed. "But, Daddy, he's my husband. You're my father. I'm not Mother, I'm Anne." She added, desperate to clarify, "Mother died, don't you remember?"

The anger was slow to leave his face, though the point seemed taken. His eyes narrowed with a legal canniness. "Allegedly," he said.

Martin had laughed at that, and the two of them led him back to his bed. But they were as little able to get back to sleep as if they had, indeed, been lovers and the man thrashing in the adjacent bedroom was the wronged husband. She perceived only later an irony of that night: the man who was with her didn't want to be. Martin's affair with Harriet had begun, and his willingness to try living with her father was his last kindness of their married life. She remembered later his great relief when she announced it wouldn't work. While her father, back in his own house, grew more puzzled and rebellious, passing from a succession of housekeepers to a live-in couple to a burly male nurse, her husband confessed more and more, and asked to separate. Once the old man was safely placed in a nursing home, Martin left. Then, abandoned, Anne perceived the gallantry of her father's refusal to submit to dying. As his reason fell away, he who had been so mild and legal had become violent and lawless; his lifelong habit of commanding respect was now twisted into a tyrannical rage, a defiant incontinence, a hitting of nurses with his fists, a struggle against a locked geriatric chair until both toppled. In his pugnacity and ferocity Anne saw the force, now naked, that had carved out of the world a shelter for his four females and had urged respectability upon them. With Martin's leaving, she, too, was naked. Herself helpless, she at last loved her father in his helplessness. Her love made all the more shameful her inability to stay with him, to lull his panic at the passage facing him as he had once lulled her panic at entering womanhood.

For three days after her commended decision, Anne came and went, marvelling at the fury of her father's will to live. His face, parched and unfed, grew rigid. His mouth made an O like a baby's at the breast. His breathing poured forth a stench like a stream of inexpressible scorn. His hand lived in hers. He could not die, she could not stay; as with the participants of a great and wicked love, there was none to forgive them save each other.

He died unobserved. Shortly a nurse noticed and drew the sheet up over his face and called his nearest relative. Anne had been raking leaves from her frostbitten lawn, thinking she should be with him. The world, which had made a space of privacy and isolation around them, then gathered and descended in a fluttering of letters and visits, of regards and reminiscences; her father's long, successful life was rebuilt in words before her. The funeral was a success, a rally of the surviving, a salute to the useful and presentable man who had passed away some time ago, while his body had still lived. Her sisters descended from airplanes and cried more than she could. Elderly faces that had floated above her childhood, her father's old friends, materialized. Anne was kissed, hugged, caressed, complimented. Yet she had been his executioner. There was no paradox, she saw. They were grateful. The world needed death. It needed death exactly as much as it needed life.

After the burial service, Martin went home with her and the children. "I'm surprised," Anne said to him as soon as they were alone, "Harriet wasn't there."

"Did you want her to be? We assumed you didn't."

"That was correct."

"She would have liked to be, of course. She admired what you did."

Anne saw that for him the funeral had been an opportunity for Harriet's advancement. In his mind he had leaped beyond their separation, beyond the divorce, to some day when she, his first wife, would be gracious to his second, repaying this supposed admiration. How small, Anne thought, he had grown: a promoter, a liaison man. "I did nothing," she said.

"You did everything," he responded, and this, too, was part of his game: to sell her herself as well as Harriet, to sell her on the idea that she was competent and independent; she could manage without him.

Could she? Not for the first time since the nurse had given her, over the telephone, the awaited gift of her father's death did Anne feel in her new freedom an abysmal purposelessness; she glimpsed the possibility that her father had needed her as none of the living did, that her next service to everyone, having killed him, was herself to die. Martin was lethal in his new manner, all efficient vitality, hugging the children ardently, talking to each with a self-conscious and compressed attentiveness unknown in the years when he had absent-mindedly shared their home. He even presumed to tap Anne on the bottom as she stood at the stove, as if she were one more child to be touched like a base. In the hour before dinner, he raced around the house changing light bulbs, bleeding the furnace, replacing window shades that had fallen from the temperamental little sockets. His virtuoso show of dutifulness—his rapid survey of the photographs the boys had developed in their darkroom, the brisk lesson in factoring he administered to his younger daughter—to Anne felt intended to put her to shame. His removal, rather than bringing her and the children closer together, had put distance between them. They blamed her for losing him. They blamed themselves. Night after night they sat wordless around the dinner table, chewing their guilt. Now he was here, pulling the wine cork, celebrating her father's death. "Anne, dear"—a locution of Harriet's he had acquired—"tell us all why you can't seem to replace the burned-out light bulbs. Is it the unscrewing or the screwing in that frightens you?" Lethal, but attractive; Harriet had made of him something smaller but more positive, less timorous and diffuse. Before, he had been in the house like the air they unthinkingly breathed; now he manifested himself among them as a power, his show of energy and duty vindictive—the display of a treasure they had wasted.

Anne told him, "I've been so busy getting my father to die I didn't notice which bulbs were on and which were off. I haven't even read a newspaper for days."

Martin ignored her defense. "Poor Grandpa," he said, gazing about at the children as if one more parental duty fallen to him was to remind them to mourn.

Hate, pure tonic hatred of this man, filled her and seemed to lift her free; he sensed it, from his end of the table, through the candlelit mist of children, and smiled. He wanted her hate. But it flickered off, like a bad light bulb. She was not free.

He helped her do the dishes. Living alone, Martin had learned some habits of housework: another new trick. As he moved around her, avoiding touching her, drying each dish with a comical bachelor care, she felt him grow weary; he, too, was mortal. In his weariness, he had slipped from Harriet's orbit back into hers. "Want me to go?" he asked, shyly.

"Sure. Why not? You always do."

"I thought, Grandpa dead and everything, you might get too depressed alone."

"Don't you want to go tell Harriet all about the marvellous funeral she missed?"

"No. She doesn't expect it. She said to be nice to you."

So his offer came from Harriet, not him. He was being given a night out, like the vulgarest of lower-class husbands. And Anne was herself too weary to fight the gift, to scorn it.

"The children are all here," she told him. "There's no extra bed. You'll have to sleep with me."

"It won't kill us," he said.

"Who's us?" Anne asked.

Months had passed since she had felt his body next to hers in bed. He had grown thinner, harder, more precisely knit, as if exercised by the distance he strained to keep between them. Perhaps only at first had it been a strain for him. When with a caress she offered to make love, he said, "No. That would be too much." In her fatigue, she was relieved. Sleep came to her swiftly, even though his presence barred her from the center of the bed, to which she had grown accustomed. In a dream, she was holding her father's hand, and he horrified her by sitting up energetically and beginning to scold, in that sardonic way Anne felt he had always reserved for her, the oldest; he showed her younger sisters only his softer side. She awoke and found her husband twisting next to her. It did not surprise her that he was there. Surprise came the other nights, when the bed was empty. Martin was up on one elbow, trying to plump his pillow. *"Why,"* he asked, as if they had been talking all along, "have you given the kids all the airfoam pillows and left yourself with these awful old feather things? It's like trying to sleep with your head on a pancake."

"Can't you go to sleep?"

"Of course not."

"Have I been asleep?"

"As usual."

"What do you think's the matter?"

"I don't know. Guilt, I suppose. I feel guilty about Harriet. Sleeping with you."

"Don't tell me about it. This was your idea, not mine."

"Also, I feel rotten about Grandpa. He was so *good.* He knew something was wrong, but he couldn't put his finger on it. The way he said 'allegedly' that time. And that day we took him to the nursing home—the way he accepted me as the boss. So brave and quiet, like a child going off to camp. This big Boston lawyer, who had always looked at me as sort of a chump, really. I had become the boss. Remember, how he kept telling me to watch out for the other cars? He had become—what's the word?—deferential."

"I know. It was pathetic."

"He didn't want me to hit another car, though. He wanted good care of himself taken."

"I know. I loved his will to live. It put me to shame. It puts us all to shame."

"Why?"

His blunt question startled her: the new Martin. The old one and she had understood each other without ever trying. She understood him now: he was saying, *Put yourself to shame, put yourself to death, but don't include me: I'm alive. At last.* She tried to explain, "I feel very disconnected these days."

"Well, I guess you are."

"Not just from you. Disconnected from everybody. The sermon today, I couldn't cry. It had nothing to do with Daddy, with anybody real. I couldn't keep my eyes off you and the boys. The way the backs of your heads were all the same."

He twisted noisily, and looped his arm around her waist. Her heart flipped, waiting for his hand to enclose her breast, his old habit. It didn't happen. It was as if his arm had been sliced off at the wrist. He said, in a soft, well-meant voice, "I'm sorry. Of course I feel guiltiest about you. Lying here is very conflicting. I felt conflicted all week, you calling me every hour on the hour to say your dear father hadn't kicked the bucket yet."

"Don't exaggerate. And don't say 'dear.' "

"You called a lot, I thought. And it went on and on, he just wouldn't die. What a tough old farmer he turned out to be."

"Yes."

"You were in agony. And there I sat in Back Bay, no use at all. I hated myself. I still do."

His confession, Anne saw, was an opportunity another woman—Harriet, certainly—would seize. His taut body wanted to make love. But, as had happened so many nights when they were married, by the same mechanism whereby the television news had lulled her, commercials and disasters and weather and sports tumbling on with the world's rotation, so her awareness of Martin's wishing to make love—of male energy alive in the world and sustaining it—put her to sleep, as her father's once sitting by her bedside had.

When Anne awoke again, he was still fighting with the pillow. By the quality of the moonlight, time had passed, but whether two minutes or an hour she couldn't tell. She knew she had failed once more, but the quality of this, too, was different. It was not so grievous, because everything was steeped and flattened in the moonlight of grief. She asked, "How can you be still awake?"

"This is a very unsuccessful experiment," he said, with satisfaction, of their sleeping together. "You do something to the bed that makes me nervous. You always did. With Harriet I have no problem. I sleep like a baby."

"Don't tell me about it."

"I'm just reporting it as a curious physiological fact."

"Just relax. Re-lax."

"I can't. Evidently you can. Your poor father's being dead must be a great relief."

"Not especially. Lie on your back."

He obeyed. She put her hand on his penis. It was warm and silky-small and like nothing else, softer than a breast, more fragile than a thought, yet heavy. Together, after a minute, they realized it was not rising, and would not rise. For Martin, it was a triumph, a proof. "Come on," he taunted. "Do your worst."

For Anne it had been, in his word, an experiment. Among her regrets was one that, having held her dying father's hand so continuously, she had not been holding it at the moment in which he passed from life to death; she had wanted, childishly, to know what it would have felt like. It would have felt like this. "Go to sleep," someone was pleading, far away. "Let's go to sleep."

Still of Some Use

WHEN FOSTER helped his ex-wife clean out the attic of the house where they had once lived and which she was now selling, they came across dozens of forgotten, broken games. Parcheesi, Monopoly, Lotto; games aping the strategies of the stock market, of crime detection, of real-estate speculation, of international diplomacy and war; games with spinners, dice, lettered tiles, cardboard spacemen, and plastic battleships; games bought in five-and-tens and department stores feverish and musical with Christmas expectations; games enjoyed on the afternoon of a birthday and for a few afternoons thereafter and then allowed, shy of one or two pieces, to drift into closets and toward the attic. Yet, discovered in their bright flat boxes between trunks of outgrown clothes and defunct appliances, the games presented a forceful semblance of value: the springs of their miniature launchers still reacted, the logic of their instructions would still generate suspense, given a chance. "What shall we do with all these games?" Foster shouted, in a kind of agony, to his scattered family as they moved up and down the attic stairs.

"Trash 'em," his younger son, a strapping nineteen, urged.

"Would the Goodwill want them?" asked his ex-wife, still wife enough to think that all of his questions deserved answers. "You used to be able to give things like that to orphanages. But they don't call them orphanages anymore, do they?"

"They call them normal American homes," Foster said.

His older son, now twenty-two, with a cinnamon-colored beard, offered,

"They wouldn't work anyhow; they all have something missing. That's how they got to the attic."

"Well, why didn't we throw them away at the time?" Foster asked, and had to answer himself. Cowardice, the answer was. Inertia. Clinging to the past.

His sons, with a shadow of old obedience, came and looked over his shoulder at the sad wealth of abandoned playthings, silently groping with him for the particular happy day connected to this and that pattern of colored squares and arrows. Their lives had touched these tokens and counters once; excitement had flowed along the paths of these stylized landscapes. But the day was gone, and scarcely a memory remained.

"Toss 'em," the younger decreed, in his manly voice. For these days of cleaning out, the boy had borrowed a pickup truck from a friend and parked it on the lawn beneath the attic window, so the smaller items of discard could be tossed directly into it. The bigger items were lugged down the stairs and through the front hall; already the truck was loaded with old mattresses, broken clock-radios, obsolete skis and boots. It was a game of sorts to hit the truck bed with objects dropped from the height of the house. Foster flipped game after game at the target two stories below. When the boxes hit, they exploded, throwing a spray of dice, tokens, counters, and cards into the air and across the lawn. A box called Mouse-trap, its lid showing laughing children gathered around a Rube Goldberg device, drifted sideways, struck one side wall of the truck, and spilled its plastic components into a flower bed. A set of something called Drag Race! floated gently as a snowflake before coming to rest, much diminished, on a stained mattress. Foster saw in the depth of downward space the cause of his melancholy: he had not played enough with these games. Now no one wanted to play.

Had he and his wife avoided divorce, of course, these boxes would have continued to gather dust in an undisturbed attic, their sorrow unexposed. The toys of his own childhood still rested in his mother's attic. At his last visit, he had crept up there and wound the spring of a tin Donald Duck; it had responded with an angry clack of its bill and a few stiff strokes on its drum. A tilted board with concentric grooves for marbles still waited in a bushel basket with his alphabet blocks and lead airplanes—waited for his childhood to return.

His ex-wife paused where he squatted at the attic window and asked him, "What's the matter?"

"Nothing. These games weren't used much."

"I know. It happens fast. You better stop now; it's making you too sad."

Behind him, his family had cleaned out the attic; the slant-ceilinged rooms stood empty, with drooping insulation. "How can you bear it?" he asked, of the emptiness.

"Oh, it's fun," she said, "once you get into it. Off with the old, on with the new. The new people seem nice. They have *little* children."

He looked at her and wondered whether she was being brave or truly hardhearted. The attic trembled slightly. "That's Ted," she said.

She had acquired a boy friend, a big athletic accountant fleeing from domestic embarrassments in a neighboring town. When Ted slammed the kitchen door two stories below, the glass shade of a kerosene lamp that, though long unused, Foster hadn't had the heart to throw out of the window vibrated in its copper clips, emitting a thin note like a trapped wasp's song. Time for Foster to go. His dusty knees creaked when he stood. His ex-wife's eager steps raced ahead of him down through the emptied house. He followed, carrying the lamp, and set it finally on the bare top of a bookcase he had once built, on the first-floor landing. He remembered screwing the top board, a prize piece of knot-free pine, into place from underneath, so not a nailhead marred its smoothness.

After all the vacant rooms and halls, the kitchen seemed indecently full of heat and life. "Dad, want a beer?" the bearded son asked. "Ted brought some." The back of the boy's hand, holding forth the dewy can, blazed with fine ginger hairs. His girl friend, wearing gypsy earrings and a NO NUKES sweatshirt, leaned against the disconnected stove, her hair in a bandanna and a black smirch becomingly placed on one temple. From the kind way she smiled at Foster, he felt this party was making room for him.

"No, I better go."

Ted shook Foster's hand, as he always did. He had a thin pink skin and silver hair whose fluffy waves seemed mechanically induced. Foster could look him in the eye no longer than he could gaze at the sun. He wondered how such a radiant brute had got into such a tame line of work. Ted had not helped with the attic today because he had been off in his old town, visiting his teen-aged twins. "I hear you did a splendid job today," he announced.

"They did," Foster said. "I wasn't much use. I just sat there stunned. All these things I had forgotten buying."

"Some were presents," his son reminded him. He passed the can his father had snubbed to his mother, who took it and tore up the tab with that defiant-sounding *pssff*. She had never liked beer, yet tipped the can to her mouth.

"Give me one sip," Foster begged, and took the can from her and drank a long swallow. When he opened his eyes, Ted's big hand was cupped under Mrs. Foster's chin while his thumb rubbed away a smudge of dirt along her jaw which Foster had not noticed. This protective gesture made her face look small, pouty, and frail. Ted, Foster noticed now, was dressed with a certain comical perfection in a banker's Saturday outfit—softened blue jeans, crisp tennis sneakers, lumberjack shirt with cuffs folded back. The youthful outfit accented his age, his hypertensive flush. Foster saw them suddenly as a touching, aging couple, and this perception seemed permission to go.

He handed back the can.

"Thanks for your help," his former wife said.

"Yes, we do thank you," Ted said.

"Talk to Tommy," she unexpectedly added, in a lowered voice. She was still sending out trip wires to slow Foster's departures. "This is harder on him than he shows."

Ted looked at his watch, a fat, black-faced thing he could swim under water with. "I said to him coming in, 'Don't dawdle till the dump closes.' "

"He loafed all day," his brother complained, "mooning over old stuff, and now he's going to screw up getting to the dump."

"He's very sensi-tive," the visiting gypsy said, with a strange chiming brightness, as if repeating something she had heard.

Outside, the boy was picking up litter that had fallen wide of the truck. Foster helped him. In the grass there were dozens of tokens and dice. Some were engraved with curious little faces—Olive Oyl, Snuffy Smith, Dagwood—and others with hieroglyphs—numbers, diamonds, spades, hexagons—whose code was lost. He held out a handful for Tommy to see. "Can you remember what these were for?"

"Comic-Strip Lotto," the boy said without hesitation. "And a game called Gambling Fools there was a kind of slot machine for." The light of old payoffs flickered in his eyes as he gazed down at the rubble in his father's hand. Though Foster was taller, the boy was broader in the shoulders, and growing. "Want to ride with me to the dump?" Tommy asked.

"I would, but I better go." He, too, had a new life to lead. By being on this forsaken property at all, Foster was in a sense on the wrong square, if not *en prise*. He remembered how once he had begun to teach this boy chess, but in the sadness of watching him lose—the little furry bowed head frowning above his trapped king—the lessons had stopped.

Foster tossed the tokens into the truck; they rattled to rest on the metal. "This depresses you?" he asked his son.

"Naa." The boy amended, "Kind of."

"You'll feel great," Foster promised him, "coming back with a clean truck. I used to love it at the dump, all that old happiness heaped up, and the seagulls."

"It's changed since you left. They have all these new rules. The lady there yelled at me last time, for putting stuff in the wrong place."

"She did?"

"Yeah. It was scary." Seeing his father waver, he added, "It'll only take twenty minutes." Though broad of build, Tommy had beardless cheeks and, between thickening eyebrows, a trace of that rounded, faintly baffled blankness babies have, that wrinkles before they cry.

"O.K.," Foster said. "You win. I'll come along. I'll protect you."

The City

HIS STOMACH began to hurt on the airplane, as the engines changed pitch to descend into this city. Carson at first blamed his pain upon the freeze-dried salted peanuts that had come in a little silver-foil packet with the whiskey sour he had let the stewardess bring him at ten o'clock that morning. He did not think of himself as much of a drinker; but the younger men in kindred gray business suits who flanked him in the three-across row of seats had both ordered drinks, and it seemed a way of keeping status with the stewardess. Unusually for these days, she was young and pretty. So many stewardesses seemed, like Carson himself, on second careers, victims of middle-aged restlessness—the children grown, the long descent begun.

A divorced former business-school math teacher, he worked as a sales representative for a New Jersey manufacturer of microcomputers and information-processing systems. In his fifties, after decades of driving the same suburban streets from home to school and back again, he had become a connoisseur of cities—their reviving old downtowns and grassy industrial belts, their rusting railroad spurs and new glass buildings, their orange-carpeted hotels and bars imitating the interiors of English cottages. But always there was an individual accent, a style of local girl and a unique little historic district, an odd-shaped skyscraper or a museum holding a Cézanne, say, or a Winslow Homer that you could not see in any other place. Carson had never before visited the city into which he was now descending, and perhaps a nervous apprehension of the new contacts he must weld and the persuasions he must deliver formed the seed of the pain that had taken root in the center of his stomach, just above the navel.

He kept blaming the peanuts. The tempting young stewardess, with a tender boundary on her throat where the pancake makeup stopped, had given him not one but two packets in silver foil, and he had eaten both—the nuts tasting tartly of acid, the near engine of the 747 haloed by a rainbow of furious vapor in a backwash of sunlight from the east as the great plane droned west. This drone, too, had eaten into his stomach. Then there was the whiskey sour itself, and the time-squeeze of his departure, and the pressure of elbows on the armrests on both sides of him. He had arrived at the airport too late to get an aisle or a window seat. Young men now, it seemed to him, were increasingly corpulent and broad, due to the mixture of exercise and beer the culture kept pushing. Both of these specimens wore silk handkerchiefs in their breast pockets and modified bandit mustaches above their prim, pale, satisfied mouths. When you exchanged a few words with them, you heard voices that knew nothing, that were tinny like the cheapest of television sets.

Carson put away the papers on which he had been blocking in a system —computer, terminals, daisy-wheel printers, optional but irresistible color-graphics generator with appropriate interfaces—for a prospering little manufacturer of electric reducing aids, and ran a final check on what could be ailing his own system. Peanuts. Whiskey. Crowded conditions. In addition to everything else, he was tired, he realized: tired of numbers, tired of travel, of food, of competing, even of self-care—of showering and shaving in the morning and putting himself into clothes and then, sixteen hours later, taking himself out of them. The pain slightly intensified. He pictured the pain as spherical, a hot tarry bubble that would break if only he could focus upon it the laser of the right thought.

In the taxi line, Carson felt more comfortable if he stood with a slight hunch. The cool autumn air beat through his suit upon his skin. He must look sick: he was attracting the glances of his fellow-visitors to the city. The two young men whose shoulders had squeezed him for three hours had melted into the many similar others with their attaché cases and tasseled shoes. Carson gave the cabdriver not the address of the manufacturer of reducing and exercise apparatus but that of the hotel where he had a reservation. A sudden transparent wave of nausea, like a dip in the flight of the 747, had suddenly decided him. As he followed the maroon-clad bellhop down the orange-carpeted corridor, not only were the colors nauseating but the planes of wall and floor looked warped, as if the pain that would not break up were transposing him to a set of new coördinates, by the touch of someone's finger on a terminal keyboard. He telephoned the exercise company from the room, explaining his case to an answering female and making a new appointment for tomorrow morning, just before he was scheduled to see the head accountant of another booming little firm, makers of devices that produced "white noise" to shelter city sleep.

The appointment jam bothered Carson, but remotely, for it would all be taken care of by quite another person—his recovered, risen self. The secretary he had talked to had been sympathetic, speaking in the strangely comforting accent of the region—languid in some syllables, quite clipped in others—and had recommended Maalox. In the motion pictures that had flooded Carson's childhood with images of the ideal life, people had "sent down" for such things, but during all the travelling of his recent years, from one exiguously staffed accommodation to the next, he had never seen that this could be done; he went down himself to the hotel pharmacy. A lobby mirror shocked him with the image of a thin-limbed man in shirt sleeves, with a pot belly and a colorless mouth tugged down on one side like a dead man's.

The medicine tasted chalky and gritty and gave the pain, after a moment's hesitation, an extra edge, as of tiny sandy teeth. His hotel room also was orange-carpeted, with maroon drapes that Carson closed, after peeking out at a bare brown patch of park where amid the fallen leaves some boys were playing soccer; their shouts jarred his membranes. He turned on the television set, but it, too, jarred. Lying on one of the room's double beds, studying the ceiling between trips to the bathroom, he let the afternoon burn down into evening and thought how misery itself becomes a kind of home. The ceiling had been plastered in overlapping loops, like the scales of a large white fish. For variation, Carson stretched himself out upon the cool bathroom floor, marvelling at the complex, thick-lipped undersides of the porcelain fixtures, and at the distant bright lozenge of foreshortened mirror.

Repeated violent purgations had left undissolved the essential intruder, the hot tarry thing no longer simply spherical in shape but elongating. When vomiting began, Carson had been hopeful. The hope faded with the light. In the room's shadowy spaces his pain had become a companion whom his constant interrogations left unmoved; from minute to minute it did not grow perceptibly worse, nor did it leave him. He reflected that his situation was a perfect one for prayer; but he had never been religious and so could spare himself that additional torment.

The day's light, in farewell, placed feathery gray rims upon all the curved surfaces of the room's furniture—the table legs, the lamp bowls. Carson imagined that if only the telephone would ring his condition would be shattered. Curled on his side, he fell asleep briefly; awakening to pain, he found the room dark, with but a sallow splinter of street light at the window. The soccer players had gone. He wondered who was out there, beyond the dark, whom he could call. His ex-wife had remarried. Of his children, one, the boy, was travelling in Mexico and the other, the girl, had disowned her father. When he received her letter of repudiation, Carson had telephoned and been told, by the man she had been living with, that she had moved out and joined a feminist commune.

He called the hotel desk and asked for advice. The emergency clinic at the city hospital was suggested, by a young male voice that, to judge from its cheerful vigor, had just come on duty. Shaking, lacing his shoes with difficulty, smiling to find himself the hero of a drama without an audience, Carson dressed and delicately took his sore body out into the air. A row of taxis waited beneath the corrosive yellow glare of a sodium-vapor streetlight. Neon advertisements and stacked cubes of fluorescent offices and red and green traffic lights flickered by—glimpses of the city that now, normally, with his day's business done, he would be roving, looking for a restaurant, a bar, a stray conversation, a possibility of contact with one of the city's unofficial hostesses, with her green eye-paint and her short skirt and tall boots and exposed knees. He had developed a fondness for such women, even when no deal was struck. Their brisk preliminaries tickled him, and their frank hostility.

The hospital was a surprising distance from the hotel. A vast and glowing pile with many increasingly modern additions, it waited at the end of a swerving drive through a dark park and a neighborhood of low houses. Carson expected to surrender the burden of his body utterly, but instead found himself obliged to carry it through a series of fresh efforts—forms to be filled out, proofs to be supplied of his financial fitness to be ill, a series of waits to be endured, on crowded benches and padded chairs, while his eye measured the distance to the men's-room door and calculated the time it would take him to hobble across it, open the door to a stall, kneel, and heave away vainly at the angry visitor to his own insides.

The first doctor he at last was permitted to see seemed to Carson as young and mild and elusive as his half-forgotten, travelling son. Both had hair so blond as to seem artificial. His wife, the doctor let it be known, was giving a dinner party, for which he was already late, in another sector of the city. Nevertheless the young man politely examined him. Carson was, he confessed, something of a puzzle. His pain didn't seem localized enough for appendicitis, which furthermore was unusual in a man his age.

"Maybe I'm a slow bloomer," Carson suggested, each syllable, in his agony, a soft, self-deprecatory grunt.

There ensued a further miasma of postponement, livened with the stabs of blood tests and the banter of hardened nurses. He found himself undressing in front of a locker so that he could wait with a number of other men in threadbare, backwards hospital gowns to be X-rayed. The robust technician, with his standard bandit mustache, had the cheerful aura of a weight lifter and a great ladies' (or men's) man. "Chin here," he said. "Shoulders forward. Deep breath: hold it. Good boy." Slowly Carson dressed again, though the clothes looked, item by item, so shabby as to be hardly his. One could die, he saw, in the interstices of these procedures. All around him, on the benches and in the bright, bald holding areas of the hospital's innumerable floors, other suppliants, residents of the city and mostly black, served as models of stoic calm; he tried to imitate them, though it hurt to sit up straight and his throat ached with gagging.

The results of his tests were trickling along through their channels. The fair-haired young doctor must be at his party by now; Carson imagined the clash of silver, the candlelight, the bare-shouldered women—a festive domestic world from which he had long fallen.

Toward midnight, he was permitted to undress himself again and to get into a bed, in a kind of emergency holding area. White curtains surrounded him, but not silence. On either side of him, from the flanking beds, two men, apparently with much in common, moaned and crooned a kind of tuneless blues. When doctors visited them, they pleaded to get out and promised to be good henceforth. From one side, after a while, came a sound of tidy retching, like that of a cat who has eaten a bird bones and all; on the other side, internes seemed to be cajoling a tube up through a man's nose. Carson was comforted by these evidences that at least he had penetrated into a circle of acknowledged ruin. He was inspected at wide intervals. Another young doctor, who reminded him less of his son than of the shifty man, a legal-aid lawyer, who had lived with his daughter and whom Carson suspected of inspiring and even dictating the eerily formal letter she had mailed her father, shambled in and, after some poking of Carson's abdomen, shrugged. Then a female physician, dark-haired and fortyish, came and gazed with sharp amusement down into Carson's face. She had an accent, Slavic of some sort. She said, "You don't protect enough."

"Protect?" he croaked. He saw why slaves had taken to clowning.

She thrust her thumb deep into his belly, in several places. "I shouldn't be able to do that," she said. "You should go through the ceiling." The idiom went strangely with her accent.

"It did hurt," he told her.

"Not enough," she said. She gazed sharply down into his eyes; her own eyes were in shadow. "I think we shall take more blood tests."

Yet Carson felt she was stalling. There was a sense, from beyond the white curtains, percolating through the voices of nurses and policemen and agitated kin in this emergency room, of something impending in his case, a significant visitation. He closed his eyes for what seemed a second. When he opened them a new man was leaning above him—a tall tutorial man wearing a tweed jacket with elbow patches, a button-down shirt, and rimless glasses that seemed less attachments to his face than intensifications of a general benign aura. His hair was combed and grayed exactly right, and cut in the high-parted and close-cropped style of the Camelot years. Unlike the previous doctors, he sat on the edge of Carson's narrow bed. His voice and touch were gentle; he explained, palpating, that some appendixes were retrocecal—that is, placed behind the large intestine, so that one could be quite inflamed without the surface sensitivity and protective reflex usual with appendicitis.

Carson wondered what dinner party the doctor had been pulled from, at this post-midnight hour, in his timeless jacket and tie. Carson wished to make social amends but was in a poor position to, flat on his back and nearly naked. With a slight smile, the doctor pondered his face, as if to unriddle it, and Carson stared back with pleading helpless hopefulness, mute as a dog, which can only whimper or howl. He was as weary of pain and a state of emergency as he had been, twelve hours before, of his normal life. "I'd like to operate," the doctor said softly, as if putting forth a suggestion that Carson might reject.

"Oh yes, *please,*" Carson said. "When, do you think?" He was very aware that, though the debauched hour and disreputable surroundings had become his own proper habitat, the doctor was healthy and must have a decent home, a family, a routine to return to.

"Why, right *now,*" was the answer, in a tone of surprise, and this doctor stood and began to take off his coat, as if to join Carson in some sudden, cheerfully concocted athletic event.

Perhaps Carson merely imagined the surgeon's gesture. Perhaps he merely thought *Bliss,* or really sighed the word aloud. Things moved rapidly. The shifty legal-aid lookalike returned, more comradely now that Carson had received a promotion in status, and asked him to turn on one side, and thrust a needle into his buttock. Then a biracial pair of orderlies coaxed his body from the bed to a long trolley on soft swift wheels; the white curtains were barrelled through; faces, lights, steel door lintels streamed by. Carson floated, feet first, into a room that he recognized, from having seen its blazing counterpart so often dramatized on films, as an operating room. A masked and youthful population was already there, making chatter, having a party. "There are so many of you!" Carson exclaimed; he was immensely happy. His pain had already ceased. He was transferred from the trolley to a very narrow, high, padded table. His arms were spread out on wooden extensions and strapped tight to them. His wrists were pricked. Swollen rubber was pressed to his face as if to test the fit. He tried to say, to reassure the masked crew that he was not frightened and to impress them with what a "good guy" he was, that somebody should cancel his appointments for tomorrow.

At a point and place in the fog as it fitfully lifted, the surgeon himself appeared, no longer in a tweed jacket but in a lime-green hospital garment, and now jubilant, bending close. He held up the crooked little finger of one hand before Carson's eyes, which could not focus. "Fat as that," he called through a kind of wind.

"What size should it have been?" Carson asked, knowing they were discussing his appendix.

"No thicker than a pencil," came the answer, tugged by the bright tides of contagious relief.

"But when did you sleep?" Carson asked, and was not answered, having overstepped.

Earlier, he had found himself in an underground room that had many stalactites. His name was being shouted by a big gruff youth. "Hey Bob come on Bob wake up give us a little smile that's the boy Bob." There were others besides him stretched out in this catacomb, whose ceiling was festooned with drooping transparent tubes; these were the stalactites. Within an arm's length of him, another man was lying as motionless as a limestone knight carved on a tomb. Carson realized that he had been squeezed through a tunnel—the arm straps, the swollen rubber—and had come out the other side. "Hey, Bob, come on, give us a smile. *Thaaat's* it." He had a tremendous need to urinate; liquid was being dripped into his arm.

Later, after the windy, glittering exchange with the surgeon, Carson awoke in an ordinary hospital room. In a bed next to him, a man with a short man's sour, pinched profile was lying and smoking and staring up at a television set. Though the picture twitched, no noise seemed to be coming from the box. "Hi," Carson said, feeling shy and wary, as if in his sleep he had been married to this man.

"Hi," the other said, without taking his eyes from the television set and exhaling smoke with a loudness, simultaneously complacent and fed up, that had been one of Carson's former wife's most irritating mannerisms.

When Carson awoke again, it was twilight, and he was in yet another room, a private room, alone, with a sore abdomen and a clearer head. A quarter-moon leaned small and cold in the sky above the glowing square windows of another wing of the hospital, and his position in the world and the universe seemed clear enough. His convalescence had begun.

In the five days that followed, he often wondered why he was so happy. Ever since childhood, after several of his classmates had been whisked away to hospitals and returned to school with proud scars on their lower abdomens, Carson had been afraid of appendicitis. At last, in his sixth decade, the long-dreaded had occurred, and he had comported himself, he felt, with passable courage and calm.

His scar was not the little lateral slit his classmates had shown him but a rather gory central incision from navel down; he had been opened up wide, it was explained to him, on the premise that at his age his malady might have been anything from ulcers to cancer. The depth of the gulf that he had, unconscious, floated above thrilled him. There had been, too, a certain unthinkable intimacy. His bowels had been "handled," the surgeon gently reminded him, in explaining a phase of his recuperation. Carson tried to picture the handling: clamps and white rubber gloves and something glistening and heavy and purplish that was his. His appendix had indeed been retrocecal—one of a mere ten percent so located. It had even begun, microscopic investigation revealed, to rupture. All of this retrospective clarification, reducing to cool facts the burning, undiscourageable demon he had carried, vindicated Carson. For the sick feel as shamed as the sinful, as fallen.

The surgeon, with his Ivy League bearing, receded from that moment of extreme closeness when he had bent above Carson's agony and decided to handle his bowels. He dropped by in the course of his rounds only for brief tutorial sessions about eating and walking and going to the bathroom—all things that needed to be learned again. Others came forward. The slightly amused dark Slavic woman returned, to change his dressing, yanking the tapes with a, he felt, unnecessary sharpness. "You were too brave," she admonished him, blaming him for the night when she had wanted to inflict more blood tests upon him. The shambling young doctor of that same night also returned, no longer in the slightest resembling the lawyer whom Carson's daughter had spurned in favor of her own sex, and then the very blond one; there materialized a host of specialists in one department of Carson's anatomy or another, so that he felt huge, like Gulliver pegged down in Lilliput for inspection. All of them paid their calls so casually and pleasantly—just dropping by, as it were—that Carson was amazed, months later, to find each visit listed by date and hour on the sheets of hospital services billed to him in extensive dot-matrix printout—an old Centronics 739 printer, from the look of it.

Hospital life itself, the details of it, made him happy. The taut white bed had hand controls that lifted and bent the mattress in a number of comforting ways. A television set had been mounted high on the wall opposite him and was obedient to a panel of buttons that nestled in his palm like an innocent, ethereal gun. Effortlessly he flicked his way back and forth among morning news shows, midmorning quiz shows, noon updates, and afternoon soap operas and talk shows and reruns of classics such as Carol Burnett and *Hogan's Heroes*. At night, when the visitors left the halls and the hospital settled in upon itself, the television set became an even warmer and more ingratiating companion, with its dancing colors and fluctuant radiance. His first evening in this precious room, while he was still groggy from anesthesia, Carson had watched a tiny white figure hit, as if taking a sudden great stitch, a high-arching home run into the second deck of Yankee Stadium; the penetration of the ball seemed delicious, and to be happening deep within the tiers of himself. He pressed the off button on the little control, used another button to adjust the tilt of his bed, and fell asleep as simply as an infant.

Normally, he liked lots of cover; here, a light blanket was enough. Normally, he could never sleep on his back; here, of necessity, he could sleep no other way, his body slightly turned to ease the vertical ache in his abdomen, his left arm at his side receiving all night long the nurturing liquids of the I.V. tube. Lights always burned; voices always murmured in the hall; this world no more rested than the parental world beyond the sides of a crib.

In the depths of the same night when the home run was struck, a touch on his upper right arm woke Carson. He opened his eyes and there, in the quadrant of space where the rectangle of television had been, a queenly smooth black face smiled down upon him. She was a nurse taking his blood pressure; she had not switched on the overhead light in his room and so the oval of her face was illumined only indirectly, from afar, as had been the pieces of furniture in his hotel room. Without looking at the luminous dial of his wristwatch on the bedside table, he knew this was one of those abysmal hours when despair visits men, when insomniacs writhe in an ocean of silence, when the jobless and the bankrupt want to scream in order to break their circular calculations, when spurned lovers roll from an amorous dream onto empty sheets, and soldiers abruptly awake to the metallic taste of coming battle. In this hour of final privacy she had awakened him with her touch. No more than a thin blanket covered his body in the warm, dim room. *I forgive you,* her presence said. She pumped up a balloon around his arm, relaxed it, pumped it up again. She put into Carson's mouth one of those rocket-shaped instruments of textured plastic that have come to replace glass thermometers, and while waiting for his temperature to register in electronic numbers on a gadget at her waist she hummed a little tune, as if humorously to disavow her beauty, that beauty

which women have now come to regard as an enemy, a burden and cause
for harassment. Carson thought of his daughter.

Although many nurses administered to him—as he gained strength he
managed to make small talk with them even at four in the morning—this
particular one, her perfectly black and symmetrical face outlined like an
eclipsed sun with its corona, never came again.

"Walk," the surgeon urged Carson. "Get up and walk as soon as you
can. Get that body moving. It turns out it wasn't the disease used to kill a
lot of people in hospitals, it was lying in bed and letting the lungs fill up
with fluid."

Walking meant, at first, pushing the spindly, rattling I.V. pole along
with him. There was a certain jaunty knack to it—easing the wheels over
the raised metal sills here and there in the linoleum corridor, placing the
left hand at the balance point he thought of as the pole's waist, swinging
"her" out of the way of another patient promenading with his own gan-
gling chrome partner. From observing other patients Carson learned the
trick of removing the I.V. bag and threading it through his bathrobe sleeve
and rehanging it, so he could close his bathrobe neatly. His first steps, in
the moss-green sponge slippers the hospital provided, were timid and brittle, but as the days passed the length of his walks increased: to the end of
the corridor, where the windows of a waiting room overlooked the distant
center of the city; around the corner, past a rarely open snack bar, and into
an area of children's diseases; still farther, to an elevator bank and a
carpeted lounge where pregnant women and young husbands drank Tab
and held hands. The attendants at various desks in the halls came to know
him, and to nod as he passed, with his lengthening stride and more erect
posture. His handling of the I.V. pole became so expert as to feel debonair.

His curiosity about the city revived. What he saw from the window of
his own room was merely the wall of another wing of the hospital, with
gift plants on the windowsills and here and there thoughtful bathrobed
figures gazing outward toward the wall of which his own bathrobed figure
was a part. From the windows of the waiting room, the heart of the city
with its clump of brown and blue skyscrapers and ribbonlike swirls of
highway seemed often to be in sunlight, while clouds shadowed the hospital grounds and parking lots and the snarl of taxis around the entrance.
Carson was unable to spot the hotel where he had stayed, or the industrial
district where he had hoped to sell his systems, or the art museum that
contained, he remembered reading, some exemplary Renoirs and a priceless Hieronymus Bosch. He could see at the base of the blue-brown mass of
far buildings a suspension bridge, and imagined the dirty river it must

cross, and the eighteenth-century fort that had been built here to hold the river against the Indians, and the nineteenth-century barge traffic that had fed the settlement and then its industries, which attracted immigrants, who thrust the grid of city streets deep into the surrounding farmland.

This was still a region of farmland; thick, slow, patient, pious voices drawled and twanged around Carson as he stood there gazing outward and eavesdropping. Laconic, semi-religious phrases of resignation fell into place amid the standardized furniture and slippered feet and pieces of jigsaw puzzles half assembled on card tables here. Fat women in styleless print dresses and low-heeled shoes had been called in from their kitchens, and in from the fields men with crosshatched necks and hands that had the lumpy, rounded look of used tools.

Illness and injury are great democrats, and had achieved a colorful cross section. Carson came to know by sight a lean man with cigar-dark skin and taut Oriental features; his glossy shaved head had been split by a Y-shaped gash now held together by stitches. He sat in a luxurious light-brown, almost golden robe, his wounded head propped by a hand heavy with rings, in the room with the pregnant women and the silver elevator doors. When Carson nodded once in cautious greeting, this apparition said loudly, "Hey, man," as if they shared a surprising secret. Through the open doorways of the rooms along the corridors, Carson glimpsed prodigies—men with beaks of white bandage and plastic tubing, like those drinking birds many fads ago; old ladies shrivelling to nothing in a forest of flowers and giant facetious get-well cards; and an immensely plump mocha-colored woman wearing silk pantaloons and a scarlet Hindu dot in the center of her forehead. She entertained streams of visitors—wispy, dusky men and great-eyed children. Like Carson, she was an honorary member of the city, and she would acknowledge his passing with a languid lifting of her fat fingers, tapered as decidedly as the incense cones on her night table.

The third day, he was put on solid food and disconnected from the intravenous tubing. With his faithful I.V. pole removed from the room, he was free to use both arms and to climb stairs. His surgeon at his last appearance (dressed in lumberjack shirt and chinos, merrily about to "take off," for it had become the weekend) had urged stair climbing upon his patient as the best possible exercise. There was, at the end of the corridor in the other direction from the waiting room from whose windows the heart of the city could be viewed, an exit giving on a cement-and-steel staircase almost never used. Here, down four flights to the basement, then up six to the locked rooftop door, and back down two to his own floor,

Carson obediently trod in his bathrobe and his by now disintegrating green sponge slippers.

His happiness was purest out here, in this deserted and echoing sector, where he was invisible and anonymous. In his room, the telephone had begun to ring. The head of his company back in New Jersey called repeatedly, at first to commiserate and then to engineer a way in which Carson's missed appointments could be patched without the expense of an additional trip. So Carson, sitting up on his adaptable mattress, placed calls to the appropriate personnel and gave an enfeebled version of his pitch; the white-noise company expressed interest in digital color-graphics imaging, and Carson mailed them his firm's shiny brochure on its newest system (resolutions to 640 pixels per line, 65,536 simultaneous colors, image memory up to 256K bytes). The secretary from the other company, who had sounded sympathetic on the phone five days ago, showed up in person; she turned out to be comely in a coarse way, with bleached, frizzed hair, the remnant of a swimming-pool tan, and active legs she kept crossing and recrossing as she described her own divorce—the money, the children, the return to work after years of being a pampered suburbanite. "I could be one again, let me tell you. These women singing the joys of being in the work force, they can *have* it." This woman smoked a great deal, exhaling noisily and crushing each cerise-stained butt into a jar lid she had brought in her pocketbook. Carson had planned his afternoon in careful half-hour blocks—the staircase, thrice up and down; a visit to the waiting room, where he had begun to work on one of the jigsaw puzzles; a visit to his bathroom if his handled bowels were willing; finally, a luxurious immersion in last month's *Byte* and the late innings of this Saturday's playoff game. His visitor crushed these plans along with her many cigarettes. Then his own ex-wife telephoned, kittenish the way she had become, remarried yet with something plaintive still shining through and with a note of mockery in her voice, as if his descending into a strange city with a bursting appendix was another piece of willful folly, like his leaving her and his ceasing to teach mathematics at the business school—all those tedious spread sheets. His son called collect from Mexico on Sunday, sounding ominously close at hand, and spacy, as long awkward silences between father and son ate up the dollars. His daughter never called, which seemed considerate and loving of her. She and Carson knew there was no disguising our essential solitude.

He found that after an hour in his room and bed he became homesick for the stairs. At first, all the flights had seemed identical, but by now he had discovered subtle differences among them—old evidence of spilled paint on one set of treads, a set of numbers chalked by a workman on the wall of one landing, water stains and cracks affecting one stretch of rough yellow plaster and not another. At the bottom, there were plastic trash cans and a red door heavily marked with warnings to push the crash bar only in case of emergency. At the top, a plain steel door, without handle or window, defied penetration. The doors at the landings in between each gave on a strange outdoor space, a kind of platform hung outside the door leading into the hospital proper; pre-poured cement grids prevented leaping or falling or a clear outlook but admitted cool fresh air and allowed a fractional view of the city below.

The neighborhood here was flat and plain—quarter-acre-lot tract houses built long enough ago for the bloom of newness to have wilted and for dilapidation to be setting in. The hospital wall, extending beyond the projecting staircase, blocked all but a slice of downward vision containing some threadbare front yards, one of them with a tricycle on its side and another with a painted statue of the Virgin, and walls of pastel siding in need of repainting, and stretches of low-pitched composition-shingled roof —a shabby, sort of small-town vista to Carson's eyes, but here well within the city limits. He never saw a person walking on the broad sidewalks, and few cars moved along the street even at homecoming hour. Nearest and most vivid, a heap of worn planking and rusting scaffold pipes and a dumpster coated with white dust and loaded with plaster and lathing testified to a new phase of construction as the hospital continued to expand. Young men sometimes came and added to the rubbish, or loudly threw the planking around. These efforts seemed unorganized, and ceased on the weekend.

The drab housing and assembled rubble that he saw through the grid of the cement barrier, which permitted no broader view, nevertheless seemed to Carson brilliantly real, moist and deep-toned and full. Life, this was life. This was the world. When—still unable to climb stairs, the I.V. pole at his side—he had first come to this landing, just shoving open the door had been an effort. The raw outdoor air had raked through his still-drugged system like a sweeping rough kiss, early-fall air mixing summer and winter, football and baseball, stiff with chill yet damp and not quite purged of growth. Once, he heard the distant agitation of a lawnmower. Until the morning when he was released, he would come here even in the dark and lean his forehead against the cement and breathe, trying to take again into himself the miracle of the world, reprogramming himself, as it were, to live —the air cold on his bare ankles, his breath a visible vapor, his bowels resettling around the ache of their healing.

* * *

The taxi took him straight to the airport; Carson saw nothing of the city but the silhouettes beside the highway and the highway's scarred center strip. For an instant after takeoff, a kind of map spread itself underneath him, and then was gone. Yet afterwards, thinking back upon the farm voices, the distant skyscrapers, the night visits of the nurses, the doctors with their unseen, unsullied homes, the dozens of faces risen to the surface of his pain, he seemed to have come to know the city intimately; it was like, on other of his trips, a woman who, encountered in a bar and paid at the end, turns ceremony inside out, and bestows herself without small talk.

The Lovely Troubled Daughters of Our Old Crowd

WHY DON'T THEY GET MARRIED? You see them around town, getting older, little spinsters already, pedalling bicycles to their local jobs or walking up the hill by the rocks with books in their arms. Annie Langhorne, Betsey Clay, Damaris Wilcombe, Mary Jo Addison: we've known them all since they were two or three, and now they've reached their mid-twenties, back from college, back from Year Abroad, grown women but not going anywhere, not New York or San Francisco or even Boston, just hanging around here in this little town letting the seasons wash over them, walking the same streets where they grew up, hanging in the shadows of their safe old homes.

On the edge of a Wilcombe lawn party, their pale brushed heads like candles burning in the summer sunlight, a ribbon or a plastic barrette attached for the occasion—I can see them still, their sweet pastel party dresses and their feet bare in the grass, those slender little-girl feet, with bony tan toes, that you feel would leave rabbit tracks in the dew. Damaris and Annie, best friends then and now, had been coaxed into carrying hors d'oeuvres around; they carried the tray cockeyed, their wrists were so weak, the devilled eggs slipping, their big eyes with their pale-blue whites staring upward so solemnly at your grinning grown-up face as you took your devilled egg and smiled to be encouraging. We were in our late twen-

ties then, young at being old—the best of times. The summer smells of bug
spray on the lawn and fresh mint in the gin; the young wives healthy and
brown in their sundresses, their skin glowing warm through the cotton; the
children still small and making a flock in the uncut grass beyond the lawn,
running and tumbling, their pastel dresses getting stained with green, their
noise coming and going in the field as a kind of higher-pitched echo of
ours, creating their own world underfoot as the liquor and the sunlight
soaked in and the sky filled with love.

I can still see Betsey and my own daughter the night we first met the
Clays. They had just moved to town. A cousin of Maureen's had gone to
school with my wife and sent us a note. We dropped by to give them the
name of our dentist and doctor and happened to hit it off. April, it must
have been, or May. Cocktails dragged on into dark and Maureen brought a
pickup dinner out to the patio table. The two baby girls that had never met
before—not much more than two years old, they must have been—were
put to sleep in the same bed. Down they came into the dark, down into the
cool air outdoors, hand in hand out of this house strange to the two of
them, Betsey a white ghost in her nightie, her voice so eerie and thin but
distinct. "See moon?" she said. Unable to sleep, they had seen the moon
from the bed. The Clays had moved from the city, where maybe the moon
was not so noticeable. "See moon?": her voice thin and distinct as a distant
owl's call. And of course they were right, there the moon was, lopsided
and sad-faced above the trees just beginning to blur into leaf. Time (at last)
to go home.

Now Betsey works at the paint-and-linoleum store on Second Street and
gives guitar lessons on the side. She fell in love with her elderly married
music teacher at Smith and went about as far as she could go with classical
guitar, even to Spain for a year. When the Episcopal church sponsored a
refugee Cuban family last winter, they called in Betsey for her Spanish.
She lives with her mother, in that same house where she saw the moon, a
gloomy place now that Maureen has closed off half the rooms to save on
heat. The Clays broke up it must be all of ten years ago. There were some
lovely times had on that patio.

Betsey sings in the Congregational choir alongside Mary Jo Addison,
who after that bad spell of anorexia in her teens has gotten quite plump
again. She has those dark eyebrows of her mother's, strange in a freckled
fair face—shaped flat across and almost meeting in the middle. Both the
Addisons have remarried and left town, but Mary Jo rents two rooms
above the Rites of Passage travel agency and collects antiques and reads
books of history, mostly medieval. My daughter invited her over for

Christmas dinner but she said no, she'd rather just sit cozy by her own fire, surrounded by her things. "Her nice old things," was how it was reported.

Evelyn Addison liked nice things, too, but in her case they had to be modern—D.R. sofas covered in Haitian cotton, Danish end tables with rounded edges, butterfly chairs. Where are they, I wonder, all those heavy iron frames for the worn-out canvas slings of those butterfly chairs we used to sit on? A man could straddle one of the corners, but a woman just had to dump herself in, backside first, and hope that when the time came to go her husband would be around to pull her out. They had an authentic 1690 house, the Addisons, on Salem Street, and curiously enough their modern furniture fit right into those plain old rooms with the exposed beams and the walk-in fireplaces with the big wrought-iron spits and dark brick nooks the Puritans used to bake bread in. It may be that's what Mary Jo is trying to get back to with her antiques. She dresses that way, too: dusty-looking and prim, her hair pulled into a tight roll held by a tortoiseshell pin. Her mother's auburn hair, but without the spark rinsed into it. None of these girls, the daughters of our old crowd, seem to wear makeup.

The New Year's right after Fred had moved out, I remember walking Evelyn home from the Langhornes' up Salem Street just before morning, an inch of new snow on the sidewalk and everything silent except for her voice, going on and on about Fred. There had been Stingers, and she could hardly walk, and I wasn't much better. The housefronts along Salem calm as ghosts, and the new snow like mica reflecting the streetlights. We climbed her porch steps, and that living room, with its wide floorboards, her tree still up, and a pine wreath hung on an oak peg in the fireplace lintel, hit me as if we had walked smack into an old-fashioned children's book. The smell of a pine indoors or a certain glaze on wrapping paper will do that to me, or frost in the corner of a windowpane: spell Christmas. We sat together on the scratchy D.R. sofa so she could finish her tale about Fred and I could warm up for the long walk back. Day was breaking and suddenly Evelyn looked haggard; I was led to try to comfort her and right then, with Evelyn's long hair all over our faces, and her strong eyebrows right under my eyes, we heard from on high Mary Jo beginning to cough. We froze, the big old fireplace full of cold ashes sending out a little draft on our ankles and, from above, this coughing and coughing, scoopy and dry. Mary Jo, about fifteen she must have been then, and weakened by the anorexia, had caught a cold that had turned into walking pneumonia. Evelyn blamed Fred's leaving her for that, too—the pneumonia. Coughing and coughing, the child, and her mother in my arms smelling of brandy and tears and Christmas. She blamed Fred but I would have blamed him less than the environment; those old wooden houses are drafty.

Thinking of upstairs and downstairs, I think of Betsey Clay at the head of her stairs, no longer in a white nightie seeing the moon but in frilly lemon-colored pajamas, looking down at some party too loud for her to sleep through. We had come in from the patio and put on some old Twist records and there was no quiet way to play them. I was sitting on the floor somehow, with somebody, so the angle of my vision was low, and like a lesson in perspective the steps diminished up to her naked feet, too big to leave rabbit tracks now. For what seemed the longest time we looked at each other—she had her mother's hollow-eyed fragile look—until the woman I was with, and I don't think it was Maureen, felt my distraction and herself turned to look up the stairs, and Betsey scampered back toward her room.

Her room would have been like my daughter's in those years: Beatles posters, or maybe of the Monkees, and prize ribbons for horsemanship in local shows. And dolls and Steiff animals that hadn't been put away yet sharing the shelves with Signet editions of Melville and *Hard Times* and Camus assigned at day school. We were all so young, parents and children, learning it all together—how to grow up, how to deal with time—is what you realize now.

Those were the days when Harry Langhorne had got himself a motorcycle and would roar around and around the green on a Saturday night until the police came and stopped him, more or less politely. And the Wilcombes had put a hot tub on their second-story porch and had to run a steel column up for support lest we all go tumbling down naked some summer night. In winter, there was a lot of weekend skiing for the sake of the kids, and we would take over a whole lodge in New Hampshire: heaps of snowy boots and wet parkas in the corner under the moose head, over past the beat-up player piano, and rosy cheeks at dinner at the long tables, where ham with raisin sauce was always the main dish. Suddenly the girls, long-legged in their stretch pants, hair whipping around their faces as they skimmed to a stop at the lift lines, were women. At night, after the boys had crumped out or settled to Ping-Pong in the basement, the girls stayed up with us, playing Crazy Eights or Spit with the tattered decks the lodge kept on hand, taking sips from our cans of beer, until at last the weight of all that day's fresh air toppled everyone up toward bed, in reluctant bunches. The little rooms had dotted-swiss curtains and thick frost ferns on the windowpanes. The radiators dripped and sang. There was a dormitory feeling through the thin partitions, and shuffling and giggling in the hall on the way to the bathrooms, one for girls and one for boys. One big family. It was the children, really, growing unenthusiastic and resistant, who stopped the trips. That, and the divorces as they began to add up.

Margaret and I are about the last marriage left; she says maybe we missed the boat, but can't mean it.

The beach picnics, and touch football, and the softball games in that big field the Wilcombes had. Such a lot of good times, and the kids growing up through them like weeds in sunshine; and now, when the daughters of people we hardly knew at all are married to stockbrokers or off in Oregon being nurses or in Mexico teaching agronomy, our daughters haunt the town as if searching for something they missed, taking classes in macramé or aerobic dancing, living with their mothers, wearing no makeup, walking up beside the rocks with books in their arms like a race of little nuns.

You can see their mothers in them—beautiful women, full of life. I saw Annie Langhorne at the train station the other morning and we had to talk for some minutes, mostly about the antique store Mary Jo wants to open up with Betsey, and apropos of the hopelessness of this venture she gave me a smile exactly like her mother's one of the times Louise and I said goodbye or faced the fact that we just weren't going to make it, she and I —pushing up the lower lip so her chin crinkled, that nice wide mouth of hers humorous but downturned at the corners as if to buckle back tears. Lou's exact same smile on little Annie, and it was like being in love again, when all the world is a hunt and the sight of the woman's car parked at a gas station or in the Stop & Shop lot makes your Saturday, makes your blood race and your palms go numb, the heart touching base.

But these girls. What are they hanging back for? What are they afraid of?

Unstuck

IN HIS DREAM, Mark was mixing and mixing on an oval palette a muddy shade of gray he could not get quite right, and this shade of gray was both, in that absurd but deadpan way of dreams, his marriage and the doctrinal position of the local Congregational church, which was resisting the nationwide merger with the Evangelical and Reformed denominations. He was glad to wake up, though his wife's body, asleep, silently rebuked his. They had made love last night and again she had failed to have her climax.

As the webs of gray paint lifted and the oppressive need to get *the exact precise shade* dawned upon him as unreal, a color from childhood infiltrated his eyes. The air of his bedroom was tinted blue. The ceiling looked waxy. The very sheen on the wallpaper declared: snow. He remembered: it had begun to spit late yesterday afternoon and was streaming in glittering parallels through the streetlamp halo when, an hour earlier than usual, they went to bed.

A car passed, its chains chunking. Farther away, a stuck tire whined. The bedside clock, whose glassy face gleamed as if polished by the excitement in the air, said six-fifty-five. The windowpanes were decorated with those concave little dunes that Mark had often counterfeited in cotton. By profession he was a window decorator, a display man, for a department store in a city fifteen miles away. He eased from the bed and saw that the storm was over: a few final dry flakes, shaken loose by an afterthought in the top twigs of the elm, drifted zigzag down to add their particles to the white weight that had transformed the town—bewigged roofs, bearded clapboards, Christmas-card evergreens, a STOP sign like a frosted lollipop —into one huge display.

The steeple of the Congregational church, painted white, looked spotlit against the heavy grayness that was fading northward into New Hampshire, having done its work here. Over a foot, he guessed. On the street below their windows the plows had been busy; perhaps it had been their all-night struggle that had made his dreams so grating. Scraped streaks of asphalt showed through, and elsewhere the crust had been rutted and beaten into a gloss by the early traffic. So the roads were all right; he could get to work if he could get the car out of the driveway.

Now, at seven, the town fire horn blew the five spaced blasts that signalled the cancellation of school for the day—a noise that blanketed the air for miles around. Mark's wife opened her eyes in alarm, and then relaxed. They had not been married long and had no children. "What fun," she said. "A real storm. I'll make waffles."

"Don't be too ambitious," he said, sounding more sour than he had meant to.

"I want to," she insisted. "Anyway, the bacon's been in the fridge for weeks and we ought to use it up."

She wanted to make a holiday of it. And she wanted, he thought, to bury the aftertaste of last night. He showered and dressed and went out to rescue his car, which was new. Last evening, after watching the forecast on television, he had prudently reparked it closer to the road, pointed nose outward. No garage had come with this big—needlessly big—old house they had recently bought. Their driveway curved in from Hillcrest Road at the back of the yard. The plows had heaped a ridge of already dirty, lumpy snow between his bumper and the cleared street. The ridge came up to his hips, but he imagined that, with the momentum his rear tires could gather on the bare patch beneath the car body, he could push through. Snow is, after all, next to nothing; he pictured those airy six-sided crystals so commonly employed as a decorative motif in his trade.

But, getting in behind the steering wheel, he found himself in a tomb. All the windows were sealed by snow. The motor turned over readily and he thanked God for this miracle of ignition. As the motor idled, he staggered around the automobile, clearing the windows with the combination brush and scraper the car dealer had given him. When he cleared the windshield, the wipers shocked him by springing to life and happily flapping. He had left them turned on last night. He got back in behind the wheel and turned them off. Through the cleared windshield, the sky above his neighbor's rooftop was enamelled a solid blue. The chimney smoked a paler blue and a host of small brown birds scuffled and settled for warmth in the dark bare patch in its lee. His neighbor herself, a woman wearing a checkered apron, came out of the front door and began banging a broom around on her porch. She saw Mark through the windshield and waved; he grudgingly waved back. She was middle-aged, lacked a husband, wore her lipstick too thick, and seemed excessively willing to be friendly to this young couple new in the neighborhood.

He put the car into first gear. Snow had blown in beneath the sides of the automobile, so the momentum he had hoped to achieve was sluggish in coming. Though his front tires broke through the ridge, the underside dragged and the back tires slithered to a stop in the shallow gutter that ran down the side of Hillcrest Road. He tried reverse. The rear of the car lifted a fraction and then sagged sideways, the wheels spinning in a void. He returned to first gear, and was gingerly on the accelerator, and gained for his tact only a little more of that sickening sideways slipping. He tried reverse again and this time there was no motion at all; it was as if he were trying to turn a doorknob with soapy hands. An outraged sense of injustice, of being asked to do too much, swept over him. "Fuck," he said. He tried to push open the door, discovered that snow blocked it, shoved savagely, and opened a gap he could worm through backwards. Stepping out, he took an icy shock of snow into his loose galosh.

His neighbor across the street called, "Good morning!" The sound made a strip of snow fall from a telephone wire.

"Isn't it lovely?" were her next words.

"Sure is," was his answer. His voice sounded high, with a squeak in it.

Her painted lips moved, but the words "If you're young" came to him faint and late, as if, because of some warping aftereffect of the storm, sound crossed the street from her side against the grain.

Mark slogged down through his back yard, treading in his own footsteps to minimize his desecration of the virgin snow. The bushes were bowed and splayed like bridesmaids overwhelmed by flowers. Chickadee feet had crosshatched the snow under the feeder. The kitchen air struck his face with its warmth and the almost excessive smells of simmering bacon and burning waffle mix. He told his wife, "I got the damn thing stuck. Get out of your nightie and come help."

She looked querulous and sallow in her drooping bathrobe. "Can't we eat breakfast first? You're going to be late anyway. Shouldn't you be calling the store? Maybe it won't be open today."

"It'll be open, and anyway even if it isn't I should be there. Easter won't wait." The precise shade of gray he had been mixing in his dream perhaps belonged to some beaverboard cutouts of flowering trees he was preparing for windows of the new spring fashions.

"The *schools* are closed," she pointed out.

"Well, let's eat," he conceded, but ate in his parka, to hurry her. As he swallowed the orange juice, the snow in his galosh slipped deeper down his ankle. Mark said, "If we'd bought that ranch house you were too damn sophisticated for, we'd have a garage and this wouldn't happen. It takes years off the life of a car, to leave it parked in the open."

"It's smoking! Turn the little thing! On the left, the left!" She told him, "I don't know *why* I bother to try to make you waffles; that iron your mother gave us has never worked. Never, never."

"Well, it should. It's not cheap."

"It sticks. It's awful. I hate it."

"It was the best one she could find. It's supposed to be self-greasing, or some damn thing, isn't it?"

"I don't know. I don't understand it. I never have. I was trying to make them to be nice to *you.*"

"Don't get so upset. The waffles are fine, actually." But he ate them without tasting them, he was so anxious to return to the car and erase his error. If a plow were to come along, his car would be jutting into its path, evidence of ineptitude. Young husbands, young car owners. He wondered if the woman across the street had been laughing at him, getting it stuck. Just that little ridge to push through. He had been so sure he could do it. "I don't suppose," he said, "this will cancel the damn church thing tonight."

"Let's not go," she said, scraping the last batch into the garbage, poking the crusts from the waffle grid with a fork. "Why do we have to go?"

"Because," he stated firmly. "These Reformeds, you know, are high-powered stuff. They're very strict about things like the divinity of Christ."

"Well, who isn't? I mean, you either believe it or you don't, I would think."

He winced, feeling himself to blame. If he had given her a climax, she wouldn't be so irreligious. "This is a wonderful breakfast," he said. "How do you make the bacon so crisp?"

"You put it on a paper bag for a minute," she said. "Did you *really* get the car stuck? Maybe you should call the man at the garage."

"It just needs a little push," he promised. "Come on, bundle up. It'll be fun. Old Mrs. Whatsername across the street is out there with the birds, sweeping her porch. It's beautiful."

"I *know* it is," she said. "I used to *love* snowstorms."

"But not now, huh?" He stood and asked, "Where's the fucking shovel?"

She went upstairs, the belt of her sad bathrobe trailing, and he found the snow shovel in the basement. The furnace, whirring and softly stinking to itself, reminded him pleasantly that snow on the roof reduced the fuel bill. The old house needed insulation. Everything needed something. On his way out through the kitchen he noticed a steaming cup of coffee she had poured for him, like one of those little caches one explorer leaves behind for another. To appease her, he took two scalding swallows before heading out into the wilderness of his brilliant back yard.

By the time Mark's wife joined him, looking childish and fat and merry in her hood and mittens and ski leggings and fur-topped boots, he had shovelled away as much of the snow underneath and around the car as he could reach. The woman across the street had gone back into her house, the birds on her roof had flown away, and a yellow town truck had come down Hillcrest Road scattering ashes. He had leaned on the shovel and waved at the men on the back as if they were all comrades battling together in a cheerful war.

She asked, "Do you want me to steer?"

"No, you push. It'll just take a tiny push now. I'll drive, because I know how to rock it." He stationed her at the rear right corner of the car, where there happened to be a drift that came up over her knees. He felt her make the silent effort of not complaining. "The thing is," he told her, "to keep it from sloughing sideways."

"Sluing," she said.

"Whatever it is," he said, "keep it from doing that."

But slue was just what it did; though he rammed the gearshift back and forth between first and reverse, the effect of all that rocking was—he could feel it—to work the right rear tire deeper into the little slippery socket on the downhill side. He assumed she was pushing, but he couldn't see her in the mirror and he couldn't feel her.

His stomach ached, with frustration and maple syrup. He got out of the car. His wife's face was pink, exhilarated. Her hood was back and her hair had come undone. "You're closer than you think," she said. "Where's the shovel?" She dabbled with it around the stuck tire, doing no good that he could see.

"It's that damn gutter," he said, impotently itching to grab the shovel from her. "In the summer you're not even conscious of its being there."

She thrust the shovel into a mound so it stood upright and told him, "Sweetheart, now you push. You're stronger than I am."

Grudgingly, he felt flattered. "All right. We'll try it. Now, with the accelerator—don't gun it. You just dig yourself deeper with the spinning tires."

"That's what *you* were doing."

"That's because you weren't pushing hard enough. And steer for the middle of the street, and rock it back and forth gently, back and forth; and don't panic."

As she listened to these instructions, a dimple beside the corner of her mouth kept appearing and disappearing. She got into the driver's seat. A little shower of snow, loosened by the climbing sun, fell rustling through a nearby tree, and the woman across the street came onto her porch without the broom, plainly intending to watch. Her lipstick at this distance was like one of those identifying spots of color on birds.

Mark squatted down and pressed his shoulder against the trunk and gripped the bumper with his hands. A scratch in the paint glinted beneath his eyes. How had that happened? He still thought of their car as brand new. Snow again insinuated its chill bite into his galosh. Nervous puffs of soiled brown smoke rippled out of the exhaust pipe and bounced against his legs. He was aware of the woman on the porch, watching. All the windows of the neighborhood he believed to be watching.

The woman in the driver's seat eased out the clutch. The tires revolved, and the slippery ton of the automobile's rear end threatened to slide farther sideways; but he fought it, and she fed more gas, and they seemed to gain an inch forward. Doing what she had told him, she rocked the car back, and at the peak of its backwards swing gunned it forward again, and he felt their forward margin expand. *Good girl.* He heaved; they paused; the car rocked back and then forward again and he heaved so hard the flat muscles straddling his groin ached. Mark seemed to feel, somewhere within the inertial masses they were striving to manage, his personal strength register a delicate response, a feminine flicker in the depths. The car relaxed backwards and in this remission he straightened and saw through the rear window the back of the driver's head, her thin neck bolt upright under an oval of loosened hair. The wheels spun again, the car dipped forward through the trough it had worn, and its weight seemed to hang, sustained by his strength, on the edge of release. "Once more," he shouted, trembling through the length of his legs. The car sagged back through an arc that had noticeably distended, and in chasing its forward swing with his pushing he had to take steps, one, two . . . *three!* The rear tires, frantically excited and in their spinning spitting snow across his lower half, slithered across that invisible edge he had sensed. The ridge was broken through, and, if he continued to push, it was with gratuitous exertion, adding himself through sheer affection to a delicious, irresistible momentum. They were free.

Feeling this also, she whipped the steering wheel to head herself downhill and braked to a stop some yards away. The car, stuttering blue exhaust smoke, perched safe in the center of the ash-striped width of Hillcrest Road. It was a 1960 Plymouth SonoRamic Commando V-8, with fins. Its driver, silhouetted with her nose tipped up, looked much too small to have managed so big a thing.

Mark shouted "Great!" and leaped over the shattered ridge, brandishing the shovel. The woman on the porch called something to him he couldn't quite catch but took kindly. He walked to his car and opened the door and got in beside his wife. The heater had come on; the interior was warm. He repeated, "You were great." He was still panting.

She smiled and said, "So were you."

A Constellation of Events

THE EVENTS felt spaced in a vast deep sky, its third dimension dizzying. Looking back, Betty could scarcely believe that the days had come so close together. But, no, there, flat on the calendar, they were, one after the other —four bright February days.

Sunday, after church, Rob had taken her and the children cross-country skiing. They made a party of it. He called up Evan, because they had discussed the possibility at the office Friday, while the storm was raging around their green-glass office building in Hartford, and she, because Evan, a bachelor, was Lydia Smith's lover, called up the Smiths and invited them, too; it was the sort of festive, mischievous gesture Rob found excessive. But Lydia answered the phone and was delighted. As her voice twittered in Betty's ear, Betty stuck out her tongue at Rob's frown.

They all met at the Pattersons' field in their different-colored cars and soon made a line of dark silhouettes across the white pasture. Evan and Lydia glided obliviously into the lead; Rob and Billy, the son now almost the size of the father, and Fritzie Smith, who in imitation of her mother was quite the girl athlete, occupied the middle distance, the little Smith boy struggling to keep up with this group; and Betty and her baby—poor bitterly whining, miserably ill-equipped Jennifer—came last, along with Rafe Smith, who didn't ski as much as Lydia and whose bindings kept letting go. He was thinner than Rob, more of a clown, fuller of doubt, hatchet-faced and green-eyed: a sad, encouraging sort of man. He kept telling Jennifer, "Ups-a-daisy, Jenny, keep in the others' tracks, now you've got the rhythm, oops," as the child's skis scrambled and she toppled down again. Meanwhile, one of Rafe's feet would have come out of his binding and Betty would have to wait, the others dwindling in the distance into dots.

The fields were immense in their brilliance. Her eyes winced, taking them in. The tracks of their party, and the tracks of the Sno-Cats that had frolicked here in the wake of the storm, scarcely touched the marvellous blankness—slopes up and down, a lone oak on a knoll, rail fences like pencilled hatchings, weathered NO TRESPASSING signs not meant for them. Rob had done business with one of the Patterson sons and would bluff a challenge through; the fields seemed held beneath a transparent dome of Rob's protection. A creek, thawed into audible life, ran where two slopes met. Betty was afraid to follow the tracks of the others here; it involved stepping, in skis, from snowbank to snowbank across a width of icy, confident, secretive water. She panicked and took the wooden bridge fifty yards out of their way. Rafe lifted Jennifer up and stepped across, his binding snapping on the other side but no harm done. The child laughed for the first time that afternoon.

The sun came off the snow hot; Betty thought her face would get its first touch of tan today, and then it would not be many weeks before cows grazed here again, bringing turds to the mayflowers. Pushing up the slope on the other side of the creek, toward the woods, she slipped backwards and fell sideways. The snow was moist, warm. "Shit," she said, and was pleasurably aware of the massy uplifted curve of her hip in jeans as she looked down over it at Rafe behind her, his green eyes sun-narrowed, alert. "Want to get up?" he asked, and held out a hand, a damp black mitten. As she reached for it, he pulled off the mitten, offering her a bare hand, bony and pink and startling, so suddenly exposed to the air. "Ups-a-daisy," he said, and the effort of pulling her erect threw him off balance, and a binding popped loose again. Both she and Jenny laughed this time.

At the entrance of the path through the woods, Rob waited with evident patience. Before he could complain, she did: "Jennifer is going crazy on these awful borrowed skis. *Why* can't she have decent equipment like other children?"

"I'll stay with her," her husband said, both firm and evasive in his way, avoiding the question with an appearance of meeting it, and appearing selfless in order to shame her. But she felt the smile on her face persist as undeniably, as unerasably, as the sun on the field. Rob's face clouded, gathering itself to speak; Rafe interrupted, apologizing, blaming their slowness upon himself and his defective bindings. For a moment that somehow made her shiver inside—perhaps no more than the flush of exertion meeting the chill blue shade of the woods, here at the edge—the two men stood together, intent upon the mechanism, her presence forgotten. Rob found the misadjustment, and Rafe's skis came off no more.

In the woods, Rob and Jennifer fell behind, and Rafe slithered ahead, hurrying to catch up to his children and, beyond them, to his wife and Evan. Betty tried to stay with her husband and child, but they were too maddening—one whining, the other frowning, and neither grateful for her company. She let herself ski ahead, and became alone in the woods, aware of distant voices, the whisper of her skis, the soft companionable heave of her own breathing. Pine trunks shifted about, one behind another and then another, aligned and not aligned, shadowy harmonies. Here and there the trees grew down into the path; a twig touched her eye, so lightly she was surprised to find pain lingering, and herself crying. She came to an open place where paths diverged. Here Rafe was waiting for her; thin, leaning on his poles, he seemed a shadow among others. "Which way do you think they went?" He sounded breathless and acted lost. His wife and her lover had escaped him.

"Left is the way to get back to the car," she said.

"I can't tell which are their tracks," he said.

"I'm sorry," Betty said.

"Don't be." He relaxed on his poles, and made no sign of moving. "Where is Rob?" he asked.

"Coming. He took over dear Jennifer for me. I'll wait, you go on."

"I'll wait with you. It's too scary in here. Do you want that book?" The sentences followed one another evenly, as if consequentially.

The book was about Jane Austen, by an English professor Betty had studied under years ago, before Radcliffe called itself Harvard. She had noticed it lying on the front seat of the Smiths' car while they were all fussing with their skis, and had exclaimed with recognition, of a sort. In a strange suspended summer of her life, the summer when Billy was born, she had read through all six of the Austen novels, sitting on a sun porch waiting and waiting and then suddenly nursing. "If you're done with it."

"I am. It's tame, but dear, as you would say. Could I bring it by tomorrow morning?"

He had recently left a law firm in Hartford and opened an office here in town. He had few clients but seemed amused, being idle. There was something fragile and incapable about him. "Yes," she said, adding, "Jennifer comes back from school at noon."

And then Jennifer and Rob caught up to them, both needing to be placated, and she forgot this shadowy man's promise, as if her mind had been possessed by the emptiness where the snowy paths diverged.

* * *

Monday was bright, and the peal at the door accented the musical dripping of the icicles ringing the house around with falling pearls. Rafe was
hunched comically under the dripping from the front eaves, the book held
dry against his parka. He offered just to hand it to her, but she invited him
in for coffee, he seemed so sad, still lost. They sat with the coffee on the
sofa, and soon his arms were around her and his lips, tasting of coffee,
warm on her mouth and his hands cold on her skin beneath her sweater,
and she could not move her mind from hovering, from floating in a golden
consciousness of the sun on the floorboards, great slanting splashes of it,
rhomboids broken by the feathery silhouettes of her houseplants on the
windowsills. From her angle as he stretched her out on the sofa, the shadows of the drips leaped upward in the patches of sun, appearing to defy
gravity as her head whirled. She sat up, pushed him off without rebuke,
unpinned and repinned her hair. "What are we doing?" she asked.

"I don't know," Rafe said, and indeed he didn't seem to. His assault on
her had felt clumsy, scared, insincere; he seemed grateful to be stopped.
His face was pink, as his hand had been. In the light of the windows
behind the sofa his eyes were very green. An asparagus fern hanging there
cast a net of shadow that his features moved in and out of as he apolo-
gized, talked, joked. "Baby fat!" he had exclaimed of her belly, having
tugged her sweater up, bending suddenly to kiss the crease there, his face
thin as a blade, and hot. He was frightened, Betty realized, which banished
her own fear.

Gently she maneuvered him away from her body, out of the door. It was
not so hard; she remembered how to fend off boys from the college days
his book had brought back to her. In his gratitude he wouldn't stop smiling. She shut the front door. His body as he crossed the melting street
fairly danced with relief. And for her, again alone in the empty house, it
was as if along with her fear much of her soul had been banished; feeling
neither remorse nor expectation, she floated above the patches of sun being
stitched by falling drops, among the curved shining of glass and porcelain
and aluminum kitchen equipment, in the house's strange warmth—strange
as any event seems when only we are there to witness it. Betty lifted her
sweater to look at her pale belly. Baby fat. Middle age had softened her
middle. But, then, Lydia was an athlete, tomboyish and lean, swift on skis,
with that something Roman and androgynous and enigmatic about her
looks. It was what Rafe was used to; the contrast had startled him.

She picked up the book from the sofa. He was one of those men who
could read a book gently, so it didn't look read. She surprised herself, in
her great swimming calmness, by being unable to read a word.

* * *

Tuesday, as they had planned weeks ago, Rob took her to Philadelphia. She had been born there, and he had business there. Taking her along was his tribute, he had made it too plain, to her condition as a bored housewife. Yet she loved it, loved him, once the bumping, humming terror of the plane ride was past. The city in the winter sunlight looked glassier and cleaner than she remembered it, her rough and enormous dear drab City of Brotherly Love. Rob was here because his insurance company was helping finance a shopping mall in southern New Jersey; he disappeared into the strangely Egyptian old façade of the Penn Mutual Building—now doubly false, for it had been reconstructed as a historical front on a new skyscraper, a tall box of tinted glass. She wandered window-shopping along Walnut Street until her feet hurt, then took a cab from Rittenhouse Square to the Museum of Art. There was less snow in Philadelphia than in Connecticut; some of the grass beside the Parkway even looked green.

At the head of the stairs inside the museum, Saint-Gaudens's great verdigrised Diana—in Betty's girlhood imagination the statue had been somehow confused with the good witch of fairy stories (only naked, having shed the ball gown and petticoats good witches usually wear, the better to swing her long legs)—still did pose on one tiptoe foot at her shadowy height. But elsewhere within the museum, there were many changes, much additional brightness. The three versions of *Nude Descending a Staircase* and the sadly cracked *Bride Stripped Bare by Her Bachelors, Even* no longer puzzled and offended her. The daring passes into the classic in our very lifetimes, while we age and die. Rob met her, just when he had promised, at three-thirty, amid the Impressionist paintings; her sudden love of him, here in this room of raw color and light, felt like a melting. She leaned on him, he moved away from her touch, and in her unaccustomed city heels Betty sidestepped to keep her balance.

They had tea in the cafeteria, out of place in their two dark suits among the students and beards and the studied rags that remained of the last decade's revolution. Here, too, the radical had become the comfortable. "How do you like being back?" Rob asked her.

"It's changed, I've changed. I like it where I am now. You were dear to bring me, though." She touched his hand, and he did not pull it away on the smooth tabletop, whose white reminded her of snow.

Happiness must have been on her face, glowing like a sunburn, for he looked at her and seemed for an instant to see her. The instant troubled him. Though too heavy to be handsome, he had beautiful eyes, tawny and indifferent like a lion's; they slitted and he frowned in the unaccustomed exercise of framing a compliment. "It's such a pity," he said, "you're my wife."

She laughed, astonished. "Is it? Why?"

"You'd make such a lovely mistress."

"You think? How do you know? Have you ever had a mistress?" She was so confident of the answer she went on before he could say no. "Then how do you know I'd make a lovely one? Maybe I'd make an awful one. Shrieking, possessive. Better just accept me as a wife," she advised complacently. The table was white and cluttered with dirty tea things between them; she could hardly wait until they were home, in bed. His lovemaking was like him, firm and tireless, and it always worked. She admired that. Once, she had adored it, until her adoration had seemed to depress him. And something in her now, at this glittering table, depressed him—perhaps the mistress he had glimpsed in her, the mistress that he of all the men in the world was barred from, could never have. She stroked his hand as if in acknowledgment of a shared sorrow. But happiness kept mounting in her, giddy and meaningless, inexplicable, unstoppable, though she saw that on its wings she was leaving Rob behind. And he had never seemed solider or kinder, or she more fittingly, as they rose and paid and left the museum together, his wife.

On the flight back, to calm her terror, she pulled the book from her handbag and read, *As Lionel Trilling was to say in 1957 (before women had risen in their might), "The extraordinary thing about Emma is that she has a moral life as a man has a moral life"; "A consciousness is always at work in her, a sense of what she ought to be and do."*

Rob looked over her shoulder and asked, "Isn't that Rafe's book?"

"One just like it," she answered promptly, deceit proving not such a difficult trick after all. "You must have seen it on the front seat of his car Sunday. So did I, and I found a copy at Wanamaker's this morning."

"It looks read."

"I was reading it. Waiting for you."

His silence she took to be a satisfied one. He rattled his newspaper, then asked, "Isn't it awfully dry?"

She feigned preoccupation. A precarious rumble changed pitch under her. "Mm. Dry but dear."

"He's a sad guy, isn't he?" Rob abruptly said. "Rafe."

"What's sad about him?"

"You know. Being cuckolded."

"Maybe Lydia loves him all the better for it," Betty said.

"Impossible," her husband decreed, and hid himself in the *Inquirer* as the 727, rumbling and shuddering, prepared to crash. She clutched at

Rob's arm with that irrational fervor he disliked; deliberately he kept his eyes on the newspaper, shutting her out. Yet in grudging answer to her prayers he brought the plane down safely, with a corner of his mind.

In her dream she was teaching again, and among her students Rafe seemed lost. She had a question for him, and couldn't seem to get his attention, though he was not exactly misbehaving; his back was half turned as he talked to some arrogant skinny girl in the class. . . . It was so exasperating she awoke, feeling empty and slightly scared. Rob was out of the bed. She heard the door slam as he went to work. The children were downstairs quarrelling, a merciless sound as of something boiling over. Wednesday. When she stood, a residue of last night's lovemaking slid down the inside of her thigh.

The children gone to school, she moved through the emptiness of the house exploring the realization that she was in love. Like the floorboards, the doorframes, the wallpaper, the fact seemed not so much pleasant as necessary, not ornamental but functional in some way she must concentrate on perceiving. The snow on the roof had all melted; the dripping from the eaves had ceased, and a dry sunlight rested silently on the warm house, the bare street, the speckled rooftops of the town beyond the sunstruck, dirty windows. Valentines the children had brought home from school littered the kitchen counter. The calendar showed the shortest month, a candy box brimming with red holidays. Rafe's office number was newly listed in the telephone book. She dialled it, less to reach him than to test the extent of her emptiness. Alarmingly, the ringing stopped; he answered. "Rafe?" Her voice surprised her by coming out cracked.

"Hi, Betty," he said. "How was Philly?"

"How did you know I went?"

"Everybody knows. You have no secrets from us." He stopped joking, sensing that he was frightening her. "Lydia told me." Evan had told her; Rob had told him at work. There was a see-through world of love; her bright house felt transparent. "Was it nice?" Rafe was asking.

"Lovely." She felt she was defending herself. "It seemed . . . tamer, somehow."

"What did you do?"

"Walked around feeling nostalgic. Went to the museum up on its hill. Rob met me there and we had tea."

"It does sound dear." His voice, by itself, was richer and more relaxed than his physical presence, his helpless, humiliated clown's air. Her silence obliged him to say more. "Have you had time to look into the book?"

"I love it," she said. "It's so scholarly and calm. I'm reading it very slowly; I want it to last forever."

"Forever seems long."

"You want to see me?" Her voice, involuntarily, had thickened.

His answer was as simple and sharp as his green glance when she had exclaimed, "Shit." "Sure," he said.

"Where? This house feels so conspicuous."

"Come on down here. People go in and out of the building all day long. There's a hairdresser next to me."

"Don't you have any clients?"

"Not till this afternoon."

"Do I dare?"

"I don't know. Do you?" More gently, he added, "You don't have to *do* anything. You just want to *see* me, right? Unfinished business, more or less."

"Yes."

Downtown, an eerie silence pressed through the movement of cars and people. Betty realized she was missing a winter sound from childhood: the song of car chains. Snow tires had suppressed it. Time suppressed everything, if you waited. Rafe's building was a grim brick business "block" built a century ago, when this suburb of Hartford had appeared to have an independent future. An ambitious blazon of granite topped the façade, which might someday be considered historical. The stairs were linoleum and smelled like a rainy-day cloakroom. A whiff of singeing and shampoo came from the door next to his. He was waiting for her in his waiting room, and locked the door. On his sofa, a chill, narrow, and sticky couch of Naugahyde, beneath a wall of leatherbound laws, Rafe proved impotent. The sight of her naked seemed to stun him. Through his daze of embarrassment, he never stopped smiling. And she at him. He was beautiful, so lean and loosely knit, but needed to be nursed into knowing it. "What do you think the matter is?" he asked her.

"You're frightened," she told him. "I don't blame you. I'm a lot to take on."

He nodded, his eyes less green, here in this locked, windowless anteroom. "We're going to be a lot of trouble, aren't we?"

"Yes."

"I guess my body is telling us there's still time to back out. Want to?"

On top of one set of bound statutes, their uniform spines forming horizontal streaks like train windows streaming by, lay a different sort of book, a little paperback. In the dim room, where their nakedness was the brightest thing, she made out the title: *Emma*. She answered, "No."

And, though there was much in the aftermath to regret, and a harm that would never cease, Betty remembered these days—the open fields, the dripping eaves, the paintings, the law books—as bright, as a single iridescent unit, not scattered as is a constellation but continuous, a rainbow, a U-turn.

Deaths of Distant Friends

THOUGH I WAS BETWEEN MARRIAGES for several years, in a disarray that preoccupied me completely, other people continued to live and to die. Len, an old golf partner, overnight in the hospital for what they said was a routine examination, dropped dead in the lavatory, having just placed a telephone call to his hardware store saying he would be back behind the counter in the morning. He owned the store and could leave a clerk in charge on sunny afternoons. His swing was too quick, and he kept his weight back on his right foot, and the ball often squirted off to the left without getting into the air at all; but he sank some gorgeous putts in his day, and he always dressed with a nattiness that seemed to betoken high hopes for his game. In buttercup-yellow slacks, sky-blue turtleneck, and tangerine cashmere cardigan he would wave from the practice green as, having driven out from Boston through clouds of grief and sleeplessness and moral confusion, I would drag my cart across the asphalt parking lot, my cleats scraping, like a monster's claws, at every step.

Though Len had known and liked Julia, the wife I had left, he never spoke of my personal condition or of the fact that I drove an hour out from Boston to meet him instead of, as formerly, ten minutes down the road. Golf in that interim was a haven; as soon as I stepped off the first tee in pursuit of my drive, I felt enclosed in a luminous wide sanctuary, safe from women, stricken children, solemn lawyers, disapproving old acquaintances —the entire offended social order. Golf had its own order, and its own love, as the three or four of us staggered and shouted our way toward each hole, laughing at misfortune and applauding the rare strokes of relative brilliance. Sometimes the summer sky would darken and a storm arise, and we would cluster in an abandoned equipment shed or beneath a tree that seemed less tall and vulnerable to lightning than its brothers. Our natural nervousness and our impatience at having the excitements of golf interrupted would in this space of shelter focus into an almost amorous heat—the breaths and sweats of middle-aged men packed together in the pattering rain like cattle in a boxcar. Len's face bore a number of spots of actinic keratosis; he was going to have them surgically removed before they turned into skin cancer. Who would have thought that the lightning bolt of a coronary would fall across his plans and clean remove him from my tangled life? Never again (no two snowflakes or fingerprints, no two heartbeats traced on the oscilloscope, and no two golf swings are exactly alike) would I see his so hopefully addressed drive ("Hello dere, ball," he would joke, going into his waggle and squat) squirt off low to the left in that unique way of his, and hear him exclaim in angry frustration (he was a born-again Baptist, and had developed a personal language of avoided curses), "Ya dirty ricka-fric!"

I drove out to Len's funeral and tried to tell his son, "Your father was a great guy," but the words fell flat in that cold, bare Baptist church. Len's gaudy colors, his Christian effervescence, his hopeful and futile swing, our crowing back and forth, our fellowship within the artificial universe composed of variously resistant lengths and types of grass were all tints of life too delicate to capture, and had flown.

A time later, I read in the paper that Miss Amy Merrymount, ninety-one, had at last passed away, as a dry leaf passes into leaf mold. She had always seemed ancient; she was one of those New Englanders, one of the last, who spoke of Henry James as if he had just left the room. She possessed letters, folded and unfolded almost into pieces, from James to her parents, in which she was mentioned, not only as a little girl but as a young lady "coming into her 'own,' into a liveliness fully rounded." She lived in a few rooms, crowded with antiques, of a great inherited country house of which she was constrained to rent out the larger portion. Why she had never married was a mystery that sat upon her lightly in old age; the slender smooth beauty that sepia photographs remembered, the breeding and intelligence and (in a spiritual sense) ardor she still possessed must have intimidated as many suitors as these virtues attracted and must have given her, in her own eyes, in an age when the word "inviolate" still had force and renunciation a certain prestige, a value whose winged moment of squandering never quite arose. Also, she had a sardonic dryness to her voice and something restless and dismissive in her manner. She was a keen self-educator; she kept up with new developments in art and science, took up organic foods and political outrage when they became fashionable, and liked to have young people about her. When Julia and I moved to town with our babies and fresh faces, we became part of her tea circle, and in an atmosphere of tepid but mutual enchantment maintained acquaintance for twenty years.

Perhaps not so tepid: now I think Miss Merrymount loved us, or at least loved Julia, who always took on a courteous brightness, a soft daughterly shine, in those underheated and window-lit rooms crowded with spindly, feathery heirlooms once spread through the four floors of a Back Bay town house. In memory the glow of my former wife's firm chin and exposed throat and shoulders merges with the ghostly smoothness of those old framed studio photos of the Merrymount sisters—there were three, of whom two died sadly young, as if bequeathing their allotment of years to the third, the survivor sitting with us in her gold-brocaded wing chair. Her face had become unforeseeably brown with age, and totally wrinkled, like an Indian's, with something in her dark eyes of glittering Indian cruelty. "I found her rather disappointing," she might dryly say of an absent mutual acquaintance, or, of one who had been quite dropped from her circle, "She wasn't absolutely first-rate."

The search for the first-rate had been a pastime of her generation. I cannot think, now, of whom she utterly approved, except Father Daniel Berrigan and Sir Kenneth Clark. She saw them both on television. Her eyes with their opaque glitter were failing, and for her cherished afternoons of reading (while the light died outside her windows and a little fire of birch logs danced in the brass-skirted fireplace) were substituted scheduled hours tuned in to educational radio and television. In those last years, Julia would go and read to her—Austen, *Middlemarch,* Joan Didion, some Proust and Mauriac in French, when Miss Merrymount decided that Julia's accent passed muster. Julia would practice a little on me, and, watching her lips push forward and go small and tense around the French sounds like the lips of an African mask of ivory, I almost fell in love with her again. Affection between women is a touching, painful, exciting thing for a man, and in my vision of it—tea yielding to sherry in those cluttered rooms where twilight thickened until the white pages being slowly turned and the patient melody of Julia's voice were the sole signs of life—love was what was happening between this gradually dying old lady and my wife, who had gradually become middle-aged, our children grown into absent adults, her voice nowhere else hearkened to as it was here. No doubt there were confidences, too, between the pages. Julia always returned from Miss

Merrymount's, to make my late dinner, looking younger and even blithe, somehow emboldened.

In that awkward postmarital phase when old friends still feel obliged to extend invitations one doesn't yet have the presence of mind to decline, I found myself at a large gathering at which Miss Merrymount was present. She was now quite blind and invariably accompanied by a young person, a round-faced girl hired as companion and guide. The fragile old lady, displayed like peacock feathers under a glass bell, had been established in a wing chair in a corner of the room beyond the punch bowl. At my approach, she sensed a body coming near and held out her withered hand, but when she heard my voice her hand dropped. "You have done a dreadful thing," she said, all on one long intake of breath. Her face turned away, showing her hawk-nosed profile, as though I had offended her sight. The face of her young companion, round as a radar dish, registered slight shock; but I smiled, in truth not displeased. There is a relief at judgment, even adverse. It is good to think that somewhere a seismograph records our quakes and slippages. I imagine Miss Merrymount's death, not too many months after this, as a final, serenely flat line on the hospital monitor attached to her. Something sardonic in that flat line, too—of unviolated rectitude, of magnificent patience with a world that for over ninety years failed to prove itself other than disappointing. By this time, Julia and I were at last divorced.

Everything of the abandoned home is lost, of course—the paintings on the walls, the way shadows and light contend in this or that corner, the gracious burst of evening warmth from the radiators. The pets. Canute was a male golden retriever we had acquired as a puppy when the children were still a tumbling, pre-teen pack. Endlessly amiable, as his breed tends to be, he suffered all, including castration, as if life were a steady hail of blessings. Curiously, not long before he died, my youngest child, who sings in a female punk group that has just started up, brought Canute to the house where now I live with Lisa as my wife. He sniffed around politely and expressed with only a worried angle of his ears the wonder of his old master reconstituted in this strange-smelling home; then he collapsed with a heavy sigh onto the kitchen floor. He looked fat and seemed lethargic. My daughter, whose hair is cut short and dyed mauve in patches, said that the dog roamed at night and got into the neighbors' garbage, and even into one neighbor's horse feed. This sounded like mismanagement to me. Julia's new boy friend is a middle-aged former Dartmouth quarterback, a golf and tennis and backpack freak, and she is hardly ever home, so busy is she keeping up with him and trying to learn new games. The house and lawn are neglected; the children drift in and out with their friends and once in a while clean out the rotten food in the refrigerator. Lisa, sensing my suppressed emotions, said something tactful and bent down to scratch Canute behind one ear. Since the ear was infected and sensitive, he feebly snapped at her, then thumped the kitchen floor with his tail, in apology.

Like me when snubbed by Miss Merrymount, my wife seemed more pleased than not, encountering a touch of resistance, her position in the world as it were confirmed. She discussed dog antibiotics with my daughter, and at a glance one could not have been sure who was the older, though it was clear who had the odder hair. It is true, as the cliché runs, that Lisa is young enough to be my daughter. But now that I am fifty every female under thirty-five is young enough to be my daughter. Most of the people in the world are young enough to be my daughter.

A few days after his visit, Canute disappeared, and a few days later he was found far out on the marshes near my old house, his body bloated. The dog officer's diagnosis was a heart attack. Can that happen, I wondered, to four-footed creatures? The thunderbolt had hit my former pet by moonlight, his heart full of marshy joy and his stomach fat with garbage, and he had lain for days with ruffling fur while the tides went in and out. The image makes me happy, like the sight of a sail popping full of wind and tugging its boat swiftly out from shore. In truth—how terrible to acknowledge—all three of these deaths make me happy, in a way. Witnesses to my disgrace are being removed. The world is growing lighter. Eventually there will be none to remember me as I was in those embarrassing, disarrayed years when I scuttled without a shell, between houses and wives, a snake between skins, a monster of selfishness, my grotesque needs naked and pink, my social presence beggarly and vulnerable. The deaths of others carry us off bit by bit, until there will be nothing left; and this, too, will be, in a way, a mercy.

Pygmalion

WHAT HE LIKED about his first wife was her gift of mimicry; after a party, theirs or another couple's, she would vivify for him what they had seen, the faces, the voices, twisting her pretty mouth into small contortions that brought back, for a dazzling instant, the presence of an absent acquaintance. "Well, if I reawy—how does Gwen talk?—if I *re*-awwy cared about conserwation—" And he, the husband, would laugh and laugh, even though Gwen was secretly his mistress and would become his second wife. What he liked about *her* was her liveliness in bed, and what he disliked about his first wife was the way she would ask to have her back rubbed and then, under his laboring hands, night after night, fall asleep.

For the first years of the new marriage, after he and Gwen had returned from a party, he would wait, unconsciously, for the imitations, the recapitulation, to begin. He would even prompt: "What did you make of our hostess's brother?"

"Oh," Gwen would simply say, "he seemed very pleasant." Sensing with feminine intuition that he expected more, she might add, "Harmless. Maybe a little stuffy." Her eyes flashed as she heard in his expectant silence an unvoiced demand, and with that touching, childlike impediment of hers she blurted out, "What are you reawy after?"

"Oh, nothing. Nothing. It's just—Marguerite met him once a few years ago and she was struck by what a pompous nitwit he was. That way he has of sucking his pipestem and ending every statement with 'Do you follow me?' "

"I thought he was perfectly pleasant," Gwen said frostily, and turned her back to remove her silvery, snug party dress. As she wriggled it down over her hips she turned her head and defiantly added, "He had a *lot* to say about tax shelters."

"I bet he did," Pygmalion scoffed feebly, numbed by the sight of his wife frontally advancing, nude, toward him as he lay on their marital bed. "It's awfully late," he warned her.

"Oh, come on," she said, the lights out.

The first imitation Gwen did was of Marguerite's second husband, Marvin; they had all unexpectedly met at a Save the Whales benefit ball, to which invitations had been sent out indiscriminately. "Oh-ho-*ho,*" she boomed in the privacy of their bedroom afterwards, "so you're my noble predecessor!" In an aside she added, "Noble, my ass. He hates you so much you turned him on."

"I did?" he said. "I thought he was perfectly pleasant, in what could have been an awkward encounter."

"Yes, in*dee*dy," she agreed, imitating hearty Marvin, and for a dazzling second she allowed the man's slightly glassy and slack expression of forced benignity to invade her own usually petite and rounded features. "Nothing awkward about *us,* ho-ho," she went on, encouraged by her husband's laughter. "And tell me, old chap, why *is* it your child-support check is never on time anymore?"

He laughed and laughed, entranced to see his bride arrive at what he conceived to be a proper womanliness—a plastic, alert sensitivity to the human environment, a susceptible responsiveness tugged this way and that by the currents of Nature herself. He could not know the world, was his fear, unless a woman translated it for him. Now, when they returned from a gathering, and he asked what she had made of so-and-so, Gwen would stand in her underwear and consider, as if onstage. "We-hell, my dear," she would announce in sudden, fluting parody, "if it weren't for Portugal there *rally* wouldn't be a *bear*able country left in Europe!"

"Oh, come on," he would protest, delighted at the way her pretty features distorted themselves into an uncanny, snobbish horsiness.

"How did she do it?" Gwen would ask, as if professionally intent. "Something with the chin, sort of rolling it from side to side without unclenching the teeth."

"You've got it!" he applauded.

"Of course you *knoaow,*" she went on in the assumed voice, "there *used* to be Greece, but now all these dreadful *Ar*abs . . ."

"Oh, yes, yes," he said, his face smarting from laughing so hard, so proudly. She had become perfect for him.

In bed she pointed out, "It's awfully late."

"Want a back rub?"

"Mmmm. That would be reawy nice." As his left hand labored on the smooth, warm, pliable surface, his wife—that small something in her that was all her own—sank out of reach; night after night, she fell asleep.

More Stately Mansions

Its webs of living gauze no more unfurl;
    Wrecked is the ship of pearl!
    And every chambered cell,
Where its dim dreaming life was wont to dwell,
As the frail tenant shaped his growing shell,
    Before thee lies revealed,—
Its irised ceiling rent, its sunless crypt unsealed!
              —Oliver Wendell Holmes,
                "The Chambered Nautilus"

ONE OF MY STUDENTS the other day brought into class a nautilus shell that had been sliced down the middle to make a souvenir from Hawaii. That's how far some of these kids' parents get on vacation, though from the look of the city (Mather, Massachusetts; population 47,000 and falling) you wouldn't think there was any money in town at all.

I held the souvenir in my hand, marvelling at the mathematics of it—the perfect logarithmic spiral and the parade of increasing chambers, each sealed with a translucent, curved septum. I held the shell up to show the class. "What the poem doesn't tell you," I told them, "is that the nautilus is a nasty, hungry blob that uses its outgrown chambers as propulsion tanks to maneuver up and down as it chases its prey. It's a killer."

I sounded sore; the students stared, those that had been listening. They know your insides better than you do, often. The shell had reminded me of Karen. Karen Owens, former wife of the late Alan. She had loved Nature

—its fervent little intricacies, all its pretty little survival kits and sexy signallings. There was a sheen to the white-and-pale-orange nacre, here in the staring light of the tall classroom windows, that was hers. As I diagrammed on the blackboard the spiral, and some up and down arrows, and the dainty siphuncle whereby the nautilus performs its predatory hydrostatic magic, I was remembering how she, to arouse me in the brightness of the big spare bedroom at the back of her house, would softly drag her pale-orange hair and her small white breasts across my penis.

Arousal wasn't always instant; I would be nervous, sweaty, guilty, stealing time from the lunch hour or even—so urgent did it all seem—ducking out of the school in a free period (classes run fifty minutes in our system) to drive across town to spend twenty minutes with her and then drive the fifteen minutes back again, screeching that old Falcon Monica's parents had given us into the high-school parking lot under the eyes of the kids loafing and sneaking cigarettes out by the bike racks. They may have wondered, but teachers come and go; kids have no idea what it takes or doesn't take to keep the world running, and though studying us is one of their main ways of using up energy, they can't really believe the abyss that adult life is: that what they dream, we do. They couldn't know, no matter what their lavatory walls said, that Karen's musk was really on my fingertips and face and that behind my fly lurked a pearly ache of satisfaction.

She and Alan lived in the Elm Hill section, where the mill-owners and their managers had built big Victorian clapboard houses. The high school, new in 1950, had been laid out on an old farm on the other side of the river. With less than the whole dying downtown between us, we might have had time to share a cigarette afterwards or talk, so that I might have come to understand better what our affair meant from her side, what she was getting out of it and where she saw it going. My father had worked in those empty mills. He had me late in life and had coughed and drunk himself to death by the time I was twenty, and a kind of rage at the mills and him and all of Mather would come over me when, in a panic to be back to my next class, I would get stuck in the overshadowed streets down in the factory district. The city fathers had made them all one-way in some hopeless redevelopment scheme.

My grandfather came over from Italy to help build those mills, brick by brick. My oldest brother is a former auto mechanic who now owns a one-third share in a parts-and-supplies store and never touches a tool except to sell it. Our middle brother sells real estate. They had me set to become a Boston doctor, but with the lint's getting my father's lungs so early I was lucky to get through college. I picked up the education credits and an easy master's and now teach general science to ninth- and tenth-graders. A while ago I was made assistant principal, which means two classes a day less and afternoons in the office. I had hoped originally to get out of Mather, but here is where our connections were—my father's old foreman was on the school board when they hired me—so here I still am. Fall is our best season, and in recent years some high-tech has overflowed Route 128 and come into the local economy, giving it a shot in the arm. It needs it. But cities aren't like people; they live on and on, even though their reason for being where they are has gone downriver and out to sea.

Alan's father, old Jake Owens, had owned Pilgrim, one of the smaller mills and about the last along the river to close down. That was the late Forties, long after the bigger outfits had all sold their machinery south. Some in town said Jake showed a touching loyalty to Mather and its workers; others said the Owenses never had had much head for business. They were drinking and shooting men, with a notion of themselves as squires, at home in their little piece of industrial valley with its country club, its Owens Avenue, its hunting and skiing an hour or two north in New Hampshire. When his father died in the mid-Sixties, Alan came home from the West Coast with his Stanford law degree and his red-haired wife.

Karen was from Santa Barbara, thirtyish, pretty, but parched somehow. All that Pacific sun was beginning to produce crow's-feet and little creases fanning out from her quick, maybe too quick, smile. She was small, with a tight cute figure that had been on a lot of beaches. She had majored in psychology and had a California teacher's certificate and put her name in at the high-school office as a substitute. That was where I first saw her, striding along our noisy halls, her hair bouncing between her shoulder blades. She was no taller than many of the girls but different from them, a different animal, with the whippy body and seasoned voice of a woman.

When we did talk, Karen and I, it was out in the open, on opposite sides of the fence, about the war. There was a condescending certainty about her pacifism that infuriated me, and a casual, bright edge of militance that possibly frightened me. I can't imagine now why I imagined then that the U.S.A. couldn't take care of itself. I felt so damn motherly toward, of all people, LBJ. He looked so hangdog, even if he was a bully.

"Why do you talk of people being *for* the war?" I would ask Karen in the teachers' room, amid the cigarette smoke and between-the-acts euphoria of teachers offstage for fifty minutes. "It puts you people in such a smug no-lose position, being not for the war. Nobody's for any war, in the abstract; it's just sometimes judged to be the least of available evils."

"When is it the least?" she asked. "Tell me, Frank." She had a tense way of intertwining her crossed legs with the legs of the straight wooden school chair so that her kneecaps jutted out, rimmed in white. This was the heyday of the mini-skirt; female underpants, sure to be seen, had sprouted patterns of flowers. When she crossed her legs like that, her skirt slid up to reveal an oval vaccination scar her childhood doctor had never thought would show. There were a number of awkward, likable things about Karen in spite of the smug politics: she smoked a lot, and her teeth were stained and slightly crooked, in an era of universal orthodontia. Her hands had the rising blue veins of middle age, and a tremor. I loved the expensive clothes that what with the Owens money she couldn't help but wear. Though her sweaters were cashmere, they always looked tugged slightly awry, so that a background of haste and distress seemed to lie invitingly behind her smooth public pose.

"Maybe you don't realize the kind of town you've moved to," I told her. "The VFW is where we have our Saturday dances. Our kids aren't pouring pig blood into draft-board files. Their grandparents were damn glad to get here, and when their country asks them to go fight, they go. They're scared, but they go."

"Why does that make it right?" Karen asked gently. "Explain it to me." The old psychology major. She was giving up the debate and babying me, as a kind of crazy man.

Her hair in its long brushed flower-child fall was not exactly either orange or red, it was the deep flesh color of a whelk shell's lip; and the more you looked, the more freckles she had. She was giving me an out, of sorts—a chance to shift out of this angry gear that discussion of the war always shoved me into. LBJ had been a schoolteacher, as I was now, and it seemed to me that the entire class, from coast to coast, just wasn't *listening*. And he was trying to be so good, so suffering-on-our-behalf—our crooked Christ from Texas.

"It just *does*," I told Karen, in my very lameness accepting her offer, surrendering. "I love these kids." This was a lie. "I grew up just like them." This was half a lie; I had been much the youngest child, pampered by my brothers, prepared for something better, out of Mather. "They give us great football teams." This was the truth.

The peace movement in Mather amounted to a few candle-bearing parades led by the local clergy, the same clergymen who would invoke the blessings on Memorial Day before the twenty-one-gun salute shattered the peace of the cemetery. When the first local boy died in Vietnam, he got a new elementary school named after him. When the second died, they took a street intersection in his part of town, called it a square, and named it after him. For the third and the fourth, there wasn't even an intersection. The Owenses' house on the hill had a big living room overlooking the city through tall, proprietorial windows. It had walnut wainscoting and a maze of ball-and-stick woodwork above the entranceways; the room could easily hold meetings of fifty or sixty, and did. At Karen's invitation, black men imported from Roxbury spoke here, and white women imported from Cambridge. Civil rights and feminism and the perfidy of the Pentagon and the scheming, polluting corporations had become one big all-purpose issue, and the Owenses had become the local chieftains of discontent, at least in the little circle Monica and I were drawn into. CMC, we called ourselves: Concerned Mather Citizens.

Monica and I had both been raised Catholic. I let it go in about my sophomore year of college, when my father died, but Monica kept it up until she went on the Pill. Our three children had been born in the first four years of our marriage. At first she attended Mass, though she couldn't take Communion; then she stopped even that. I was sorry to see it—it had been a part of her I had understood—and to hear her talk about the Church with such bitterness. That's how women can be, mulling something over and getting madder and madder about it, all in secret, and then making a sudden quantum jump: revolutionaries. My impression was that Karen had courted Monica at the teachers' Christmas party, asking her to come over during the holidays and help address circulars. Monica jumped right in. She stopped getting perms and painting her fingernails. She pulled her springy black hair back into a ponytail and wore sneakers and jeans not only around the house but out to shop. She stopped struggling against her weight. Monica bloomed, I suppose; she had been a jock at Mather High (field hockey, girls' basketball) and a cheerleader, and now, fifteen years later and fifteen pounds heavier, that old girlish push, that egging-on fierceness, had come back. I didn't much like it but wasn't consulted. Somehow in all this I had become the oppressor, part of "the system," and the three children we had "given" each other, as they used to say, had been some kind of dirty trick. She said the Pill was carcinogenic and I should get a vasectomy. I told her to go get her tubes tied if she was into mutilation and she said that was what Karen Owens had advised. I asked angrily, hungrily, if Karen Owens's tubes were tied and Monica replied with a certain complacence that, no, that wasn't the reason Karen and Alan didn't have children; she knew that much, and knew I'd be interested. I ignored the innuendo, excited to think of Karen in this way and alarmed by Monica's tone. It was one thing to stop going to Mass—after all, the Church had betrayed us, taking away Latin and Saint Christopher and fish on Friday—but this was beginning to feel evil.

Still, I went to the meetings with her, across town through the factory district and up Elm Hill. Support the Blacks, Stop the War, Save Ecology

—Karen often sat up beside the speaker, entwining her legs with the chair legs so her kneecaps made white squares and, in a kind of V for Victory, resting the tips of her middle and index fingers at the corners of her lips, as if enjoining herself not to say too much. When she did talk, she would keep tucking her hair behind her ears, a gesture I came later to associate with our lovemaking. Sometimes she laughed, showing her engagingly imperfect teeth. She hadn't been born rich, I deduced.

Alan would sit in one of the back rows of the chairs they had assembled, looking surly and superior, already by that time of evening stupid with booze but backing her up in his supercilious deep voice when she needed it. As a lawyer in town he had already taken on enough fair-housing and draft-resistance cases to hurt his practice with the people who could pay. It was hard to know how unhappy this made him; it was hard to decipher what he saw, slumped down in the back, watching with sleepy eyes. He had great long lashes, and hardly any eyebrows, and a high, balding forehead sunburned in summer.

I disliked him. He took up my oxygen when he was in the room. He was tall, tall as the rich get, plants with no weeds around them. When he looked down at me, it wasn't as if he didn't see me, he saw me too well; his eyes—with their lashes like an ostrich's and a yellowish cast to the whites —flicked through and away, having taken it all in and been instantly bored. Whatever had happened to him out there on the West Coast, it had left him wise in a way that made the world no longer very useful to him. Yet he also had Karen, and this Victorian mansion, and golf clubs and shotguns and tennis presses in the closets, and his father's deer heads in the library, and a name in the town that would still be worth something when this war and its protest had blown over.

In fairness, Alan could be entertaining, if he hadn't drunk too much. After the meetings a favored few of us would stay to tidy up, and Alan might get out his banjo and play. As a teen-ager, off at private schools since he was eleven, he had been a bluegrass freak and had taught himself this lonely music, fashionable then. When he got going, cracking his voice and yowling, I would see green hills, and a lone hawk soaring, and the mouths of coal mines, and feel so patriotic that tears would sting my corneas; all the lovely country that had been in America would come rushing back, as it was before we filled the land too full. Tipping back his head to keen the hillbilly chorus, Alan exposed his skinny throat as if to be cut.

While Monica and I would sit enthralled, joining in on the choruses, Karen would keep moving about, picking up the glasses and ashtrays, her determined manner and small set smile implying that this was an act Alan saved for company. First it had been her turn to howl; now it was his. When his repertoire ran out, she took over again, organizing word games, or exercises to enhance our perceptions. She had brought these games and exercises from California. One Saturday night, I remember, all the women there hid behind a partition of blankets and extended one hand for the men to identify, and to my embarrassment I recognized Karen's, its blue veins, and couldn't find Monica's—it was thicker and darker than it should have been, with a hairier wrist.

In many ways I did not recognize my wife. Her raised consciousness licensed her to drink too much, to stay up too late. She never wanted to go home. The Owenses, the times, had corrupted her. However my own heart was wandering, I wanted to have her at home, raising the children, keeping order against the day when all this disturbance, this reaching beyond ourselves, blew over. I had been attracted to what was placid in Monica, the touch of heaviness already there when she was seventeen, her young legs glossy and chunky in the white cheerleader socks. She had an athlete's slow heartbeat and fell asleep early. When I came to sleep with Karen, in the bright back bedroom of her big ornate house, I had trouble accepting the twittery fervor she brought to acts that with Monica possessed a certain solemn weight, as of something yielded. Monica had once confessed to me that she held back out of dread of losing her identity in the sex act; Karen seemed to be pushing toward just such a loss. Her quick, dry lips, kissing mine for the first time in the hazardous privacy of the teachers' room, took their style (it crossed my mind) from the adolescents thundering all around us. I couldn't be worth, surely, quite such an agitation of lips and tongue, quite so hard a hug from this slender, overheated person, whose heart I could feel tripping against my own through my coat and shirt and tie, and the wool of her sweater, and the twin cages of our ribs. Even in this moment of first surrender I observed that the wool was cashmere. It crossed my mind that she had mistaken me for a stud, an obediently erect conscript from the working class. I was a little repelled by the something *schooled* in her embrace—something pre-readied and too good to be true. But in time I accepted this as simply her metabolism, her natural way. She was love-starved. So was I.

Days when she didn't substitute became our days, set up with sweaty phone calls from the pay phone outside the cafeteria, which the kids had usually clogged with gum or clumsy slugs. The Owenses' house backed up to some acres of woods that they owned. Bird-chirp and pine-scent would sift through her windows. The abundant light was almost pornographic; I was used to the uxorious dark. She kept an aquarium and a terrarium back here, to take advantage of the sun, and wildlife posters all around: *we* were wildlife, naked and endangered. The bestial efficiency of our encounters had to do for tenderness. She knew to the minute when I would arrive and was ready, clothes off and the phone off the hook. She knew to the minute when I must go. When one of my free periods backed onto the lunch hour, and we had more time, we wasted it in bickering. When LBJ announced he would not run, I told her this would bring in Nixon, and hoped she was happy. I taunted her with this while the happiness of our lovemaking was still in her eyes. She had light-hazel eyes that darkened when we made love. She had a way of looking me over, of examining me as reverently as she did the toad and garter snake in her terrarium, flicking back her hair to get a closer look, or to take me into her mouth. I, with my foreskin and sexual hunger and blue-collar resentments, was simply life to her, a kind of treasure.

And she to me? Heaven, of a sort. When I sneaked in the back, past the plastic trash cans smelling of Alan's empties, Karen would be standing at the head of the back stairs like a bright, torn piece of sky. Up close, her body was a star map, her shoulders and shins crowded with freckles. Even those patches of skin shaped like the pieces of a bathing suit revealed to inspection a dark dot or two where the sun had somehow pricked.

"You really ought to go, darling," she would soon say. More practiced than I (I hated to think this, but it must have been the case), Karen was the policeman of our affair. I began to feel disciplined, and to resent it.

At school, when she came to substitute, it drove me wild to see her in the halls, her red hair bouncing on her back, her whippy little body full of our secrets. The Movement was in the air even here now; our young Poles and Portuguese were no longer willing to be drafted unquestioningly, and the classes in government and history, even in general science, had become battlefields. At Columbia and in Paris that spring, students were rioting. Whole masses of rooted presumption were being torn up around me, but I no longer cared. I felt so foolishly proud, linking myself with Karen in those minutes between classes, in the massive shuffle smelling of perfume and chewing gum and bodily warmth.

She warned me: "I love your touch, but, Frank, you mustn't touch me in public."

"When did I?"

"Just now. In the hall." We were in the teachers' room. She had lit a cigarette. She seemed extra nervous, indignant.

"I wasn't aware," I told her. "I'm sure nobody noticed."

"Don't be stupid. The children notice everything."

It was true. I had seen our names pencilled together, with the correct verb, on a lavatory wall. "You care?"

"Of course I care. So should you. We could both be hurt."

"By whom? The school board? The American Legion? I thought the revolution was on and there was naked dancing in the streets. I'm all for it; watch."

"Frank. Someone could come in that door any second."

"We used to neck in here like mad."

"That was before we had our days."

"Our half-hours. I'm sick of rushing back to the table of elements in a post-coital coma."

"You are?"

The fear in her face insulted me. "Yes," I told her, "and I'm sick of the hypocrisy. I'm sick of insomnia. I can't sleep anymore, I want you beside me. Only you. I thrash around, I take Sominex. Sometimes I cry, for a change of pace."

She tucked her hair behind her ears. Her face looked narrow, its skin tight at the sides of her eyes, a glaze across the tiny wrinkles. "Has Monica noticed?"

"No, she slumbers on. Nothing wakes her up. Why? Has Alan noticed any difference in you?"

"No, and I don't want him to."

"You don't? Why not?"

"Need you ask?" The sarcasm made her face look quite evil. There was a set of smug assumptions behind it that I hated.

My voice got loud. "You bet your sweet ass I need to ask." I repeated, "Why the hell not?"

"Shh. He's my husband, that's why."

"That seems simplistic. And rather reactionary, if I may say so."

Betty Kurowski, first-year algebra and business math, opened the door, looked at our faces, and said, "Oh. Well, I'll go smoke in the girls' lavatory." As she was closing the door we both begged her to come back.

"We were just arguing about Vietnam," Karen told her. "Frank wants to bomb South China now."

For summer employment, Monica and I were counselors at a day camp in New Hampshire, about forty minutes' drive from Mather. As if this were not separation enough, Karen and Alan spent a month in Santa Barbara visiting her family. I had been wrong about her not being rich; the parents lived in a million-dollar house near the beach. She would wear a bikini all day long. At night, while Monica slept, I masturbated like a kid. Even during the day, amid the *plockety-pock* of table tennis and the shouts of horseplay from our little brown lake, I could not stop thinking of Karen

—her freckled flesh, the sunlight in her room, the way she fed on me with her eyes and mouth. I was weary of children, including my own, yet part of my fantasy was that I would give her a child. A child with her hazel eyes and my black hair: an elf child that would never need to have its diapers changed.

In August the Owenses returned from their month away, and Monica telephoned them the first night, as if she had been missing them, too. She and Karen arranged to have Karen come up to the camp one day to lead a nature walk. She fixed up a bottle with a jeweller's loupe so that the children could peer into a sample of pond water and see the frenzy of minute life there—little transparent ovals and cylinders bumping around like Dodg'em cars, trying to find something to eat without being eaten. She was honeycolored from the California sun, and her hair had been bleached to the pallor of an orange-juice stain on a tablecloth, but her teeth were still slightly crooked, and her knees bony and intense.

In the aftermath of this visit, this glimpse of her functioning with such sweet earnestness as a teacher, I wrote her on our camp stationery, which was beige, with a green letterhead spelling out the camp name in little birch logs. I came across some stolen sheets of it a few years ago, when we changed houses, and had to laugh. My letter recounted details of our lovemaking and proposed that we break out of our marriages and get married to each other. More a violent dream than a proposal: the surge of writing, in a corner of the picnic pavilion while Monica was out on the lake with a canoeing class, carried me into it, and the fact that I was out of Mather, writing a letter back into it. It was what they call now an out-of-body experience. I could see myself, very small, back in Mather, and I was easy to manipulate, into a life of love with this other doll. I held off mailing it for a day. But on rereading, the words seemed frightening but true, like the cruel facts of pond life.

Once that blue mailbox gathering dust at the side of that three-lane New Hampshire highway had closed its iron mouth, I sensed that I had overstepped. There were limits, and proprieties, like the glass walls of her terrarium, within which Karen had given me freedom. Outside those limits there was danger, and death.

Not that there was much danger of Alan's intercepting the letter. I knew the mail arrived at the Owenses' house around eleven, when he would be at his office or still in bed from the night before. Alcohol was worming deeper and deeper into his system and making it hard for him to sleep at night. He and I both, for different reasons, were feeling our lives turn upside down.

Days of silence went by. At first I was relieved. But when camp ended, and we were in town all day as well as evenings, I had expected some message from Karen, at least a social gesture toward the two of us. Late-summer muddle—New England squeezing the last drops of fun out of its few warm months—was all around us, and school would soon begin again. In Chicago, the Democrats had nominated Humphrey while Johnson hid in the White House. The police were clobbering protesters while people like me cheered. That Thursday morning a call from Karen at last came through; she and Alan were having some of the CMC over to watch the riots and Humphrey's acceptance on television. The convention went on and on, everything sacred unravelling before our eyes, and we kept pace with brandy and beer and white wine. Instead of junk-food snacks, Karen served little saucers of health foods—raisins, sesame and sunflower seeds, even macadamia nuts, which nobody else could afford. Alan concentrated on the bourbon, and somehow around eleven I was delegated to go downtown and get him another bottle. The package stores were closed, but he was sure I could wangle a fifth from the bartender's at Rudy's. Rudy's was the main dive in the factory district; my father had been a regular. I resented the errand—I had resented my father's long evenings at Rudy's—but performed it, counting out Alan his change to the penny. He said I could have kept the change. When he saw, foggy as he was, how badly this went over, he tried to cover up with jokes about connections. He told me, "It must be great, Frank, to have connections. My problem in town is, I don't have the connections." He meant this to be a joke: the Owenses were well connected and my people were nobodies. But in fact it was true: Mather, sluggish as it was, changed a bit from year to year, and had slipped away from the Owenses.

Around midnight the other concerned citizens began to drift home. Around one-thirty the four of us were left sitting at the four sides of the antique kitchen table, a cherrywood drop-leaf, made in Mather in the 1840s by the Shaker community that had existed here. The night was hot, with a last-gasp heat; along the coast, sea breezes lighten the summer, but in our river valley it hangs heavy until the maples start to turn. Crickets were singing outside the screen door. I had had insomnia the night before, and Monica had to get up early to take our son Tommy to the orthodontist, but we didn't make a move to go.

"So where are we?" Alan abruptly asked. He seemed to be focussed on Karen, across the table from him. Monica and I sat on his either side.

"Here and there," Monica said, giggling. She had had plenty to drink and was more mischievous, more wakeful, than I was used to seeing her. Her liberated Catholic hair had a bushy outward thrust that was the coming look—tough, cheerful, ethnic. Karen's look, the long ironed hair, the nervous vulnerability, belonged to a fading past.

"Let's talk turkey," Alan persisted through his blur, his long lashes blinking, his rather pretty mouth fixed helplessly in a sneer.

"Oh, what a good idea!" Monica said, glancing at me to see how I was taking all this.

"Alan, explain what you *mean,*" Karen said. Her voice with children sometimes had a wheedling tone. She was the least drunk of us all, and in a flash of alcoholic illumination I saw her as pedantic. He was being naughty and she was set to baby him, Socratically, as she had babied me about the kids going off to fight. Using her psychology. "Don't hide behind your liquor," she went on after Alan. "Explain what you *mean.*" Some old grievance between them seemed to be surfacing while the crickets droned.

It appeared to me he didn't mean very much; he was just drunkenly making conversation. I was interested in the tremor of Karen's stringy freckled hands as she maneuvered a cigarette to her mouth and was therefore slow to notice Monica's plump hand on top of Alan's. Accustomed to seeing her comfort children at the camp, I dismissed it as more Alan-babying, from his other side.

"He's a Virgo," Karen told Monica, smiling now that her cigarette was lit. "Virgos are *so* withholding."

He looked at his wife with his fishy, starry, stunned eyes and I saw that he loathed the brightness that I loved. Much as I disliked him, my thought was that he must have reasons. He opened his mouth to speak and she prompted "Yes?" too eagerly; her sharp smile chased him back into his shell.

He hunched lower over the table, and Hubert Humphrey's high-pitched old-womanish voice came out of his mouth. "Let's put America back on track," Alan said, imitating the acceptance speech we had heard, interspersed with shots of the violence outside. "Let's not talk about the green belt." Karen's latest project had been to arouse community interest in creating a green belt around our tired little city. "Let's talk about—"

"Below the belt," Monica finished for him, and she and I laughed. Across the table from me she looked enlarged, her hair puffed out and her face broadening under its genial film of alcohol. Her mother was fat, with a distinct mustache, but I had never thought Monica would grow to resemble her. Now that she had, I didn't mind; I felt she would take care of me, even though I had recently flung into the mailbox a letter offering to leave her. Her glances toward me were like holes in the haze that the Owenses were generating, working something out between themselves. She and I and, in his way, Alan were in tune with the crickets and the occasional swish of cars passing, but our camaraderie was weakened by something resistant in Karen and by our common fatigue; watching too much televi-

sion, we, too, had become staticky and unreal. We kissed one another good
night then, Karen and I primly—what a dry little mouth she gave me!—
and Alan and Monica lingeringly, like a pair of sentimental drunks. Out
on his porch, he did not want to let go of Monica's hand. A warm drizzle
had begun. My wife fell asleep in the car beside me as the windshield
wipers swept away the speckles of rain. Downtown was deserted, the great
empty factories looking majestic and benevolent, asleep. We lived across
the river, in a development a mile beyond the high school.

That was our last evening with the Owenses. Next morning, Karen
called the house when she knew Monica would be off with Tommy. "I told
him," she told me.

"You did?" A great numbness hit my heart and merged with my hang-
over. "But why?" I had answered on the upstairs phone and could see on
the curving street below, under the development saplings, a few yellow
leaves, the first fallen, lying in spots of damp from last night's rain.

Karen's voice, husky from lack of sleep, picked its way carefully, as if
spelling out things to a child. "Didn't you under*stand* what *Alan*"—I
hated the slightly strengthened way she pronounced the sacred name of
Alan—"was *say*ing last night? He was saying he wanted to go to bed with
your wife."

"Well, something like that. So?"

Karen didn't answer.

I supplied, "You think he should have asked her in private, instead of
making it a committee matter."

She said, "The reason he couldn't get it out, he didn't think you'd accept
me in exchange." Her voice snagged, then continued, roughened by tears,
"He's only ever seen us quarrel. About Vietnam."

"That's touching," I said. I didn't find Alan touching, actually. But she
was enrolling me in her decision.

"I couldn't bear it, Frank. His being so innocent."

"How did he take the news?"

"Oh, he was exhilarated. He kept me up all night with it. He couldn't
believe—I shouldn't tell you this—he couldn't believe I'd sleep with a
townie."

Downstairs my two younger children had grown bored with television
and were punching each other. I said, "But with a non-townie he'd believe
it? How many non-townies have you slept with?"

"Frank, don't." She hesitated. "You know how I am. He doesn't give me
shit, Frank. He's *sink*ing."

"Well, let him." A coldness, the cold of death, had come over me.

"I can't."

"O.K. I don't think it was very nice of you to turn us in without even warning me," I said, all weary dignity.

"You would have argued."

"You bet. I love you. Loved you."

"I did it for you, too. For you and Monica."

"Thanks." The day outside was bright, with a rinsed brightness, and I thought, *When she hangs up, I must open the window and let in some air.* "Did you get my letter?" I asked her.

"Yes. That was another thing. It frightened me."

"I meant it to be a nice letter."

"It *was* nice. Only—a little possessive?"

"Oh. Maybe so. Pardon me." *I'll never sleep with her again, never, ever,* I thought, and the window whose panes I stared through seemed a translucent seal barring me from great volumes of possibility, I on one side and my life on the other, my life and the naked bright day.

Karen was crying, less in grief, I thought, than in exasperation. "I *wanted* to talk to you about it, but there wasn't any way to get *to* you; I haven't even had a chance to give you the present I brought from Santa Barbara."

"What was it?"

"A shell. A beautiful shell."

"That you found on the beach?"

"No, those are too ordinary. I bought it in a shop, a shell from the South Seas. A top shell, silvery white outside with pink freckles underneath. You know how you go on about my freckles."

"Your gorgeous freckles," I said.

Karen didn't substitute-teach that fall; she went into Boston and worked long days for the peace movement. Friends of ours who had remained in the Owenses' inner circle told us that some nights she didn't come home. If you look at the memoirs of the celebrity-radicals of that time, a lot of it was sex. Liberals drink and smoke, radicals use dope and have sex. Karen and Alan split up finally, sometime between when Nixon and Kissinger finagled our troop withdrawal and when South Vietnam collapsed. His drinking became worse; he ceased to function as a lawyer at all, though the name stayed up in the lobby of the office block downtown where he had rented space. She went back to the West Coast; he stayed with us, like the gutted factories. Though I didn't see him from one year to the next, I thought of him often, always with joy at his fall. Monica and I had moved, actually, into his neighborhood; we allowed ourselves a fourth child before she got her tubes tied, and, with heating oil going higher and higher, we were able to pick up very reasonably—my brother was the realtor—a big turn-of-the-century house on Elm Hill, with a finished third floor and a porch on two sides. We've closed off some of the rooms and put in a wood-burning stove in the living room.

Betty Kurowski's mother cleaned, twice a week, the Owens house two blocks farther up the hill. It was Betty who told me how bad Alan was getting. "A skeleton," she said. "You should go see him, Frank. I went in there last week and talked with him and he asked about you. He saw in the paper how you've become assistant principal."

"Why would I want to go see that snide bastard?"

Betty looked at me knowingly, under those straight black eyebrows that didn't go with her bleached hair. "For old times' sake," she said, straight-faced.

I asked Monica to go with me and she said, "It's not me he wants to see."

"It was you he liked."

"That was pathetic, that was his attempt to fight back. He's not fighting back anymore. Poor Alan Owens. That whole family was just too good for this world." She sounded like her mother. But Monica hasn't gotten fat. She counts those calories and is taking a night course in computer science. She's been working mornings as receptionist and biller for a photo-developing lab that has taken half a floor of the old Pilgrim mill, and they want her to learn to use the computer. I'm proud of her, seeing her go off nights in her trim skirt and blouse. She's tough. Old cheerleaders keep that toughness. Win or lose, is the way they figure. The truth about Karen and me, when it came out, simply made her determined to win.

Karen sends us mimeographed Christmas letters. She's remarried, has a son and a daughter, and got a degree in landscape architecture. Alan had been holding her back, but a dozen years ago she was too uncertain of herself to know that. It hadn't occurred to me, then, that being sexy could be a woman's way of repressing her other problems.

Nobody answered my knock. The Owens house has a front door as wide as a billiard table, with gray glass sidelights into which a lacy pattern of frosting has been etched, so people can peek in only in spots. The clapboards in the shelter of the porch were pumpkin-colored, but those out in the weather were faded pale as wheat, and peeling. There were dry leaves all over the porch; it was that season again. Advertising handouts had been allowed to collect on the welcome mat. The door was unlocked and swung open easily. The downstairs showed Mrs. Kurowski's work; indeed, it was uncannily clean and tidy in the big rooms, as if no one ever walked through. The long kitchen, with its little Shaker table, looked innocent of meals. Two tangerines in a pewter bowl had turned half green with mold.

"Alan?" I was sorry I had come; being in their house after so many years awakened in my stomach the sour tension of those noontime visits that would never come again. Sun slanted in at the kitchen windows the way it always had, making the scratched lip of the aluminum sink sparkle, drying out the bar of soap in its cracked rubber dish. She had liked those stained-glass flowers and butterflies people use as shade-pulls, and a few of these were still hanging here, picking up the light. I stood at the foot of the dark back stairs at whose head naked Karen used to flicker like a piece of sky, and called again, "Alan?"

Frighteningly, his voice came. "Come on up, Francis." He had always had a deeper, more melodious voice than one would have expected out of his skinny, slumped frame, and there was still timbre in his voice, though it sounded frayed and quavery, like an old woman's. I remembered his imitation of Hubert Humphrey. I climbed the stairs, my belly remembering how my eyes would possess her, her ankles, her knees, her amber triangle, each step carrying me higher toward the level of her fluttering, excessively pleased embrace, her heart through her arched ribs thumping against my classroom clothes, my tie and the coarse cotton of my button-down shirt crushed against the cool-warm silk of her.

"In here," his voice came, already weaker. I had feared he would be in the bright back room that she and I had used, but he was in the bedroom that had been theirs, at the front of the house, darkened by the mass of the two big beeches outside. And the shades were drawn. The dim room was soaked in a smell that at first I took to be medicinal but that then came clear as whiskey, the flat and shameful smell it has in the empty bottle. Alan was sitting in the center of his tousled bed in striped pajamas and an untied blue bathrobe, in the lotus position, smoking a cigarette. He looked dreadful—emaciated, with a patchy beard inches long. He had lost the hair on the top of his head in a clean swath, but the rest hung down nearly to his shoulders. His skin was as dull and thin as tracing paper; there was something radiant about the blue-white tops of his naked feet. The room was hot, the thermostat turned way up—in this day and age, a bit of swank in that.

"Alan," I managed to get out. "How do you feel?"

"Not bad, Francis. How do I look?"

"Well, thin. Aren't you eating?"

He put the cigarette to his lips the way children learning to smoke do, trying to follow the tip with his eyes. Yet the gesture with which he took it away and exhaled was debonair. "I've been having a little war with my stomach," he said. "I can't keep anything down."

"Have you seen a doctor?"

"*Aaah.*" A little flip of his hand, all bones now. His gestures had become effete, unduly flexible. "They always say the same thing. I know what I've got—a stomach bug that's been going around. A touch of the flu."

"What is it that they always say?" I asked. "The doctors."

His hands were so emaciated, the hairs on their backs seemed to be growing with a separate life. He turned his head away, toward the dusty frame of sunlight around the drawn shade nearest his bed; dim as it was, the light made him squint, and a cutting edge of bone was declared by a shadow scooped at his temple. He turned back toward me and tipped his head flirtatiously. "You know, you son of a bitch," he drawled, trying to be pleasant. "To taper off on the sauce. But the sauce has never hurt me. It's when I taper off that the horrors begin." His eyes widened, remembering. His voice for a moment was flattened into honesty.

There must be fear of death in there somewhere, I thought; but as a gentleman he wanted to shield me from it. The result was a kind of grisly puppetry: so gaunt, with his face spread wide by alcoholic bloat, he looked like a lollipop with a Rasputin beard. Fear was my emotion, mixed in with that thrill of importance witnesses to disaster have.

I found the courage to tell him, "Alan, you can't keep on like this. You'll get dehydrated. You really must *do* something."

It was what he had wanted me to say, so he could spurn it. He sneered and made a soft hawking noise that put me in my place. "I'm not that much of a doer. Let's talk about you. I see where you got a promotion."

"It happens, if you're there long enough."

"Always modest," he said. "And you've moved in down the street."

"You mind?"

It wasn't clear that he heard me. His next speech came out as if it had been recorded on tape; his head wobbled as he drawled it out. "I always knew you'd make it big in a half-ass way. One of those sleek slobs in three-piece suits eating steak every Friday night over at the River House, hopping up from your table to go across and pal it up with some school-board member, everybody jolly, saying sure you'll head up the door-to-door drive for the new hospital wing, go peddle tickets for the K of C clambake and all that public-spirited crap. That's what I used to tell Karen, he'll wind up one of those sleek wop slobs in a three-piece suit. Where's the third piece?" He whined, "You look so fucking preppy, Frank."

I laughed. I was wearing a jacket and gray flannels. His twitching head, his eyes oddly theatrical with their big lashes, seemed actually to be searching the corners near the ceiling for the third piece. He wanted me to laugh, really. The atmosphere of this room was rich, with the gloom and bad smells, and there was a certain grandeur in his ruin, none of his scorn for all of us concealed anymore. "Yeah," I said. "Karen told me at the time you couldn't believe she'd sleep with a townie."

"Wop. I think I said wop."

"No doubt you did."

"You owe me one for that. You owe me one, brother."

"It was a long time ago. What happened between you two then?"

He looked toward the window shade again, as if he could see through it. "Karen was . . . greedy." The words came out of him as if dictated from behind, by a prompter's voice he had to hear and then echo. "You owe me one, brother," he repeated, fuddled.

"Alan, what can I do for you?" My own voice seemed to boom. "I'm not a doctor, but I'd say you need one." That third piece he mentioned, the vest, seemed to be on my chest, making me thicker, armored, ruthless in my health.

He fended me off with effeminate, flustered gestures. "You can do a little shopping for me," he said. "This damn flu, I can hardly make it to the john. My legs don't want to work right."

"Can't Betty's mother shop for you?"

"She drags in loathsome stuff. Breakfast cereal. Orange juice. She doesn't know . . ."

"Doesn't know what, Alan?"

"What's good for flu."

"What is? Bourbon?"

He gave me a straight dark helpless look. "Just to tide me over until I get my legs back."

"On one condition, Alan. You call your doctor."

"Oh, sure. Absolutely. I know he'll just say it's the flu. My wallet's on the bureau over there—"

"My treat." As he said, I owed him one. No embarrassing deal with the bartender at Rudy's this time; I paid $18.98 over the counter for a glass-handled half-gallon of Wild Turkey's best, 101 proof, at the liquor super-market at the new shopping mall on the other side of Elm Hill. Back up the hill, back up the stairs: my siphuncle was working overtime. Alan wasn't in his bed, he was in the bathroom; I listened a moment and heard the noise of dry heaves. I left the bottle in the center of his bed.

Who can say that that was the bottle that killed him? A parade of bottles killed him, going back to his spoiled teens. It was not the next morning but the next week that they found him curled over, stiffened in the lotus position beside the toilet bowl. When they opened the door (Betty's mother had called the police, guessing what was behind it), his body fell over in one piece, like a husk. Dehydration, internal bleeding, heart failure. Betty told us there were empty bottles everywhere—under the bed, in the closet. I pictured mine in my mind's eye, drained, lying on its side on the floor, gleaming when they raised the shades at last. Maybe it was that bottle I thought of when the student brought in the nautilus shell. Or the shell Karen never got to give me. Or that big house with all its rooms and this naked freckled woman waiting in one of its chambers.

Thinking I should strike a more positive note, I held up the souvenir again and told the class, "There's a clear lesson here in this shape. Who knows what it is?"

Nobody did.

"Growth," I said. "We all have to *grow.*"

Learn a Trade

"MOBILES?" Fegley echoed over the telephone, with a sinking feeling. He was an internationally known junk sculptor whose annual income ran well into six figures, but in his mind he was still an unpopular and ill-coördinated adolescent walking out to a rural mailbox in Missouri to place in it a brown envelope containing cartoons and addressed to *Collier's,* or else to discover there a brown envelope returned from the same magazine with a rejection slip. Partch, Hoff, Rea—he imitated them all, and yet everything came back. Once, he tried to sell the nearest city's only newspaper a comic strip and then took the same cartoons to the local department store, as the possible basis for an advertising scheme. His mother went with him into the city that day, since he was too young to drive, and a street photographer snapped a picture of them walking together, she clutching her purse, he holding his portfolio under a skinny arm, both of them looking distracted and tired. His mother had sponsored his "creativity," indulged it. Almost his first memory of her was of a young woman sitting on the threadbare carpet with him, crayoning solid a space at the top of a page of the coloring book on the floor before him; it seemed marvellous to the child that she, sitting opposite him, could color upside down, as well as with such even, gentle strokes, which never strayed outside the printed outlines. Fegley's father, who supplemented the income from the farm by working as a non-union carpenter, wrung his hands to think of his son's wasting his life on hopeless ambitions. "Learn a trade," he begged the boy. "Get a solid trade, and then you can fool around with this artsy-craftsy stuff." One night in bed, Fegley, shortly before going off to a New York art school, overheard his father confide to his mother downstairs, "They'll just break his heart."

Overhearing this, the boy had inwardly scoffed. And eventually, moving from cartooning, by way of imitating the playful sculpture of Picasso and Ipoustéguy, into a world of galleries and spacious duplexes and expectant museum spaces that his father had never dreamed existed, he proved the old man wrong. Yet the older that Fegley himself grew, the more it seemed his father had been essentially right.

In the pattern of his generation he had married young, had four children, and eventually got a divorce. His first wife, met at the art school, had been herself artistic: Sarah painted delicate impressionistic still-lifes and landscapes that were often abandoned before the corners were filled. There was usually something wrong with the perspective, though the colors were remarkably true. He sometimes blamed himself, in their years together, for not encouraging her more; but in truth all "this artsy-craftsy stuff" depressed him, and he hoped that his children would become scientists. He plied the two boys, especially, with telescopes and microscopes, chemistry sets and books of mathematical puzzles; they squinted at Saturn's rings for an evening and at magnified salt granules for an afternoon, and then the expensive tubes of brass and chrome drifted toward the closets already full of deflated footballs and gadgets whose batteries had given out. Fegley's two daughters, as they grew into women, with the distances and silences of women, took watercolor brushes and pads on their sunbathing expeditions, and at home solemnly inscribed haiku on pebble board with crow-quill pens. Their mother encouraged all this, having set the example by her own dabbling, which fitfully continued into her middle age; the house was strewn with Sarah's half-completed canvases. Fegley did his powerful, successful sculpture—most famously, the series of giant burnished insects fabricated from discarded engine blocks and transmission systems—in an old machine shop he rented two miles from the house, down low along the Hudson. He did not encourage his children to visit him there, and even had his subscription to *Artnews* directed to that address. He was like a man who, having miraculously survived a shipwreck, wants to warn all others back at the edge of the sea. As the two boys grew older, he congratulated himself that they seemed more concerned with putting their feet to leather balls and car accelerators than with setting implements to paper. Unlike his youthful self, they were popular and well-coördinated, and expert at sports. The older went off to college determined to make the football varsity, having been a spectacularly shifty tight end for his boarding school, but somewhere under the cloud of his parents' divorce proceedings he dropped out of athletics and into film studies; he took courses (college courses! for credit!) that analyzed the cutting rhythm in old Laurel and Hardy comedies and the advance of camera mobility in musical comedies of the Forties. Now he was living in a squalid Manhattan loft with several other aspirants to the world of film, lost young souls stoned on media, pounding the sidewalks and virtually (who knows?—maybe actually) selling their bodies for the whisper of a promise of becoming an assistant grip's assistant in a public-television documentary on the African killer bee. Fegley's daughters had also faded into the limbo of artistic endeavor; one was in northern California making "pinch pots" out of her lover's back-yard clay, and the other was editing a journal of genealogy in Cincinnati while working on a highly ambitious feminist novel called *Ever Since Eve*. This left uncontaminated by creativity only the younger son, Warren. Warren was a broad-shouldered brown-eyed nineteen-year-old who had once collected butterflies and rock specimens and who was clever with his hands; he had even given signs of becoming a carpenter, working alongside his grandfather for a few summers, before the old man died. Here at last, Fegley had thought, was my practical, down-to-earth child.

So it was with a sinking feeling that Fegley heard that the boy was making mobiles this summer. "But what about his job?" he asked.

"I don't think he ever called that number Clara gave him," Sarah said.

Clara, Fegley's present wife, was a civil engineer with a firm in White Plains and had given her stepson a lead on a summer job with a road-repair crew.

"What do you mean exactly, mobiles?" Fegley asked.

"They're lovely," the distant voice answered. "They really must be seen to be believed. You should come look." Her voice was fading; one of her annoying habits, which he had not been much aware of as long as they lived together, was that of dropping the telephone mouthpiece to her chin as she talked.

"All right, damn it: I'll be right over," Fegley said. "I want to *talk* to Warren. Clara went to a lot of trouble to find a contractor who had filled his minority quota." He left his new studio, an abandoned gas station in Port Chester, with its friendly mounds of junk and pleasant, unifying stench of the acetylene torch, and swung his Porsche up onto the battered road, into that overtrafficked grid interconnecting Westchester County's hidden green hives of plenty. He drove the thirty minutes across 287 to his old suburb.

It was strange, to be in his former home. The large Tarrytown house, once so full of children and their music and clutter, was silent now, and its furniture only half familiar. The former Mrs. Fegley had a new husband, a hearty pipe-smoker whose spoor and scent were everywhere. Like Clara, the man led a useful inartistic life and worked all day. Sarah still painted and, what was hurtful, had improved; her recent still-lifes were filled to the corners, and the perspective was tight as a drum. Apologetically she announced, "Warren said he'd be right back. I told him you were coming."

"Aha. Where did he go, ostensibly?"

"He said downtown to buy some more copper wire. His mobiles take a lot of it."

"I bet. Do you know what copper wire costs these days?"

"Of course. Who do you think gives him the money?"

"Then why do you let him?"

"I let *you,*" she said, and looked lightly away—the equivalent of allowing the telephone mouthpiece to slip down to her chin. It was true: she had let him do what he could. She had indulged him. For a time she had supported them both, working as a salesgirl in the old Fifth Avenue Bonwit's.

Sarah had put on weight, without impairing a certain absent-minded grace that flitted into the air from foci in her wrists and ankles. Adjusted to the sight of her and the ambience of the house, Fegley remembered the kindergarten crayon scrawls posted on the refrigerator with magnets, the driftwood sculptures brought home from their summer rentals, the collages of beach glass, the crow-quilled haiku, the linoleum cuts at Christmastime, the cardboard circuses. Once, Fegley had bought the children a set of Cuisenaire rods to inculcate number theory, and the baby daughter, then about four years old, had taken two of the units for number one—tiny wood cubes—and pencilled dots on them to make dice. She had made little cats of the rectangular rods representing number two, dogs of the longer threes, people with faces and bow ties of the still longer fours, and skyscrapers, with pencilled windows and canopied doorways, of the fives. Sarah had gone ecstatic over this show of "creativity." The child, Fegley saw now, should have been spanked. A delayed fury spoke in him: "You've brought these kids up to live in a never-never land. All this stuff, the world doesn't *need* it. It needs practical nurses. It needs securities analysts. You should *tell* them."

"I never told *you,*" she said, in that same mild and distant voice. "Why should I say it to *them?*"

"I was different," he said. "I was ignorant. I was desperate to get out of Missouri. Our children aren't desperate, they're just kidding around."

Sarah shrugged. "Who's to say? He's been *so* excited. I've never seen him work this hard—down in the cellar all day and into the night, pounding and sawing."

Fegley's father's hands, he remembered, had combined the hardened traces of chisel-nicks and saw-slips with a spotty bubbling of brown warts on the backs. Those hands had done honest work, Fegley used to think, admiring them; and now his own hands, scarred by metal, looked much the same. The image of his broad-shouldered son in the cellar, captive to an illusion, and of a once young and slender woman standing on sore feet behind a counter at Bonwit's, and of his own young mother sitting opposite him carefully crayoning in the depths of the Depression—these superimposed images afflicted him with a pathos and sense of waste that were paralyzing. His former wife had to prompt, "Why don't you go down and look at them?"

"I don't want to see the damn things. I came to see *him.*"

"It might be a while before he comes back, frankly. I think he was scared of what you'd say to him, that's why he took off." Warren had inherited his brown eyes from her, with those same elusive golden flecks.

"Poor little Warren," Fegley said, and descended the steps to his former cellar. Scrap lumber and stray junk from the long ago when he had worked at home had mysteriously disappeared; his old workbench supported an unfamiliar litter of pliers and snippers, coiled wire, cut tin, glue, tape, and mutilated sheets of plastic and cardboard. A new fluorescent tube brightened the work space, but Warren had hung the finished mobiles in the dimness that stretched beneath the cobwebbed pipes and floor stringers to the faint far stone foundation wall. Each mobile embodied a different idea: some suggested the flight of birds, others the scales of a dragon; some were twirled of copper wire into terminations like the heads of fiddlehead ferns, and some held at the ends of invisible black-wire arms cardboard paddle shapes, or crescents or circles, ranged in sequences drifting outward in precarious spacy cascades that gently moved as the creator's mother's footsteps, heavy with fatality, descended the stairs.

"See?" Sarah asked.

Each mobile by itself might have looked spindly, but the effect of so many, hanging unsold, unrequested by the world, waiting here in the dark, was of a leafy forest or a firmament of stars twinkling one behind the other in a recession as good as infinite.

"Yeah," Fegley had to say, half to himself. His former wife came and stood beside him, to get the same perspective. "That's right," he said. "Keep breaking my heart."

The Ideal Village

OUR PARTY had of course long known of the existence of the village; yet there was fear that our pilots, Fidel and Miguel, would be unable to locate its clearing in the vastness of the jungle. Not a month before, dusk had overtaken a supply plane aiming for the landing strip of some Lutheran missionaries still farther to the south, and the pilot had panicked and made a run for the lights of the coast. His fuel had carried him as far as the Montes de Ferro, where the scar of his crash was (we saw from the air) indistinguishable from a mining tip. And our second plane, piloted by Miguel, did drop from radio contact in the clouds—those strange clouds that in this part of the world form directly above the vaporous rivers, so that the sky seems to be full of enormous snakes—but it later developed that he had merely tuned in to the band of reggae music ceaselessly transmitted from the large rebel encampment in the Montes del Oro. (The encampment lies just over the border and seeks, of course, to overthrow not our exemplary and democratic government but that of the neighboring country, with its deplorable regime.) Fifteen minutes after we landed, Miguel's Cessna materialized in the sky as a speck no bigger than a buzzard, and as indolent in motion. We cheered. Even the chief cheered, though he had seen much pain in his years in the city as a chiropractor, and had always his dignity to think of.

He and the radical priests had come forward to greet us, but as it were reluctantly, long after our engines had been cut and the unpacking of our baggage—our backpacks and *chinchorros* and Styrofoam wine coolers—had already created small mountains on the packed earth in the shadows of our wings. The landing strip was also the main street of the village, and our backwash had stripped wands of grass from the conical roofs, and our engine noise had made short work of the afternoon siesta. Of the two priests, one was tall and pale and elegant, his accent the Spanish lisp, and the other shorter and darker, his mixed blood churning in him like a suppressed vivacity. The chief, of course, had pure Indian features, though sagged and soured by his years of metropolitan experience. In late middle age he had been rallied by the nobility of this experiment—communism and ethnicity seamlessly combined—to return to the village of his origins. He wore the tribal parrot-feather girdle, which did not quite cover his buttocks, and the armbands of monkeyskin that blazoned his rank, and the vest of a gray three-piece suit. Miguel brought his little red-striped Cessna in on the money and trundled to a stop, trailing a crowd of children. Some of the children were naked, some wore blue jeans, but all appeared healthy, cheerful, and unalarmed, in contrast to the children of the unideal villages we had visited previously. There was no begging, and only on the part of the onyx-eyed infants was any tactile curiosity expressed in our apparatus or the sleek and shiny urban costume of the females in our party.

We were shown to our quarters, where some male villagers strung our *chinchorros* to the overhead beams, using the knots that only they knew, and so swiftly that even Ortega, the knot expert among us, could not follow the twists. Each tribe, in a culture based upon vines and fibers, and which thirty years ago astounded the pioneer anthropologists with the intricacies of its woven fishnets and suspension bridges, boasts a secret language of knots—a flurry of brown fingers and thumbs capped, as the knot is cinched, with a guffaw, half defiance and half celebration, out of mouths disfigured by the perpetual wad of green tobacco.

We were afforded time to freshen, and then given the expected tour of the artichoke fields, the acres of experimental cotton, the long hut where the women on looms powered by the village generator mass-produce the ancestral patterns, the small huts where the old men carve from kapok wood the same unvarying figures of coati, capybara, jaguar, and centipede, to be sold at airport souvenir shops a thousand miles away. Such an industry, the taller priest explained in his epicene Catalan, is of course less than ideal, since the zoömorphs thus manufactured are acknowledged by the hand that whittles them to have lost their sacred animistic purpose. We are in transition here. These old men—his gesture flicked across the bent, partly shaved heads—can create only these forms, which their fathers seriously confused with living creatures. The next generation, he hoped, would be quite free of the old shadows and produce wood carvings expressive of both their own individual genius and the beauty of the common weal.

Whether such figures would be popular in the airport shops remained to be seen. We advance here by trial and error, he said; we do not disdain half-measures. Only in our ultimate goals are we doctrinaire.

These goals, it did not need to be said, were liberty, equality, fraternity; worker control of the means of production; freedom from oppression, subtle or overt. A social contract, in short, that had no binding edges. The smaller priest laughed, with his half-breed exuberance, out here in the artichoke fields, where the shadows were beginning to thicken, leaf upon leaf; his plump hands, slightly cupped, momentarily formed in front of his cassock a mystical shape, an intangible social form whose edges did not bind.

We swam in the river. There were no piranhas along this stretch, we were assured, and the alligators were in their *sazón de letargo*—their season of torpor. Conchita and Esmeralda looked piquant in their bikinis, slender and sallow and nervous. The opaque beige water swallowed their flesh at the knees like some magically thin paint; yet we emerged the same color as before, and uneaten. The vegetation along the riverbanks was monotonous and tall. Many tropical species, our botanist, Fernando, explained, had been shaped by nature to look almost exactly alike. An explorer from Mars, he went on to elaborate, even were he to land at our icebound poles would find microbes and lichen, so abundant—so frantically, hysterically abundant—is life on this permissive planet.

As, wrapped in our towels, we crossed the wide plaza of earth at the center of the village, between the feasting hut and the hut of adolescent initiation, we were struck by the large smooth stones dotted about without apparent pattern, and casting long shadows as evening approached. Luis, our anthropologist, surmised that these were counters in some ritual or game. He was not far wrong; the melancholy chief merrily explained that the young men of the village tested their strengths by lifting these stones. Against our polite but unemphatic protests, the present champion was called forth: a rather fat boy in blue jeans and stencilled T-shirt *(Bata Shoes,* his shirt advertised, though he was barefoot) who had to be urged forward like a bashful girl by his companions. He removed his shirt, displaying a soft-looking, rounded, almost female chest. He approached a stone—presumably the heaviest, a champion in its own stolid and mindless way—and with sudden decisiveness tugged at one end so that the monolith stood upright. Upended, it looked heavier, its shadow having become so much longer. The boy squatted and embraced the stone as a father would embrace a toddling child who had just demonstrated a need for affection. Then he attempted to stand with his burden, and the entire crowd (for our

inner arc of witness had been multiplied and made into a complete circle
by the arrival of much of the village population) grew tensely silent in
empathy with his effort. On first attempt, the stone outbalanced him and
he had to release it abruptly, dancing back lest his bare toes be crushed. On
second try, he wrestled it up onto his thighs and then higher, so that the
stone, like some massive slithering parasite, seemed to be searching for an
entry into his body; at last, his bashful smile awash with strain, the champion had the monster on his shoulders. He turned once to face the complete circle of his audience and then dumped the stone to the ground with
a thud swallowed in the burst of applause. The speed with which the boy
melted into the shadows seemed modestly to state that his gift was not his
own, but a divine blessing that had happened to alight on him; he had been
pushed forward just as a crowd of loiterers at a street corner in my native
North America might offer up one of their own to be questioned by Fernando's hypothetical explorer from Mars.

The chief and the two priests had witnessed the demonstration and,
observing our pleasure, arranged now for a blowpipe to be produced and
for an especially proficient villager—a bow-legged elderly man with several
front teeth ornamentally extracted and a chevron of welts on each cheek—
to strike with its tufted darts small targets (a folded leaf, a Ping-Pong ball)
dropped many paces away on the plaza. The blowpipe was at least ten feet
long. Our shadows, too, had elongated remarkably, as an evening chill
enwrapped our wet bodies; goosebumps, each with its own minute shadow,
had appeared on Conchita's thighs, and the fine hairs stood up on Esmeralda's forearms like the feathery fringes of a tropical *rara avis*. Nevertheless, invited to try the blowpipe ourselves, we each obliged, amusing the
crowd with our puffed cheeks and wide misses.

The whole thing, it should be stressed, was done with a tact, a fine
lightness, not always present at such cultural intersections. Quickly,
lightly, the crowd dispersed. Cooking smoke, both sweet and acrid, fla-
vored the air. A translucent gibbous moon had appeared in the still-ceru-
lean sky above us. We went to our quarters to prepare for the feast.

The feast! Anteater and coati meat swimming in a sauce peppered with
bits of ground insect, plus side dishes of artichoke paste and boiled
Pijiguao fruit, all served at the long plank table in the banquet hut, amid a
plethora of toasts to progress, amity, and the overthrow of imperialism—
the meal passed in a blur. Afterwards, we took chairs outdoors, into the
moonlight; the earth of the plaza was as firm and level as the floor of a
parlor. The native priest reached down and affectionately scratched the
neck of a hairless dog that, like a few naked children, had come silently to

join us. The chief had disappeared. Our pilots had retired with some onyx-eyed girls met by the river. The tall pale priest, a child in arms when his parents fled Franco, outlined his vision and responded to our questions. The rapid, segmented Spanish words—*comunidad, economía, avenimiento, modos de producción*—flowed like sparkling water across my ears. A wine bottle cast its half-empty shadow on the blanched earth, in the amazing moonlight. The dog curled himself into an intense ball, like an armadillo, beside the plump priest's shoes, whose polished tips gleamed. The hands of the other priest in their impassioned gestures appeared elegant and white, flitting like bats in a negative film, but his voice never rose above a gentle, cautious, explanatory monotone. The moon above, sunstruck, seemed to dye a great realm of the heavens around it a lavender that drowned the very stars. The fringe of jungle at a distance around us was low, and as total as the horizon of the ocean. To think that this was the only such conversation within a thousand or more square miles—the luxury of it, the calm human grandeur. "All we ask of the government," our host proclaimed, with his soft yet urgent melody, "is to be let alone!"

When the good priests took themselves off to bed, another bottle of wine materialized. Like children let out of school, we went for a walk that became a run. The moonlit stretch of village street that doubled as an airplane runway invited speed: our footsteps pattered; our suppressed laughter became the ecstasy of breathlessness; we flew. Pepé and Ortega and Raoul, our linguistics expert, led the way. Conchita and Esmeralda, surprisingly quick and lithe, followed hand in hand, giggling. Fernando and I and Salvador, our earthbound agronomist, ploddingly brought up the rear.

Then we stopped, at the place where the jungle trees, drawing close, grew tall. Their liana-interlaced crowns bent over us like solicitous giant heads. A clicking, whispering life could be heard behind their wall of darkness, and the soft tireless roar of the cataracts in the river far to our left. Beyond this wall the depth of forest loomed as practically infinite, like the depth of night sky above us. Looking backwards, we saw the runway as a pilot must see it in the instant before touchdown—as a cone of luminous safety framed by fatal vague shapes. Its isolation was an essential part of the plan of the ideal village. Any less far, the contaminating hand of government would reach, and the chief would not have bothered to abandon his chiropraxis and don his girdle of feathers.

Predictably, we slept badly in our *chinchorros*: each movement produced a sickening sway and there was no turning over onto one's stomach. Early in the morning, in the silky black hour between moonset and sunrise, something or someone outside our windows repeatedly tittered. Departure proved to be a hurried, graceless process. The pilots were visibly suffering from post-coital depression as well as anxiety concerning the miles and miles of green wilderness they must droningly traverse. The chief showed up without his gray vest, which apparently had been put on out of deference to our supposed sense of decency. Conchita was given a necklace of tapir teeth; Esmeralda was allowed to purchase a carved coati at discount. We said our farewells and kept waving as our two planes banked in unison back across the plaza of baked earth and over the river and away.

It was not until weeks afterwards, collating our diaries in the course of preparing our report to the government, that we discovered how happy each of us had been to leave. Man was not meant to abide in paradise.

One More Interview

THE ACTOR'S TOUR had taken him to a Midwestern city fifteen miles from the small town where he had grown up, and an interviewer called suggesting that they visit there together. "It would provide, you know," he said, "an angle." The newspaper the interviewer worked for was the only one left in the city, and this gave it an aura of absolute power, of final opportunity. The actor was at that awkward age almost too old for romantic leads but not old enough for character parts. Opportunity, his agent had more than once told him, doesn't knock forever. He could use the publicity.

"I can't stand interviews," he said.

The prospective interviewer said nothing, just waited.

"They're so intrinsically imprecise," the actor went on. "So sadly prurient." The presence on the other end of the line stuck to its silence. The female exclamations of another conversation faintly wafted into the braided wires. "O.K.," the actor said, and they set a time to meet on the hotel parking lot.

The interviewer stood beside a little mustard-colored car; he wore dun bell-bottoms and a denim jacket cut as short as a waiter's jacket. He was a trim, tight young man with an exceptionally small mouth and wiry black hair that had about it, without being exactly kinky, a glisten of contained energy, a kind of silent acrylic crackle that declared it would never decompose. There would be no mercy, the actor saw. He would have to watch what he said as carefully as if he were in court. Unfortunate words had a way of passing into print from a single absent-minded nod politely granted an impudent question. The actor had a number of former wives, each equipped with vigilant lawyers, and he moved through the dark skies of private life, it sometimes seemed to him, like a comet trailing stiff white envelopes of legal stationery. So: no politeness today, no ridiculous "givingness," no charming sharing of indiscretions with this person to whom he was not a person, after all, but a name, an object to be exploited, a walking slag heap to be sifted for ore one more time.

"Would you like me to drive, so you can take notes?" the actor asked. He was a big-boned, coarse-skinned man offstage, and he took pleasure in menacing at the outset, with such extravagant coöperation, his wiry little persecutor.

"Why, yes, that might be nice, come to think of it."

The car was a Japanese model, as cunning and tawdry as a music-box. It had four forward gears and a reverse tucked somewhere in the lower right quadrant, where New Zealand is on a map. The dashboard hummed and spelled out monosyllables of instruction and warning. The actor felt clumsy. "I don't drive much anymore," he explained. "I'm just dragged around by these limousines."

"What about at your summer place in Amagansett?" the interviewer asked, having already produced a notebook.

"My last wife got that, as you probably know. The place, the Porsche, the works."

"No, I didn't know." The man wrote busily.

"Don't put that in—Christ," the actor begged, shifting from first gear straight into fourth, with a fearful laboring of the engine.

"It's on the record, isn't it, elsewhere?"

"Well, let's not put it on again. Makes it look as though I have nothing else to talk about."

"Of course," the interviewer said. He put the notebook away and gazed out the window.

The actor didn't like this swift, prim docility, either; it seemed stagy. From the side, the other man's mouth was a mere irritated nick in his profile; he resented having been ousted from the driver's seat.

"This wasn't meant to be so much a personal piece about you and your, uh, affairs," the interviewer said, "as about the place. You in regard to the place you grew up in."

"It's not much of a place, that was its charm," the actor said, and added, "Don't put that in, either."

The miles went by. Inner suburbs gave way to outer, and then there was something like countryside, behind the roadside gas stations and the old stone farmhouses with reflecting balls in their front yards. The interviewer sat silent, in what seemed to be a sulk. The strange impression grew upon the actor that this man had been a high-school athlete, a second-baseman: quick on the pivot and pesky at the plate. Determined to be entertaining, to charm away the sulk, the actor talked about the play he was in, leading actresses he had worked with, his theories of stagecraft, his philosophy of professional ups and downs. The interviewer kept his notebook tucked away. The little automobile had become quite responsive to the actor's touch, and began to swing along curves he knew by heart, having driven them as a child, first with his father at the wheel and then with himself in control. "Of course," the actor explained, as they approached the town limits, "all this was trees and fields then. That mall didn't exist. That mess of ticky-tacky houses over there was just a dairy farm with a little creek that ran through a pasture where my mother's quainter relatives used to gather watercress. There was a dam and a pond back in there where the tough boys and the pretty girls used to go swimming. I never did. My mother thought I might drown or lose my virginity or have people think I did, which would be even worse."

"Uh-huh," the interviewer said, as though he had heard this before.

"Don't put that in about my mother and virginity," the actor asked. "She still has cousins in the area, in nursing homes mostly. There used to be a diner here," he announced abruptly, "that stayed open all night. At two in the morning you could go there, after a date, all lightheaded and your face full of lipstick, and eat a hamburger. That was my idea of the sophisticated life, eating a hamburger at two in the morning. A man called Smoky Moser ran it. He never seemed to sleep. We kids loved him. Loved him like a father, you could say. He was the father I yearned for."

"Is that a fact?"

"I exaggerate a little. Smoky was O.K., though. Died young, of some disease nobody would ever name. Better skip that: he may have a widow."

Grudgingly the interviewer had got out his notebook and made a few notes. The gravel lot that had surrounded the diner was occupied now by a great cube of brown-tinted glass, the branch of a statewide bank. Yellow arrows painted on the smooth asphalt told automobiles how to proceed to the drive-in windows. The actor studied the faces of the people moving in and out of the bank and recognized none of them, though there was something he did recognize—a tone, a pallor and density of flesh in their arms and faces, a way of suddenly looking behind and above them, unsmilingly, fearing the worst out of the sky, the weather of the world. "Up here, there was a feed mill, where . . ."

Where some of the faster girls had supposedly let it be done to them, that fabled thing, in the weedy area between two asbestos-shingled walls.

The actor was surprised, after the more than a decade since he had last visited, by how sexy the town was, how saturated with love and that psychosomatic quickening which love brings. The cotton-wool sky, the heavy dusty trees, the very tone of dull red in the bricks arrived in unison at something like one's own exact body temperature. Surrounded by farm country, it was a kind of hill town, divided in the middle by an avenue that followed the curve of an abandoned railroad bed. The town's lower part, south of the avenue, had been built solid in the years just before the Depression in rows of brick semi-detached houses, houses with symmetrical big living-room windows and square-pillared front porches. There was a security here, in these ruddy rows, block after block, each with its little apron of terraced lawn, and two concrete steps leading up to the first terrace, and little pansy beds or barberry hedges along the walk. The rectilinear, repetitive streets were high-crowned, and the actor was made to remember the rhythm imparted to a car, the soft braking and dipping, as the intersections were cautiously traversed. Many an afternoon, many a Sunday, he had cruised these streets in his parents' old tan Dodge, and then in the navy-blue Chrysler with the iridescent touched-up patch on the fender, looking for the action, for a familiar car parked outside a house he knew, which might signal an afternoon of canasta or an evening of laughing at Liberace or the roller derby on that new toy called television. Any excuse for a party, a party wherever two or three got together.

"This side of town hasn't changed much at all," he told the interviewer. "How could it? They didn't leave any vacant lots." Each of the thickset duplexes was like a married couple, it occurred to him now, the rumblings and spats on one side of the wall impossible not to hear on the other. "For some reason," the actor said, "the terrific-looking girls all tended to live over in this section. My family lived in a house all alone on its lot, on the older side of town. There's a distinct change once you cross the avenue. The houses, a lot of them, are wood, and look—how can I say?—gaunt. Pinched. Scary, even. Don't put that in."

He steered the nimble little car through a stoplight that hadn't been there thirty years ago and drove uphill, out of the cozy low-lying area of red brick rows, into the slanting neighborhood where he had been raised. "That used to be a barber shop," he said, driving up Liberty Street. "You can still see the striped pole, though Jake's been dead for years now. Apoplexy, if memory serves. Can you spell it?" Haircuts—the long wait and then the sitting so still as metal gnashed across your scalp—had filled the actor as a child with a gloom and suspense bordering on terror. There had been a big plate-glass window, and as the scissors interminably clicked, the sunshine and the traffic on the other side had seemed an unattainable paradise. Now that big window held Venetian blinds and a sign proclaiming that gold and silver could be bought and sold here. He suddenly remembered the octagonal green-and-cream pattern of the linoleum floor, dotted with hair clippings, where Jake would tap-dance. Not tap-dance, perhaps, but do a spry and comical shuffle-and-slide on that slick floor. Jake had hated Roosevelt—the thought of the man had made him apoplectic—and in the fury of his shrill tirades must have felt the danger of driving customers away, for he would suddenly relent, and change the poisoned subject, and go into his little comical steps, sometimes with the broom as partner. "And where you see that marquee with 'Bingo' on it was the old movie house, where I learned to dream," the actor said. "To dream and to pose, you could put it." Actually, the sign said INGO, and the look of disuse in its new role as a gambling hall had overtaken the theatre. The old glass cases where the movie posters—Alan Ladd, Lana Turner, Lassie—had been different every week were empty of any advertisement and had been defaced with illegible spray-painted swirls.

"Which was your house?" the interviewer asked.

"That one."

"Which one?"

"You missed it. It looks just like the ones around it."

"I thought you said it stood so alone on its lot."

"They were small lots." Why was he being perverse, the actor wondered —denying this infielder the small intrusion of gazing upon his averagely shabby and plain birthplace? Was it that the house itself, in his own quick glimpse of it, seemed to beg that he not give it away? It was wearing a new color of paint—a bright lime green—like a desperate disguise. Or was it that he himself was ashamed, of it, because it in fact had *not* been just like the ones around it? The house had been and still was slightly smaller than its flanking neighbors, those better-kept and higher-gabled houses owned in his boyhood by the Behns and the Murchisons, who looked down on them, his mother had felt, because his father worked with his hands, because his father was unemployed, because his father came home drunk and could be heard cursing out on the lawn. . . . There were many reasons why the Behns and the Murchisons might look down on them.

The actor's furtive glimpse had not been so quick, however, that he did not spy in the shrubbery around the front porch, with its jigsawed banister uprights, the invisible ghosts that had kept him company when he hid there, there where the earth had been too packed and sheltered to give weeds a purchase, like a hard floor. The spaces between the bushes had been like a set of little rooms only he lived in, and where he entertained voices. Who had these presences been that had spoken back to the voice inside his head? They were still there, crowded around the porch, calling out to him. There were even a few at the side of the house, where his mother had tried to grow peonies against the brick foundation, and it had proved too shady. Or had she planted the roots too deep? Mrs. Behn told her she had, and they didn't speak for a year. Imagine, his mother had said, her spying down on me from those parlor windows and not saying a word until it was too late and the peonies were dug in. The cement walk along here, in the shadows, used to accumulate anthills in the cracks, as well as neighborhood bitterness. Out back, there had been a sandbox, and its little ridges had been dunes in the Sahara, and the green lead tanks had been chasing Rommel. The voices the actor had heard while playing in the sandbox had been different; they had been news voices, broadcast from overseas.

"You said you learned to dream and to pose in the movie house," the interviewer prompted.

They were driving down another block, and his old home was sealed safe behind them. "And in the high school," the actor said. "I'll take you by it. They built it up on top of the hill; the only thing higher in town is the cemetery. Here's a confession for you. You like confessions, don't you?"

That silence again.

"I had terrible acne as a kid, from about fourteen on. Just like my father. He was all pockmarked. Well, when I put on makeup for some assembly play in about ninth grade, my own skin disappeared! For as long as I was onstage, I was like everybody else: I was human. So I said to myself, 'Hey. The actor's life for me.' "

"Many adolescent boys have acne, don't they?" There seemed a reprimand in this, a call back to relativity.

"I don't know. Did you?"

"Not so bad, actually."

"Well, then. I bet you were quite a smooth jock in your time."

"Well, I was . . ."

"Don't be modest. You played second base, didn't you?"

"Center field, usually."

"Same idea. Anyway, I didn't care what other boys had. They were them and I was me. Leave that grammar just the way I said it."

"Yes. I don't know that I can use everything you say; you've already been quite generous with your time."

"Also, I loved having a role; it wasn't just the makeup. The whole role was like a mask, a spiritual mask I was safe behind. If people laughed, it wasn't at me, exactly. I loved to hear them laugh. Let's hear you laugh."

Silence.

"Come on. For me."

It was a dry, embarrassed noise.

"I love it," the actor complimented him. "There you see the high school. The old style, Roman pillars and all. They say when you come back to a place things look smaller, but it looks bigger than ever to me. It looks huge. I hear they don't have students to fill it now." He swung the corner, racily. "This little bug really has some zip, doesn't it? There used to be a variety store here, with the steps at an angle and the little overhang, and paper pumpkins in the window at the appropriate time of year, and then Christmas cards and Easter eggs. . . . It was a kind of 3-D calendar you could walk into and take a stool. There was a counter we could sit up at and smoke. And look at ourselves smoking in the mirror. I bet you never smoked, did you?"

"No. As you guessed, I was big into sports."

"God, I used to smoke. Anything to keep a mask in front of my face. It's gone now. The store."

The new owners had painted everything white, even the display windows, so no one could look in. Somebody must be living behind those blank windows. The people who had descended upon the town to live in it since the actor had left were aliens from space; he could not imagine their lives. "Now we're getting into a part of town that was new then—rich houses, we thought they were, though they don't look so rich now. The section was called Oak Slope. To live in Oak Slope was about the ritziest thing I could imagine, to live in Oak Slope and have huge closets of clothes, with a different corduroy shirt for every day of the week. Corduroy shirts—that dates me. And we used to wear reindeer sweaters; I don't suppose you know what a reindeer sweater was, do you?"

"I can imagine."

"I'm not sure you can. The sharp guys, there was a word then, 'snazzy,' s-n-a-z-z-y, the snazzy guys, whose fathers sold real estate or were foremen at the mill, owned a lot of them, beautifully knitted, with different things, it wasn't just reindeer—snowflakes, butterflies. . . ."

"They're still around."

"It's not the same. I used to wear the one I had inside out some days, as if it was another sweater. It didn't fool anybody but made me feel slightly, you could say, snazzy. I'll be honest about it: I was pathetic. More than that, I was obnoxious. With acne yet. Just driving around Oak Slope makes me *feel* obnoxious. How am I acting?" He got no answer. "Now, down here," the actor announced, "this curving street, when I was a lad— another funny old-fashioned word, l-a-d—past the last new house built, there used to be a kind of dirt road that didn't go anywhere much and was a great place to park, if you had a girl."

At the age of seventeen, he had acquired a girl, Ermajean Willis. "For heaven's sake," the actor exclaimed, without acting, his exclamation honest. "It's still here. I would have thought it'd been built up ages ago."

The necking place. The spatial feeling of the spot—with a tall bank of earth on one side, freshly bulldozed then and still rather raw and scraggly now, and a lower rise on the other side, deep green from the time when this had been a hillside hayfield—was unaltered, uncorrupted, sexy. In his excitement the actor braked; the interviewer glanced over, worried. "Amazing," said the actor, spacing his syllables, back in performance. "I wonder if it's still used."

"I see a few beer bottles," said the interviewer uneasily.

"You don't understand what a lovely surprise this is. For a space like this to last, in modern America. The cops used to check it out once in a while and shine a flashlight in the windows." The little unpaved road that generations of furtive, love-craving cars had worn into the earth continued for a few yards between the two sheltering grassy shoulders and then dipped down to rejoin a side street called Button. Button led into Maple, Maple crossed the avenue, and two more blocks took you into Sycamore; Ermajean used to live at the corner of Sycamore and Pierce. A kind of hazy warmth, as when he would show up after midnight at Smoky's diner, had been laid across the actor's face. Without his realizing it, the little Japanese car had under his hands driven itself along the remembered route, into that inviting red realm of the two-family brick houses in rows. The car had come to the corner of Pierce and Sycamore, to the big house whose retaining walls were ornamented with mossy concrete balls and whose side entrance was a set of steps with an iron railing he had often grasped; he softly braked. She would come down those very steps for a date, all starchy and perfumed and hopeful, though what had he had to offer her but a second-run movie and an ice-cream soda afterwards? As she hurried across the street to the old Chrysler with the patched fender, her pastel dress would be flattened against her thighs by her hurrying, by the soft wind she made in her haste to be with him.

"My girl friend used to live here," he confessed to his interviewer.

"You had only one?"

"Well, yes. How many do you recommend? I thought I was lucky to have even one. She was a grade behind me at school, and after I graduated I lost track of her. Married, I suppose, somewhere." The actor was incredulous that the interviewer could be blind to the glory around them, the railings and retaining walls and little laplike lawns of these solid, unchang-

ing homes, rows that at any moment might release Ermajean, racing
lightly toward them with her hair in barrettes and her round young legs
tipped by the kind of open-toed white heels women in Hollywood comedies wore—Jean Arthur, Rosalind Russell. The actor felt swamped by
love; he was physically sickened, to think that such a scene had once been
real, and that a self of his had been there to play a part.

His foot eased the clutch back in, and the car moved off reluctantly.
"Let me show you some more of the town," he offered. "There's a quarry
where we used to ice-skate. And a playground. A block from here, where
they put the new annex on the town hall, there used to be the strangest
little structure, like something out of Disneyland, a sort of stone tower
where you paid your water bills."

Ermajean loved butter-pecan ice cream, he remembered, in a vanilla
soda, and always debated with him whether she should have onion on her
hamburger. If he would, she would. And her skin—all of his life since, he
had been dealing with women who were doctoring their skins—vitamin-E
cream, pancake makeup, moisturizers. Ermajean's skin had been utterly
neutral in shade, neutral and natural, tinted by nothing, pure trusting
female skin beneath her pastel clothes. The actor's face felt hot; he wanted
to cruise forever through this half of town, the car dipping in a kind of
obeisance at every intersection.

The interviewer cleared his throat and said, "I think maybe I've seen
enough. This is only for a sidebar, you know."

"Wait. How about coming with me to my old luncheonette and having a
bite to eat? How about some butter-pecan ice cream?"

The other man laughed, stiffly, as when commanded to laugh before.
"And then there's a time problem," he said. "If I don't get this in tonight,
your show won't still be around."

"That's O.K. The luncheonette is a flower shop now anyway. Please,
don't put my old girl friend's name in the article."

"You never mentioned it."

"Ermajean Willis. E-r-m-a-j-e-a-n. Isn't that a wonderful funky name?"

"Maybe it'd be easier if I drove now."

"No. Keep your pencil out. You son of a bitch, I'm going to tell you the
names of every family that used to live in this entire block."

The Other

HANK ARNOLD met Priscilla Hunter at college in the Fifties, and the fact that she was a twin seemed to matter as little as the fact that she had been raised as an Episcopalian and he as a Baptist. How blissfully little did seem to matter in the Fifties! Politics, religion, class—all beside the point. Young lives then, once Eisenhower had settled for a draw in Korea and McCarthy had self-destructed like a fairy-tale goblin, seemed to be composed of timeless simplicities and old verities, of weather and works of art on opposite sides of a museum wall, of ancient professors, arrogant and scarcely audible from within the security of their tenure, lecturing from yellowing notes upon Dante and Kant while in the tall windows at their backs sunlight filtered through the feathery leaves of overarching elms. In those days Harvard Yard was innocent of Dutch elm disease. And in those days a large and not laughable sexual territory existed within the borders of virginity, where physical parts were fed to the partner a few at a time, beginning with the lips and hands. Strangely, Hank and Priscilla had been traversing this territory for several weeks before she confided to him that she was an identical twin. One of her breasts, clothed in an angora sweater and the underlying stiffness of a brassiere, was held in his hand at the time. Their faces were so close together that he could smell the mentholated tobacco in the breath of her confession. "Henry, I ought to tell you. I have a sister who looks just like me." Priscilla seemed to think it slightly shameful, and in fact it was an exciting idea.

Her twin, the other, was named Susan, and attended the University of Chicago, though she, too, had been admitted to Radcliffe. Their parents—

two Minneapolis lawyers, the father a specialist in corporation law and the mother in divorce and legal-aid work—had always encouraged the girls to be different; they had dressed them in different clothes from the start and had sent them to different private schools at an early age. A myth had been fostered in the family that Priscilla was the "artistic" one and Susan the more "practical" and "scientific," though to the twins themselves their interests and attitudes seemed close to identical. As children, they had succumbed simultaneously to the same diseases—chicken pox, mumps— and even when sent to different summer camps had a way, their conversations in September revealed, of undergoing the same trials and initiations. They learned to swim the same week, in widely separated lakes, and had let themselves be necked with in different forests. They fell in love with the same movie star (Montgomery Clift), had the same favorite song ("Two Loves Have I," as sung by Frankie Laine), and preferred the same Everly brother (Don, the darker and slicker-looking). Hank asked Priscilla if she missed her twin. She said, "No," but to have said otherwise might have been insulting, for she was lying entangled with him, mussed and over-heated, in his fifth-floor room, with its single dormer window, in Winthrop House.

Hank was an only child, with a widowed mother, and asked, "What does it feel like, having a twin?"

Priscilla made a thoughtful mouth; prim little creases appeared in her pursed upper lip. "Nice," she answered, after a long pause that had dried the amorous moisture from her eyes. They were brown eyes, a delicious candy color, darker than caramel but paler than Hershey's kisses. "You have a backup, seeing the same things you do. A kind of insurance policy, in a funny way."

"Even when you're sent to different schools and all that?"

"That doesn't matter so much, it turns out. Suzie and I always knew we weren't the other and were going to have to lead different lives. It's just that when I'm with her there's so much less explaining to do. Maybe that's why I'm not much good at explaining things." She added, a bit challeng-ingly, "*Sor*ry." Her face was still pink from the soft struggle they had been having on his bed.

"You're good enough," Hank said, and dropped the subject, for it had interrupted this slow journey they were making into one another. She had, Priscilla, a lovely athletic figure, long-muscled and hippy and with wide sloping shoulders, yet narrowed to a fine boniness at the ankles and wrists. His pleasure at seeing her undressed disconcerted her, at first, in its inten-sity, and time passed before she could accept it as her due and, still a virgin, coolly give him, in his room, in the narrow space between his iron frame bed and standard oak desk, little one-woman "parades." Though they could not, for all those good Fifties reasons (pregnancy, the social worth of female chastity), make love, he had talked her into this piece of display. She held her chin up bravely and slowly turned in mock-model style, showing all sides of herself; the sight was so glorious Hank could scarcely stand it and had to lower his eyes, and then saw how her bare feet, fresh from chilly boots and rimmed in pink, looked as they slowly pivoted on the oval rug of braided rags his mother had given him, to make his room more "cozy." When his minute of drinking in Priscilla was up, she would scramble, suddenly blushing and laughing at herself, into bed beside him, under rough blue blankets that Harvard issued in those days as if to soldiers or monks. They would try to read from the same book; they were taking a course together—Philosophy 10, "Idealism from Plato to White-head."

Once she had told him that she was a twin, Hank could not forget it, or quite forgive her. The monstrous idea flirted at the back of his head that she was half a person; there was something withheld, something hollow-backed and tinny about the figure she cut in his mind even as their court-ship proceeded smoothly toward marriage. He wanted to become a lawyer; she was doubly the daughter of lawyers and in all things ideal, given the inevitable small differences between two individuals. She had been raised rather rich and he rather poor. Hank's drab and pious upbringing embar-rassed him. He had felt indignantly drowned on that absurd day when, dressed in a sleazy white gown, he had submitted to the shock of immer-sion, the scandal of being tipped backward and all the way under by the murderous firm hands of a minister wearing hip waders; whereas Priscilla kept in her room, like a girlhood Teddy bear, the gold-stamped prayer book given her upon confirmation, and sometimes she carried it, in white-gloved hands, to services at the old wooden gray Episcopal church across from Cambridge Common. Both young people were for Stevenson in 1956, but she seemed secretly pleased when Eisenhower won again, whereas Hank had wished Henry Wallace were still running. He wanted to become a lawyer for a perverse reason: to avenge his father. His father, not yet fifty when he died of Hodgkin's disease, in the days before chemotherapy, had been an auto mechanic who had borrowed heavily to open a garage of his own, and it had been lawyers—lawyers for the bank and other creditors—who had briskly, with perfect legality, administered the financial debacle and thwarted the dying man's attempts to divert money to his survivors.

None of this at the time seemed to matter; what mattered was Priscilla's beauty and Hank's ardor and gratitude and her cool appraisal of the future value of his gratitude as she dazzlingly, with a silver poise faintly resembling cruelty, displayed herself to him. The fact of her being a twin put a halo around her form, a shimmer of duplication, a suggestion, curiously platonic, that there was, somewhere else, unseen, another version of this reality, this body.

Priscilla's parents lived in Saint Paul, in a big, cream-colored, many-dormered house a few blocks from the gorge holding the Mississippi, which was not especially wide this far north. Though Hank several times travelled there to display himself, in his best clothes, to his prospective in-laws, he did not meet Susan until the wedding. She had always been away —on a package tour of Europe or waitressing in southern California, a part of the world where she had been led by some of her racier University of Chicago friends. When Hank met her at last, she had come from Malibu Beach to be Priscilla's maid of honor. Though it was early June and cool in Minnesota, she had a surfer's deep tan and a fluffy haircut short as a boy's. A stranger to the family might not have spotted her, amid the welter of siblings and cousins, as the bride's twin. But Hank had been long alerted, and as he clasped her thin feminine hand the current of identity stunned him to wordlessness. Her face was Priscilla's down to the protruding, determined cut of her upper lip and the slightly sad droop of the lashes at the outside corners of her eyes. In a sense, he had seen her undressed. He reddened, and imagined that Susan did, though her manner with him was instantly ironical—bantering and languid in perhaps the West Coast manner. Enclosed within Priscilla's known body, the coolness of a stranger seemed rude, even hostile. Hank noted what seemed to be a ray or two less of caramel in Susan's irises, a smoother consistency of chocolate. These darker eyes made her seem more passionate, more impudent and flitting, as she moved through her old home with none of a bride's responsibilities. And she was, Hank estimated, appraising Susan through the social flurry, distinctly bigger, if only by a centimeter and an ounce.

His impressions, Priscilla told him when they were alone, were wrong: Susan had expected to like him and did, very much. And though she had been the firstborn, she had never been, as often happens, the stronger or heavier. Their heights and weights had always been precisely the same. Priscilla thought that, indeed, Suzie had lost some weight, chasing around with that creepy crowd of beach bums out there. Their parents were up in arms because she had announced her intention to do graduate work in art history at UCLA, where there really wasn't any art, when there was that entire wonderful Chester Dale collection at the Art Institute, along with everything else in Chicago. Or why not go east, like Priscilla? Their parents had hoped Susan would become a physicist, or at least a psychologist.

Hank liked hearing Priscilla, not normally much of an explainer, run on this way about her sister; being near her twin did seem to embolden her, to loosen her tongue. He enjoyed the profusion of an extensive, ambitious family, amid whose many branches his own mother, their guest for the weekend, seemed a wan, doomed graft. The big house was loaded with overstuffed sateen furniture and expensive vacation souvenirs; his mother found a safe corner in a little-used library and worked at a needlepoint footstool cover she had brought with her from North Carolina.

In church, the twins, the one majestic in white tulle and the other rather mousy in mauve taffeta, were vividly distinguishable. Hank, however, standing at the altar in a daze of high Episcopalianism, the musk of incense in his nostrils and a gold-leafed panel of apostles flickering off to the side, had a disquieting thrill of confusion—the mocking-eyed maid of honor might be his intimate from Winthrop House days and the mysterious figure on their father's arm a woman virtually unknown to him, tanned and crop-haired beneath her veil and garland of florets. Susan's voice was just a grain or two the huskier, so he knew it was Priscilla who, in a shy, true voice, recited the archaic vows with him. At the reception, amid all the kissing, he kissed his sister-in-law and was surprised by the awkwardly averted, rather stubbornly downcast cheek; Hank had reflexively expected Priscilla's habituated frontal ease. And when they danced, Susan was stiff in his arms. Yet none of this marred her fascination, the superior authenticity she enjoyed over the actual reality as the wedding night untidily proceeded through champagne and forced cheer to its trite, closeted climax. Susan was with them (her remembered stiffness and silence in his arms, as if she and Hank had had too much to say to dare a word, and her imagined slightly greater size) during the botch of defloration; she excited him, urging him on through Priscilla's pain. Though he knew he had put an unfortunate crimp in this infant marriage, and had given his long-cherished ardor a bad name, he fell asleep with happy exhaustion; his guilt seemed shifted onto the body of a twin of his own.

Hank was not accepted at Harvard Law School; but good-hearted Yale took him. It was all for the best, for if Cambridge in those years was the path to Washington, New Haven was closer to New York and Wall Street, where the real money was. After a few years in the city, the Arnolds settled in Greenwich and had children—a girl, a boy, and a girl. Having married a San Diego builder of multi-unit dwellings, Susan kept pace with a girl, a boy, and then another boy. This break in symmetry led them both, it seemed, to stop bearing children. Also, the Pill had come along and made birth control irresistible. Kennedy had been shot, and something called rock blasted from the radio however you twisted the dial. The twins, though, had their nests safely made. Susan's husband was named Jeb Herrera; he claimed descent from one of the old Spanish ranching families of Alta California, but in joking moods asserted that his great-great-grandfather had been a missionary's illegitimate son. He was a curly-haired, heavy, gracious, enthusiastic man, a bit too proclaimedly, for Hank's taste, in love with life. His small, even teeth looked piratical, when he smiled through the black curls of his beard. He was one of the first men Hank knew to wear a full beard and to own a computer—a tan metal box taller than a man, a freestanding broom closet that spat paper. Jeb had programmed it to respond to the children's questions with jokes in printout. His office was a made-over wharf shed where dozens shuffled paper beside canted windows full of the Pacific. None of his employees wore neckties. Though the twins, as they eased into matronhood, might still be mistaken for each other, there was no mistaking the husbands. Susan, it would appear, had the artistic taste, and Priscilla had bet on practicality. Hank had become a specialist in tax law, saw his name enrolled in the list of junior partners on the engraved firm stationery, and forgot about avenging his father.

The growing families visited back and forth; there was something concordant about the homes, though one was white clapboard set primly on watered, terraced lawn, and the other was redwood wedged into a hillside where fat little cactuses intricate as snowflakes flourished among studiously arranged rocks. Both houses were cheerful for children, offering back stairs and odd nooks and a certain sportive airiness. The Arnolds had a long sunroom with a Ping-Pong table and, above it on the second floor, a sleeping porch with a hammock. As soon as they could afford it, they crowded a composition tennis court into the space between the garage and the line fence, where the lawn had always been scruffy anyway and the vegetable garden had gone to weeds every July. The Herreras' La Jolla house, which overlooked the fifteenth fairway of a golf course, shuffled the indoors and the outdoors with its sliding glass panels and cantilevered deck and its family-sized hot tub out on the deck.

Hank first saw his sister-in-law naked one warm evening in Christmas vacation when Susan let fall a large white towel behind her and slid her silent silhouette into this hot tub. Hank and his wife were already in, coping with the slithering, giggling bodies of their small children; so the moment passed almost unnoticed amid the family tumble. Almost. Susan was distinctly not Priscilla; their skins had aged differently on the two different coasts. Priscilla's was dead pale this time of year, its summer tan long faded, whereas there was something thickened and delicately crinkled and permanently golden about Susan's. With an accustomed motion she had eased her weight from her buttocks into the steaming wide circle of water. Her expression looked solemn, dented by shadow. Rob remembered the same resolute, unfocussed expression on Priscilla's face in the days when she would grant him her little "parade" in the shadows of his narrow college room. Both sisters had brown eyes in deep sockets and noses that looked upturned, with long nostrils and sharp central dents in their upper lips. Both were wearing bangs that winter. Their heads and shoulders floated side by side. Susan's breasts seemed the whiter for the contrast with her year-round bathing-suit tan.

"How much do you do this sort of thing?" Priscilla asked her twin, a touch nervously, glancing toward Hank.

"Oh, now and then, with people you know, usually. You get used to it— it's a local custom. You sort of let yourself dissolve."

Yet she, too, gave Hank an alert glance. He had already passed into dissolution, his vapor of double love one with the heat, the steam, the abundant dinner wine, the scent of the eucalyptus trees towering above the deck, the stars beyond them, the strangeness of this all being a few days before Christmas. Immersed, their bodies had become foreshortened stumps of flesh, comical blobs of mercury. Jeb appeared on the deck holding a naked baby—little Lucas—in one crooked arm and a fresh half-gallon of Gallo Chablis in the other. Early in his thirties, Jeb had a pendulous belly. He descended to them like a hairy Neptune; the tub overflowed. When the water calmed, his penis drifted under Hank's eyes like a lead-colored fish swimming nowhere.

The families stopped travelling back and forth in complete units as the maturing children developed local attachments and summer jobs. The two oldest cousins, Karen and Rose, had been fast friends from the start, though there was no mistaking them for twins: Karen had become as washed-out and mild-faced a blonde as Hank's mother (now dead), and Rose was so dark that boys on the street catcalled to her in Spanish. The two older boys, Henry and Gabriel, made a more awkward matchup, the one burdened with Hank's allergies and a drowsy shyness all his own, and the other a macho little athlete with a wedge-shaped back and the unthinking cruelty of those whose bodies are perfectly connected to their wills. The girl and the boy that completed the sets, Jennifer and Lucas, claimed to detest each other, and, indeed, did squabble tediously, perhaps in defense against any notion that they would some day marry. The bigger the children became, the harder they pulled apart, and the more frayed the lines between their parents became. Once little Lucas became too big to hold in one arm and strike a pose with, Jeb's interest began to wander away from families and family get-togethers. There were late-night long-distance calls between the sisters, and secrets kept from the children.

Susan suddenly had more gray hair than Priscilla. Hank felt touched by her, and drawn to her in a new fashion, when she would visit them for a few weeks in the summer without Jeb, with perhaps an inscrutable Rose and a resentful Lucas in tow. More than once, Hank met the L.A. red-eye at LaGuardia and was kissed at the gate as if he were Susan's savior; there had been drunks on the plane, college kids, nobody could sleep, Lucas had insisted on watching a ghastly Jerry Lewis movie, Rose threw up over Nebraska somewhere, they had gone way north around some thunder-heads, an old lech in an admiral's uniform kept trying to buy her drinks at three in the morning, my God, never again. As Hank gently swung the car up the lush green curves of the Merritt Parkway, Susan nodded into sleep, and seemed his wife. Priscilla's skin, too, now sagged in those defenseless puckers when she slept.

As a guest in their home, Susan slept on the upstairs porch. The swish of cars headed toward the railroad station, and the birds—so much more aggressive, she said, than those on the West Coast—awakened her too early; and then at night the Arnolds took her to too many parties. "How do you stand it?" she would ask her twin.

"Oh, it gets to be a habit. Try taking a nap in the afternoon. That's what I do."

"Jeb and I hardly go out at all anymore. We decided other people weren't helping our marriage." This was a clue, and far from the only one. There was a hungry boniness to her figure now. Like a sick person willing to try any cure, Susan drank only herbal tea—no caffeine, no alcohol—and ate as little meat as she politely could. Whereas Priscilla, who had once appeared so distinctly a centimeter smaller, now was relatively hefty. Broad of shoulder and hip, she moved through parties with a certain roll, a practiced cruiser who knew where the ports were—the confiding women and the unhappy men and the bar table in the corner. Sometimes after midnight Hank watched her undress in their bedroom and thought of all the Martinis and Manhattans, the cream-cheesed celery sticks and bacon-wrapped chicken livers that had gone into those impressive haunches and upper arms.

"Other people don't help *it*," was Priscilla's answer to Susan. "But they might do something for *you*. You, a woman. Aren't you a woman, or are you only a part of a marriage?" She had never forgiven him, Hank feared, for that unideal wedding night.

Poor Susan seemed a vision of chastity whom they would discover each morning at the breakfast table, frazzled after another night's poor sleep, her hair drooping onto the lapels of a borrowed bathrobe, her ascetic breakfast of grapefruit and granola long eaten, the *Times* scattered about her in pieces read with a desperate thoroughness. Hank wanted to urge eggs and waffles upon her, and to make up good news to counteract the bad news that had been turning her hair gray. Priscilla knew what it was, but was no good at explaining. "Jeb's a bastard," she would say simply in their bedroom. "He always was. My parents knew it, but what could they do? She had to get married, once I did. And all men are bastards, more or less."

"My, you've gotten tough. He was always very dear with the kids, I thought. At least when they were little. And he builds those nice shingled rental villages, with solar panels and wading pools."

"Not so much anymore he doesn't," she said. As she pivoted on their plush carpet, yellow calluses showed at her heels.

"What do you mean?"

"Ask *her*, if you're so interested."

But he never could. He could no more have asked Susan to confide her private life than he could have tiptoed onto the sleeping porch and looked down at—what he held so clearly in his mind—his wife's very face, transposed into another, chastened existence, fragilely asleep in this alien house, this alien climate and time zone. So magical a stranger might awake under the pressure of his regard. He would have trespassed. He would have spoiled something he was saving.

The little 1975 recession gave Jeb's tottering, overextended business the last push it needed; everything coming undone at once, the Herreras began to divorce amid the liquidation. When Susan visited Hank and Priscilla in the bicentennial year, it was as a single woman, her thinness now whittled toward a point, a renewed availability. But not, of course, available to Hank; the collapse of one twin's marriage made the other doubly precious.

As in other summers, Hank was touched by Susan's zeal with the children, ushering as many as could be captured onto the train and into the city for a visit to the Museum of Natural History or to see the tall ships that beautiful hazy July day. Rose was not with her; the girl had drawn closer to her father in his distress, and was waitressing in a taco joint in downtown San Diego. And Karen, now stunning with her flaxen hair and pale moonface and lithe dancer's body, was above everything except boys and ballet. One Saturday, while Priscilla stayed home, having contracted for a lunch at the club with one of those boozy women she called "girl friends," Hank accompanied Susan on an excursion she had cooked up for the just barely willing Jennifer and Lucas, all the way to New Haven to see the Beinecke Library, with its translucent marble and the three marvellously simple Noguchis in their sunken well. Hank had not seen these wonders himself; they had come to Yale after his time. And he rather enjoyed these excursions with his sister-in-law; all that old tumble of family life had fallen to them to perpetuate. He let her drive his Mercedes and sat beside her, taking secret inventory of all the minute ways in which she differed from Priscilla—the slight extra sharpness to the thrust of her upper lip, the sea scallop of shallow wrinkles the sun had engraved at the corner of her eye, the hair or two more of bulk or wildness to her eyebrow on its crest of bone. The hair of her head, once shorter, then grayer, was now dyed too even a dark brown, with unnatural reddish lights. She turned to him for a second on a long straightaway. "You've never asked about me and Jeb," she said.

"What was to ask? Things speak for themselves."

"I loved that about you," Susan pronounced. Her verb alarmed him; "love" was a word he associated with the embarrassing sermons of his youth. "It's been a nightmare for years," she went on, and he realized that she was offering to present herself in a new way to him, as more than a strange ghost behind a familiar mask. She was opening herself. But he, after nearly two decades of playing the good husband, had discovered affairs, and had fallen in love locally. The image of his mistress—she was one of Priscilla's "girl friends"—rose up, her head tipped back, her lipstick smeared, and deafened him to the woman he was with; without hearing the words, he saw Susan's mouth, that distinctive complicated mouth the sisters shared, making a pursy, careful expression, like a schoolteacher emphasizing a crucial point.

Lucas, in the back seat, was listening, and cried out, "Mom, stop bitching about Dad to Uncle Hank—you do it to *everybody!*"

Jennifer said, "Oh, listen to big man here, protecting his awful daddy," and there was a thump, and the girl sobbed in spite of her scorn.

"You make me barf, you know that?" Lucas told her, his own voice shakily full of tears. "You've always been the most god-awful germ, no kidding."

"Daddy," Jennifer said, with something of womanly aloofness. "This little spic just broke my arm."

The adult conversation was not resumed. A few days later, Priscilla drove her sister back to LaGuardia, to begin a new life. Susan was planning to take her half of what money was left when the La Jolla house was sold and move with the two younger children to the Bay area and study ceramics at Berkeley.

"I told her she's crazy," Priscilla said to Hank. "There's nothing but gays in San Francisco."

"Maybe she's not as needful of male consolation as some."

"What's that supposed to mean? You're not above a little consolation yourself, from what I've been hearing."

"Easy, easy. The kids are upstairs."

"Karen isn't upstairs; she's in New York, letting that cradle robber she met at the club take her to the Alvin Ailey. Wake up. You know what your trouble has always been? You're an only child. You never loved me, you just loved the idea of sneaking into a family. You loved my family, the idea of there being so many of us, rich and Episcopalian and all that."

"I didn't need the Episcopalian so much. I thought I was going to sneeze all through the wedding. Incense, I couldn't believe it."

"You poor little Baptist boy. You know what my father said at the time? I've never told you this."

"Then don't."

"He said, 'He'll never fit in. He's a redneck, Prissy.' "

"Wow. Did he really say 'redneck'? And fit into what—the Saint Paul Order of the Moose? Gee, I always rather liked him, too. Especially early in the mornings, when you could catch him sober."

"He de*spised* you. But then Suzie picked Jeb, and he was so much worse."

"That *was* lucky."

"He made you look good, it's a crazy fact."

"Yes, and you make Suzie look good, so it evens out. Come on, let's save this for midnight. Here comes Henry."

But the boy, six feet tall suddenly, was wearing earphones plugged into a satchel-sized radio; on his way to the sunroom he gave his parents a glassy oblivious smile.

Any smugness the Arnolds may have felt in relation to the Herreras' disasters lasted less than a year. An ingenious tax shelter that Hank had directed a number of clients into was ruled invalid by the IRS, and these clients suddenly owed the government hundreds of thousands of dollars, including tens of thousands in penalties. Though they had been duly cautioned and no criminal offense was charged, the firm could not keep him; his divorce soon followed. One of the men Priscilla had been seeing had freed himself from his own wife and was prepared to take her on; Hank wondered what Priscilla did now, all hundred and fifty pounds of her, that was worth the trouble. To think that he had started her off on the sexual road with those formalized, chaste "parades."

She resettled with the children in Cos Cob. Having fouled his professional nest in the East, Hank accepted with gratitude the offer of a former colleague to join a firm in Los Angeles, as less than a junior partner. He had always been happy on their family visits to southern California and, though a one-bedroom condo in Westwood wasn't a redwood house overlooking a fairway in La Jolla, old Mr. Hunter had been right: he fitted in better here. Southern California had a Baptist flavor that helped him heal. The people mostly came from small Midwestern towns, and there was a naïveté in even the sin—the naked acts in the bars and the painted little-girl hookers in jogging shorts along Hollywood Boulevard. The great stucco movie theatres of the Thirties had been given over to X-rated films; freckle-faced young couples watched while holding hands and eating popcorn. In this city where sex was a kind of official currency, Hank made up for the fun he had missed while catching the train and raising the children in Greenwich, and evened the score with his former wife. Los Angeles was like that earlier immersion, at the age of religious decision, which coincided with puberty; that bullying big hand had shoved him under and he had come up feeling, as well as breathless and indignant, cleansed and born-again.

One day downtown on the escalator from Figueroa Street up to the Bonaventure, he found himself riding behind a vivid black-haired girl whom he slowly recognized as his niece, Rose. He touched her bare shoulder and bought her a drink in the lobby lounge, amid all the noisy, curving pools. She was twenty-four years old now; he could hardly believe it, though Karen was the same age. She told him her father had a job as foreman for another builder and had bought himself a stinkpot and kept taking weekend runs into Mexico; his dope-snorting friends that kept putting a move on her drove her crazy, so she had split a while ago. Now she worked as a salesgirl in a failing imported-leather-goods shop in the underground Arco Plaza while her chances of becoming an actress became geometrically smaller with each passing year. These days, she explained, if you haven't got your face somewhere by the time you're nineteen you're *finito*. And indeed, Hank thought, her face was unsubtle for a career of pretense; framed by a poodle cut of tight black curls, it had too much of Jeb's raw hopefulness, a shiny candor somehow coarse. Hank was excited by this disappointed young beauty, but women her age, with their round breasts and enormous pure eye whites, rather frightened him, like machines that are too new and expensive. He asked about her mother, and was given Susan's address. "She's doing real well," Rose warned him.

An exchange of letters followed. Susan's handwriting was a touch rounder than Priscilla's, but with the same "g"s that looked like "s"s and "t"s that had lost their crossings, like hats blown off by the wind. One autumn Saturday, Hank flew up to the Bay area. Three hundred miles of coast were cloudless and the hills had put on their inflammable tawny summer coats, that golden color the Californian loves as a New Englander loves the scarlet of turning maples. Berkeley looked surprisingly like Cambridge, once you ascended out of Oakland's slough: big homes built by a species of the middle class that had migrated elsewhere, and Xeroxed protest posters in many colors pasted to mailboxes and tacked to trees. Susan lived in the second-floor-back of a great yellow house that, but for its flaking paint and improvised outside stairways, reminded him of her ancestral home in Saint Paul. She had been watching for him, and they kissed, awkwardly, halfway up her access stairs.

The apartment was dominated by old photos of her children and by examples of her own ceramics—crusty, oddly lovely things, with a preponderance of turquoise and muddy orange in the glazes. She was even selling a few, at a shop a friend of hers ran in Sausalito. A female friend. And she taught part-time at a private elementary school. And still took classes—the other students called her Granny, but she loved them; their notions of what mattered were so utterly different from what ours were at that age. All this came out in a rapid voice, with a diffident stabbing of hands and a way of pushing her hair back from her ears as if to improve her hearing. Her manner implied that this was a slightly tiresome duty he had invented for them. He was an ex-relative, a page from the past. She was thinner than ever and had let her hair go back to gray, no longer just streaked but solidly gray, hanging down past the shoulders of a russet wool turtleneck sweater such as men wear in ads for Scotch whiskey. Hank had never seen Priscilla look anything like this. In tight, spattered jeans, and bony bare feet, Susan's skinniness was exciting; he wanted to seize her before she dwindled away entirely.

She took him for a drive, in her Mazda, just as if they still had children to entertain together. The golden slashed hills interwoven with ocean and lagoons, the curving paths full of cyclists and joggers and young parents with infants in backpacks looked idyllic, a vision of the future, an enchanted land not of perpetual summer, as where he lived, but of eternal spring. She had put on spike heels with her jeans and a vest of sheepskin patches over her sweater, and these additions made her startlingly stylish. They went out to eat at a local place where tabbouleh followed artichoke soup. Unlike most couples on a first date, they had no lack of things to talk about. Reminiscence shied away from old grievances and turned to the six children, their varying and still-uncertain fates; fates seemed so much slower to shape up than when they had been young. Priscilla was hardly mentioned. As the evening wore on, Priscilla became an immense hole in their talk, a kind of cave they were dwelling in, while their voices slurred and their table candle flickered. Was it that Susan was trying to spare him acknowledging what had been, after all, his male failure to hold Priscilla's love; or was Hank trying not to cast upon her a shadow of comparison, an onus of being half a person? She took him back to her apartment; indeed, he had not arranged for anywhere else to go.

She kicked off her shoes and turned on an electric heater and dragged a magnum of Gallo from the refrigerator. She was tired; he liked that, since he was, too, as though they had been pulling at the same load in tandem all these years. They sat on the floor, on opposite sides of a glass coffee table in whose surface her face was mirrored—the swinging witchy hair, the deep eye sockets and thoughtful upper lip. "You've come a long way," she announced, in that voice which had once struck him as huskier than another but that in this room felt as fragile as the pots blushing turquoise on the shelves.

"How do you mean?"

"To see me. *Do* you see me? *Me,* I mean."

"Who else? I've always liked you. Loved, should I say? Or would that be too much?"

"I think it would. Things between us have always been . . ."

"Complicated," Hank finished.

"Exactly. I don't want to be just your way of correcting a mistake."

He thought a long time, so long her face became anxious, before answering, "Why not?" He knew that most people, including Susan, had more options than he, but he had faith that in our affluent nation a need, honestly confessed, has a good chance of being met.

This being the Eighties, she was nervous about herpes and all those other awful new diseases. She didn't know what-all he'd been doing in L.A.; she really would have to know him a lot better before sleeping with him. He didn't argue, but meekly said there *was* something she could do he would be very grateful for. Seeing her undress and move self-consciously, chin up, through a little "parade" in the room, Hank thought her majestic, for being nearly skeletal. Plato was wrong; what is is absolute. Ideas pale. The delay Susan imposed, the distances between them that could not be quickly altered, helped him grasp the blissful truth that she was just another woman.

Slippage

A NOT QUITE SLIGHT EARTHQUAKE—5.4 on the Richter scale—afflicted Morison's area early one morning: at 6:07, it said later over the news. He awoke abruptly, nauseated without knowing why. Then the last shudder made the bedside lamp give out a delicate buzzing noise, a kind of tingle, and in the little heave, as if the bed were a boat sluing in a wave trough, he looked about the room wide-eyed, to see what damage there was. There appeared to be none; the crisp low plaster ceiling was intact to its corners, no broken glass showed on the windowsills, the water glass and alarm clock and folded spectacles had not abandoned their stations beneath his lamp. His wife at his side had not stirred. Only the top of her head showed —long blond wisps, mussed. She always slept deep under the covers, her face off the pillow, as if in the night she had slipped down toward the foot of the bed. Her body under the covers was flattened frighteningly, like something dead on the road. He pressed his own body more securely against the mattress and waited, eyes open, for the room's motion to renew itself; he waited for the end of the world. But the little earthquake had subsided, and within an hour had become an amusing item on the televised news, the kind that lets the anchormen, after tense recitation of international massacres and negotiations, relax their faces and segue kiddingly into the weatherman.

No significant damage had been reported. The center of the disturbance lay in the thinly populated mountains eighty miles to the north. Area residents had flooded the station with calls.

"Interesting," Morison said to his wife over their second cup of coffee, "that people call television stations now."

"Instead of what?" She was much younger than he, and seemed cranky as a child in the mornings, her face still imprinted with the creases of the wrinkled bedsheet. "What *should* they call?"

"Oh, I don't know. Police stations. City Hall. They seem to think authority now is vested in the television station."

"There's no point in calling *any*body about an earthquake anyway," she said irritably.

"I agree," Morison quickly said, feeling the conversation slipping toward a quarrel.

"Did you really wake up seasick, or are you just imagining things again?"

His memory extended so much further back in time than hers that she liked to dismiss its superior content as imagination. She was getting them both ready, he sometimes felt, for his senility, though he was barely sixty. "I certainly did. The whole room shook. The bed absolutely jumped. *You,*" he added in an accusatory tone, "slept right through, like a"—he didn't want to say "baby"—"like a log."

"I was *tired,*" she whined, reaching for another cigarette. She knew the sight of her smoking pained him, and hurried lighting the match. "All these end-of-the-year parties with drunken professors. Keuschnig last night got all sentimental with me about the Anglo-Saxons. Their valor, the comitatus, I forget all what. His hand kept creeping to my knee, and I could have sworn at one point there were tears in his eyes." All this was volunteered by way of making up, after her unconscious offense of sleeping through his earthquake.

Morison's wife had been a student of his. He was a history professor, and today he concluded the spring term of his survey course, "Europe on the Rise: 1453–1914." The students customarily applauded the last lecture, and today the applause went on longer, it seemed to him, than usual, wave upon wave, with a warmth and valedictory enthusiasm that kept renewing itself. In a little trough between two waves of applause it came to Morison, smiling and bobbing his gray head uneasily, that this noise was indeed goodbye: his work was essentially done. Though he had written a notable monograph or two and, with a colleague now dead, a general account of the Austrian Empire still considered standard, the revolutionary thesis, the sweeping and unifying insight that would have forever pinned his name to history's turning wheel, had never come to him. As a young assistant professor he had felt it well within his grasp—a little more study, a sabbatical spent in inspired scribbling at his desk, and he would have it, one of those radical perceptions that in hindsight loom as inevitable as those of a Weber or a Burckhardt. The possibility had been there, fair as a willing young woman, and he failed to nail it. His specialty, Austria-Hungary, had turned out to be a comic-opera patchwork, a muddle of "provisional absolutism," an empire without a coronation ceremony, a reactionary monarchy tottering through a paper blizzard of decrees and concessions, a study in inertia and fragmentation. Yet, for all that, Morison continued to think, a model of human arrangements. The students' compassionate fond applause was wrapping him up, sealing him into his coffin; his mind had made its run, and at a deep level that his body had yet to detect he was exhausted. He was, with his old-fashioned tweed jacket and gray flannels, his memories of the last good war and of the intellectual gold rush that had come with the GI Bill, his dated "slant" and late-capitalist liberal humanism, himself now history, a flake of consciousness lost within time's black shale.

A tug of nausea returned with this perception. The applause spattered to a close. Morison gathered his worn lecture notes, the pages frayed with repeated handling and the typed text spidery where second and third thoughts (none of them recent) had spun over the years a web of insertions. Like a person who takes a backache or a love pang onto a crowded bus, Morison moved with his queasiness out among the exiting, pushing students. They were bright-faced and noisy and clad in light rags. June was almost here. A boy in denim cutoffs and a tank top, one of the pushers, seeking professorial intimacy right to the edge of exam period, voiced puzzlement and a disposition to quarrel with the somewhat ironical portrait Morison had painted of a Europe halcyon and the envy of the globe in 1914, until Austria-Hungary's doddery decision to launch war against Serbia for the sake of an assassinated prince everyone had disliked. "But, sir, what about the poverty and sweatshops? What about the abortive revolutions, like in 1905?" Morison brushed past the boy as if he were shouting in a foreign language. The professor had no heart left for history; his retrospect was obsessed by that immense, subtle tremble in whose arms he had hours ago awoken.

Sex, Morison thought as the day wore on. Sex was what had slid away. Not the fact of it—his young wife, though she needed her sleep, was less fussily obliging than any woman of Morison's generation would have been —but the hope, the expectancy that used to draw all days and hours to a point. In his untenured years, he would look forward all day to a dinner party, to seeing Mrs. R. or combative Miss B. or languorous Madame de L. of the Department of Romance Languages in a silk or satin party dress, and watching the skins of such females flush and their gestures widen under the influence of drink and food and what the behavioral scientists called socialization, and hearing their voices rise and grow adorably raucous and reckless. The air then was full of signs, of meanings, of flashing immaterial knives. Now at dinner parties he would sit and be amazed that there was not one woman at the table he wanted to sleep with. It was a kind of deafness, a turning down of the sound on a television set. The mouths around the table moved absurdly, like the mouths of fish. Politely, animatedly even, he and his colleagues—his comitatus—were going through the motions. It was, Morison supposed, what Freud had meant by civilization; no one healthy, really, had ever had much use for it.

Students, too, emitted their signals, their secondary meanings of pose and glance—pitfalls, at times, of delicious hazard. Now the girls in their provoking undress were to Morison like foliage, blandly thronging the sides of his vision as he walked the campus paths. Though only thrice wed, in a profession notorious for its marital casualties, he had been, all those years when the great theory, the seminal statement, waited to be discovered, in a constant fever of love, talking to one female or another in his head incessantly, making her the unwitting witness of his being—his lectures, his conferences, his reading of term papers, his carpentry, his leafraking, even his lovemaking to another. Now, if he thought of women, in a moment of silent occupation, or while falling off to sleep, it was of his daughters, with great pity and sorrow and, obscurely, self-blame. He had had three, by the first two wives, and all three were adult, and lived alone in tiny rented rooms in various ungrateful cities. When he thought of a daughter, he pictured a pea suspended in the center of an empty cube, waiting to be found, a tiny, hard, slightly shrivelled core of disappointment floating in a room whose one window gave on identical, other windows. The picture had the sadness of a Magritte. So it would startle him, confronting one of his daughters in actuality, to find her large and hearty and solicitous toward *him;* he was aging, he would read in her eyes. To them he appeared a fragile relic of the past they had shared, when they had been giggling babies and he dark-haired and omnipotent. Morison would have wept, if he could weep as easily as Keuschnig, over his daughters.

His daughters and his teeth. A left lower bicuspid, having long ago lost the molar behind it, now was wearying of carrying a gold bridge, and stood with its root all but completely exposed by the eroding jawbone, and felt palpably loose to Morison's tongue. And he could not stop touching it, testing to what degree the looseness was fact and to what degree morbid illusion—his imagining things, as his wife put it.

In his office, he pawed through stacks of term papers pounded out under the inspiration of cram notes and NoDoz. He made few marginal remarks; these final papers were often not even retrieved, but left to gather dust on a chair in his locked office all summer. Outside, the afternoon glided by with a waxy brilliance. The sky was cloudless, showing heaven's independence of earth. The motion of the bed this morning, produced by subterranean thunder, in Morison's mind had become less like a boat sluing, less large: more of a nervous, sharp motion, as if the bedposts had been socketed in cups of grease. His tongue pressed against the weakening tooth once more. There was another dinner party tonight, and his failure to feel excitement seemed another slight softening, an installment of eventual total loss.

Yet it was here, at this party in the home of a younger colleague—a disciple of Braudel deep into the statistics of Midwestern grain and cattle shipment in the 1880s—that she appeared, the exciting woman. She was an unscheduled guest, the visiting sister of a geologist. Slender, tall, her hair a gaudy orange and teased into a compact airy ball around her face, she marched into the room erect as a soldier, chin up and an arm extended before her toward the hostess in a gesture almost balletic, as if her fingers held a wand. No husband accompanied her. To Morison she seemed so precious, so precarious and knifelike a vision in her pale-green sheath of a dress, that he shied from talking to her. Only in the second hour of pre-dinner drinks, the small crowd around her mysteriously dispersing, did they come face to face. Her eyes, like her dress, were pale green, and they fastened on his with an intensity that suggested they had met before, in circumstances that had been discreditable. The tilted-back angle of her bony, bright face looked a little unnatural and tense, up close. "Are you retired?" she asked, unsmiling.

He provided the smile. "Not quite yet. Do I look as though I should be?"

It was her chance to flirt, but she said with a hiss, "Yes."

He changed the subject. "Your brother is a geologist."

"My brother," the woman said, "is a bully." The muscles at the points of her jaw kept jumping, and her long throat was composed of rigid vertical cords.

"I was curious to know what he thought about the earthquake this morning. Has he expressed anything to you? Any theories? Is this the beginning of a cataclysmic trend?"

She said nothing, merely stared at him with a face about to fling itself into outrage; it was as if he were daring to speak to her in a sacred code, as if he were violating the terms of an agreement they had arrived at in secret. Yet she was lovely, Morison noticed, in her bones, the widely spaced cheekbones and jaw points, and in the tilt of her nose and the blooded darkness of her narrow, pink-rimmed nostrils. She was vivid as a wild animal; he needed only to find the tone that would settle her down.

"Did you notice it?" he asked, softer-voiced. "This morning? My lazy wife slept right through, but it was all over television, and the afternoon papers."

"I don't want to be here," this woman in green explained, wagging her jaw slightly from side to side and barely unclenching her teeth, as if afraid of vomiting. "It's my brother's idea. I have a lovely home. But my crazy husband—"

"Your husband?"

"He says I shouldn't talk about it." For the first time; her eyes left his, and her head swivelled, surveying the room so rapidly her ball of teased hair bounced under the stress of rotation.

"Your husband says?"

"My *brother.*" The corners of her lips, which were very long and somewhat imprecisely painted a purplish red, bent upwards in a cramped attempt at a smile. "He's taking it from me, my *beau*tiful home, and now my children, oh my God, he has *law*yers, and *doc*tors, he *buys* people, and gets them to *lie*—"

"This is not your brother, this is your husband," Morison said. It was a stupid, professorial effort to keep things clear, but he was becoming frightened.

The woman looked at him with astonishment. He had the irrational fear her face might fly apart, like an explosion of shrapnel, its cheekbones and nostrils and the eyes that seemed bones of a different color. "You're *wonderful,*" she pronounced at last, and silently laughed, a huge ghost of a laugh, her mouth opening wider than he would have thought possible, so that from his angle he saw the ribs of the roof of her mouth and the gutter of black fillings running back through her molars.

She was, he realized, quite mad; her defiant entry into this party, her situation as she described it were suddenly explained, and the mystery of why the people around her had dispersed, leaving Morison to face her. And she, seeing what must have been a change, a slippage, in his own face, tipped back her face in triumph and attached herself to him with a slim, nervous, hard hand. For the rest of the evening, she followed him with her gaze and her voice, seating herself beside him at the table, staring, pleading that he understand her, that the code they had worked out in the fathomless past continue to bind them together and become the basis for her rescue. The vague human appeal that always hangs gaseously in the air of parties had become suffocatingly solid; the ceiling of the room seemed to be lowering and chasing him from corner to corner, from group to group, as the woman circled in her hunt.

"What a nightmarish evening," Morison said to his wife when at last it was over and they were home.

"She *did* take quite a shine to you," she said. "Poor soul. Apparently she was quite brilliant and lovely once, and just flipped. Her brother was saying they don't want to have to do any more shock treatments."

"I thought nobody did those anymore." The idea slightly sickened him. Would they shave off her hair? Had that hair been a wig? "It was terrifying," he confessed, "to realize suddenly that she wasn't *there,* in the way that people normally are. I must have looked foolish."

"No more," she said, "than old guys on the make ever look." Having mussed her own hair in pulling off her dress, she tossed her head with petulant violence, like a child who doesn't want her snarls combed out; thus shaken, this hair, blond and long, loosened of its own down her back. In bed, by way of making up, she smoothed his eyebrows, which had grown bushy with the years, and massaged the front of his skull as if to ease the creases from his forehead. "Everybody at the party thought you were heroic," she said loyally.

This all formed a signal, and Morison wanted to respond, for his wife now seemed a treasure, sleepy but at least sane; but the moment when he should have nailed her, as it were, passed, and she slipped in his arms into forgetfulness of him.

He lay in the wide bed and waited. Though the ceiling had receded to its proper distance, his memory of that mouth, so suddenly, avidly flexible, with its ribbed cave roof and black back teeth, afflicted him. His tongue touched his own tooth, testing the give; perhaps he was imagining it. He thought of Franz Josef, punctilious to the end, arising on the day of his death at three-thirty as usual, for the usual rubdown with cold water by a valet, and donning his medals; feverish, feeble, the world beyond his windows brought to ruin by the disastrous miscarriage of his ultimatum to Serbia, the old monarch examined and signed papers all day at Schönbrunn, though too weak in the evening to kneel to his prayers. Sedl, the bishop of the Hofburg, came at eight-thirty and put the ancient Hapsburg cross to the Emperor's lips; his mistress, Katherina Schratt, was called too late, and placed on the bed where Franz Josef's corpse lay two white roses, which were buried with him. Morison thought of his daughters in their empty rooms, and of the thinly populated mountains to the north. Suddenly, the mattress seemed to slue a bit sideways, to give a little flirtatious tug; but the bedlamp didn't tingle, so he must have imagined it.

Poker Night

THE PLANT has been working late, with the retailers hustling to get their inventories up for Christmas even though this is only August, so I grabbed a bite on the way to the doctor's and planned to go straight from there to poker. The wife in fact likes my not coming home now and then; it gives her a chance to skip dinner and give her weight problem a little knock.

The doctor has moved from his old office over on Poplar to one of these new medical centers, located right behind the mall, where for years when I was a kid there was a field where I can remember the Italians growing runner beans on miles and miles of this heavy brown string. The new center is all recessed ceiling lighting and there's wall-to-wall carpet everywhere and Muzak piped into the waiting room, but if you look at their doors you could put a fist through them easily and can hear the other doctors and patients through the walls, everything they say, including the breathing.

What mine said to me wasn't good. In fact, every time I tried to get a better grip on it it seemed to get worse.

He provided a lot of cheerful energetic talk about the treatments they have now, the chemotherapy and then cobalt and even something they can do with platinum, but at my age I've seen enough people die to know there's no real stopping it, just a lot of torment on the way. If it wasn't for company insurance and Medicaid you wonder how many of these expensive hospitals would still be in business.

I said at least I was glad it hadn't been just my imagination. I asked if he thought it could have been anything to do with any of the chemicals they have to use over at the plant, and he said with this prim mouth how he really couldn't venture any opinion about that.

He was thinking lawsuit, but I had been just curious. Me, I've always figured if it isn't going to be one thing it'll be another; in this day and age you can stand out on a street corner waiting for the light to change and inhale enough poison to snuff out a rat.

We made our future appointments and he gave me a wad of prescriptions to get filled. Closing the door, I felt somebody could have put a fist through me pretty easily, too.

But drugstores are bright places, and while waiting I had a Milky Way and leafed through a *People,* and by the time the girl behind the counter had the medicine ready you could tell from her smile and the way the yellow Bic-click stuck out of her smock pocket that nothing too bad was going to happen to me, ever. At least at a certain level of my mind this seemed the case.

Moths were thick as gnats under the streetlights and there was that old sound of summer happiness in the swish of car tires on sticky tar and the teen-agers inside the cars calling out even to people they didn't know. I got into my own car and after some thinking about it drove in the Heights direction to poker.

I wanted to be sharing this with the wife but then they were counting on me to be the sixth and a few hours couldn't make much difference. Bad news keeps: isn't that what the old people used to say?

The group has been meeting every other Wednesday for thirty years, with some comings and goings, people moving away and coming back. We've even had some deaths, but up to now none of the regulars, just substitutes—brother-in-laws or neighbors called in to round out the table for just that one night.

It was at Bob's tonight. Bob's a framer, in his own shop downtown: it's amazing what those guys get now, maybe forty, fifty bucks for just some little watercolor somebody's aunt did as a hobby, or some kid's high-school diploma.

Jerry does mechanical engineering for an outfit beyond the new mall, Ted's a partner in a downtown fruit store, Greg manages the plumbing business his father founded way back, Rick's a high-school guidance counsellor believe it or not, and Arthur's in sales for Doerner's Paints and Stains. Arthur had to be on the road tonight, which is why they needed me to make six.

It all began when we were newlyweds more or less starting up our families in the neighborhood between Poplar and Forrest, on the side of the avenue away from what used to be the great old Agawam Wallpaper factory, before they broke it up into little commercial rental units. One April night I got this call from Greg, a guy I hardly knew except everybody knew his old man's truck.

I thought Alma would make resistance: both Jimmy and Grace must have been under two at the time and she was still trying to give piano lessons in the evenings. But she said go ahead, I'd been working pretty hard and she thought I could use the relaxation.

Now none of us live in the neighborhood except me and Ted, and he talks about moving to a condo now that the kids are out of the house, except he hates the idea of fighting the traffic into town every day. From where he is now he can walk to the fruit store in a blizzard if he has to, and that crazy Josie of his never did learn how to drive.

For years Arthur has been over on the Heights too, about three of these curving streets away from Bob's place, and Rick is over on the other side of town toward the lake, and Jerry has gone and bought himself some rundown dairy farm south of the mall; he's fixing up the barn as a rental property, doing most of the work himself on weekends. Also over the years there have been a few changes as to wives and business situations.

But the stakes haven't changed, and with inflation and our moving more or less up in the world the dimes and quarters and even the dollar bills look like chips, flipping back and forth. It really *is* pretty much relaxation now, with winning more a matter of feeling good than the actual profit.

I arrived maybe ten minutes late because of the wait in the drugstore. The little paper bags in the pocket rattled when I threw my jacket on the sofa and the sound scraped in my stomach, reminding me.

Did you ever have the strong feeling that something *has* to be a dream, and that tomorrow you'll wake up safe? It used to come to me as a kid, whenever I'd be in real trouble, like the time Lynn Pechilis said she was pregnant or when they caught us stealing the comic books from Woolworth's.

I got a beer and settled in at the table between Ted and Rick. The five faces, all lit up already with beer and the flow of the cards, looked like balloons, bright pink balloons in that overhead light Bob has rigged up in his den, a naked 100-watt bulb on an extension cord propped up there among the exposed two-by-eights.

He's been working on his den for years, bringing the ceiling down and the walls in for better insulation. But the framing business keeps him downtown Saturdays as well as evenings, and the plasterboard sheets and lumber and rolls of insulation have been leaning around so long in this den it always gives us something to rib him about.

I thought, *I'll never see this room finished.* The thought hit me like lead in the gut; but I figured if I sat perfectly quiet and drank the first beer fast the balloons of their faces would slowly take me up with them, to where I could forget my insides.

And it worked, pretty well. The cards began to come to me, under the naked bulb, the aces and deuces and the queens with their beautiful cold faces, and I really only made two mistakes that night.

The one was, I hung on with two pair, jacks and eights, all the way into the dollar-raise stage of a game of seven-card high-low when Jerry had four cards of a straight showing and only two of the nines, the card he needed, were accounted for. But I figured he would *have* to bet as if he had it whether he did or not; as it turned out, he *did* have it, and I wasn't even second best, since Greg had been sitting there sandbagging with three kings.

The other was, in the last round, when what with the beer the pots really build, I folded a little full house, fives and treys, in a game of Twin Beds, because so many pairs were already out there on the board I figured somebody had to have me beat. I was wrong: Rick won it with an ace-high heart flush.

Can you imagine, winning Twin Beds with a flush? It's in my character to feel worse about folding a winner than betting a loser; it seems less of a sin against God or Nature or whatever.

Maybe my concentration was off; it did seem silly, at moments, sitting here with these beered-up guys (it gets pretty loud toward the end) playing a game like kids killing a rainy Sunday afternoon when I'd just been told my number was up. The cards at these moments when I thought about it looked incredibly thin: a kind of silver foil beaten to just enough of a thickness to hide the numb reality that was under everything.

My cards as it happened were generally pretty dull, so I had time to look around. The guys' faces looked like pink balloons but their hands as they reached on the table were another story altogether: they were old guys' hands, withered long wrinkled white claws with spots and gray hair and stand-up veins.

We had grown old together. We were all drawing near to death, and I guess that was the comfort of it, the rising up with them.

Ted spilled his beer as he tends to do as the evening wears on, reaching for some cards or the popcorn basket or his bifocals (it's an awkward length: you can see your own cards fine with the short vision but the cards in the middle tend to blur, and vice versa) and everybody howled and kidded him as they always do, and my throat began to go rough, they were all so damn sweet, and I'd known them so damn long, without ever saying much of anything except this clowning around and whose deal was it;

maybe that was the sweetness. Their faces blurred and came up in starry points like that out-of-focus thing they do with television cameras now—the false teeth and glasses and the shiny high foreheads where hair had been—and the crazy thought came to me that people wouldn't mind which it was so much, heaven or hell, as long as their friends went with them.

Ted has these slightly swollen-looking hands, nicked around the fingers and fat at the sides of the palms, from handling the crates I suppose, and you would think, deft as he must have to be every day in the fruit store, picking out plums and tomatoes for the lady customers, he would be the last one of us to be knocking his beer glass over. But he's always the one, just like Rick is the one to hang in there with junk and Jerry the one to catch that one card in the deck he needs.

I wound up about five dollars down. If I'd had the guts to stay with that little full house I might have been five dollars ahead.

I put on my jacket and the rustling in the pocket reminded me again of the prescriptions and the doctor. Woolworth's didn't prosecute, and it turned out Lynn just wanted to give me a scare.

The wife wasn't up. I didn't expect her to be, at quarter to twelve.

But she wasn't asleep, either. She asked me from the bed in the dark how I did.

I said I broke about even. She asked me what the doctor had said.

I asked her if she'd like to come down to the kitchen and talk. I don't know exactly why I didn't want anything said in the bedroom, but I didn't.

She said she'd love to, she had skipped supper tonight and was starving. There was some leftover lasagna in the fridge she could warm in the microwave in a minute; she'd been lying there in the dark thinking about it.

Alma isn't fat exactly; solid is more how I think of it. When you're with her in bed, you can feel she still has a waist.

We went downstairs and turned on the light and she in her bathrobe heated the Pyrex dish half full of lasagna and I thought about one more beer and decided against it. Then the lasagna was so hot—amazing, how those microwaves do it; from the inside out, they say, vibrating the molecules—I went and got the beer just to soothe my mouth.

I told her everything as much like the doctor had told me as I could. His exact words, his tone of voice as if it wasn't him saying this but a kind of pre-recorded announcement; the look of the recessed lights about his examining table and his steel desk and of his fake hardboard wood-grained wainscoting all revived in me as if I'd just come from there, as if I hadn't been to poker at all.

Alma did and said all the right things, of course. She cried but not so much I'd panic and came up with a lot of sensible talk about second opinions and mysterious remissions and modern medicine and how we'd take it a day at a time and had to have faith.

But she wasn't me. I was me.

While we were talking across the kitchen table there was a barrier suddenly that I was on one side of and she was on the other, overweight and over fifty as she was, a middle-aged tired woman up after midnight in a powder-blue bathrobe but with these terribly alive dark eyes, suddenly. I had handed her this terrible edge.

You could see it in her face, her mind working. She was considering what she had been dealt; she was thinking how to play her cards.

Made in Heaven

BRAD SCHAEFFER was attracted to Jeanette Henderson by her Christianity; at an office Christmas party, in Boston in the Thirties, in one of those eddies of silence that occur amid gaiety like a swirl of backwater in a stream, he heard her crystal-clear voice saying, "Why, the salvation of my soul!"

He looked over. She was standing by the window, pinned between a hot radiator and Rodney Gelb, the office Romeo. Outside, behind the black window, it had begun to snow, and the lighted windows of the office building across Milk Street were blurring and fluttering. Jeanette had come to the brokerage house that fall, a tidy secretary in a pimento wool suit, with a prim ruffled blouse. For this evening's event she had ventured open-toed shoes and a dress of lavender gabardine, with zigzag pleats marked at their points by flattened bows. The flush the party punch had put in her cheeks helped him to see for the first time the something highly polished about her compact figure, an impression of an object finely made, down to the toenails that peeked through the tips of her shoes. Her profile showed pert and firm as she strained to look up into Rodney's overbearing, beetle-browed face. Brad stepped over to them, into the steamy warmth near the radiator. The snow was intensifying; across the street the golden windows were softening like pats of butter.

Jeanette's face turned to her rescuer. She was lightly sweating. The excited blush of her cheeks made the blue of her eyes look icy. "Rodney was saying," she appealed, "that only money matters!"

"Then I asked this crazy little gal what mattered to *her*," Rodney said, giving off heat through his black serge suit. A sprig of mistletoe, pale and withering, had been pinned to his lapel.

"And I told him the first thing I could think of," Jeanette said. Her hair, waved and close to her head, was a soft brown that tonight did not look mousy. "Of course a *lot* of things matter to me," she hurried on, "more than money."

"Are you Catholic?" Brad asked her.

This was a question of a more serious order than Rodney's badinage. Her face composed itself; her voice became secretarial, factual. "Of course not. I'm a Methodist."

Brad felt relief. He was free to love her. In Boston, an aspiring man did not love Catholics, even if he came from Ohio with the name of Schaeffer.

"Did I sound so silly?" she asked, when Rodney had gone off in search of another cup of punch and another little gal.

"Unusual, but not silly." In his heart Brad did not expect capitalism to last another decade, and it would take with it what churches were left; he assumed religion was already as dead as Marx and Mencken claimed. There was a gloom in the December streets, and in the statistics that came to the office, that made the cheer of Christmas carols sound obscene. From the deep doorways of Boston's business buildings, ornamented like little Gothic chapels, people actually starving peered out, too bitter and numb to beg. Each morning the Common was combed for frozen bodies.

"I *do* believe," Jeanette went on, as if apologizing. The contrast between her blue eyes and rosy, glazed skin had become almost garish. "Ever since I can remember, even before anything was explained to me. It seems so natural, so necessary. Do you think that's strange?"

"I think that's lovely," he told her.

By Lententime they were going together to church. It was his idea, to accompany her; he liked seeing her in new settings, in the new light each placed her in. At work she was drab and brisk, a bit aloof from the other "girls," and dressed in a way that made her look older than she was. At her ancestral home in Framingham, with her parents and brothers, she became girlish and slightly drunk on family atmosphere, as she had been on punch; Brad greedily inhaled the spicy air of this old house, with its worn Orientals and sofas of leather and horsehair, knowing that this was the aroma of her childhood. On the streets and in restaurants, Jeanette was perfectly the lady, like a figure etched on a city scene, making him, in their scenic anonymity, a gentleman, an escort, a gallant. Her smiling face gleamed, and the satin lapels of her melton-cloth coat, and the pointed tips of her patent-leather boots. Involuntarily his arm encircled her waist at crossings, and he could not let go even when they had safely crossed the street. Her bearing was so nicely honed in every move—the pulling off, for instance, finger by finger, of her doeskin gloves in Locke-Ober's—that Brad would sometimes clown or feign clumsiness just to crack her composed expression with a blush or a disapproving frown.

It did not occur to him, when, during a rapt *pianissimo* moment in Symphony Hall, he nudged her and whispered a joke, that he was rending something precious to her, invading a fragile feminine space. In church, he loved standing tall at her side and hearing her frail, crystalline voice lift up the words of the hymns. He basked in her gravity, which had something shy about it, and even uncertain, as if she feared an excess of feeling might leap from the musty old forms and overwhelm her. He knew the forms; he had been raised as a Presbyterian, though only his mother attended services, and then only on those Sundays when she wasn't needed in the fields or at the barn. Jeanette had resisted, at first, his accompanying her. It would be, she murmured, distracting. And it was true; her shy, uncertain reverence made him, perversely, want to turn and hug her and lift her up with a shout of pride and animal gladness.

He was twenty-eight, and she was twenty-five—old enough that marriage might have slipped her by. Her composure, the finished neatness of her figure, already seemed a touch old-maidenly. She shared rooms with another young woman on Marlborough Street; he lived on Joy, on the dark, Cambridge Street side of Beacon Hill. She had been going to church at the brick Copley Methodist over on Newbury Street, with its tall domed bell tower and its Byzantine gold-leaf ceiling. Brad found within an easy walk of his own apartment—down Chambers Street as it curved, and then up a little court opposite the Mayhew School—a precious oddity, a Greek Revival clapboard church tucked among the brick tenements of the West End. Built by the Unitarians in the 1830s and taken over by the Wesleyans during their post–Civil War resurgence, the little building had box pews, small leaded panes of gray glass, and an oak pulpit shaped somewhat like a bass viol. Brad was to recall fondly all of his life coming here with Jeanette for the Wednesday-night Lenten services, on raw spring nights when the east wind was bringing the smell of brine in from the harbor. The narrow dim streets bent and resounded as he imagined old quarters in Europe did; the young courting couple walked through the babble and the cooking odors of Jewish and Italian and Lithuanian families, and then came to this closet of Protestantism, this hushed, vacant space—scarcely a dozen heads in the pews, and the church so chilly that overcoats were left on. There was no choir, and each shift of weight on a pew seat rang out like a cough. Perhaps Brad was still an unbeliever at that point, for he relished (as if he were whispering a joke to Jeanette) the emptiness, the chill, the pathos of the aged minister's trite and halting sermon as once again the old clergy-man, set down to die in this dying parish, led his listeners along the worn path to the Crucifixion and the bafflement beyond. During these pathetic sermons Brad's mind would range wonderfully far, a falcon scouting his future, while Jeanette sat at his side, compact and still and exquisite. She would lift him up, he felt. In the virtual vacancy of this old meetinghouse she seemed most intimately his.

Roosevelt was newly President then, and Curley was still mayor; their boasts came true, the country survived. The precious little hollow church, with its wooden Ionic columns and viol-shaped pulpit, was swept away in the Fifties along with the tenements of the West End. By this time Brad and Jeanette had moved with their children to Newton and become Epis-copalians.

On their wedding night, hoping to please her, he had held her body in his arms and prayed aloud. He thanked God for bringing them together, and asked that they be allowed to live fruitful and useful lives together. The prayer in time was answered, though on this occasion it did little to relax Jeanette. Always his love of her, when distinctly professed, made her a bit reserved and tense, as if a certain threat was being masked, and a trap might be sprung.

Their four children were all born healthy, and Brad's four years as a naval officer passed with no more injury to him than the devastating im-pression the black firmament of spattered stars made when seen from the flight deck of an aircraft carrier, in the middle of the Pacific. How little, little to the point of nothingness, he was beneath those stars! Even the great ship, the *Enterprise*, that held him a tall building's height above the all-swallowing ocean was reduced to the size of a pinpoint in such a per-spective. And yet it was he who was witnessing the stars; they knew noth-ing of themselves, so in this dimension he was greater than they. As far as he could reason, religion begins with this strangeness, this standstill; faith tips the balance in favor of the pinpoint. So, though he had never had Jeanette's smiling intuitions or sensations of certainty, he became in his mind a believer.

Ten years later, in the mid-Fifties, he suggested they become Epis-copalians, because the church was handier to the Newton house—a shin-gled ark full of corridors for vanished servants and with even a cupola. Narrow stairs wound up to a small round room that became Jeanette's "retreat." She installed rugs and pillowed furniture, did crocheting and watercolors. From its curved windows one could see to the east the red warning light topping the spire of the John Hancock Building. Brad did not need to say that his associates and clients tended to be Episcopalians, and that this church held more of the sort of people they should get to know. Although he never quite grew accustomed to the droning wordiness of the service, and the awkward and repetitive kneeling, he did love the look of the congregation—the ruddy men with their blue blazers and ever-fresh haircuts, the sleek Episcopal women with their furs in winter and in summer their wide pastel garden hats that allowed a peek of the backs of their necks when they bowed their heads. He loved Jeanette among them, in her black silk dress and the strand of real pearls, each costing as much as a refrigerator, with which he had paid tribute to their twentieth anniversary. Money gently glimmered on her fingers and ears. All capitalism had needed, it had turned out, was an infusion of war. The postwar stock market climbed; even plumbers and grocers needed a stockbroker now. Shares Brad had picked up for peanuts in the Depression doubled and redoubled and doubled again in value.

Jeanette never took quite so active a role in the life of the church as he had expected. He himself taught Sunday school, passed the plate, sat on the vestry, read the lesson. It was like an extension of his business life; he felt at home in the committee room, in the linoleum-floored offices and robing rooms that mere worshippers never saw. There was always some practical reason for him to be at the church Sunday mornings, whereas in growing season Jeanette often stayed home to garden, much as Brad's mother had worked in the fields. Her body had added a mature plumpness to that polished, glossy quality that had first enchanted him. Her Christianity, as he imagined it, was, like water sealed into an underground cistern, unchangingly pure. Standing beside her in church, hearing her small, true voice lifted in song, he still felt empowered by her fineness, her faith; in the jostle after the service his arm involuntarily crept around her waist, and he would let go only to shake the minister's overworked hand.

"I wish you wouldn't paw me in church," she said one Sunday as they drove home. "We're too middle-aged."

"I wasn't so much pawing you as steering you through the mob," he offered, embarrassed.

"I don't *need* to be steered," Jeanette said. She tried to stamp her foot, but the gesture was ineffectual on the carpeted car floor.

Here we are, Brad thought, in our beige Mercedes, coming home from church, having a quarrel; and he had no idea why. He saw them from afar, with the eyes of aspiration, like a handsome mature couple in a four-color ad. "If I can't help touching you," he said, "it's because I still love you. Isn't that nice?"

"It is," she said sulkily, then added, "Are you sure it's me you love or just some idea you have of me?"

This seemed to Brad a finicking distinction. She was positing a "real" her, a person apart from the one he was married to. But who would this be, unless it was the woman who took a cup of tea and went up the winding stairs to her cupola at odd hours? This woman disappeared. And no sooner did she disappear, when he was home, than two children began fighting, or the dry cleaner's delivery truck pulled into the driveway, and she had to be called down again.

"Did it ever occur to you," she asked now, "that you love me because it suits you? That for you it's an exercise in male power?"

"My God," he said indignantly, "who have you been reading? Would you rather I loved you because it *didn't* suit me?"

After a pause for thought, she admitted, in her smallest, tidiest voice, "That *would* be more romantic." He took this for a conciliatory joke, and believed their mysterious lapse of harmony to have been caused by her "change of life."

He became head of the vestry, and spent hours at the church, politicking, smoothing ruffled feathers. After the last of the children had been confirmed and excused from faithful attendance, Jeanette began to go to the eight o'clock service, before Brad was fully awake. She would return, shiny-faced, just as he was settling, a bit foggily, to a second cup of coffee and the sheaves of the Sunday *Globe.* She loved the lack of a sermon, she said, and the absence of that oppressive choir with those Fred Waring–like arrangements. She did not say that she enjoyed being by herself in church, as she had been in Boston many years ago. At the ten o'clock service, he missed her, the thin sweet piping of her singing beside him. He felt naked, as when alone on the deck of the imperilled *Enterprise.* He explained to Jeanette that he would happily push himself out of bed and go with her to the eight o'clock, but the committee people he had to talk to expected him to be at the ten o'clock. She relented, gradually, and resumed her place at his side. But she complained about the length of the sermon, and winced when the choir came on too strong. Brad wondered if their sons, who had become more or less anti-establishment, and incidentally anti-church, had infected her with their rebellion.

Ike was President, and then JFK. Joseph Kennedy, when Brad was young, had been a man to gossip about in Boston financial circles—a cocky mick with the bad taste not only to make a pot of money but then to leave Boston and head up the SEC under Roosevelt and his raving liberals. The nuances of the regional Irish-Yankee feud escaped Brad, since to his Midwestern eyes the two inimical camps were very similar—thin-skinned, clubby men from damp green islands, fond of a nip and long malicious stories. Brad never could catch the New England accent, never bring himself to force his "a"s and to say "Cuber" and "idear" the way the young President did so ringingly on television.

With their own young, the Schaeffers were lucky—the boys were a bit too old to fall into the heart of the drugs craze, and the girls were safely married before just living together became fashionable. One boy didn't finish college and became a carpenter in Vermont; the other did finish, at Amherst, but then moved to the West Coast to live. The two girls, however, stayed in the area, and provided new grandchildren at regular intervals. Brad's wedding-night prayer was, to all appearances, still being answered, decade after decade.

But as the Sixties wore into the Seventies, some misfortunes befell the Schaeffers as well as the nation. Both daughters went through messy divorces, involving countersuing husbands, scandalous depositions, and odd fits of nocturnal violence on the weedless lawns and in the neo-colonial bedrooms of Lynnfield and Dover. Freddy, the son on the West Coast, kept failing to get what could be called a job; he was always "in" things—in real estate, in public relations, in investments—without ever drawing a salary or making, as far as Brad could determine, a profit. Like Brad, Freddy had turned gray early, and suddenly there he was, well over thirty, a gray-haired boy, sweet-natured and with gracious, expensive tastes, who had never found his way into the economy. It worried Jeanette that to keep him going out there they were robbing the other children, especially the carpenter son, who by now had become a condo contractor and part-owner of a ski resort. They were grieved but at some level not surprised when poor Freddy was found dead in Glendale, of what was called an accidental drug overdose. A cocaine habit had backed him, financially, to the wall. He was found neatly dressed in a blue blazer and linen slacks—to the end, a gentleman, something Brad, in his own mind, had never become.

The Newton house huge and empty around them, the couple talked of moving to an apartment, but it seemed easier to turn off the radiators in a few rooms and stay where they were. Amid the ramparts of familiar furniture were propped and hung photographs of the children at happy turning-points—graduations, marriages, trips abroad. This grinning, tinted population extended now into the third generation, and was realer, more present, than the intermittent notes and phone calls from the children themselves. Brad knew in the abstract that he had changed diapers, driven boys to hockey and girls to ballet, supervised bedtime prayers, paternally stood by while tears were being shed and games were being played and the traumas of maturation endured; yet he could not muster much actual sensation of parenthood—those years were like a television sitcom during which he sat sleepily watching himself play the father. More vivid, returning in such unexpected detail that his eyes watered and the utter lostness of it all made him gasp, were moments of his and Jeanette's Boston days in the L-shaped apartment on Saint Botolph Street and then in the fifth-floor Commonwealth Avenue place—its leaky skylight, its peek at the Charles between chimney pots, its birdcage elevator—and of old times at the firm, before it moved from the walnut-panelled offices on Milk Street to a flimsy, flashy new skyscraper over on State. Certain business epiphanies—workday afternoons when an educated guess paid off in spades or a carefully cultivated friendship produced a big commission—could still put the taste of triumph into his mouth. Fun like that had fled the business when the Sixties' bull market collapsed. The people he had looked up to, the crusty Yankee money managers with names like Loring and Batchelder, were all retired. Brad himself retired at the age of sixty-eight, the same summer that Nixon resigned. In his loneliness those first months, in his guilty unease at being out of business uniform, he would visit Jeanette in her cupola.

She did not say she minded, but everything seemed to halt when he climbed the last, pie-slice-shaped steps, so the room had the burnished silence of a clock that has just stopped ticking. She sat lit from all sides, surrounded by windows, her soft brown hair scarcely touched by gray and the wrinkles of her face none of them deep, so that her head seemed her youthful head softened by a webbed veil. The rug she had been hooking was set in its frame at the side of her armchair, and a magazine lay in her lap, but she did not seem to be doing anything—so deeply engaged in gazing out a window through the tops of the beeches that she did not even turn her head at his entrance. Her motionlessness slightly frightened him. He stood a second, getting his breath. Where once just the tip of the old Hancock Building had showed above the treetops, in the distance, now a silvery cluster of tall glass boxes reflected the sun. He had always been nervous in high places, and as his eyes plunged down, parallel with her gaze, through the bare winter branches toward the dead lawn three stories below, his thighs tightened and he shuffled self-protectively toward the center of the room.

Since she said nothing, he asked, "Do you feel all right?"

"Of course," Jeanette answered, firmly. "Why wouldn't I?"

"I don't know, my dear. You seem so quiet."

"I like being quiet. I always have. You know that."

"Oh yes." He felt challenged, and slightly dazed. "I know that."

"So let's think of something for you to do," she said, at last turning, with one of her usual neat motions, to give him her attention. And she would send him back down, down to the basement, say, to repair a framed photograph that had fallen from its nail one night, when no one was looking, and broken its glass. It was strange, Brad reflected, that in this room of her own Jeanette had hung no pictures of the children, or of him. But, then, there was little wall space between the many windows, and the cushioned window seats, two-thirds of the way around the room, were littered with old paintings, crocheted cushions, and books whose cloth covers the circling sun had bleached. He thought of it as her meditation room, though he had no clear idea of what meditation was; in even the silent seconds inserted between rote petitions at church, his own brain skidded off into that exultant plotting which divine service stimulated in him.

Her illness came on imperceptibly at first, and then with cruel speed. They were watching television one night—the hostages had been taken in Iran, and every day it seemed something *had* to happen on the news. Suddenly Jeanette put her hand on his wrist. They were sitting side by side on the red upholstered Hepplewhite-style love seat that they had impulsively bought at Paine's in the late Forties, during a blizzard, before the move to Newton. Because of the storm, the vast store was nearly empty, and it seemed they must do something to justify their presence, and to celebrate the weather. His love for her always returned full force when it snowed. "What?" he asked now, startled by her unaccustomed gesture.

"Nothing." She smiled. "A tiny pain."

"Where?" he asked, monosyllabic as if just awakened. The news at that moment showed an interview with a young Iranian revolutionary who spoke fluent, Midwestern-accented English, and Jeanette's exact answer escaped Brad. If in the course of their marriage there was one act for which he blamed himself—could identify as a sin for which he deserved to be punished—it was this moment of inattention, when Jeanette first, after weeks of hugging her discomforts to herself, began to confide, in her delicate voice, what she would rather have kept hidden.

The days that followed, full of doctors and their equipment, lifted all secrecy from the disease and its course. It was cancer, metastasizing from the liver, though she had never been a drinker. For Brad these days were busy ones; after the five years of retirement, of not knowing quite what to do with himself, he was suddenly housekeeper, cook, chauffeur, switchboard operator, nurse. Isolated in their big house, while their three children anxiously visited and then hurried back to their own problems, and their friends and neighbors tried to tread the thin line between kindness and interference, the couple that winter had a kind of honeymoon. An air of adventure, of the exotic, tinged their excursions to clinics and specialists tucked into sections of Boston they had never visited before. They spent all their hours together, and became more than ever one. His own scalp itched as her soft hair fell away under the barrage of chemotherapy; his own stomach ached when she would not eat. She would greet with a bright smile the warmth and aroma of the food he brought to the table or her bed, and she would take one forkful, so she could tell him how good it was; then, with a magical slowness meant to make the gesture invisible, Jeanette would let the fork slowly sink back to the plate, keeping her fingers on the silver handle as if at any moment she might decide to use it again. In this position she sometimes even dozed off, under the sway of medication. Brad learned to treat her not eating as a rebuff he must overlook. If he urged the food upon her, sternly or playfully, real anger, of the petulant and surprisingly bitter kind that a child harbors, would break through her stoical, drugged calm.

The other irritant, strangely, seemed to be the visits of the young Episcopal clergyman. He had come to the church this year, after the long reign of a hearty, facetious man no one had had to take seriously. The new rector possessed a self-conscious, honey-smooth voice, and curly pale hair already receding from his temples, young as he was. Brad, who had been privy to the infighting among the search-committee members that had preceded his selection, admired his melodious sermons and his conservative demeanor; ten years ago a clergyman his age would have been trying to radicalize everybody. But Jeanette complained that his visits to the house—though they rarely extended for more than fifteen minutes—tired her. When she became too frail, too emaciated and constantly drowsy, to leave her bedroom, and the young man proposed that he bring Communion to her, she asked Brad to tell him, "Another time."

The room at Mass. General Hospital to which she was eventually moved overlooked, across a great air well, a concrete wall of steel-rimmed windows. The wing was modern, built on the rubble of the old West End. It was late March, the first spring of a new decade. Though on sunny days a few giggling nurses and hardy patients took their lunches on cardboard trays out to the patio at the base of the air well, the sky was usually an agitated gray and the hospital heat was turned way up. During his visits Brad often removed his suit coat, it was so hot in Jeanette's room.

Dressed in a white hospital johnny and a pink quilted bed jacket with ribbons, she looked pretty against her pillows, though on a smaller scale than the woman he had known so long. Her cheeks still had some plumpness, and her fine straight nose and clear eyes and narrow arched brows—old-fashioned eyebrows, which looked plucked though they weren't—still made the compact, highly finished impression that had aways excited him, that kindled a fire within him. Her hair was growing back, a cap of soft brown bristle, since chemotherapy had been abandoned. Only her hands, laid inert and fleshless on the blanket, betrayed that something terrible was happening to her.

One day she told him, with a touch of mischief, "Our young parson was in from Newton this morning, and I told him not to bother anymore."

"You sent the priest away?" Brad's aged voice seemed to rumble and crackle in his ears, in contrast to Jeanette's, which sounded crystalline and distant.

" 'Priest,' for heaven's sake," she said. "Why can't you just call him a minister?" It had been a joke of sorts between them, how High Church he had become. When on occasion they visited the Church of the Advent on Brimmer Street, she had ridiculed the incense, the robed teams of acolytes. "He makes me tired," she said now.

"But don't you want to keep up with Communion?" It was his favorite sacrament; he harbored an inner image, a kind of religious fantasy, of the wafer and wine turning, with a muffled explosion, to pure light in the digestive system.

"Like 'keeping up' an insurance policy," she sighed, and did sound tired, tired to death. "It seems so pointless."

"But you *must,*" Brad said, panicked.

"I must? Why must I? Who says I must?" The blue of her challenging eyes and the fevered flush of her cheeks made a garish contrast.

"Why, because . . . you know why. Because of the salvation of your soul. That's what you used to talk about when I first met you."

She looked toward the window with a faint smile. "When I used to go alone to Copley Methodist. I loved that church; it was so bizarre, with its minaret. Dear old Doctor Stidger, on and on. Now it's just a parking lot. Salvation of the soul." Her gaunt chest twitched—a laugh that didn't reach her lips.

He lowered his eyes, feeling mocked. His own hands, an old man's gnarled, spotted claws, were folded together between his knees. "You mean you don't believe?" In his inner ear he felt all the height of space concealed beneath the floor, down and down.

"Oh, darling," she said. "Doesn't it just seem an awful lot of bother?"

"Not a bit?" he persisted.

Jeanette sighed again and didn't answer.

"Since when?"

"I don't know. No," she said, "that's not being honest. We should start being honest. I do know. Since you took it from me. You moved right in. It didn't seem necessary, for the *two* of us to keep it up."

"But . . ." He couldn't say, so late, how fondly he had intended it, enlisting at her side.

She offered to console him. "It doesn't matter, does it?" When he remained silent, feeling blackness all about him, to every point on the horizon, as on those nights in the Pacific, she shifted to a teasing note: "Honey, why does it matter?"

She knew. Because his death was also close. He lifted his eyes and saw her as enviably serene, having wrought this vengeance. A nurse rustled at the door, her syringe clinking in its aluminum tray, and across the air well in the blue spring twilight the lights had come on, rectangles of gold. It had begun, a few dry flakes, to spit snow.

Though she had asked that there be absolutely no religious service, Brad and the young minister arranged one, following the oldest-fashioned, wholly impersonal rite. Jeanette would have been seventy-one in May, and Brad was three years older. He continued to go to the ten o'clock service, his erect figure carrying his white hair like a flag. But it was sheer inert motion; there were no falcon flights of his mind anymore, no small, true voice at his side. There was nothing. He wished he could think otherwise, but he had believed in her all those years and could not stop now.

Getting into the Set

FOR THE FIRST YEARS that Nick and Katie Higginson lived in the little New England town, they were preoccupied with their house, an early-eighteenth-century saltbox that had been allowed to drift perilously close to complete dilapidation. The beams in the dirt cellar were powdery with dry rot; the lovely old fireplaces, with their wrought-iron spits and inset bake ovens, had been bricked and boarded over. The floors—the irreplaceable broad pine floorboards—had been painted dark hard colors and, in the room that became the Higginsons' dining room, covered with several layers of linoleum. The house, though not large, had been divided; to accommodate the families that lived in both halves, upstairs rooms had been partitioned, downstairs doors had been removed, and makeshift arrangements of plumbing and wiring had been pushed and cut through the precious old woodwork. Some raised-field panelling had been, incredibly, wallpapered over, and layers of poisonous green paint had all but obscured the beauty of the exquisite shell cupboard to the left of the fireplace in the living room—the house's gem, with its serpentine shelves and curved back panels, all framed in bolection-molded trim and stop-fluted pilasters. Nick and Katie scraped and refinished, and what they could not do paid others to do. The floors, worn in visible troughs near the doorways and along the central hall, were pried up board by board and relaid and sanded level. A downstairs bathroom was built into the space of an abandoned stairway. Unobtrusive baseboard hot-water heating replaced the ponderous cast-iron radiators, whose paint had been peeled by their own steam; dainty twelve-over-twelve sash windows were restored where a previous owner had barbarously installed casemented Thermopane.

Through her new windows Katie would gaze out at the street, one of the town's main streets; a block away, the shops began, and people shopping downtown often had to park in front of the Higginsons'. There was, she realized those first years, a set of people in town about her and Nick's age, who saluted one another on the sidewalk and even embraced, as if a jovial reunion were constantly in progress. They wore, these young adults in their early thirties, a ramshackle and reckless yet well-heeled air; they seemed, in winter sunshine or summer shade, in quilted parkas or cotton shorts, to be always between parties. She and Nick had joined the available organizations, the conservation group and the Congregational church and the historical society, and yet no parties forthcame. She learned the names of some of the set—Brick Matthews and his wife, Felicia; Tory Riddle and her husband, Trevor; the Ledyards, Joan and Kenneth—but not the way in.

Katie was a tall woman with a high glossy forehead that made her seem somewhat brittle and prim. Yet her figure was good, and her spirit unsatisfied. She had married Nick when she was only twenty, not finishing college, and two children, a boy and a girl, had arrived rapidly, exhausting her breeding instinct. Now that both children were in school, her days stretched long; she had taken to doing household tasks better suited to an elderly spinster. Nick's parents had died rather prematurely, leaving the young couple a great deal of handsome antique furniture, including a mahogany double-pedestal-base dining table and six Chippendale dining chairs whose old crewelwork seats had over the years become threadbare and stained. Katie picked six harmonizing but not identical floral needlepoint patterns and set about the long task of executing them—as if she needed some endless chore to fill the time between now and the grave. Nick had found such a chore for himself: he was paving the old cellar, mixing a few bags of sand and cement at a time, often descending after dinner and coming up, begrimed and blinking, well after Katie, wearied by the nightly rituals of putting the children to bed, had herself fallen asleep. The needlepointing hurt her eyes after an hour, but at her tender age she was resisting getting close-distance glasses.

The children made possible the first step, on the beach. Katie's confidence was enhanced in a bathing suit; furthermore, there was a kind of emboldening democracy at the beach, so sunstruck and broad and murmurous. The tame tumult of its surf merged in the ear with the hum of bathers, the hundreds of exclamations and conversations all testifying to some central treasure, some hidden honey. Her eight-year-old, Chris, had joined another boy in building a sand castle; this boy, when the castle was undermined by a lunge of the tide, joined a group of children and mothers that included Felicia Matthews and Joan Ledyard. Chris followed his new friend into their midst, and Katie hesitantly trailed after him, in case he was being a nuisance. "Not at all," the elegantly brown Matthews woman told her, staring upwards with eyes scrunched small as diamonds in the sun.

There were several young mothers Katie didn't know by sight, and she felt ungainly, standing. She was putting the others in her shadow. "Sit down if you'd like," the Ledyard woman said, after a pause in which, Katie imagined, a silent debate had been held in the air. Katie sat inelegantly on the damp sand and listened as the other women chattered. Chris soon got bored; the boy whose castle he had helped build ignored him in favor of the more familiar playmates who clustered in this nest of beach chairs and reclining women. When Chris rejoined his sister, on a distant blanket, his mother had to follow. Katie tried to express in her goodbyes how grateful she was for these ten minutes of shared company; the responding farewells sounded faint and perfunctory, like wind chimes.

But a step had been made. She described, that evening, the encounter to Nick. "They seemed just terribly nice, and quite funny, really, their way of putting things."

"For example."

"Oh, I don't know, it's hard to remember. A lot of it has to do with the tone of voice. The way Felicia called her husband 'the old man,' and spoke of her children as 'the littles.' It doesn't sound so funny when I say it, but in the context . . ."

"O.K.," Nick said, anxious to get to his basement. Though fearful of rats, she had more than once gone down the cellar steps with him and tried to share his delight and sense of gradual triumph, each day's gobs hardened by next day into an adamant gray chunk of floor. It was like an army —his army of particles, consolidating, spreading to all the dark, cobwebbed corners. The foundation of the house had been made of fieldstones, laid up without mortar, and after the floor was finished Nick intended to cement and point all these stones, fixing them in place rigidly.

Now at the beach Katie sometimes dared sit with one or two of the wives of the set, if there were not too many. A group bigger than three she declined to join, imagining that she was winning points with her tact. Even when there were just two or three, she was aware of worlds of allusion that her presence was suppressing, allusions to scandals brewing or brewed, to gatherings that had taken place or would take place. The set in season played tennis and paddle tennis, went sailing and skiing and picnicking. In the late spring, Katie had gathered, there was an annual canoe trip down the river as far as the factory and the falls, and on Sundays in the autumn, the men played touch football in somebody's field. "Oh, Nick played football in high school!" she volunteered one August day, when the subject had slipped into conversation; over these summer weeks Felicia and Tory and Joan had become a bit careless of their gossip in her presence. Katie had once regaled them with a word-picture of Nick and his basement and, since a comic husband seemed to be a ticket to acceptance by these women, she offered it again. "He played a floating end, or whatever they call those people who aren't very strong and can't throw the ball, either."

There was a silence, washed across by the desultory sounds of the dying summer—the waves becalmed, the crowds thinned. "They may not be doing it this year," Joan Ledyard at last said. "They're all a year older."

"But if they do and need somebody," Katie persisted, blushing at her own shamelessness, "they should call Nick; it would be so *good* for him."

When, a month later, the call did come, Katie was startled, even frightened, by the gravelly, barking man's voice at the other end of the line. He didn't identify himself and asked for Nick; she called her husband up from the cellar. Nick spoke to the man in grudging monosyllables. "Who on earth was it?" Katie asked when he had hung up.

His eyes, she thought, looked fishy behind the plastic goggles he wore to protect them from cement dust. "Some guy called Trevor Riddle. He'd heard I'd like to play touch football. I don't know where he got that idea; I hate the damn game. I nearly got my neck broken playing football in high school."

"You didn't say no!"

"You heard me talking. I thanked him and said I'd keep it in mind. That's as good as saying no."

Katie was determined not to cry, though she felt as if a door had been slammed in her face. Nick lifted his goggles to see her better; she flounced away. That night, she dressed for bed not in the sheer persimmon-colored shortie that he liked and that was something of a Saturday-night tradition for them, but in the long-sleeved flannel nightgown he said made her look like an old lady.

The next day turned out to be an invitingly brisk September Sunday, with the smell of apples and hay in the air. After lunch, though he had promised the children a bicycle ride, Nick put on some old corduroys and a sweatshirt and his jogging shoes, and went off to play touch football. When he came back, he was limping; he had sprained his ankle. Also, his speech was slightly loud and slurred. There had been drinks, afterwards, at someone's house. Again, Katie resisted tears; she had not been invited. He explained, "Only some of the wives came, and others weren't there; I couldn't figure out the system, and figured I'd have a quick sip and be right home. Then I got to talking to some guy called Leadman, Leadbelly . . ."

"Ken Ledyard."

"Right. About siding. He says they have a new Fiberglas clapboard now that breathes just like wood."

"Nick, you're drunk, and you're not going to ruin this lovely old house with Fiberglas siding! It's bad enough what you've done in the basement, smothering all the nice old dirt!" She dashed from the room as if to hide tears; but in truth she had remembered that she had turned down the lamb in the oven when Nick was so late coming home. It needed to be turned up again. And Katie needed to be alone with her new information, and to contemplate her next step.

"You should offer to have drinks here," she told Nick one Sunday after he had hobbled home with grassy knees and glazed eyes. The post-football drinks rotated from house to house, he reported; he had been playing for six weeks, and it was nearly November. "I don't know," he said. "It might seem pushy."

"Why wouldn't it just seem courteous?"

"They seem pretty happy with things the way they are."

"It's all very well for you to say—you see them every week."

"They're not so great, actually. Kind of noisy and silly, really, and can't talk about anything except each other. Why don't you just come over sometime, toward the end of the game, and watch, and then tag along? A lot of the wives do that. I made a terrific catch today, you should have seen it—over the shoulder, running full tilt."

"I wouldn't *dream* of going anywhere where I wasn't invited."

"They don't really in*vite,* you know. It's just who's there, and what develops."

"Oh, you're so *in* it's killing. You could invite them next Sunday for the following."

"Well . . . it's awkward."

"Exactly. Awkward is just how I find it, too," Katie said, feeling her angry blush rise from her cheeks, through her forehead to her hairline.

The next Sunday he reported, "Brick Matthews said it sounded nice, but he wasn't sure there'd still be touch football. It depends on the frost. They don't like to play once there's frost in the ground; it gets too slippery."

"It sounds to me," Katie said, "that it's Brick Matthews who's slippery. There's plenty of lovely weather left, right through Thanksgiving. I've changed my mind. I don't want them to come. They're *your* friends—you go take them all to the bar at the Amvets."

The next Sunday afternoon, however, just in case, she tidied up the downstairs and prettily improvised a bar in the shell cupboard, with newly bought bottles and plastic glasses and paper cocktail napkins. The needle-point was beginning to sting her eyes in the dusk, when the porch resounded with many heavy footsteps. The house trembled. Then there was a clamorous rapping of the door knocker, insistent and rude; but she opened the door smilingly. Nick, pale-faced and standing on one leg, was being supported between two large, muddy, red-faced men. "He's sprained it again," she said, before any of them could speak. More cars were drawing up to the curb, releasing men in sneakers and wives in quilted parkas and wool slacks. November had turned cold; there had been frost for several nights. This crowd stood on the sidewalk, staring up at the house—its many-mullioned shiny new windows, its freshly painted and gilded blue-and-gold eagle plaque above the formal Georgian doorway—while the party on the porch negotiated.

"It may be worse than that," one of the men supporting Nick told her, with a sheepish air of collusion. His was the rough voice that had alarmed Katie over the phone: Trevor Riddle.

"I heard something snap," Nick said in that irritating whine he put on when he had a cold or a bad day at work. "Turned to make a catch and some clumsy bastard plowed right into me."

"That was me," the other supporting man explained. Katie recognized him, belatedly, as Brick Matthews; she had only seen him before at the historical society, in a three-piece gray business suit. Now he was wearing a dirty yellow cable-knit sweater and his hair stood out all around his head in stiff cedar-colored curls. "I tried to cut back, and slipped on the mud. The frost, you know, gets into the ground, and then it melts on the top."

"I'm sure it's just that same sprain," Katie said. "Why don't you all come in for a drink?"

Entering the house, the men seemed enormous, scarcely a one under six feet and all exuding animal warmth and a confident tang of sweat. The women, too, out of their bathing suits and into sweaters, bulked larger than Katie remembered. They moved toward the bar in a herd. While she rushed into the kitchen to replenish the ice, Tory Riddle and a dark-haired woman she didn't know fussed over Nick, setting him up in the bargello wing chair and easing under his wounded ankle the silk-covered Newport footstool with the cabriole legs. Inherited furniture that, because of its desiccated delicacy, Nick and Katie rarely used was suddenly thrust this way and that under a surge of friendly bodies. Two canework side chairs were brought forward from their basically ornamental position flanking the veneered card table that stood with half of its round folding top leaning silhouetted against the wall. The dark japanned chest that rested beneath one window, and off of whose golden, ghostly scene of men with bows and arrows hunting a maneless lion Katie was always clearing newspapers that Nick carelessly left there, now offered a perch for Joan Ledyard, who was using the little Minton porcelain basket as an ashtray. Neither Nick nor Katie smoked; suddenly there was a widespread need for ashtrays. Some of the men even puffed big cigars. On her way to the kitchen to look for suitable receptacles, she saw that the party had spilled over into the dining room, and that several wet rings were already whitening the table's mahogany surface while Felicia Matthews and some tall man whose name Katie didn't know were huddled close in conversation. As she was hurrying back down the hall with a paper towel, a tablecloth, and some saucers for ashtrays, Brick Matthews locked his furry hand around her forearm. "Why don't you have a drink and relax?" he asked.

Something about him made her leap into *non sequiturs*. "I'm so worried about Nick," she said. "Suppose his ankle is broken, like he said?"

"Suppose it is; another hour won't make any difference. He's on his second drink and feeling no pain. What about you?"

"Me?" Her thought was still aimed at wiping those rings before they sank into the finish.

"All summer my wife's been raving to me about what a terrific figure this woman has down at the beach."

"If you're looking for your wife, she's in the dining room talking to somebody."

"Don't I know it. What can I get you, Katie?"

"Get me?" He was one of those men whose chest hair comes up very high; above the neck of his sweatshirt there was a froth the color of pencil shavings.

"G-and-t, whiskey, Bloody Mary . . ."

"Just a white-wine spritzer," she said. "Very weak."

"I might have guessed," he said, with cheerful disgust, and did not follow her into the dining room. Felicia's conversation in there had deepened; averting her face as the tall, sulky-looking man poured words into her ear, she was plucking petals from the bowl of chrysanthemums Katie had arranged as a centerpiece and was rolling them into thin tubes she dropped one by one on the tabletop. Katie quickly, apologetically spread the cloth over the mess and retreated to the living room.

A thick blue stratum of tobacco smoke hung beneath the newly plastered ceiling. The noise level had risen; the touch-football game was being replayed in one conversation, and the recent town election was being deplored in another. The two children had come downstairs from watching television and stood like tiny guards, bewildered but watchful, by the arms of Nick's wing chair. He looked up with a glazed smile while Trevor Riddle's harsh guffaw soared above him; the joke must have been at Nick's expense, for he reluctantly joined in. The noise, Katie thought, was like that hive of voices at the beach, brought closer and pressed against the ear. Brick Matthews handed her a wineglass of pale fluid that the first taste proved to be not a spritzer but a Martini. "White wine's all gone," he told her.

"How awful; let me look in the fridge."

"Relax. I already did. Ken's gone home for some, and another fifth of gin. Now, tell me what you do to keep in such great shape."

"I do needlepoint," she said, knowing the reaction this would get, but minding less than she would have even an hour ago his hot, forced laugh, his determined effort to get her gaze to meet his watery eyes, his slightly painful grip on her forearm. She downed the Martini quickly, since she hated the taste, and stood at the side of several excited conversations to which she had nothing to contribute. Another Martini was handed to her, and she began to have things to say. Time speeded up, so that though some people left, and others seemed to rearrive, and she later remembered herself taking the children upstairs and tucking them in, it felt like an abrupt miracle that nine o'clock had come to the brass face of the tall walnut case clock that Nick's greatgrandfather had once brought from Philadelphia. Nick was no longer in the flame-stitched wing chair. Only the dark-haired woman was left in the living room. She had exotic olive skin, as even in color as if painted on. She introduced herself to Katie with a firm handshake: "I'm Vivian Crewes. My husband has been in the dining room all this time. Brick's going to round them up so we can all go. You've been wonderful. This is such a lovely house, and you've done such good things with it. I do hope Nickie's trip to the hospital doesn't produce any bad news."

"Nick's at the hospital?"

"I think you were in the kitchen trying to get the icemaker to work. The swelling seemed to be getting worse, and he was losing feeling in the toes. Ken Ledyard took him, in the Matthewses' car, since Joan had to go home and feed the children."

From the dining room came a spurt of muffled male grunts, and then a crash, a sound of wood sliding and breaking, followed by the somehow dispassionate tinkle of glass. Katie tried to move through her alcoholic

laziness to see what the damage was, but the hallway was blocked by Brick
Matthews, dragging something behind him that turned out to be Felicia.
He had seized her by one arm and she was bumping along on her bottom,
her heels kicking at the pine floor as she writhed to regain her feet. Brick
winked at Katie. "My wife loves parties," he said. "I always have to drag
her away." The joke made, he allowed Felicia to get to her feet; he kept
squinting on one side of his big red face, in case she decided to hit him.

The tall man followed them. He was caressing his mouth; his lips were
pouting and possibly bruised. "The awfullest thing is, dear," he told his
own wife, "we all have to go in our car, since the damn fools gave Ken
theirs!"

The dark-haired woman squeezed one of Katie's hands between her two;
her olive hands were thin and cool yet tremulous, as if propelled by the
pulse of a hummingbird. "Please excuse us," she said. "This was darling.
You and Nick must come to our house, soon."

The last car roared away from the curb, where Katie had more than
once seen members of the set embrace. Where Felicia's heels had kicked
the soft old pine boards there were long gray dents. In the dining room, the
woman's agitation had consumed a whole chrysanthemum, its petals
turned into tubes that littered the tablecloth. The cloth had been tugged to
one side, and wet plastic glasses and a quarter of a lime rested on the
luminous wood. One of the Chippendale chairs, one of the two with a
completed needlepoint covering, had been knocked onto its side by the
men's struggle and, worse, the new window had buckled: several of the fine
"period" mullions, specially milled, had snapped and three panes of glass
had broken.

In the living room, where the smell of smoke would cling to the draper-
ies for weeks, the damage was subtler. Salted peanuts and chips for the
onion dip had been dropped and heedlessly ground into Nick's mother's
lovely old blue Tabriz. The men had all been wearing these running shoes
with patterned soles that pack dirt between their little cleats, and everywhere, on the rug and the wide pine floorboards, were grid prints and
crumbs of dried mud. The japanned chest, sure enough, showed a crack in
its heavily varnished lid, cutting across the floating golden mountains. The
silk cushion of the footstool was soaked from melted ice applied to Nick's
ankle.

The ash-laden saucers could be emptied and washed and the plastic
glasses picked up and thrown away, but what of the cigarette burns? Not
one but several people, getting drinks for themselves at the bar set up in
the shell cupboard, had put down cigarettes and let them burn past the
molded serpentine edges of the reddish pearwood shelves. There were so

many of these charred lines in a row it seemed a game had been played, or an initiation rite enacted. Katie knew every curved inch of these shelves; she and Nick had spent hours at the cupboard, their heads swimming with the fumes of paint remover, the careful scraping of their tools the only sound between them. She turned, to face the wrecked room with hot eyes. The tears could come now, now that they were tears of happiness.

The Wallet

FULHAM had assembled a nice life—blue-eyed wife still presentable and trim after thirty-three years of marriage, red-haired daughter off in the world and doing well, handsome white house in one of the older suburbs—yet the darkness was not quite sealed out. Dread would attack him, curiously, in movie theatres, during the showing of escapist kiddie films at that. He had, at the age of sixty-five, an eleven-year-old grandson, Tod, and a nine-year-old granddaughter, Antoinette, and on those not uncommon weekends when the grandparents were asked to babysit, his contribution to the entertainment would be to take them to a Saturday- or Sunday-afternoon movie.

The theatre complex at the nearby mall had been built as four theatres, and then further partitioned to make six; the walls, masked by giant psychedelic drapes, were so insubstantial that the rumble of one film's climax easily penetrated into the hushed moments of another. For some reason of constructional economy the movie screens were not exactly square to the rows of seats, and the audiences therefore settled to one side of the theatre, like passengers on a cruise boat at sunset. These viewing conditions constituted just enough hardship to amuse Fulham, along with the remarkable stickiness of the floors, which were so saturated in spilled soft drink as to release the soles of his shoes with an audible snap. He was also amused by the remarkable youth of the other moviegoers—gum-chewing, frizzy-haired girls in stencilled T-shirts and buttock-hugging cutoffs, and boys the menace of whose ragged tank tops and punk haircuts was belied by an androgynous softness of form and a quizzical mildness of expression worlds removed from the truly menacing, Depression-hardened toughs of the aging man's own youth.

His moviegoing had begun in a small Massachusetts town, in a theatre with vaguely Mexican decor and huge fake organ pipes. Since his parents worked late in the family drugstore, he went to the movies a great deal; he even had a favorite seat—back row, extreme left—and a famous laugh. Older people he scarcely knew would tell his parents over the drugstore counter that their boy had been at the show last night, they had heard him. He loved the black-and-white world that Hollywood manufactured in those years; he took pleasure in following the minor actors, Guy Kibbee and Edward Everett Horton and Adolphe Menjou and Charles Coburn, from role to role, a huge family of familiar, avuncular faces and rapid, mock-furious voices. Then Fulham's moviegoing had shifted to the khaki-filled rec halls of Southern army bases and, during his Boston days of college and courtship, to art-film houses where one waited in espresso-scented lobbies to absorb the latest postwar bulletins from the troubled spirits of Bergman and Antonioni, Fellini and Buñuel. With marriage and children and the advent of television, Fulham became ever more homebound, one more member of that vast lost audience which Hollywood at first courted with desperate displays of skin and blood and finally quite abandoned. Sitting drowsily with his wife through some chopped, commercial-riddled rerun of a film they had both sentimentally cherished, Fulham was struck by how feeble and cynically mechanical these pre–wide-screen classics were, these creaky old vehicles that once had lifted him far out of himself and whose high moments had lingered in millions of brains like his in lieu of religious visions.

The world is pitched toward the ignorant young, he could only realize now that he was no longer young. In the company of his grandchildren he went to movies rated G or PG—lavishly engineered romances involving spaceships and slapstick, special effects and mystical puppets, with abrupt allusions to marijuana and sex tossed in, Fulham supposed, to flatter the teen-agers in the audience. His pre-pubescent grandson laughed hard at these naughty bits, with a piercing eager laugh that reminded Fulham of his childish own, while the little girl, robotically feeding popcorn into her face, refused to smile at what she did not understand. She had inherited her mother's very fine, shiny, carrot-colored hair.

Sitting between these small heads in the flickering light, while on the screen some mechanical dragon unfolded its wings or starships did special-effects battle with supposed laser beams, Fulham would be visited by terror: the walls of the theatre would fall away, the sticky floor become a chasm beneath his feet. His true situation in time and space would be revealed to him: a speck of consciousness now into its seventh decade, a mortal body poised to rejoin the minerals, a member of a lost civilization that once existed on a sliding continent. The curvature of the immense Earth beneath his chair and the solidity of the piece of earth that would cover Fulham's grave would become suffocatingly real to him, all in an instant; he would begin to sweat. There was a *seriousness* to human existence, an absolute irreversibility, from which all our social arrangements and entertainments attempt to divert us. No, there was no "us" to it, no "our"—it was *his* existence, his in his totally lonely possession of it, that was so sickeningly serious.

Why? Why should he be afflicted here? The images and music emanating from the screen were somehow the means of conveying to his apprehension these leaden, unbearable truths. Movies had always been realler than life to him, bright gaps in the daily, dutiful fog. These "kiddie" movies were coarsely mythic; they portrayed other worlds, he reasoned, and death, toward which he was headed, was another world. All these films had in them episodes involving heights, great spaces, places one might never get back from. To be out there, among the stars! One of his earliest memories was a fear of not getting home on time, of being stuck in a wrong place. His mother had been a tyrannical worrier, his dose-measuring father a fiend for punctuality. Now Fulham had few years left to live, and here he was in a sticky movie house, wasting a priceless afternoon, when he could have been trimming his bushes or bringing his accounts up to date. Such self-analysis slowly diluted the premonition of extinction thrust upon him as he sat sunk between his grandchildren, with their towering life expectancies. By the time the villains had all been detonated and the credits were rolling and the lights came on, Fulham had nursed himself back to the appearance and manner of a normal, cheerful grandfather.

Tod would then beg for a quarter to play a video game in the lobby. Fulham marvelled at the dexterity with which the child manipulated the swift electronic phantoms as they beeped and buzzed. Today, he cajoled his grandfather into playing. "You play, Grandpa."

"I'd just as soon not, thank you kindly."

"Ah, go ahead. Give yourself a cheap thrill."

"Grandpa doesn't want to," Antoinette interposed. "He doesn't feel well."

"Who says I don't feel well?"

The little girl solemnly considered him, with her shiny eyes, beneath her shiny hair. "You look sick to your stomach," she said.

His abdominal muscles did ache, as if he had lifted something heavy. "Maybe I need some fun," he admitted.

She shrugged, and her brother showed Fulham how to operate the controls. But Fulham's little screened fighter ship, a triangular thing like a bit of luminous origami, got stuck in a corner, and nothing he could do with the confusingly numerous knobs moved it away. Instead, it twirled like a trapped animal, and when it fired its guns was annihilated by its own ricocheting rays. Shrill little Tod screamed with disbelieving hilarity. GAME CONCLUDED, the screen announced.

Fulham didn't see what was quite so funny. People in the lobby had turned their heads toward Tod's conspicuous laugh. Fulham was sweating again, and it took him some seconds to realize that the small insistent face, as round and white and incisively marked as the face of a clock, had chimed something up at him: he was being asked for another quarter. "Come on, Grandpa. It's only two bits," the child demanded.

"No," Fulham said, with considerable satisfaction, and led the children to his car and home. By the time his own child showed up with her husband, both young adults rosy-faced and loud from their tennis match or cocktail party, he was glad to see the grandchildren taken away, and his large white house in Wellesley returned to the order that he and his wife maintained.

With a history of hypertension, Fulham had taken early retirement from his brokerage firm, and managed his own investments and those of a favored few old clients in an upstairs room. He went to this room, overlooking his side yard's trimmed shrubs, every morning with his *Wall Street Journal* and second cup of decaffeinated coffee. He kept up his charts and his correspondence, made his phone calls and a daily visit to the post office; but the illusion of integration with the larger circuits of the world was harder to maintain than when he enjoyed a corner office on the nineteenth floor of a Boston skyscraper, with swift-moving secretaries to shield and buttress him and to turn his hesitant murmurs of dictation into official communications, on engraved company stationery. Now that the postmen of an increasingly lazy and insolent government were no longer permitted to walk up to a doorway more than a specified distance from the sidewalk, his mail came to him in a tin box down by his white picket fence, and this casual and hazardous housing somehow made additional light of the old pomp of finance.

For some days he had been expecting a large check, which the sender, a Houston oil company, had not chosen to send by registered mail or any of the express services now available. The check, in the low six figures, repre-

sented considerable acumen and initial investment on Fulham's part, and
he was anxious to stow it away in one of his bank accounts. Every noon,
after the mailman—a young man who with annoying musicality whistled
opera arias as he strolled along—had banged shut the lid of the box,
Fulham hurried down the long brick walk to discover, amid the wads of
bills and fourth-class solicitations, if the check had come. It had not, day
after day. Standing by the mailbox, he could feel his heart thudding, an-
noyingly, like one of those large trucks that, defying a clearly posted sign,
went by every now and then on their quiet street, making the house shudder. A week passed, and then another. Phone calls to Houston produced
only a series of drawling assurances that the check had been mailed and
had not been cashed, and undoubtedly it would show up. One lady, who
from the resonant lilt of her voice seemed to be black and, like the mailman, excessively musical, even explained to him that the company never
registered checks, on the theory that this called attention to them and in
some cases had instigated thievery, among the poorer class of postal workers.

The possibility of thievery had not in so many words occurred to Fulham; he had always thought of the postal service as an overarching entity,
like the cloud pattern projected nightly on Channel 5, which, however
unpredictable, in the last analysis inevitably delivers every bit of vapor
entrusted to it. Now the possibility had been raised that the system had
holes in it, through one of which had fallen a sum of money that should be
his, numbers that should already be punched into his bank's computer and
generating interest for his account. Each day that the check didn't arrive,
he computed, he was losing more money than it cost him and his wife to
eat. His calls to Houston rose in pitch of insistence, and his comforters
correspondingly rose in the company's hierarchy, urging him, however, in
the end, to wait a few more days before asking them—as was his privilege,
of course—to stop the check and issue another.

He slept poorly, agitated by the injustice of it. There was no one to
blame and no court in which to place an appeal—just an impenetrable
delivery system stretched airily between New England and Texas. Awake
at odd hours, he imagined footsteps softly passing on the sidewalk and
hands rattling at his mailbox. The box itself, substituted by governmental
decree for his infallibly retentive front-door letter slot, seemed a perilous
extension of himself, an indefensible outpost, subject to graffiti and casual
battering. He tried to imagine in detail the processes of the mails—the
belts, the sacks, the shufflings, the sorting machines that fling envelopes
heedlessly in all directions. He yearned to seize and shake that vast imagined system, to shake loose that stuck small fortune so blithely confided to

a scrap of paper within another, folded, scrap. The wish to shake shook him; Fulham's pulpy, intimidated heart filled his skull, the bed, and the bedroom with its thumping.

His wife, woken by his furious rotation beneath the covers, couldn't grasp the problem, the indignity. Each day, she still ate three thoughtfully chosen and prettily prepared meals; she still tended her garden in the milky morning cool of these late-summer days and then went over to the club for lunch and a swim or nine holes with her giggling, brown-legged, female foursome. For Diane, perhaps there was no abyss. She had been a schoolteacher, forty years ago, inculcating young minds with the lessons of cause and effect and of patience. "The man said," she reminded Fulham in the middle of the night, "that if it didn't show up in a few more days they'd cancel it and mail another."

"That means waiting *more* days. I should be getting interest on that amount."

"Do we need the interest so badly?"

"It's not a question of *need,* it's a question of *right.* We have a right to that money. Furthermore, every day that check is uncashed, the company is drawing interest on its undiminished balance. Not only are we losing a profit, they're *gain*ing one, thanks to their own inefficiency!"

"I think you're making too much of it. There's no issue involved, it's just one of those things. It got on the bottom of a mail sack somewhere."

She thus managed in her soothing effort to stumble on the very wasps' nest of imagery that infuriated him: the letter lost, at the bottom of a sack, forever; the flaw in the mindless system; the outrage without a perpetrator, or at least any perpetrator who could be discovered, who would declare himself; a certain horrible smugness within the Actual, imperfect and blundering though it was; an outrageous cosmic *unanswerableness.*

The perpetrator struck again, inside the home. Waking on Friday morning, Fulham discovered that his wallet was not on the top of his bureau, where he almost invariably put it upon retiring. He looked in the hip pocket of the pants he had worn the day before, and then, with growing desperation, on the closet floor, under the bed, in the bedside table, on the bathroom sink, into the pockets of all his pants hanging in the closets, and, insanely, all the pockets of all his coats, even those which had been hanging in dry-cleaning bags since June.

For the years and decades of his urban employment, Fulham had carried a breast wallet, a small leather shield above his heart, gradually thickening with the years. In his retirement, he wore coats only to go out at night, and so, in a minor rite of passage, a slight change of armor, he bought a hip wallet, to go with his new working uniform of slacks and sports shirt. Strange and forgettable at first, and a little unbalancing, the wallet soon came to feel like a friendly adjunct to his person, a reminder, in its delicate pressure upon his left buttock, of his new, freer, stage of life. It was, the wallet, almost too plump to sit upon, containing plastic charge cards for BayBank, NYNEX, Brooks Brothers, Hertz, Visa, Amoco, American Express, MasterCharge, The Harvard Coop, Filene's, the Newton-Wellesley Hospital, and Massachusetts General Hospital, plus his plasticized driver's license and paper cards signifying his membership in the Museum of Fine Arts, the Athenaeum, the Wellesley Country Club, the Tavern Club, the Harvard Club, Blue Cross/Blue Shield, and Social Security. Fulham was a sentimental and retentive man; the wallet also held, in its insert of transparent leaves, photos of his wife, daughter, and two grandchildren, and, in its various leather pockets, a card showing his last draft classification (5-A), his insurance agent's business card, six business cards of his own, a yellowed newspaper clipping recording his victory many years ago in an intercollegiate tennis championship, and a little brown photograph, taken in a booth at the Topsfield Fair, of a seventeen-year-old girl, with bangs, and dark lipstick, whom he had once loved. There were also a number of obsolete receipts (for film left at the drugstore, dry cleaning, a lawnmower to be sharpened, a watch to be repaired) and perhaps sixty dollars in cash.

The cash was the least of it; it was the other things—the irreplaceable mementos, the credit cards that were infinitely tedious to replace—whose disappearance he could not endure, could not encompass. He methodically, yet with that frantic undercurrent which defeats method, searched the large house, checking the bathroom floors, the creases behind sofa cushions, the drawers of his desk, the spaces above the books in the library. Fulham knew that on rare occasions, semi-consciously, he would find the wallet's bulk bothersome and take it from his pocket to set it on a convenient surface. He went over the quiet events of the evening before, fishing them up from his aging gray cells: dinner, a walk out into the garden to admire the late roses and the first turning leaves, a little time spent in the library leafing through the latest issue of *Barron's,* a half-hour watching, with Diane, a rerun of an old movie, *Silk Stockings,* with Fred Astaire and Cyd Charisse. The production numbers lacked grandeur on the little screen and the plot spun painfully between them. He had forgotten how high Astaire's voice was, how slight. And Charisse, whom he had also once loved, looked stiff and uneasy under the burden of her fake Russian accent. They should have left it all on Broadway, as *Ninotchka.* Fulham had gone to bed ahead of his wife, undressing, as best he could remember, in his usual pattern, and reading himself into nodding with an

Agatha Christie he may have read decades before; faint sensations of *déjà lu* teased the edges of his dissolving consciousness, as Poirot paced off precise distances in the murder-stricken drawing room.

In the morning, he recalled that there had been, between the times in the library and the television room, a call from his daughter, saying they were bringing the children over early in the morning so she and Rob could drive to Providence for a Sam Shepard play they were dying to see and then spend the night with a couple they knew in Rumford. Fulham went to the spot where he had answered the call, a nook of many small shelves just off the kitchen. Suddenly inspired, he deduced that here, amid the leaning cookbooks and rarely used hors-d'oeuvre plates, was where his wallet had to be; indeed, he *saw* it—fat, brown, with corners rubbed pale and the shape of a credit card denting the leather as sometimes a woman's underpants show in shallow relief through a very tight dress—and emitted a small crow of triumph before realizing that what he took for the wallet was an old out-of-date address book that Diane had not bothered to throw away. His hallucination rattled him and doubled the fury with which he searched the house, room by room, corner by corner. The wallet had ceased to exist.

"It's been stolen," he told his wife at lunch.

Diane had a calm patrician face, and when she lifted her chin and thus pulled smooth the loose flesh beneath, it was still beautiful, her abundant hair so utterly white as to seem an expensively sought-after effect. "How could it have been?"

"Easy. The house is big enough anybody could slip in and out in a minute without our knowing. Anyway, it's not up to me to figure out how to do it, it's up to *them*. And they've done it. The bastards have done it and I'm going to have to cancel every goddamn credit card."

She looked at him coolly, giving him her full attention for once, and said, "I've never seen you like this."

"How am I?"

"You're wild."

"It was my *wallet*. Everything is in it. Everything. Without that wallet, I'm nothing." His tongue had outraced his brain, but once he said it he realized this to be true: without the wallet, he was a phantom, flitting about in a house without walls. "And I know *why* they took it," he went on. "To get the bank card. With that bank card they can now deposit and draw on that check they stole earlier."

"Deposit it in your own account?"

"And then transfer it to their own, somehow. I don't know, I don't know how criminals do their work exactly; that's *their* job. I do know that with these computers there's no more common sense in banking—a wino off the street can walk away with ten thousand dollars if he knows how to satisfy the idiotic machine. People and institutions are being—what's the phrase these kids have?—ripped off all the time. We ourselves have just been ripped off of—" He named the amount of the lost check from Houston and her blue eyes went round as she began to believe him. "Don't you see?" Fulham pressed. "The check, and now the wallet—it's too much of a coincidence."

"I can't believe," Diane said weakly, "it's as simple as you make it sound, with all these safeguards—our code word, for instance."

He scoffed: "Hundreds of people know our code word by now—all the employees at the bank, and anybody who's ever stood behind us in line." It was irrefutably clear to him that forces out there, beyond the horizon of towering beech trees and snug slate roofs, had silently, invisibly conspired to invade his domain and steal all his treasure. Every door and window, even the little apertures of the mail slot and the telephone, were holes through which his possessions, the accumulations of a lifetime, were being pulled from him. Ruinously the world has cast property into the form of nebulous, mechanized fluidity. The cards in the missing wallet opened into slippery tunnels of credit, veins of his blood. Fulham stood, feeling drained and faint. "I'm going to call Houston and stop the check," he told his wife. "Then the bank and freeze my account."

She nodded, lowering her eyes to guide her fork while its side sliced the lettuce leaves beneath her scoop of cottage cheese.

Even as he acted, Fulham knew, his enemies, armed with his wallet, were running up giant bills—buying cars, clothes, front-seat theatre tickets, mockingly extravagant meals. Yet the girls he talked to that Friday afternoon counselled delay; they all sounded seventeen, with placid, gum-chewing voices. As a group, they seemed to have dealt with momentarily disappearing wallets before. Houston did agree to stop payment on the check, but the bank said the computer could not possibly be programmed to his account before early next week. The credit-card offices had busy phones, and differing policies, and by the time Fulham hung up in exhaustion his credit lay in a tangle, a hydra with a few of the heads cut off but most still writhing. He went through the whole house again, trying to imagine his self of yesterday in every tidy room, including the small room, once a sewing room, where they watched television. To discourage excessive watching, the Fulhams had furnished it austerely; there was only the bare set, an oval rag rug, and a cushionless Windsor settee, with a plaid blanket neatly folded against one arm. The wallet's non-existence rang out through the rooms like a pistol shot which leaves deafness in its wake; he stood stunned that an absence could be so decisive. It occurred to Fulham that the house would feel like this the day after he died.

Downstairs, the front door slammed. "Got the mail," Diane called up. In his distraction he had forgotten to make his usual noon trip to the box at the end of the brick walk. But into his subconscious had filtered, hours ago, Rodolfo's "Che gelida manina" from *La Bohème,* whistled off-key. The mail was dumped on the hall table, with the petals fallen from the summer's last roses. A long sand-colored envelope from Houston lay amid the junk and bills. It held the check, dated three weeks ago. No hidden message, no mark of misdirection or extra wear on the envelope betrayed where it had been for so long a time. In this blankness he felt a kind of magnificence, the same kind that declines to answer prayer. He found himself not consoled. Payment on the check had been stopped; it was a worthless piece of paper.

Next morning, Saturday, Fulham awoke with a soreness in his stomach, a chafing hairball of vague anxiety that clarified into the conscious thought *I am a man without a wallet.* The arrival of the check had lessened his fears of criminal conspiracy but isolated the wallet's loss upon a higher plane, where it merged with landscapes and faces that had once belonged to his life and would never be seen again, melted into the irreversible void like the sticky, oddly plausible stuff of dreams. Shame had replaced rage as his prime emotion; he had no wish to leave the house, or go to his make-shift office, or face the grandchildren, who, downstairs in the hall, were noisily arriving. His daughter's and his wife's voices twined in a brief music ended by the slam of the front door and the click of high heels briskly retreating down the walk. From an upstairs window he spied on the redheaded visitor, once his baby, as she ducked into her husband's low sports car, flashing a length of bare leg.

The children spent the morning gorging on television and at lunchtime little Tod handed Fulham his wallet. He said, "Did you want this, Grandpa? It was all folded up in the blanket."

His fat, worn wallet. His own.

"Oh, dear," Diane said, putting her hand to her cheek in a choreo-graphic gesture that seemed to Fulham to parody dismay. "When *Silk Stockings* ended I tidied up and must have folded your wallet in without realizing it. Remember, we put the blanket over our laps because of the draft?"

That made sense. The nights were getting cooler. Now Fulham recovered a dim memory of being annoyed, on the hard Windsor settee, by the lump in his back pocket. He must have removed it, while gazing at Cyd

Charisse. As if in another scene from the movie, he saw himself, close up, hold the wallet in his hand, where it vanished like a snowflake.

"Grandpa has lots of wallets," Tod's shiny-haired little sister chimed in. "He doesn't care."

"Oh, now, that's not quite true," Fulham told her, squeezing the beloved bent book of leather between his two palms and feeling very grandpaternal, fragile and wise and ready to die.

Leaf Season

OFF WE GO! Saturday morning, into our cars, children and dogs and all, driving north to Vermont in leaf season, to the Tremaynes' house on the Columbus Day weekend. It's become a custom, one of the things we all do, the four or five families, a process that can't be stopped without running the risk of breaking a spell. Threading out of greater Boston on its crowded, potholed highways, then smoothly north on 93, and over on 89, across the Connecticut River, into Vermont. At once, there is a difference: things look cleaner, sparser than in New Hampshire. When we leave 89, the villages on the winding state roads, with their white churches and irregular, casually mowed greens and red-painted country stores advertising FUDGE FACTORY or PUMPKIN OUTLET, show a sharp-edged charm, a stagy, calendar-art prettiness that wears at the eyes, after a while, as relentlessly as industrial ugliness. And the leaves, whole valleys and mountains of them—the strident pinks and scarlets of the maples, the clangorous gold of the hickories, the accompanying brasses of birch and beech, on both sides of the road, rise after rise, a heavenly tumult tied to our dull earth only by broad bands of evergreen and outcroppings of granite. We arrive feeling battered by natural glory, by the rush of wind and of small gasoline explosions incessantly hurried one into the next. The dirt driveway—really just ruts that the old wagons and carts wore into the lawn and that modern times have given a dusting of gravel—comes in at right angles off an unmarked macadam road, which came off a numbered state route, which in turn came off a federal highway; so we feel, at last arriving, that we have removed the innermost tissue covering from an ornately wrapped present, or reduced a mathematical problem to its final remainder, or climbed a mountain, or cracked a safe.

The gravel grinds and pops beneath our tires. Marge Tremayne is standing on the porch. She looks pretty good. A little older, a shade overweight, but good.

She and Ralph bought the big wheat-yellow farmhouse with its barn and twenty acres one winter when he had made a killing in oil stocks, the year of the first gas lines, and when their three children were all excited about skiing. Ralph, too, was excited—he grew a Pancho Villa mustache in imitation of the ski instructors and, with his fat cigar in the center of his mouth and his rose-colored goggles and butter-yellow racing suit and clumpy orange step-in boots, was quite a sight on the slopes. Marge, in her tight stretch pants and silver parka and Kelly-green headband and with her hair flying behind, looked rather wonderful, too; her sense of style and her old dance training enabled her to mime the basic moves gracefully enough, and down she would slide, but she wasn't a skier at heart. "I'm too much of a coward," she would say. Or, in another mood, to another listener: "I'm too much of an earth mother." She took to using the Vermont place in the summer (when Ralph had hoped to rent it) and raised vegetables by the bushel and went into canning in a big way, and into spinning wool and mushrooming, and she even began to show a talent for dowsing, serving her apprenticeship with some old mountain man from beyond Montpelier. Ralph was still working in town, and except for Augusts would drive up to his wife on weekends, five hours each way, carting children and their friends back and forth and keeping house in Brookline by himself. So this leaf-season weekend has become a visit to Marge, our chance to see what is going on with her.

Marge and the newly arrived Neusners are standing on the side porch when the Maloneys pull up. The Maloney children bound or self-consciously uncoil, depending upon their ages, out of automotive confinement. There is pleasant confusion and loudly proclaimed exhaustion, a swirling of people back and forth; the joy of an adventure survived animates the families as they piecemeal unload their baggage and collapse into Marge's care. She has a weary, slangy, factual voice, slightly nasal as if she has caught a cold. "It's girls' and boys' dormitories again this year. Men at the head of the stairs turn right, women left. Boys thirteen and older out in the barn, younger than that upstairs with the girls. The Tylers are already here; Linda's taken some littles for a leaf walk and Andy's helping Ralph load up the woodboxes. Ralph says each man's supposed to split his weight in wood. Each woman is responsible for one lunch or dinner. Breakfasts, it's a free-for-all as usual, and don't put syrupy knives and forks straight into the dishwasher, anybody. That means *you,* Teddy Maloney."

The nine-year-old boy, so suddenly singled out, laughs in nervous fright; he had been preoccupied with trying to coax the family dog, Ginger, a red-haired setter bitch, out of the car, in spite of the menacing curiosity of Wolf, the Tremaynes' grizzled chow, and Toby Neusner, an undersized black retriever.

Bernadette Maloney, embracing Marge and kissing her cheek and thinking how broad her body feels, backs off and asks her, a touch too solemnly, "How are you doing?"

Marge gazes back as solemnly, her slate-blue eyes muddied by elements of yellow. "The summer's been bliss," she confides, and averts her gaze with a stoic small shrug. "I don't know. I can't handle people anymore."

Her headband today is maroon. Her thick long dirty-blond hair over the years has become indistinguishably mixed with gray, this subtle dullness intensifying her odd Indian look, not that of blood Indians but of a pale-face maiden captured and raised in their smoky tepees, in their casually cruel customs; her face up here has turned harder and more chiselled, her unpainted lips thinner, her eyes more opaque. She has not so much a tan as a glow, a healthy matte colorlessness rubbed deep into her skin. Her body has grown wider, but with her old sense of style she carries the new weight well, in her hip-hugging jeans and a man's checked lumberjack shirt that hangs over her belt like a maternity blouse. Belly, gray hair, and all, she is still our beauty, and Ralph, when he appears—having evidently been hurried from his car straight into service, for his Brooks Brothers shirt is creased and dirtied by the logs he has been lugging and his city shoes are powdered with sawdust—is still a friendly ogre; he exudes fatherly fumes, he emits barks and guffaws of welcome. His eyes are reddened by cigar smoke, he stammers and spits in his greedy hurry to get his jokes out, he laughs aloud before the punch line is quite reached. He appears to have lost some weight. "My d-daughters' awful cooking," he explains. "Th-they're trying to, *ha,* poison the old guy."

How old are we? Scarcely into our forties. Lots of life left to live. The air here is delicious, crisper and drier than air around Boston. We start to breathe it now, and to take in where we are. The sounds are fewer, and those few are different—individual noises: a single car passing on the road, a lone crow scolding above the stubbled side field, a single window sash clicking back and forth in the gentle wind we hadn't noticed when outside unpacking the cars. The smells of the house are country smells—linoleum, ashes, split wood, plaster, a primeval cellar damp that rises through the floorboards and follows us up the steep, wear-rounded stairs to the second floor, where we see the children and their sleeping bags settled in the tangle of middle rooms. The house, like most Vermont farmhouses, has suffered many revisions over the years; they thought nothing, in the old days, of lifting out a staircase and turning it around or of walling in a fireplace to vent a Franklin stove. With our suitcases as claim markers, we stake out bunks in the two large front bedrooms that the Tremaynes, when they were most excited about skiing, had set up as single-sex dormitories.

Deborah Neusner stands by the upstairs-hall window, gazing out at the empty road, at the field across the road, at the woods beyond the field, with all their leaves. Bernadette Maloney joins her, standing so close that the two women feel each other's body warmth as well as the heat from the radiator beneath the window. "The Englehardts are coming, but late. Little Kenneth has a football game."

"Not so little, then," Deborah says dryly, not turning her thoughtful profile, with its long chin and high-bridged nose. When she does face Bernadette, her brown eyes, in the sharp Vermont light, shine on the edge of panic. The Englehardts mean different things to different people, but to all of us they—Lee so bald and earnest and droll, Ruth so skinny and frizzy and nimble and quick-tongued—make things all right, make the whole thing go. Until they arrive, there will be an uneasy question of why we are here, at the top of the map, in this chilly big wheat-yellow farmhouse surrounded by almost vulgarly gorgeous, red-and-gold nature.

The host is under the house! All afternoon, Ralph lies on the cold ground beneath the kitchen wing, wrapping yellow Fiberglas insulation around his pipes. Already there have been frosts, and last winter, when the Tremaynes were renting to skiers, the pipes froze and the people moved to a motel and later sued. He keeps the cigar in his mouth while stretched out grunting in the crawl space; Bill Maloney hopes aloud to Andy Tyler that there is no gas leak under the kitchen. Both men—Bill burly and placid, Andy skinny and slightly hyper—hang there as if to be helpful, now and then passing more insulation, or another roll of duct tape, in to their supine host. Josh Neusner is splitting his weight in wood, an unfamiliar and thus to him somewhat romantic task. The romance intensifies whenever the splitting maul bounces from an especially awkward piece of wood and digs deep into the earth inches from his feet. He is wearing thin black loafers, with tassels. Wood chips and twigs litter the barnyard around him, and white dried dung from the days when Marge tried raising chickens. The barn overhang is loosely battened; upstanding spears of light make sliding patterns as you move your head. It is like an Op Art sculpture in a gallery, but bigger, Josh thinks, and the effect has that coarse broad au-

thority of the actual, of the unintended. This whole milieu and the business
of woodchopping is so exotic to him that his awareness flickers like a bad
light bulb. Minutes of blankness—rural idiocy, Marx had called it—are
abruptly illumined by the flash of danger when the maul again sinks its
murderous edge close to the tips of his city shoes; then the pebbles, the
grit, the twigs are superillumined, vivid as the granules of paint in a
Dubuffet, and something of this startled radiance is transferred, if he lifts
his head quickly enough, to the sky, the fields, the gaudy woods.

Linda Tyler returns from her leaf walk with the children she collected
and makes them as a reward for being good some peanut-butter-and-jelly
sandwiches. Other children, late arrivals and adolescents too jaded for the
walk, slouch in from the long living room, where a fire of green wood is
smoking and where they have been dabbling with decks of greasy cards
and old board games with pennies and buttons substituted over the years
for the correct counters. Though they have been here on other Columbus
Day weekends, they are shy of the kitchen. Other years, Mrs. Tremayne
was cheerfully in charge, but this year she has withdrawn to her downstairs bedroom and shut the door; from behind it comes the whir and soft
clatter of a spinning wheel. At the sound of food being prepared in the
kitchen, the children gather like birds at a tray of seeds, and Linda hands
out cookies, apples, pretzel sticks. She is petite, with pale freckled skin and
kind green eyes, and wears baggy clothes that conceal her oddly good
figure. As not only her husband here knows, her body on its modest scale
has that voluptuous harmony, that curve of shoulder and swing of hip,
which spells urgency to the male eye. She caters to the assembled children,
warning them to leave room for the traditional big hot-dog-and-chili dinner tonight, after the Englehardts have arrived.

The children present for this weekend are: Milly, Skip, and Christine
Tremayne; Matthew, Mark, Mary, Teddy, and Teresa Maloney; Fritz and
Audrey Tyler; and Rebecca, Eve, and Seth and Zebulon (twins) Neusner.
The Englehardts will bring Kenneth, Betsey, and their unplanned one-and-
a-half-year-old, named in a jocular mood Dorothea—gift of God. The
fanciful name would have been a curse had not the child lived up to it—an
ethereal little girl with her mother's agility and that milky, abstracted blue-
eyed gaze of her father's, set beneath not his bald dome but a head of
angelic curls. The pets present are Toby Neusner, Ginger Maloney, Wolf
Tremayne, and two cats, a sleepy, vain, long-haired white and a short-
haired gray with extra toes who appears throughout the house at the
strangest places, in locked rooms and bureau drawers, like an apparition.
It is all too much, as the children get bigger. The oldest, Milly Tremayne

and Fritz Tyler, are both seventeen, and embarrassed to be here. They were embarrassed last year as well, but not so keenly.

Ralph emerges at last from underneath the house and announces, spitting smoke and amiably sputtering, that it's way past time for the softball game. "Wh-what are all you young br-bruisers lounging inside for on a gorgeous Saturday like this? Let's c-compete!" He gets down in a football lineman's crouch and, with the cigar stub in the center of his mouth like a rhinoceros horn, looks truly angry.

Softball is organized in the side field. Everyone plays, even Deborah Neusner and Bernadette Maloney, who had been murmuring upstairs for hours. What about? The absent, the present, the recent past, the near future—a liquid soft discourse that leaves, afterward, a scarcely perceptible residue of new information, which yet enhances their sense of who and where they are.

Fritz Tyler bowls Milly Tremayne over, rushing across from shortstop for a pop fly. "You bastard, didn't you hear me calling you off?" she asks him, sprawling in the long dry grass, red-faced and tousled, her upraised legs in their tight jeans looking elegant and thin. Her hair is dark like Ralph's but though not blond has the shape of Marge's, abundant and wiry and loose in a tent shape, before Marge began to braid it and pin it up like a nineteenth-century farmer's wife. Bill Maloney hits a home run, over the heads of Seth and Zebulon—they have been put in right field together, as if two little eight-year-old boys will make one good grownup fielder. Their black, loping dog, Toby, helps them hunt for the ball in the burdock over by the split-rail fence. The sky in the west, above mountains whose blush is turning blue, has begun to develop slant stripes tinged with pink, and the battered hay in the outfield is growing damp, each bent strand throwing a longer and longer shadow. Though the children are encouraged to continue the game until darkness, the grownups drift away, and in the long, narrow living room, with its plaster ceiling drooping in the center like the underside of an old bed, a fresh fire is built, of dry and seasoned logs from the woodbox beneath the stairs (the children had tried to burn freshly split wood, from beneath the barn overhang), and an impressive array of bottles is assembled on the sideboard. Bring your own, the rule is.

Marge, ostentatiously drinking unfermented cider, sits on the sofa, which is faded and plaid and has wide wooden arms, and knits a sweater of undyed wool she has carded and spun herself. Toward seven o'clock Linda and Bernadette go into the kitchen to feed the starving younger children. The older have scattered to their rooms upstairs, or out to the barn. By the time the Englehardts at last arrive, the adults not only are drunk but have gone through two boxes of crackers and a wedge of Vermont cheddar that was bought to last the weekend.

Cheers go up. Roly-poly, sleepy-looking Lee doffs his hunter's cap and reveals the polished dome of his perfectly smooth skull. Tall, frizzy-haired Ruth stands there and surveys the scene through her huge glasses, taking it all in. The temples of her glasses have the shape of a lightning bolt, and the bridge rides so low on her nose as to reduce it to a tiny round tip, a baby's nose. Kenneth and Betsey are lugging knapsacks and suitcases in from the car and up the stairs, including a plastic basket containing little Dorothea. "Who-who won the football game?" the host eagerly asks.

"We won," Ruth tells him, in the complex, challenging tone of a joke on herself, "but Kenny didn't play." The weariness of the long drive is still in her voice. Ruth's words are like glass sandwiches that reflect back an obvious meaning on the first level, a less obvious one on the second, and so on, as deep as you want to look. "The poor child sat on the bench," she adds.

"Oh." Ralph blinks, having evidently been tactless. His eyes slide over to Marge on the sofa, as if to seek support. Her eyes are lowered to the knitting. Wolf, who in his old age has been known to snap, sleeps at her feet. Upstairs, Kenneth and Betsey seek the company and comfort of the other children, as the Englehardts are meshed into the adult group beneath them and the hilarity, the shouting, swells by that increment.

It is hard, afterwards, to remember what was so funny. Their all being here in Vermont, in this old farmhouse with its smells from another century, is in itself funny, and the Saturday-night meal of something so hearty and Western as chili and hot dogs is funny, and the half-gallons of cheap wine that replace themselves at the table, like successive generations of bulbous green dwarfs, are part of the delicate, hallucinatory joke.

They organize two tables of bridge afterwards, and, drunk as they know themselves to be now, this is droll also. "Double," Lee Englehardt keeps saying solemnly, his shining brow furrowed, the long wisps of hair above his ears grayer than last year in the light of the paper-shaded bridge lamp that, like most of the furnishings of the house, will not be missed if ski tenants destroy it. "Four diamonds," Andy Tyler says, hoping that Deborah Neusner will have the sense to put him back into spades. The Neusners, who spent their time at college less frivolously than the others, rarely play cards of any kind, and Deborah was pressed into service only because Marge pleaded a headache and has gone back into her bedroom. Husbands and wives cannot be partners, and should not be at the same table. "Double," Lee Englehardt says. *Take me out of diamonds,* Andy Tyler thinks intensely, so intensely the message feels engraved on the smoke above his head. "Pass," Deborah Neusner says, weakly. "Four hearts," says Bernadette Maloney, feeling sorry for Deborah, knowing that being so close to Lee upsets her; the two had an affair years ago, a fling that ended up in the air, so in a sense it was never over. That is one of the En-glehardts' charms, their ability to leave things up in the air, like jugglers in a freeze-frame. "Four spades," Andy pronounces with great relief, praying that Deborah will now have the wit to pass again. "Five diamonds?" she hesitantly says.

Josh Neusner reads a very old *National Geographic* he found in the woodbox beneath the stairs. It is so old that the photos are mostly black-and-white, and the type is different, and the cultural biases are overt. These bare-breasted women and woolly chiefs with bones through their noses are clearly, cheerfully being condescended to, anthropologically. This would never do now; isn't it one of the tenets of our times that all cultural formations, even cannibalism and foot-binding, make equally good sense? Josh's neck and shoulders ache from splitting his weight in wood. He has taken a glass of dinner wine away from the table and rests it on the broad arm of the corduroy-covered armchair by the dying fire that Ralph built. Suddenly the wine seems an odious, fermented substance, and the hilarious chatter from the bridge tables inane, poisonous. Above his head, on the swaybacked ceiling, footsteps scurry and rustle like those of giant rats. The children; he wants to go upstairs to check on the girls and tuck in the twins, but during these leaf-season weekends the children are invited to make their own society, and exist like a pack of shadows in the corners of the grownup fun. Strange places, strange customs; cannibalism, he reads, is almost never a matter of hunger but of ingesting the enemy's spiritual virtues. He wonders why liquor is called spirits. The cheap wine tastes dead. The thumping and scurrying overhead slowly weakens, loses its grip. He himself, when at midnight both tables loudly announce an-other rubber, goes upstairs and puts himself into one of the upper bunk beds in the men's dormitory. The window in the upstairs hall where Debo-rah and Bernadette met and talked this afternoon now displays white, scratchy, many-tentacled frost ferns above the radiator.

The bunk isn't quite long enough for him to stretch out in. He thinks of Marge alone in her room below him, her sulky mystery, her beautiful dancer's body. She was the queen of all this and now is trying to withdraw. He could sneak down the back stairs and they could spin together. Josh cannot sleep. The noise from below, the sound of rampant spirits, is too great. And when at last the bridge concludes and people begin to clatter up the stairs, he still cannot sleep. Andy underneath him, Lee and Bill across the room in the other double bunk, all fall asleep swiftly, and snore. Lee is the most spectacular—nasal arpeggios that encompass octaves, up and down the scale—but Bill plugs steadily away, his rhythmic wheeze like a rusty engine that will not die, and Andy demonstrates, a few feet below Josh's face, the odd talent of coughing in his sleep, coughing prolongedly without waking himself. Josh feels trapped. A broadsword of light falls diagonally across the floor, and there are faint, halting footsteps. One of the Tremaynes' cats has pushed open the door and is nosing about. Josh strains his eyes and sees it is the gray one with extra toes. He reaches out from the upper bunk with his foot and nudges the door shut again. The house's huge content of protoplasm ebbs in little stages into quiet, into sleep: twenty-six other human beings—he counts them up, including the boys in the barn—soaking up restorative dreams, leaving him stranded, high and listening, his ears staring into the tense, circumambient wilderness. Never again. This is the last time he and his family are going to come for this weekend to Vermont. This is torture.

Bacon! The crisp, illicit, life-enhancing smell of it penetrates the room, his nostrils, his brain. Josh sees that the three other bunks are empty, the day is well advanced. He must have fallen asleep after all. He remembers, as the wee hours became larger and lighter, conducting mental negotiations, amid the brouhaha of the other men's snoring, with the gray cat, who seemed to be here, and then there, in the room. Now the animal is nowhere to be seen, and Josh must have dropped off for an hour or two.

The house, like a ship under way, is shaking, trembling, with the passage of feet, with activity. A maul and wedge ring: Lee Englehardt is splitting his weight in wood. Car doors slam: the Maloneys, all seven of them, are going off to Mass. They'll bring back Sunday papers and a whole list of staples—crackers, orange juice, cheddar cheese, tonic water—that Marge has pressed upon them. She seems in a better mood. She is wearing, instead of the sullen peasant skirt and sweater and shawl of last night, tight shiny red pants that make her legs look almost as thin and sexy as her daughter Milly's. Her hair is done up in a fat blond-gray pigtail that bounces on her back as she friskily, bossily prepares breakfast, wave after wave, flipping six pieces of bacon at a time with a long aluminum spatula. "Three pieces per person, and that includes you, Fritz Tyler," she says severely. "Those who like their scrambled eggs runny, come serve yourselves right now. Those who don't, get at the end of the line. We don't believe in Sugar Pops in this household, Seth Neusner. Up here in the mountains it's all bran and granola and yucky fiber. Betsey, go out to the woodpile and tell your father the baby's just spit up all over herself and your mother's in the bathroom."

Ralph comes sleepily into the kitchen, the first cigar of the day in his mouth, its lit end making a triangle with his two red eyes. He is barefoot— pathetic white feet, with ingrown yellow toenails and long toes crushed together—and is coming from the wrong direction, if we assume he slept in the master bedroom, at the front of the downstairs.

He hasn't slept in the master bedroom. Beyond the kitchen lies a small room with a few cots in it, for an overflow ski crowd. Ralph slept in there. He did not sleep with Marge! The knowledge runs silently through the mingled families, chastening them. For this weekend Marge and Ralph are like the mother and father, even of the other adults. We want them to love each other. For if they do not love each other, how can they love and take care of us?

Marge seems intent on showing that she can do it all. She ruffles Ralph's head as he sits groggily at the breakfast table. Grownups eat at the long dining-room table, where one of the bridge groups played last night, and children at the round butcher-block table in the center of the kitchen. "Achey, achey?" Marge asks, cooingly.

"T-too much grape juice, Mother," Ralph says.

They are trying to make up. We all feel better, bolder. Josh Neusner describes his terrible night, quite comically as he relives his mental negoti- ations with the mysterious cat, but Lee Englehardt, having come in from wood-splitting to care for Dorothea, without smiling states, "Jews make poor campers." We are shocked. It is the sort of thing that can be said only among intimate friends or confirmed enemies. And why would they be enemies?

Josh, remembering Lee's aggressive unconscious arpeggios, and his posi- tion at the card table next to Deborah, chooses to accept the remark as a piece of ethnology, arrived at innocently: Lee is an insurance salesman whose father was a professor of history, and as if in compensation for a lesser career he collects such small pedantic conclusions as that Jews make poor campers. Lee's charm really rests on his insecurity. Josh chooses to keep playing the clown. He covers his forehead with one hand and moans, "I can't sleep without a woman. Men are *hid*eous."

Deborah, a little later, when they meet on the stair landing, says, "Baby, I'm sorry you had such a poor night; you should have played bridge."

"I wasn't asked."

"You didn't want to be asked. I would have given you my seat. Andy Tyler kept wanting to kill me, I could tell."

"The only person I like here is Linda," Josh petulantly volunteers. "And Dorothea," he adds, to soften it.

This reminds her: "Ruth didn't sleep in the girls' dormitory last night.

Marge set her up in the living room with the baby after everybody else had gone to bed, in case Dorothea yelled. So the bunk above me is empty if you really want it. Linda and Bernadette wouldn't care."

"It would make me look like a sissy." He goes on, "And then yesterday I kept nearly cutting off my foot splitting their idiotic wood."

"Come on, honey, try to get into the spirit of things."

"It's all barbaric," he says, so lightheaded with lack of sleep that every perception has a translucent, revelatory quality. Suddenly, he is having a very good time. He goes down and has some more coffee and bacon and discusses Boston-area private schools with Linda and Lee, who are disenchanted with highly touted Brookline High.

The Maloneys return laden with the Sunday New York *Times,* the Boston *Globe,* and the Burlington *Free Press.* The children fight over the funnies, the men over the sports and financial pages. The day proceeds with that unreality peculiar to Sunday; one hour seems as long as two, and the next goes by in ten minutes. A great deal of the conversation concerns where various other people are. Marge is in the car, with her son, Skip, and her dog, Wolf, performing some errands having to do with quantities of natural fleece—uncarded, greasy-wet with lanolin—to be found at a farm fifteen miles away. It turns out that Andy Tyler has gone along for the ride. Bernadette Maloney is in Marge's garden salvaging tomatoes and zucchini from last night's frost; Mark and Mary and Teddy are helping her, by holding the paper bags with bored expressions and then by throwing the rotten vegetables at one another. Linda Tyler, having been told that her husband has disappeared with Marge, announces that she will go on a mushrooming walk in the woods; her daughter, Audrey, and Betsey Englehardt and the two Neusner girls come with her, like a procession of little witches in training. Christine Tremayne—who has inherited Marge's dull complexion and Ralph's stocky build, unfortunately—is showing Teresa Maloney the barn, and the Neusner twins tag along. The interior is awesome; some high small windows and the gaps between the slats admit shafts of light as if in a cathedral. They have all seen slides of cathedrals at school. The light reveals an atmosphere glittering with dust, dust from the hay still stacked in staircases of bales at one end, a dust that thickens the air, that makes light visible while lessening it. The children feel deep in the sea of time. Elements of old farm machinery rust in corners here and there, with pieces of lumber, ten-gallon milk cans, strawberry boxes, and glass eggs. They find an old rope-quoit set, and the four of them play until a dispute between Seth and Zebulon makes it no fun.

Milly Tremayne and Fritz Tyler—who knows where they have gone to?

Mary Maloney, having left the garden party in tearful disgust when Mark caught her right on the mouth with a rotten zucchini, has come into the house; the television set gets only one channel, and that one full of ghosts from the hills and valleys between here and the station, but she is happily watching some man with big eyebrows and a Southern accent give a sermon, and a lot of fat ladies in glitzy dresses sing hymns, until her father comes and tells her she should be outdoors in the sunshine.

What sunshine? A cloud has just passed across the sun, not a little cloud but a large dark one, with a wide leaden center and agitated, straggling edges—a cloud it seems the surrounding mountains have given birth to.

Bill Maloney and Lee Englehardt find a shovel and refresh the holes that take the posts for the volleyball net. Nature fills in the holes from one leaf season to the next. Then they find and unwind the two-by-fours and the net and the guy ropes and pegs where they have reposed all wound and tangled up in the barn since last October. As they move slowly, in the quickly moving cloud shadows, through the tedious ritual of setting up the net, Lee asks Bill, "How was Mass?"

Bill, who has a moonface and delicate pink Irish skin, looks at Lee cockeyed and says, "Like it always is. That's the beauty of it, Mr. Eng."

Lee makes a rueful nod, concluding to himself that this is the essence of male companionship: cards close to the chest.

Inside the kitchen, Bernadette and Deborah are making lunch—a cauldron of clam chowder Bernadette has lugged up from Boston; and a tuna salad Deborah is whipping up out of four cans plus chopped celery, scallions, mayonnaise, lemon juice, and a head of lettuce; and a tinned ham for those who, like most of the children, hate fish. As the two women slide and bump past each other between Marge's old-fashioned black soapstone sink and the wooden countertops on either side, they quietly talk about the situation between Marge and Ralph, which seems far gone, and that between Andy and Linda, which seems to be heading for trouble.

Ruth Englehardt comes into the kitchen with her curly-headed toddler propped on her hip and a cigarette tilting at an opposite angle out of her mouth. "So the Queen of Sheba has eloped with the handyman," she says, "the Queen of Sheba" referring to Marge and "the handyman" to Andy, not just because of his name but because of his tendency, well known to all the women, to reach out under the table and touch. "If you two were about to discuss Lee and me, I'll leave," she adds; then she begins to cough, and one eye cries from the smoke. She sets down the heavy child and watches her stagger across the worn linoleum to one of the low old mahogany counters, where Dorothea quicker than thought reaches up and flips a sharp knife down past her own ear. Ruth deftly retrieves the knife and her daughter; the little girl, as she feels herself being lifted, reflexively spreads her legs to sit astride her mother's hip. The three women talk, touching their friends with their tongues not to harm them but to give themselves pleasure; little new can be offered, mere pinches or slivers added to the salad, tiny, almost meaningless remarks or glimpses that yet do enhance the flavor. The conversation, too, serves a purpose of location, of locating the others on a continuum of happiness or its opposite, of satisfying the speakers that the others are within hailing distance in this our dark passage through life, with its mating and birthing, its getting and spending, its gathering and scattering. Some, indeed, are even closer than hailing distance, for from underneath the floor there comes a sudden grumbling and scraping: their host wrapping more insulation.

Lunch is served, then volleyball. Let's not do the volleyball. Let's just say that once there were five on a side and now the children have grown so that three eight-person teams must be fielded, and some of the boys lunge and swagger and swat as lustily as their fathers. More lustily, since these powers are new to them. Matthew Maloney knocks Audrey Tyler flat on her back, and Fritz Tyler comes down from a spike right on Deborah Neusner's toe, so that she thinks it might be broken. She thinks she heard it snap, at the still center of the swelling red cloud of pain. She hops off the court. "This hasn't been their weekend," Ruth Englehardt says *sotto voce* to Marge, who has returned from her drive to buy the wool.

"I just can't get excited about any of it," Marge confides to Ruth, under the net, while Bill Maloney, with much drolly elaborate ceremony, is winding up to serve. For all of his elaboration, the ball flies too high and sails out. The other side hoots. The sight of such a throng, in suburban shorts and halters and stencilled sweatshirts, is so unusual here in Vermont this time of year that cars and pickup trucks slow down on the little quiet unnumbered road. One truck (passing, everybody later agrees, for about the fourth time) fails to brake when the ball, hit wild by Eve Neusner, bounces under his chassis and, with a sound as sickening as that of a box turtle being crushed beneath the wheels, bursts. Then the truck brakes. Ralph slightly knows the driver, and a pleasant and apologetic palaver takes place by the fence, though the red-bearded, red-hatted face of the truck driver doesn't look apologetic. Mark Maloney has brought his soccer ball, and that is substituted, though it is enough heavier that a number of the females complain of stinging hands and sprained wrists.

So we have done the volleyball after all. The sun, momentarily appearing between the ridge of a mountain and the edge of another great cloud, throws the shadows of the poles right to the edge of the road. The smallest children—Teddy and Teri Maloney, Seth and Zebulon Neusner, even little Dorothea Englehardt, the knees of whose bib overalls are filthy and whose lips drool from sucking on a milkweed pod—scrimmage in the trampled grass and try to heave the heavy soccer ball, cunningly stitched together of pentagons, over the sagging net. The clouds have thickened and darkened so as to form a continuous ragged canopy. A cool wind blows as if through a hole in a tent.

The exercise has left the adults feeling contentious, vigorous, and thirsty. They rush to the bottles. They go upstairs one by one to take showers in the only bathroom on the second floor. Josh Neusner by now is feeling quite delirious with fatigue and is experiencing small, flashlike epiphanies of love for each of his friends as they move in and out of the living room, up the stairs, out of doors, and back in. They all look very tall to him, even the children, from where he lies on the plaid couch, fighting off the sleep that refused to come last night. He shuts his eyes a moment and when he opens them, Bill Maloney, his oldest son, Matthew, Lee Englehardt, and Josh's own wife, Deborah, are over by the far wall, where the wallpaper has been scorched and curled by the pipes of an old wood-stove that was taken away when Ralph installed the new heating system whose pipes he has been so desperately, patiently insulating. The four people over there are engaged in a contest of endurance—seeing how long each can sit against the wall, posed as if on a chair that is not there, before the muscle pain in their thighs forces them to surrender and stand. Bill Maloney times each contestant with a watch; his own son seems to be winning, until Lee Englehardt, exposing that something fanatic and needy he keeps hidden behind his mild eyes, continues to hold the pose—straight back flat on the wall, thighs at a ninety-degree angle—for the number of seconds needed to win. Bill counts off the seconds. Lee's bald head fills with blood like the bulb of a thermometer. Deborah is visibly impressed, even moved, by Lee's macho effort. Her long jaw has dropped as if she might swoon. In women, Josh thinks, admiration and pity are faces of one emotion.

Other games are introduced, other feats are performed. Andy Tyler, it turns out, slim and flexible as he is, can hold a broom in both hands and jump over it without letting go. He can then, the broom now held behind him, reverse the trick, hopping up like a handkerchief pulled through a ring. Others try, and kick the broom to the floor with a smack, or else themselves fall to the floor like misfired cannon balls. Ralph Tremayne demonstrates his ability to set a coin on his uplifted elbow and with the same hand grab it in midair. He can even do it with a small stack of quarters. Now coins are flying all over the room, and scatter into the corners. Ralph, encouraged, revives an old drill from his college football years; you squat, he eagerly explains, and fall backwards, and push off with your hands at your shoulders so that you land back on your feet. Every time he tries it, Marge's collection of stippled milk glass on the mantel trembles, and Ralph, after a tantalizing, teetering moment of near-success, drops with a plaster-cracking thud onto his back. Others also fail. Josh, amid much noisy skepticism, gets up off the sofa and succeeds at his first try. He startles himself, too. He used to be good at gym, a talent he had thought unusable in real life. In the aftermath of his exertion the roomful of people lurches slightly, like the first hesitant movement of a carrousel when all the rides are sold.

Linda Tyler introduces a contest whereby a box of matches is set on the floor a forearm's length from the kneeling person's knees. She demonstrates. Then, her hands clasped behind her, she explains that she will attempt to knock the matchbox over with her nose. She does this easily. But when Bill Maloney tries, he falls forward onto his thin-skinned moon-face. Even Lee's stubborn determination fails; his nose, grimace though he will, comes up a millimeter short. Bernadette, however, performs the trick without effort, and Deborah also. There is something affecting in the position of abasement the women assume on the floor, their hair falling forward, their hands behind them like a manacled slave's, their hips broad and round in the crouching position, their feet—bare or in little ballerina slippers—soles up beneath their hips. It's all in the hips, Linda explains, patting her nicely convex own: weight distribution. Almost no man can knock the matchbox over, and almost every woman can. Even Ruth, long and lanky as she is, condescending to try it, illustrates this sexist truth: though there is a precarious moment of balance striven for, the matchbox falls. Everybody cheers, and Dorothea, put to sleep in Marge's bedroom, cries at the sudden loud noise.

And then there is leg wrestling, man against man and man against woman, if the woman is wearing slacks. How strangely sweet and clarifying it is to be lying hip to hip, face to feet, with someone of the opposite sex while the circle of excited faces above counts, "One! Two! Three!" On the count of three, the inside legs, lifted on each count, are joined and a brief struggle ensues, brief as the mating of animals, and ends with a moment's exhausted repose side by side. And then there are ways in which a woman can lift a man, by standing back to back and hooking arms at the elbows, and ways in which two people, holding tight to each other's ankles, can somersault the length of a carpet. There seems no end to what bodies can do, but at last Bill Maloney complains that if he has another drink he will fall down and why the hell isn't there any food?

The Englehardts remember the beef casserole they were going to heat. Milly Tremayne, fortunately, with the help of Fritz Tyler, Becky Neusner, Betsey Englehardt, and Mark Maloney, has got the meal started in the oven and fed the younger, ravenous children on baloney sandwiches, chili, and tuna salad left over from other meals. The television set has been rescued from the living room and plugged in upstairs, its rabbit ears augmented with Reynolds Wrap that the Neusner twins, who are clever about such things, took from a kitchen drawer. The children also have fed the three dogs and two cats, even though, unbeknownst to all except the animals (who didn't tell), Marge had fed them earlier. She disappeared into her bedroom when little Dorothea began to cry and never, come to think of it, returned. Worn out with their drinking and wrestling, the grownups in sudden spurts of familial conscience now scold the children for being so addicted to television (some dreadful car-chase thing, totally unsuitable) and pack them into their bunk beds and cots and sleeping bags.

Dinner, served at ten o'clock, feels anticlimactic; angels of awkward silence keep passing overhead, and Linda Tyler, quite prettily, keeps yawning, showing the velvety red lining of her mouth, her tense tongue, the horseshoe arc of her lower teeth. Deborah Neusner is sure she has broken her toe; she reinjured it when the corduroy armchair tipped over while she was trying to do a headstand on it. Ruth Englehardt says, "There's a hospital in Barre," which might mean that they should drive her to it, or that it is too far to drive anyone to, or that Deborah is being ridiculous to think she has a broken toe. Ruth has not been blind to the frequency with which, in the night's tumbling, Deborah and Lee bumped or rubbed against each other. Bernadette Maloney says she just can't keep her eyes open another minute; it must be the Vermont air.

Only one table for bridge can be mustered. Bill and Lee are keen to play, and it seems Ruth might be willing but that something during the evening has offended her—perhaps being the last woman invited to knock the matchbox over, perhaps Marge's somehow taking over little Dorothea, perhaps feeling that as the mother of a child much younger than anyone else's she is not as free as they, as frivolous—and she says no, she thinks she'll put a load of dishes into the washer and then go to bed. Bernadette and Linda help her. Even Andy Tyler makes a move for the kitchen, his slim hands lifted as if to pat something agreeably yielding, but the other men coarsely, in voices that grind together like gears and gravel, insist he play bridge with them. Ralph, who at the dinner table, without warning, while plucking at his mustache, seemed to turn green and wiggly like the elephant king in *Babar,* has disappeared into the dismal room, beyond the

kitchen, where he slept last night. Ruth's helpers at the dishwasher have
taken from her the cue that the time has come in the weekend to say no,
and they, at first coquettishly and then quite firmly, resist the men's impor-
tunities to make the fourth. This leaves Deborah, who has been sitting on
the living-room floor sorrowfully inspecting her bare foot. Her feet and
legs have a certain chunkiness, a bit like that of children; the mismatch of
her doughy, low-waisted figure with the fineness of her face—the tapering
long chin, the moist brown eyes, the pensive dents at the corners of her
mouth, a hint of haughtiness in the high bridge of her nose—forms the
secret of her charm, her vulnerability. She says that with the pain in her
toe she wouldn't be able to sleep anyway, so why not? The men cheer. She
turns and explains to someone behind her, rolling her eyes so the whites
seem to leap from a Biblical tableau, "Sweetie, these men are crazy to have
me play bridge with them!"

But Josh is no longer standing there, solicitously. He has crept upstairs.
Fleeing the scene of last night's horror, so bone-weary he seems to be
floating, he crosses the hall in his pajamas and looks into the girls' dormitory, where Deborah had said there was an extra bunk. All four beds are
empty; he tries to imagine which one his wife sleeps in and, silent and light
as last night's cat, climbs into the bunk above it. A low-watt light bulb
under a brown shade patterned in pinholes is burning across the room; he
pulls the covers over his head and wishes himself invisible and very small.
There is a soft sound around him, distinct from the conversation and
scraping of chairs downstairs. A sound with its own life, with subtle pauses
and renewals and changes of mind. Of course. Rain. Those huge clouds
this afternoon.

He is not conscious of falling asleep. He is awakened by some small
noise, a delicate alteration, in the room. He opens one eye, frightened that
if he opens two he will be ousted from this haven. Linda Tyler has entered,
in a white nightgown. Her shadowy nipples tap the cloth from within. Her
entire slender body appears angelic, lifted at all its points by a lightness
that leaves her preoccupied face behind, sullen and even ugly, unaware of
being watched. This impassive sad face looms close to his eye, and van-
ishes. She has put herself into the bunk beneath him. The lamp with its
bright pinholes has been switched off. Josh can just barely make out across
the room, by the hall light that slides itself like a huge yellow letter under
the door, that Bernadette Maloney, with her splash of black hair, is asleep
in the lower bunk and some other woman, unseeable, in the top. The rain
continues its purring, its caressing of the roof shingles, its leisurely debate
with itself, drowning out the gentle breathing of the women. This is lovely.
This is bliss.

* * *

When Monday morning arrives, everyone is irritable, though the rain has stopped. Only Josh, it would seem, slept well. Evidently, Marge emerged from her bedroom when Ruth, after kibitzing at bridge for an hour, went in, to transfer Dorothea to the living room, and Marge suggested to Deborah that she switch beds with her, so the other women wouldn't be disturbed when the bridge at last was over. Also, there was something mysterious about her not being there in case Ralph "got ideas." So Marge herself must have been the unseeable woman in the other top bunk. The bridge had lasted until three. Deborah has taken so much aspirin her stomach burns and she got hardly an hour's worth of sleep, in Marge's bed, but this morning she does doubt that the toe is actually broken. If it was broken, she couldn't take a step; she demonstrates, on the kitchen floor, some limping strides, and Josh thinks of how lightly Linda moved into his vision last night, her breasts uplifted behind their veil, and how he slept all night with her beneath him, awakening once or twice with an erection but listening to the rain intermingled with the women's gentle breathing and sinking with his steely burden deep into sweet sleep again.

He volunteers, so full of energy, to go out and split some more wood. Ralph, who looks only half sick today, but with a curious pinkness around his eyes as if he were wearing his old rosy ski goggles, says one of the boys broke off the maul, up at the neck, by swinging and missing the wedge. The boy, unnamed, is Matthew Maloney, and Mark and Mary were leaders in this morning's plot to make French toast for the children's breakfast, which has left everything in the kitchen sticky with syrup. So the Maloneys as a family are in bad odor, and Bill and Bernadette go out on the porch to fight about something—his staying up till three, perhaps, or her failure to supervise the making of the French toast.

She has been gossiping, actually, over coffee in the living room with Andy Tyler. As the weekend wears on the sex distinctions wear down, as limestone statues turn androgynous in the weather. Bill's drinking, Bernadette confided to Andy, really has passed well beyond the social stage, and she is afraid it's beginning to hurt him at work. As for herself, as soon as Teresa hits kindergarten, she's going back to nursing and complete her R.N.; once you have your cap, you're ready for anything. A woman has to think that way these days, no matter what the Church says—these ridiculous old men, who have never known love or had families, telling us how to behave. Seeing her wince as she moved her head for emphasis, Andy offered to massage her neck, and she let him, not stretching out on the sofa —that would have been too much, at least at this stage—but perching on the edge of the corduroy armchair so he could get at her shoulder muscles with his thumbs. She groaned, "That feels so good. It's sleeping with a strange pillow does me in every time. My doctor says I have a very delicate cervical area. Up top, of course."

Perhaps this massage is what she and Bill were fighting about. It hasn't been a very good weekend for Bernadette, what with Deborah and Ruth between them getting such a lock on Lee. The Maloneys, at any rate, are the first to pack up and leave, though it takes them all morning. They have all sorts of yard work at home to do, and they want to beat that terrible rush, it happens every Columbus Day, on 89 and 93, especially at the Hooksett tollbooth. The Neusners wave goodbye from the porch and wonder if they, too, shouldn't be thinking about going. They are tender with each other, each having endured a night without sleep, and each having fallen more deeply in love with a person outside the marriage—with Lee, with Linda. Also, the twins have a Cub Scout party in Newton they had hoped to get to. The father of one of the pack leaders knows a linebacker for the Patriots and he's supposed to come and give the kids an inspirational message.

As for Marge and Ralph, they seem pleased to have gotten through the weekend with no more showing than did. They beg the Englehardts and Tylers not to go. The six of them, the hard core, sit around in the living room lunching on leftovers and finishing a bottle of red wine found at the back of the refrigerator. There are few leftovers, and the supply of wood also appears to have been exhausted, for what is in the fireplace smokes and fails to catch, in spite of repeated kindlings by muttering, grunting Ralph. Even the cigar in the center of his face has gone out. Every motion he makes, up or down, seems to give him pain: old football injuries. "Y-you young fellas, w-w-wait till you get to be my age," he says to Andy and Lee, though he is only a year or two older.

They are sleepily at ease, these six, the two other couples gone. They sit sprawled in a kind of spiritual deshabille, open to inspection, their dismissive remarks about the Maloneys and Neusners desultory and not unfond, their inventory of one another's failings and wounds mostly silent, an unspoken ticking-off. "I asked Bill how Mass had been," Lee complains, "and he nearly bit my head off." Andy contributes, "Bernadette gave me quite an earful, how she hates the Church. I think she's fixing to bust out of the whole shmeer." "And oh my goodness, I don't mean to be the complaining type," Ruth says, "but wasn't our little Debbie absolutely insufferable, a cat in with the catnip with all that bridge?" "They're very quick learners," Lee says, leaving who "they" are up in the air, and trusting Andy to keep silent about how little time he, Lee, spent in the boys' dormitory last night. His mild big blue eyes are still a baby's beneath his bald dome; Ruth's frizzy crown of honey-blond hair seems avid, as do her sharp nose and flexible quick mouth and the pockets of emaciated shadow beneath her cheekbones. She and Andy do most of the talking, Lee and Marge most of the appreciative laughing. Marge's good humor is striking; as the pressure of being a hostess lifts, she expands, and in her loose-hanging man's shirt distinctly shows middle-aged spread, the fleshly generosity of a beauty who has fulfilled her duties and knows herself to be, whatever shape the future will bring, basically beautiful. Her headband today is turquoise. Ralph squints at her and appears both puzzled and wise, a bloodshot old owl who can still swoop down from a branch and carry off in his claws a piping, furry treasure.

After an hour and a half of this, this complacent torpor, Linda can't stand it. She jumps up and announces she is going on another leaf walk. Do any of the littles want to go with her? Surprisingly, a few do, again all girls—Christine, Audrey, and Betsey. Also, Wolf comes; he misses Ginger and Toby. They file diagonally across the trampled softball field, leaving the barn behind them on the right, into the long strip of woods along the creek, which has grown up thick since the remote days when all this difficult land was cleared for farming. Bits of old stone wall and tumbled-in cellar holes hide in the woods. The sound of the cars on the road can barely be heard.

Linda gestures up and around her. "The bright colors we've all come all the way up here to admire are, above all, the turning leaves of the maple tree, especially the sugar maple, from which we get—?"

"Maple syrup," says Christine Tremayne, who knows she is homely, but will make up for it in life by being dutiful.

"But all the trees contribute, from the stately beech, which you can recognize by its smooth gray bark, and the birch family, of which you especially know the white, or paper, birch, from which the Indians used to make—?"

"Canoes," says Betsey Englehardt. She misses the Neusner twins, even though Zebulon did take the rope quoits and throw them down the well so nobody could play the game anymore. When she cried about it, her father explained to her at length why Jewish children are spoiled.

"The last trees to let go of their leaves are the oaks," Linda tells the children. She picks up an oak leaf and holds it out to impress upon them its lobed, deeply indented shape. "Even in the winter snows, the oak will cling to its old brown leaves. The *first* tree to let go tends to be another giant of the forest—the ash. Its leaves, the only opposite feather-compound leaves in the American forest, turn an unusual purplish-blue color, unlike anything else, and then suddenly, one day, are gone. Girls, look up and around you. Those who went walking with me Saturday, do you notice any difference?"

"More sky," says Audrey, her own daughter, who knows what answer she wants.

"That's right," Linda says, intensely grateful. "And yet, standing here, who can see a leaf fall?"

No one speaks. A minute passes. No leaf falls.

"Oh, if we stood here long enough," Linda concedes, "or if there were a wind, or a hard rain like we had last night; but normally it happens unobserved, the moment when the root of the stem, where the bud once was, decides the time has come to let go. But it happens." She looks upward and lifts her arms. The widened light falls upon her face and palms, and the little girls grow still, feeling threatened by something within the woman that she is pulling from the air, from the reds and golds trembling around them. "Nobody sees it happen, but it does. For suddenly, it seems, the woods are bare."

Beautiful Husbands

SPENCER RIDGEWAY had always liked Kirk Gunther, and even while, in the messy wake of his affair with Dulcie Gunther, he was being legally battered by him, Spencer found something to admire, something warrior-like and sterling, in the barrage of registered letters, hand-delivered summonses, and grim-voiced, telephoned ultimatums—all intended, Spencer felt, less to discomfit him than to panic Dulcie into an easy divorce settlement. Spencer had been noticing Kirk, indeed—on the train, downtown on Saturdays—long before Dulcie made any impression on him. He was taller than Spencer, with a full and fluffy head of hair gray in just the right places (temples, sideburns, a collielike frosting above the collar), whereas Spencer was going thin on top and combing the remaining strands across his pate from a parting closer and closer to the tip of one ear. Kirk had a year-round tan and one of those thin no-nonsense mouths, with two little tense buttons of muscle underneath, that Spencer envied; he had always been embarrassed by his own big, soft-looking lips. As the men and their wives happened to be, more and more, at the same cocktail parties, and on adjacent tennis courts at the club, and in the same conservation groups, the couples drew closer. Kirk laughed at Spencer's jokes—Kirk himself could not make jokes, his tongue wasn't hinged that way—and took him on as a golf partner, though he was a solid 8 and Spencer a courtesy 20.

Dulcie was a steady, up-the-middle 13—from the women's tees, of course. She had oodles of honey-gold curly hair held in place by her visor, and tidy brown legs exposed to mid-thigh by her taut khaki golf skirt. The one time Doris, Spencer's unfortunate first wife, showed up to make a

Sunday-afternoon foursome, she horrified the other three by wearing blue-jean cutoffs, with the shadow of a Sixties-style heart-patch on the backside, and muddy Adidases in place of golf shoes. All of Dulcie's costumes were impeccably Eighties-suburban. When she and Spencer first began to meet illicitly, her broad-shouldered, waistless wool suits and summer frocks of fine-striped ticking, or her scoop-necked georgette blouse with a flickering skirt of pleated crêpe de chine, gave him the thrilling impression that Kirk himself had dressed her; Spencer could picture him, sitting with his intent, humorless handsomeness in the clothing store, surrounded by multiple reflections of his fluffy, frosty hair, as Dulcie strutted out of the dressing room in one smart outfit after another. And when her furtive luncheons with Spencer blossomed into intimacy, this impression spread to her underwear—lace-trimmed bras, bikini-style panties, sexy yet not really frivolous, in military tones of beige or black—and even to her skin, which was silky-smooth with lotions that perhaps Kirk's hands had spread, especially on that unreachable, itchy area just under the shoulder blades.

In the Gunthers house, after the figurative roof fell in, Spencer would stretch his tired body and ease his battered spirit amid Kirk's heavy, leathery furniture. He admired the matching plaid walnut suite in the den lined with Books of the Month, the stereo and record cabinets expertly cut and mortised by Kirk's sharp-toothed array of power equipment in the basement, and, upstairs, the monolithic bed that consisted simply of an airfoam mattress on a low wooden platform. Perfect-seeming Kirk had had a bad back, Dulcie revealed; another unsuspected debility was that, according to her, he had been incredibly boring.

Spencer always tried to defend him. "I always found him pleasant. Not a laugh a minute, exactly . . ."

"Like incredibly darling and amusing you," she interrupted, giving him such a hug that the wooden platform creaked beneath the airfoam.

He found her adoration unexpected and, he could not but feel, undeserved. Spencer had some trouble understanding how he had come to be in this other man's wife's embrace, trying to pick a prong of her tumbling golden hair out of his eye. ". . . but hearty," he finished. "Good-natured."

"He was rigid and brutal," Dulcie insisted. "This tactic with the eviction notices is so typical; he knows how terrified I am of the police."

In truth, it was an impressive sight, to see the sheriff's new Chevrolet Celebrity coupe, with its twirling blue light and silver lettering, pull up the driveway to deliver the latest beribboned, notarized document.

"Just getting a parking ticket used to make me cry." This kind of small revelation, this little glimpse of her feminine softness, had had a slightly different quality when she was still Kirk's lawful wife. Then, it had been a peek into paradise; now, it was a mere datum. "Whereas *he* scoffed at tickets and used to rip them off the windshield and throw them into the gutter. I used to pick them up when he wasn't looking and Scotch-tape them together and pay them."

"He did?" Spencer said. "That's fascinating."

"It used to make me hysterical. He liked that. That's why he's doing all this now, to make me hysterical. It's his way of still interacting." He felt her skin take on an oily, preening texture as he mechanically rubbed below her shoulder blades.

"Oh, now," he said comfortingly. "Don't forget, he's hurting. We've badly hurt him."

"Pooh," she said, her face unseen beneath her heap of hair, except for a corner of her painted lips, where a bubble of saliva had popped with the exclamation. "I don't know," she went on woefully. "It's horrible, being a woman. Sometimes I feel you're both against me. Everything he does, you seem to defend."

"I just think we should be fair, and try to understand Kirk. All this suing and so on is just his way of dealing. We have each other, and he has nothing."

"He has his own precious pretty carcass, and that's all he ever cared about anyway."

"Yes, it was pretty," Spencer had to agree.

Even when the lawsuit for alienation of affections was far advanced, Spencer imagined he could glimpse, through the swirl of correspondence and the hours of stilted conferences with dapper lawyers, a twinkle in Kirk's eye. At one point in the actual proceedings, he found himself bumping through the padded courtroom doors at the same time as the plaintiff and made a joke ("Must have been part of a padded cell") at which Kirk curtly, grudgingly chuckled. Away from Dulcie's calorie-and-fiber-conscious cooking, the man had put on weight and looked, in the witness box, a bit jowly. He looked grim and unsympathetic; between responses, he clenched his teeth and did a lot of blinking. Spencer (who had lost seven pounds) felt disappointed by Kirk's deterioration and further disappointed by the verdict, of not guilty and no damages. The judge was a woman to whom the very charge savored of a bygone sexism. In this day and age wasn't a woman free to change men if she so desired? Was she some sort of chattel for men to bandy back and forth?

"It was sad," Spencer confided to Dulcie, "to see him come such a cropper."

"Why?" she asked, wide-eyed. "I thought it served him right. Now he says he's going after custody of the children."

There had been something lovable, Spencer had thought, in the erect dignity with which Kirk had marched away at the head of his little team of legal advisers, none of them quite so tall nor so gravely tan nor so tastefully grayed as he.

"Poor guy. I'm afraid he doesn't have much of a chance."

"Not if you make me an honest woman, he doesn't."

Married, and reduced to impecuniousness by their legal fees, Spencer and Dulcie resigned from the club and played at public courses, she giving him three strokes a side. Kirk got fatter and uglier and his legal attentions became a mere embarrassment. When he sullenly, silently came to pick up the children on alternate weekends, Spencer would spy on him from the upstairs window, or from behind the library curtains, probing his old admiration much as the tongue warily probes the socket of an extracted tooth. His heart would flutter, his face get hot. It took a long time for Kirk's silvery magic to tarnish entirely.

He loved hearing from Dulcie details of her other marriage, especially the early years—the rainy honeymoon in Bermuda, the quarrels with his possessive upstate mother, the progressively larger and less shabby living quarters spiralling out from the heart of the city into increasingly affluent and spacious suburbs. Kirk at first was almost painfully thin, a beanpole, and totally innocent about alcohol, among other things. Then there was a period of problem drinking, and flirtations with these tarty, man-hungry junior account execs at his office. But such a dear father, at least in the beginning, when the children were little and thought he was God, before this obsession with his own career, his own condition, even his clothes. "You see, Spencer dear—don't tickle like that—they didn't have the word 'yuppie' in those days, so Kirk didn't know exactly what he was until he was forty, and it was almost too late."

Spencer's own early married life had been spent in exotically different circumstances, on the other coast, in rebellion and riot, experimenting with drugs and organic farming. Doris had been a perfect hippie, hairy all over and serenely stoned. Even the divorce she had been laid-back and philosophical about. He begged Dulcie, "Tell me about the pajamas again."

"Well, darling, there's really nothing much to tell. I think I began to hate the marriage when he insisted I iron his pajamas. When we were first married, he was still such a boy he would sleep in the underwear he had worn that day, the way he would in college, and then for years he used these simple dacron pajamas with a drawstring, no monogram or anything, and it was plenty good enough if I simply folded them when they were fresh out of the dryer, before the wrinkles really, you know, set. But then we got into a-hundred-percent sea-island cotton that he said had to be hand-washed in lukewarm water, and he wanted sharp *creases* just to put himself between the covers in. And the eyeshades, and the ear stopples—I felt utterly shut out."

"And the shoes," Spencer prompted. "Did he have shoes?"

"Did he have *shoes?* They covered the entire floor of his closet, row on row, and went right up one wall. He had a separate pair for every suit, and then on the weekend, if he raked leaves it would be the suede Hush Puppies, but if I asked him to haul just one load of mulch over to the rose bed he would go back in the house and put on the shitkickers. It was like his skis, he had the pair for corn and the pair for icy conditions, and then a third kind for deep powder. And the *gloves:* if he couldn't find one certain pair of gloves, with grease stains already on them, he wouldn't touch the engine of the car, even just to add windshield-washer fluid."

"And did he take a long time in the bathroom, or a short time?" Spencer asked, knowing full well the answer. Eventually he knew all the answers, had extracted every molecule of the departed husband from his wife's memory—Kirk's odors and deodorants, his habits both annoying and endearing, the quarrels they had and the orgasms he gave her or, increasingly during the last years, failed to.

"I love kissing you," she confided to Spencer. "With him it was like putting your mouth against an automatic bank teller, where it swallows your credit card. And his hair! You had to be so careful not to muss his hair. That fluffiness wasn't natural, you know. It was *set.*" There was a limit to this sort of information. Kirk slowly became boring. The wraps of her first husband fell from her, so that Dulcie at last stood naked, fit to be loved.

Spencer loved her. Warming the dawn and evening of every day, the source and goal of every commute, the light and animator of every weekend, Dulcie was his treasure, the gold from which Kirk's dull residue had been panned away. He loved her cascading hair, her sturdy legs, her sweet, steady golf swing, which never strayed from the fairway in an ill-advised attempt to achieve more distance. They rejoined the golf club, their finances again permitting and Kirk having long ago resigned.

It was there, at the post-fourball barbecue, in the fullness of the happiness of Dulcie's team's having won the women's division, that a copper-haired woman approached Spencer. "Hi there," she said, speaking just like a name tag, "I'm Deirdre." Her handshake was a little too firm, and her gaze a shade too level. "Ol' Dulce was terrific out there, though I was the one got the gross par on the dogleg eleventh, which what with my twenty handicap made a net eagle for the team."

Dulcie had come up behind the other woman, and gave her a comradely hug. Their two curly heads were side by side, their tan faces with pale laugh crinkles at the corners of their eyes. "Isn't she terrific?" Dulcie asked, though Spencer couldn't see quite how. But, then, years ago, he remembered, he had been insensitive to Dulcie's charm. "The Greenfields have just moved to town, and I've promised to have them over."

Deirdre glanced around, rather urgently. "Let me find Ben." She hurried into the crowd, which was dressed with facetious country-club gaudiness—scarlet pants, straw hats—under the hanging cloud of mesquite-flavored smoke. Spencer felt a fateful sliding in his stomach.

"I don't want to meet any new people," he told his wife.

"You'll like him," Dulcie promised.

The aggressive copper-haired woman was dragging a man toward them —a tall, dazed sacrificial lamb with a sheepish air, an elegantly narrow and elevated nose, slicked-down black hair, and a seersucker suit that gave him, with his blue button-down shirt and striped necktie, an endearingly old-fashioned, vaguely official ambience. He was, in his way, beautiful.

Spencer, his face heating up, hardly had time to protest, "I don't want to like him."

The Other Woman

ED MARSTON awoke in the night to urinate, and as he groped his way back to bed the moonlight picked out a strange flash of white paper in his wife's top bureau drawer, which she had not quite closed. This drawer, he knew from twenty-two years of cohabitation, Carol devoted to her underthings and a small stack of folded headscarves over on the left. Paper belonged in her desk downstairs, or on the hall table, where she usually left the day's mail. She was breathing steadily, obliviously, like an invisible ocean in the dark, not ten feet away. With two fingers extended in a pincer, taking care not to rustle, Ed extracted the paper out from under the top scarf and crept back to the bathroom. He shut the door, turned on the light, and sat on the closed toilet seat. As he unfolded the concealed document, his hands were, more than trembling, jumping.

It was a homemade valentine to her from the husband of a couple they knew, a pleasant bland couple he had never much noticed, on the politer fringes of their acquaintanceship. Yet the valentine had been flamboyantly penned and phrased with a ceremonious ardor, its short text encircled by a large heart in red ink, a heart which, the writer reassured the receiver, was "even bigger this year than last."

A weapon had been placed in Ed's hands. He reread the missive more than once, and in his nervous excitement had to lift up the seat and urinate again. He switched off the bathroom light. The moonstruck snow outside the window seemed to leap bluely toward him, into him, with its smooth and expansive curves of coldness, its patches of shadow and glare. He felt toweringly tall, as if his feet rested not on the bathroom floor, which had fallen away, but on the earth itself. His trustfully sleeping wife, and her lover asleep in his house up the road, and that man's own wife, and all their combined children were in his hands.

Still trembling, he refolded the valentine. Sliding along beside the bed toward the bureau in its slant of moonlight, he soundlessly tucked it back into the drawer, beneath the top silk scarf. Tomorrow Carol might notice its slightly exposed position, and rebuke herself, and thank God that Ed had not noticed. Not that she was much one for rebuking herself, or thanking God.

Suddenly her voice, out of the darkness of the bed, asked sharply, "What are you doing?"

"Trying to find you, sweetie. I've just been to the bathroom."

She made no answer, as if she had spoken in her sleep. When he got back into the warm bed beside her, her breathing seemed as deep and oblivious as before. Gently the aroma of sleeping flesh and its soft snuffles and rasps washed over his senses. Her life was like a spring in some dark forest, constantly, murmuringly overflowing. Far away in the neighborhood, a dog barked, excited by the moonlight on the snow.

It fit, he realized: Carol's volatile moods of late, her spells of lovingness and depression, her increased drinking, her unexplained lateness in returning from certain trips into New York and from evening meetings in their suburb—meetings of a zoning commission, come to think of it, of which the other man, Jason Reynolds, was the chairman. It had been he, in fact, who had proposed Carol for membership; he had come to the house one night, after a portentous phone call, and, while Ed obligingly did the dinner dishes and put the youngest child to bed, murmured downstairs to her, at the dining-room table, of the crisis facing their suburb, of predatory builders and their corrupt brothers-in-law on the planning board, of the need for a woman on the commission who was here during the weekdays and could bring a homemaker's point of view, and so on. Carol had told Ed all this afterwards, wondering whether she should accept. It would take her out of the home, she worried; Ed told her she had put in enough time in the home. She didn't know anything about planning or building; he told her, speaking as an engineer, that there wasn't much to know.

Now he wondered if even then, over two years ago, the affair had begun and she was only pretending to vacillate, to hang back. If so, it had been a pretty piece of acting. Ed smiled appreciatively in the dark. He had urged her to accept because she had seemed to him in danger of becoming one of those suburban agoraphobes who wind up not daring leave the house even to shop, who have everything delivered while they sit sipping sherry behind the drawn curtains. Twenty-two years and five children had pretty well absorbed the venturesome subway-rider and semi-Bohemian, in sneakers and babushka, of their city days. She could hardly be persuaded, these last years, to come into town and join him for dinner and a play. Her nervousness about flying, as the children attained college age and began to fly here and there, increased to a phobia, and she no longer felt up to the trips she and Ed used to take to the Caribbean in the winter. "Anyway," she would argue, "they say now the sun is terrible for your skin." Carol was blue-eyed, with wiggly oak-pale hair.

"It's always been terrible; your skin wasn't meant to last forever. You can sit inside and read. You can use a number-fifteen sun block."

"Well, that seems to defeat the whole purpose of going. Why not just stay home and save the airfare?"

"You know something, my dear? You're becoming a real drag." Ed had urged her to accept the commission appointment because he wanted her out of the house. He wanted her, if the truth be known, out of his life.

But she had done him no harm—had done, indeed, everything he had asked. Borne him healthy children, created a home that could be displayed to colleagues and friends, served as an extension of his ego. Yet, lying beside her night after night, rising to urinate once, twice, depending on his insomnia, which expanded in spirals like a rage, he had become convinced that there must be a better life than this. A better life for the both of them. Carol had her qualities still—a flexible grace, though she had put on weight with the years, and a good-humored intuitiveness that was like the pure blue pilot light burning in an old-fashioned oven—but Ed had never dared expect that some other man might covet her. Jason Reynolds's message, in its festive red outline, had struck a tone handsomely blended of friendliness and passion, a tone of manly adoration. Carol, somehow, was loved. Realizing this made Ed, too, feel loved, and like a child in arms he fell swiftly asleep.

For days and weeks Ed did nothing with his knowledge, merely observed. How could he not have seen before? At parties, the lovers would do a long circling dance of avoidance, elaborately courteous and jolly with almost everyone else there, and only after dinner, when the shoes come off and the records go on, and the tired host brings fresh logs up from the cellar, did Carol and Jason allow themselves to drift together, and to talk quietly in that solemn way of people to whom the most trivial daily details of one another's lives have acquired the gravity of the sexual, and then to dance together with a practiced tenderness that they trusted those around them to be too drunk or sleepy to observe.

Jason was a thin and dignified man, a trust officer at a midtown bank, who observed a rigorous health regimen of exercise and diet; he had a rowing machine, played squash at lunchtime in the city, and after dinner jogged along the country roads in a reflective orange vest. It sometimes happens with such people that their bodies make their faces pay the price of aging, and so it was with him: his middle-aged face needed flesh. His fatless, taut, weather-yellowed features, his deep eye sockets and long creased cheeks and dry gray hair were those of a man ending rather than beginning his forties. Jason was forty-two, like Carol. In his arms she looked young, and her broad hips suggested a relaxed and rounded fertility rather than middle-aged spread. Though Jason's eyelids were lowered in their deep sockets, and seemed to shudder in the firelight, Carol's blue eyes were alertly round and her face as pristine and blank as a china statuette's each time the slow music turned her around so Ed could see her. It was not their faces that gave it away, it was their hands, their joined hands melting bonelessly together and Jason's other hand pressing an inch or two too low on the small of Carol's back.

Ed was not watching alone, he noticed; the flickering, dim room, cushions and chairs and fuzzy heads and stockinged legs, was lined with shadows watching Jason and Carol, or studiously not watching. People knew—had known, with the casual accuracy of detached observation, long before he had, before the night of the valentine. Until then he had existed in a kind of bubble, a courteous gap in the communal wisdom. He had been blundering with a blind smile through society while the truth, giggling, just evaded his fingertips. This, in retrospect, was hard to forgive. Did his opposite number, Patricia Reynolds, also exist in such a bubble? What did she know, or guess, or feel?

She was a short woman, with exemplary posture, who seemed wooden to Ed. Even her prettiest feature, her thick chestnut hair, seemed a shade of wood, brushed shiny and cut short in a helmet shape, with bangs. She jogged and exercised alongside Jason, but the regimen that had ravaged his face gave hers instead a bland athletic smoothness. Her chin was square, her brown eyes opaque. From a wealthy but not famous family, she had attended correct second-best schools and was thoroughly the product of her background; with a mannish upper-class accent, throatier than one expected, Pat had a good-soldier air about her, as if she had stiffened in her mission of carrying her family line into the next generation. There were two Reynolds children—a son and a daughter. Pat was slightly younger than Jason, as Carol was younger than Ed. Ed had never heard Pat say anything unpleasant or unconventional; but, then, he had rarely listened to her. At parties they tended to avoid each other. He had the feeling that he, with his rumpled, sleepless air, his incorrigible cigarettes and bossy, clownish, perhaps coarse manner, rather dismayed her; when he approached, she grew extra polite. Now, though, his eyes sought out her chiselled profile in the room, to see if she, like him, was watching.

In fact, she was seated on the floor not far away and, her face turned full away from the dancers, was discussing with another woman that most appropriate of topics for the commission chairman's wife, zoning—the tragic break-up of the local estates, the scandalous predations of the developers. Ed moved from his easy chair to the floor near her and said, "But, baby—you don't mind my calling you 'baby,' do you, Pat?—nobody wants to *live* in the old estates. The third generation is all in SoHo doing graffiti art. They can't afford the upkeep and the taxes and nobody can afford servants and they want to get their money *out* and in *hand.*"

"Well, of course that's what everybody says," Pat said, "and I suppose there's some truth to it."

"*Some* truth! It's all truth, Pat honey." Six bourbons were talking through him, not quite in synchrony. "You blame these poor hard-working Italian contractors who do the bulldozing and put up their four-hundred-thousand-dollar tract houses, but it's the rich, the *rich* who are greedy, who are dying to sell and let somebody else put the new slate roof on Daddy's old stables. Condominiumization"—he was so proud at having got the word out intact that even Pat smiled, briefly showing her dental perfection—"is the only way to save these old places from the wrecker's ball."

The woman next to Pat, Georgene Fuller, tried to come to the rescue. She was lanky and lazy and whiny, with long bleached hair loose to her shoulders. Ed had slept with her, for six months, years ago. "Still, Ed, you have to admit—"

"I have to admit nothing," he said quickly. "How about you, Pat? What do you have to admit?"

A flicker of puzzlement crossed this other woman's even features. Georgene nudged Ed in the small of his back. But she needn't have feared; it suited him to have Pat in the dark, in her bubble.

"The wrecker's ball," he resumed. "It should be the name of a song. We're gonna dance off both our shoes," he began to sing. The pressure on his back repeated, and it occurred to him he should ask Georgene to dance. Once you sleep with them, however many years go by, they fit smoothly into your arms.

But others also wished to break up the conversation between Pat and Ed; Jason and Carol suddenly loomed over them like parents above children playing on the floor. "We think you two should dance with us," Carol announced primly, and obliging Ed pushed himself up from the floor, which seemed with the bourbon to have taken on an elastic life of its own, and to bounce under his feet. Carol, rather miraculously, always felt slightly strange in his arms, as though their many years of marriage had never been. They had never quite worked out the steps, and this awkwardness made her interesting, especially now that he knew that somewhere, with somebody else, she *was* working out the steps. Her plump body felt solid with her secret, and unusually flexible to him; reaching behind her gracefully, she adjusted the position of his hand on her back. Ed had experimentally placed it an inch or two lower than usual. "Jason looks like a smooth dancer," he said.

"Not that I noticed," she answered.

"He is with Pat. Look at them go. Twirls, and everything."

"They went to the same sort of cotillions."

"But there's more to life than cotillions, huh?"

"Ed, you really shouldn't drink so much. It's what gives you insomnia— all that sugar in the blood."

"Next you'll be telling me I should take up jogging."

"Or something. It's not just you. We're *both* horribly out of shape."

He moved his hand lower again on her back and patted her solid fanny. He had his husband's prerogatives still. "To me you feel just right," he said.

Ed was an engineer, specializing in stress analysis of tall steel-frame buildings. His plan for dismantling his marriage demanded that his wife's affair remain in place, as a temporary support; otherwise, at the moment of pullout, his burden of guilt and strangeness would be too much. The children were heaviest, but the house, the town, and all the old connubial habits would weigh upon him in his moment of flight. He feared that Jason and Carol might break up out of their own dynamics, or in response to discovery from the other side; yet he wanted to allow some months to steel himself, as it were. Seeing, in the raw spring evenings, tall Jason moving with his jogger's stagger along the shadowy roads, Ed felt a pang of alarm that the precious man would be hit by a car, and the whole structure collapse.

Warm weather arrived, with its quickening of the blood, and then summer, with its promiscuous looseness, its airy weave of coming and going, of lingering light and warm darkness, of screened porches and reactivated swimming pools and pickup drinks on the patio. Everyone got browner in the summer, more frolicsome and louder; the suburban women in their bathing suits and sundresses took on the sultry hardness of high-class whores—their eyes hidden behind sunglasses, their toenails lacquered. Jason and Carol became more blatant; more than once, Ed spotted them holding hands in a corner of a cocktail party, and when asked where she had been during some unaccountable absence, she would give a teen-ager's lame, evasive answer—"Oh, out." She might add, "It's so hot I had to take a walk toward the river," or else display a half-gallon carton of skimmed milk and a packet of wheat-germ cookies as if the purchase of these had naturally consumed two hours. And Jason was always coming around to the house on more or less plausible errands, having to do with zoning or tennis or an exchange of gardening equipment. Ed, to make his tennis-court fence ten years ago, had invested forty dollars in one of those two-handled post-hole diggers, and it was surprising how many posts Jason seemed to be planting in his modest back yard, or how often, for a man who owned only a half-acre, he had to borrow Ed's chainsaw. Every errand, of course, won from Carol a hospitable offer of coffee or tea or a drink, depending on the time of day.

Pat sometimes came along on these hollow excursions, and made flawless, wooden small talk with Ed out on the screened porch while the other two were coincidentally absent within the house: Carol had had to rush into the kitchen, Jason to the bathroom or to make a phone call. The house, that summer, seemed much used. Carol kept setting up, around the excuses of the tennis court and the swimming pool, informal little parties that almost always included the Reynoldses. One day in early August, returning to the house from an emergency run to the liquor store downtown, Ed swung into the driveway as Carol and Jason were greeting another couple. They looked so natural, posed side by side in the golden late-afternoon light, so *presiding,* standing together one flagstone step up from the driveway, he with his gray hair and gaunt stoop and she with her matronly round arms and shoulders, that Ed felt abolished, already gone; he secretly shared their joy in each other, and yet primitive indignation contributed to his energy as he marched toward them with the rattling bags of liquor. Carol looked toward him; she seemed unfeignedly happy to see him. Or was it the liquor she was happy to see? She was wearing only a wraparound denim skirt over her black bathing suit, and in the chill of approaching evening was hugging herself; the homeyness of this ageless gesture, and the familiar small sight, as she stepped down and reached forward to take one of the bags from him, of the downy hairs standing erect with goosebumps on her bare forearms, wounded him unexpectedly —activated random stress within a situation he had considered thoroughly analyzed.

The season was ebbing. Ed had to make his move. The children were conveniently scattered to summer jobs and to friends' houses, but for the youngest, who after dinner wrapped himself in the mumble of television in his room upstairs. Ed invited Carol to take a walk with him. Her eyes widened, into their china-doll look, and she hurried to get a jacket from the closet; the tone of his voice, without his willing it, had spoken to her guilt. They walked along the broad grassy path, favored by joggers and snowmobilers, kept open above the Croton Aqueduct, which poured water south in a line parallel to the river and the railroad tracks. The city's gravity pulled everything toward it. The Marstons walked uphill, between clumps and groves of maples and beeches, and past school grounds seen through wire fencing; back yards abutted on the right-of-way, and Ed and Carol felt themselves moving like ghosts through family cookouts and badminton games and the domestic music of chugging dishwashers and the evening news.

He described to her the night he had discovered the valentine, and what he had observed since. She listened and did not interrupt; in the corner of his vision, against the moving background of leaves and fence slats, her pale face seemed a motionless image projected from a slide upon a skidding, flickering screen. He proposed this to her: he would leave, take an apartment in the city, and take her secret with him. In return for his silence, she would present the separation to their children and friends as a mutual decision. He would provide financial support, and in a year they would see how things stood.

She spoke at last. "I'll give him up."

"Oh, don't do that."

"Why not?" Her eyes had grown watery, seeking his.

"You love him."

"Maybe I love you, too."

"You think that now, but in the long run . . ." The sentence trailed off. He summoned up a little indignation. "Anyway, I don't want to be loved *too*. Come on, Carol," he said. "We've given it a good try, had some nice kids and nice times; you wouldn't have taken up with Jason if things were what they should be. You and he, you really seem to have it."

She could have denied it. But she simply said, "He has Pat."

Ed sighed. "Yes, well. I can't take care of everybody."

This was a Saturday. The next day, with the sickening new condition of their marriage drying everywhere like an invisible paste, and the children and the pets and the furniture all still unknowing, Carol surprised Ed by still wanting to be taken to a Sunday-afternoon concert at a local church. The Reynoldses were also there, in a pew on the far side of the nave; they all mingled over punch afterwards, in the ladies' parlor. It was thrilling, for a connoisseur of stress, to see Carol lightly bantering with Jason and making valiant small talk with Pat. As Ed drove her home, she began to cry, and he asked her why she had wanted to come. "It was my only chance to see Jason," she confessed, as bluntly as if to a counsellor, and not bothering to hide the reverent way her voice fell in pronouncing her lover's name. So quickly, Ed had become her accomplice. He felt his heart shiver and harden. "He knows I know?"

"Not the details, just the fact."

"How did you manage that?"

"I slipped a note to him. Didn't you see?"

Ed felt trapped and betrayed. With the other man knowing, there was less chance of backing out. "No."

"I thought you'd become such a great observer."

He asked her, sarcastic in turn, "Aren't you two afraid of Pat catching you out in some of these shenanigans?"

"She doesn't want to catch us out," Carol told him. He glanced over, and her eyes, though red-rimmed, had a twinkle. She seemed to be adjusting to his departure faster than he was.

That fall, Ed entered into the strange new status of half-husband. He found a small apartment in the West Eighties and went home weekends to rake and put up storm windows and entertain the kids. Some nights, he slept over in the guest room, where the children didn't like to find him. They wanted him back in Mommy's bed. That creepy Mr. Reynolds was always coming around, red-faced and panting, in his jogging shoes. They called him Big Foot. "Big Foot's just clumped up!" one of the children would shout from downstairs, and Ed, involved in a game of Trivial Pursuit in his oldest daughter's room, would see Carol sail past the door, her quick step silent, her whole body lightened by expectation.

In this cozy atmosphere, with their conspiracy now widened to include the children, Ed asked Carol, in curiosity as much as envy, what Jason did for her that he had not. "It's very peculiar," she admitted, spacing her words. "He just thinks I'm amazingly wonderful." And she had the grace, this valuation being so clearly excessive, to look down into her drink and blush.

"Well, who doesn't?" he asked, himself blushing. Since leaving her, Ed was all flattery.

She looked up sharply. Did he imagine it, or had her blue eyes become darker, snappier in her months of living alone, of being her own woman? Certainly her hair, its oak color loaded with gray, had become wigglier. *"You* didn't," she told him. "You never did. I was just *there* for you, like an

I-beam or something. Any other beam would have done just as well. I'm
sure you've laid some in place already."

"No," he said slowly, almost truthfully. For in fact Ed was enjoying the
shabby austerity, the modest purity, of bachelor life. He had married so
young he had never had to cook for himself before, or make his own bed.
These skills had seemed arcane to him, and now they proved learnable,
and he understood why women were healthier, with all that reaching and
stirring and industrious attention to the texture of things. His crowded,
clamorous, only slightly dangerous block near upper Broadway spoke to
him more intimately, of small decisions and services, groceries and laun-
dry, than the suburbs ever had. Keeping himself fed and tidy and half-
running Carol's household forty minutes to the north took most of his
energy. Living alone makes one methodical; his drinking had eased off,
and the weekend slices of his old social life tasted sour and flat.

He had rarely seen their friends except on weekends anyway, and in
these days of domestic confusion his defection and part-time reappearance
were casually accepted. The Reynoldses, of the couples they had known
together, were kindest and most attentive to Carol in her singleness, and
came by the house oftenest. Pat and she shared garden-club trips, aerobics
classes, a night course in the English Romantic poets at the local community college. The Marston children gave Pat the logical nickname of Little
Foot, as if by verbal magic to knit the Reynoldses closer together. "The
Feet are here again," one would shout, and Ed, if he was caught in the
house, would sometimes have to make a fourth at tennis.

He always insisted that he and Pat be partners. That way, the sides were
most even. Jason was a well-schooled but lumbering player, and Carol's
insouciance, her good-humored indifference to the exact outcome, undermined her natural grace at the game. Ed had a weak backhand but killer
instinct at the net, and little Pat played, it seemed to him, like a weakly
wound-up machine. She moved back and forth as if on tiptoe and her
movements minced in the sides of his vision. Across the net from her, Ed
would have gobbled up her ladylike forehands and pounded them back at
her. As it was, he would growl, "Let's go get 'em, Pat," and count on her
to cover the back line as he lunged from side to side, looking for the
winning volley. The matches were fun, especially when fussy, no-fat-on-me
Jason began to tut and mutter to himself, and Carol grew rosy in the face
as she tried to play to please her lover while both acknowledging Ed's
ironic glances and keeping her expression blank for Pat's benefit.

In a way, it was the three of them against Pat. Or was it the three of
them keeping her safe in her bubble of ignorance? Ed felt alternately that
they were a deceit machine, chewing her up, and a kind of cradle, holding

her above the abyss. For what, really, he asked himself, would telling her the truth have done but force her to act and perhaps plunge them all into disaster? How much did Pat suspect? Nothing, it appeared, which seemed incredible to Ed; just looking at Jason and Carol across the net, hearing their mutual encouragements, feeling the easy warmth their partnership gave off should have told Pat the tale. Once he joked to her, "You know what they look like, those two? Mr. and Mrs. Jack Sprat." It was true: in the stress of their long affair, Jason had become even thinner and Carol plumper. Pat laughed politely but emptily, intent on her serve. Though her strokes lacked fire, she did like to win; this much was human about her, and intelligible, and likable.

She was the youngest, their baby, not quite forty; and Ed, at forty-five, felt like the daddy, only playing at playing. His sense of their spatial relations, out on the court, was of himself enclosing the three others and of keeping them, with transparent lines of force, apart, as if under his direction had been struck one of those balances of gravity and inertia, rigidity and mass that form islands of stability within the universe. Pat's ignorance, he decided, was a function of her social complacence, and thus more annoying than pitiable. She had snobbishly willed herself to be sexually blind.

Only once, that long sunny fall they shared, was he physically stirred by her; after three sets she complained of a blister, and on the bench by the side of the court took off her sneaker and sock. Little Foot. The neatness that through the rest of her body seemed rather wooden and mechanical here in her bare, pale foot was exquisite; here in the long low late-afternoon rays that slanted upon them, imprinting their sweaty bodies and tennis outfits with the fencing's shadowy lozenges, Pat's sharp, small anklebones and metatarsal tendons and unpainted toenails roused in Ed a desire to kneel in slobbering self-abasement and to kiss this tidy white piece of woman, to whose golden sole adhered a few cinnamon-red grains of clay-court topping.

Pat felt his eyes feasting on her foot and looked up as if he were a shoe salesman who had failed to answer a perfectly reasonable question. The moment passed.

"Doesn't she think it strange," Ed asked Carol, "always getting stuck with us, always being dragged here?"

"She likes me," Carol said, with her endearing insouciance. "She feels sorry for me."

"Does she ever ask why I left?"

"No. Not really. We don't discuss that sort of thing. I think she just sees you as a rather wild, unpredictable person and there's no accounting for what people like you do."

"As opposed to people like Jason."

"Mm-hm." Just thinking of Jason made Carol's lips draw in as though she were sucking a candy.

"What's she going to do when she finds out?"

"I don't know. Ask me to give him up, and I guess I'll have to."

"Have you ever thought of giving him up right now, before there's an ugly crisis?"

Carol sipped at her drink and reminded him, "I offered to, and you said no."

"That was in relation to us. I'm thinking of it now for your sake. Don't you ever feel terribly guilty toward her?"

"All the time," Carol confessed—rather cheerfully, Ed thought.

"Aren't you ever afraid I'm going to tell her?"

"No. That's the last thing you'd ever do."

"Why not?"

"Because you're a coward," she promptly, lightly said, and softened it to "The same reason nobody tells her—even her own children. They discuss it with mine. Ours. We're all cowards. Anyway, what would be in it for you? You got your exit visa, you don't care what happens to us back in the old country."

"Oh, but I do. I do. Apparently I wasn't a very satisfactory husband for you. I'm trying to arrange one for you that is."

"That's very kind of you, dear," Carol said. Ed couldn't tell if she was being ironic. His deceptions included this ambiguity toward Carol: was he aiming truly to be rid of her or in some circuitous way to win her back—to show her who, underneath all, was boss?

He always boarded the train south, back to his apartment and his block, with some relief to be out of the suburban cat's-cradle he had helped weave. But his life, his life as his reptile brain grasped it, was still back there, witnessing Carol's wifely blushes on the other side of the net and the other woman's exposed bare foot, like the helpless cold foot of a cadaver, in the warm sunset light. Sunday nights, in bed, he could not stop replaying the tennis match, its diagonals and elastic, changing distances. Round watching faces, children's faces in the grandstands—though in fact the children rarely came to watch; they snubbed it all—became frustratingly confused with the fuzzy balls being battered back and forth. Eventually he would fall asleep, with no boundary between insomnia and dream and no healing sense, when he awoke, of having slept soundly. Being alone in bed made even a small room seem large, and reverberant, like a great drum with the ceiling for a skin.

At last, mercifully, the weather became too cold for tennis. He did not want to face Pat anymore, however securely this woman was sealed in her bubble of unknowing. The lovers had come to accept their precarious situation as settled, and Ed's complicity as their right. His role as confidant subtly expanded to that of pander. Carol took to asking, in that casual, irresistible way of hers, if they could borrow his apartment during the day, when he was off at work. Returning through the winter dark, he would find his bed made with an alien neatness, and sometimes a bottle of wine in the refrigerator, or his Martini pitcher used as a vase for a bright bouquet of flowers, the kind of bouquet peddled, in a paper cone, at subway entrances or from gloomy traffic islands.

The city was slowly absorbing Ed. He had made a few friends, if not commitments, and asked that on weekends Carol send the children, those young enough still to be interested, in on the train. The echoing halls of the Museum of Natural History welcomed him back from his own childhood; many of the exhibits were jazzier, and pedagogic voices talked from the walls, but the extinct creatures had not aged, and the African dioramas still had the same airless, suspenseful enchantment of Christmas windows along Fifth Avenue. A dry tuft of foreground grass or a few presumably geologically accurate pebbles scattered to lend verisimilitude would fascinate him, as if these humble details, just inches inside the great glass pane, had a secret vitality denied the stiff stuffed creatures at the center of the exhibit. When, late that winter, Pat's bubble at last broke, Ed felt well removed from the crisis, which was muffled by a snowstorm in any case. Carol kept phoning him, and several times a cloud of static overwhelmed her voice, and the connection was broken.

Apparently a maiden aunt of Pat's, who lived in the next town to the south, in one of those big Hudson River houses that had not yet been condominiumized, had seen Jason and Carol in a car together, at eight-thirty on a weekday morning. Ed knew it was their habit for Jason to miss the train that Pat had dropped him off to catch, walk a block or two to where Carol would pick him up, and then take the next train from the station farther down the line; in this way they stole a half-hour for themselves. A dangerous habit, and hardly worth it, Ed had advised Carol long ago. But the little wifely act of putting Jason on a train had been precious to her. The aunt, seeing them with dim eyes from her own moving car, had thought Carol must be Pat, but heavier than she had ever seen her, with bushier hair, and the car didn't seem exactly familiar, either; yet there was no mistaking Jason—that long head, thin as a knife. Troubled by the possibility that she was going senile and seeing things, the innocent old lady telephoned to have her vision confirmed.

"Evidently," Carol told Ed, "Pat very coolly lied and said yes, she had been taking Jason to a different station because they had dropped off their other car at a gas station near the town line."

"What she could have said that would have been better," Ed pointed out, "was that Jason had accepted a ride that particular morning with a woman they both know who also commutes. It happens all the time. I assume you were driving the Honda."

"It needs its snow tires, by the way. I totally forgot to have them put on. I've been nearly getting killed."

"Then what happened?"

"Well, I guess she stewed all day, but still hoped Jason would have some explanation when he came back. But this image, of a fat woman with messy hair, she instantly connected with me. How do you like that for an insult?"

Ed saw Carol's expression as she said this, her self-mocking face, eyes rounded, corners of her lips drawn down. It occurred to him that Pat had been snobbishly unable to believe that he and Carol, messy and clownish as they were, could ever do anything that would matter, seriously, to herself and her husband. "Well, he's here. I mean, he was here. He's had to go back because she isn't *there*, it turns out." In a flurry of static, an annoyed operator came on and told them that this line was being preëmpted for an emergency call. In the imposed silence, snow continued to pile up in parallel ridges on the fire escape. The lights of upper Broadway were burning a yellow-pink patch into the streaming sky. An occasional siren could be heard, trying to clear a path for itself, but the city was inexorably filling up with a smothering, peaceable snow. Ed paced back and forth; his hands, as he mixed himself a drink, were jumping. His old calculations were being upheld, miles and miles away.

Carol got through in an hour and continued her story. "Well, she's apparently left the house. Leaving the two children there. In the middle of this blizzard. It's crazy. Jason is very upset, but I think it's just her rigid way of doing things. She has no sense," she said, in the pedagogic voice of the experienced woman, "of riding with the punches."

"Was her reaction anger, or despair, or what?"

Carol paused before selecting, "Indignation. She was indignant, first off, that her aunt had been sullied somehow; she thinks that idiotic family of hers is something sacred. Then I guess she was indignant that Jason couldn't come up with a cover story that would get us all off the hook; he says he'd just come off the train after a rotten day at the bank and was too tired to think. So instead he kind of collapsed and told her everything. What really got to her, what she couldn't get over, was how everybody except her had known or guessed about us for years. She kept reliving everything, all these little moments that came back. She had even seen us holding hands a couple of times, it turns out, but couldn't believe her eyes."

"Was she especially sore at me? It must have come out that I knew, too."

Carol paused again; Ed felt she was being tactful. "Not especially. I don't think they discussed you much. I don't want to hurt your feelings, but you're really a very minor figure in all this. It was more the notion of the community at large, of looking like a fool in front of everybody for so long."

"In her pretty bubble," Ed said. Carol had been right: he was a coward. For a year he had been dreading the phone call from Pat asking for a conference, asking him what he knew. The call had never come; in her doughty innocence she had never asked, and he had been almost grovellingly grateful to her for that. Perhaps she too had done some stress analysis. Now, evidently, she had stormed out of the house, in the thick of a blizzard. She had cracked. Ed circled the room in his triumph, in his agitation. All night, as the plows on the street kept scraping holes in his sleep, he imagined that Pat, who was missing, would rap on his door. The secret he had so long kept was off his hands, and out whirling in the world. The voice of the wind was her voice, so coolly and multiply wronged. He would comfort her, she would take off her soaked boots and be barefoot, exposing again that little foot so tidily formed and yet somehow in essence immature, a child's foot, ignorant, luminous. . . . He awoke, and it was morning, and a stark brilliance like that of an offended angel stood at the window. The sky was blank blue, and a hush as of guilt lay everywhere. With scraping shovels and whining tires, the city began to put itself back together.

Pat, it turned out, had done the conventional thing: she had fled to her mother's, on Long Island. "She drove right across greater New York," Carol explained to Ed, "along all these choked highways, through this blinding storm."

"What an epic," he said, relieved that Pat was still alive.

"I've been talking to Jason about it," Carol said, as loosely chatty as if to a psychotherapist, "and as I told him, I think it was typical. Everything with her has to be black or white; she has no feeling for gray areas."

* * *

Pat never returned to the husband or the town that had deceived her. The teen-aged children elected to stay with their schools and friends, which meant that they stayed with their father, which meant that Carol coped. The two households were gradually merged into one. Mothering the wounded and hostile Reynolds children suited Carol's talents better than the zoning commission. In the summer, Jason moved in with her—he had always coveted, Ed thought, their bigger yard, and tennis court, and the stand of woods out back, and the screen of tall arborvitae in front, between the house and the road. The Marston children coined a nickname for their mother: they called her Happy Foot. Pat at her distance disdained the new realities as she had disdained the old; though initially she had all society's sympathy and legal bias on her side, her rigid, vindictive behavior, especially toward her own children (they, too, had known, she maintained, and had kept her in the dark), eroded her advantages, and by the fall Jason's lawyer saw no insurmountable obstacle to achieving divorce and custody, though Pat had vowed to give him neither.

Ed was kept abreast of all this not only through Carol, whose calls gradually became less frequent and less confiding, but through the children and their visits, and through Georgene Fuller, his lanky friend of old, who also paid visits. His interest in the episode lessened, as toward any completed job. His former wife was happy, his children were virtually adult, and the new Mr. and Mrs. Reynolds (who honeymooned in St. Thomas) sent him, when February rolled round once again, a homemade valentine.

On a bright day one April—the squinting, wincing kind when winter's grit is swirled from the city streets and green garbage bags torn by dogs go loping down the sidewalks—Ed saw Pat Reynolds a half-block away. It was an unlikely neighborhood, the West Thirties, to bump into anyone you knew. He was hurrying to a dreaded appointment with his periodontist; he had fallen into the hands of a team of young specialists who were going to give him, in their cheery words, "a new mouth." Root canals, refashioned crowns and bridges—but the worst of all was the gum work, with tiny quick knives and sickles and scrapers, by a humming young man who wore a thick gold chain around his neck.

Pat, when Ed thought of her, was another kind of soreness, an ache as if a rib had been long ago removed or as if, that first glaring morning after the snowstorm, the side of him toward the window had been exposed to radiation. In all the world she was the person he least wanted to see. He considered ducking into a jeweller's entryway, or hiding in a store that offered souvenirs to the tourists straggling back from the Empire State Building; but his appointment wouldn't wait, and Pat's face was momentarily turned the other way. She wore a bright red scarf on her head and carried a shopping bag, which, with her sneakers and black raincoat, gave her a forlorn, wandering air. He had the irrational impression that she was in this neighborhood for some sort of medical attention also; she was hesitating right in front of the very entryway, a large mustard-colored arch, that he must pass through to have his gums cut. He had almost slipped by, squinting against the gritty wind, when she turned her head and recognized him.

"Ed! Ed Marston." Her voice had changed; the suburban little-man throatiness had become warmer, as if she, too, lived in the city now and was learning to deal in its heated, semi-European style. "Come here," she commanded, seeing his tendency to keep moving through the arch.

He went to her and she lifted herself on tiptoe to kiss him. The chiselled edges of her face had been blurred; her features had undergone that subtle bloating one sees on the faces of addicts, even when cured. Underneath the scarf her hair was the same rich chestnut, no longer a sleek helmet but unbecomingly permed into curliness. He tried to kiss her cheek but she aimed for the center of his mouth; having pressed her lips hard to one corner of his, she hung on, resting her face on his shoulder a long moment. His brain felt numbed. He asked, "How've you been?"

"*Good.*" The word was italicized; it must have been a lie, but it was offered with a fervor that would have made it true. She watched his face, waiting for another question, but since none came, asked him, "And you?"

"Terrible," he told her, which was also something of a lie. "I'm going right now to see my periodontist—they do these terrible things to your poor gums." Clowning in his embarrassment, he grimaced so that his gums showed.

Pat's eyes were solemn, shining. She nodded. Her own gums, of course, would still be perfect. With great relief Ed realized that no accusations or interrogation would be forthcoming; the bubble to that extent was still intact. A bit more small talk, a mock-desperate pointing at his wristwatch, and he had made his grateful escape. He never had had much to say to Pat. A backward glance as he pushed the elevator button showed the red of her uncharacteristic scarf (she had always gone bareheaded, even in the worst of winter, jogging along beside Jason) being sliced and battered on the far side of the revolving door.

Her kiss, so unexpectedly passionate, felt like a visible encumbrance on his mouth. What had it meant? That she had crazily forgotten who he was, and how he had betrayed her? Or that she forgave him? Or that she saw him now as just a piece of the past and had hung on to him a moment as we all wish to hang on to what is gone? Or that—and this fit best, as Ed heard his name called and stood to go in to his punishment—she was in her embrace acknowledging their closeness that night when, in an exultant, trembling moment, he had held her, too, in his hands?

A NOTE ABOUT THE AUTHOR

JOHN UPDIKE was born in 1932 in Shillington, Pennsylvania. He graduated from Harvard in 1954, and spent a year in England on the Knox Fellowship, at the Ruskin School of Drawing and Fine Art in Oxford. From 1955 to 1957 he was a member of the staff of *The New Yorker,* to which he has contributed short stories, poems, and book reviews. His books include twelve novels, five volumes of poetry, and a play. This is his eighth collection of short stories, counting two volumes of linked tales concerning the fictional writer Henry Bech, and not counting two selections in paperback, *Olinger Stories* and *Too Far to Go.* Mr. Updike has lived since 1957 in Massachusetts.